Julie Caplin is the international bestselling author of the Romantic Escapes series. Her books have hit the bestseller charts in Italy, Germany, the UK and the Czech Republic and have sold over a million copies worldwide. Her uplifting romantic comedies are set in gorgeous destinations across the globe, providing her readers the ultimate escape.

Formerly a PR director, for many years Julie swanned around Europe taking top food and drink writers on press trips to sample the gastronomic delights of the continent. It was a tough job but someone had to do it. These trips have provided the inspiration and settings for her novels.

Julie also writes romantic and historical fiction as Jules Wake.

juleswake.co.uk

twitter.com/JulieCaplin
facebook.com/JulieCaplinAuthor

Also by Julie Caplin

Romantic Escapes

THE FRENCH CHATEAU DREAM

Romantic Escapes

JULIE CAPLIN

One More Chapter
a division of HarperCollins*Publishers* Ltd
1 London Bridge Street
London SE1 9GF
www.harpercollins.co.uk
HarperCollins*Publishers*
Macken House, 39/40 Mayor Street Upper,
Dublin 1, D01 C9W8, Ireland

This paperback edition 2023
3
First published in Great Britain in ebook format
by HarperCollins*Publishers* 2023

A catalogue record of this book is available from the British Library

ISBN: 978-0-00-857923-4

This novel is entirely a work of fiction. The names, characters and incidents
portrayed in it are the work of the author's imagination. Any resemblance to
actual persons, living or dead, events or localities is entirely coincidental.

Printed and bound in the UK using 100% Renewable Electricity
by CPI Group (UK) Ltd

This book is dedicated to all those people struggling with difficult family issues — may there be light at the end of the tunnel for you.

Chapter One

Laughter bubbled up out of Hattie's mouth as she turned off the car engine and sat for a moment staring up at the building in front of her. It exceeded every expectation, dazzling her in the brilliant sunshine of the early afternoon as bright light bounced off the pale stone walls and the white coping, making her squint even behind her sunglasses. In truth, she hadn't been sure what to expect but it had definitely been more crumbling ruin than the rather magnificent façade of the Château St Martin. Gorgeous, grand, fairy-tale and her home for the next two months.

It seemed a miracle that this morning she'd set out from a very grey overcast Surrey and in just six hours, here she was in the bright sunshine, with everything around her blooming full of life. It felt as if she were coming out of hibernation herself and the spontaneous laugh was surely a good omen. Laughter had been in short supply in recent months. She'd been too busy wading through the weighty business of living.

Itching to get out and be in the moment, she opened the car door and stepped into warm, fragrant air. She had that instant punch to the senses that she wasn't in England anymore. A row of cherry trees along the drive were bursting with pink pompoms of blossom, the odd petal fluttering in the air like confetti as if to say: this is the perfect place to hold a wedding. It was tempting to pinch herself to make sure she wasn't dreaming. This last week had been horrendous and she still wasn't sure she'd done the right thing leaving Chris and her job, but the minute the train left Folkestone and she'd crossed under the Channel, it was like a physical parting from her old life. She had to focus on the now, even if she was going to have to work extremely hard for the next few weeks. She had a hell of a lot to prove. Entertaining the prospect of failure was not an option. She might not have been her cousin Gabby's first choice as wedding planner but she'd got the gig now. This was going to be a triumph, even if it killed her. It had to be. For the last few years she'd been a mere assistant, learning the ropes of the wedding planning business – she might have exaggerated a little to her uncle about her experience but she'd learned a lot answering the phone, arranging meetings and paying invoices.

She took a deep breath and smelt the fresh tang of rosemary and marjoram in the flower beds beside her. Fresh start, Hattie. Fresh start. She lifted her chin and looked at the château again.

If the inside was as spectacular as the exterior, Gabby was going to have one amazing wedding. The setting was quite, quite beautiful, as was the gorgeous countryside that she'd driven through from Reims to St Martin. The lush rolling hills were covered in uniform rows of bright green vines that undulated across the contours of the land. The never-ending lines marching across hill and field into the distance were punctuated by gnarled stumps supporting the fledgling canopy of leaves.

Hattie was fascinated by them. The vines were much

shorter than she'd imagined – but then what did she know about wine apart from it was made from grapes and she liked it? Maybe while she was here she could learn a bit about it, although she'd always been quite intimidated by wine. Her Uncle Alexander owned a half share in a wine company in London and was always very generous, bringing the posh stuff to her parents' house.

Although she'd almost spat her tea out when she'd seen the amount of money he'd deposited in her bank account. The number of zeros made her feel slightly sick and euphoric at the same time. It seemed money was no object for his daughter's wedding.

Alexander had told her that she had free rein in the château for the day of the ceremony, although he had booked an entire hotel for the guests and the bridal party. She'd also been told that there was a housekeeper in situ but she could hire any additional staff as she saw fit or bring anyone else in. Hattie had never hired staff in her life and although the thought didn't worry her – she knew she'd be more than competent at doing so – it was more that she didn't want to have to responsible for anyone else at the moment. She'd been doing that for too long.

As she was standing marvelling at the house, the front door opened and a tall man stood in the doorway.

'Are you going to knock or just stand there all day, hoping the door will open by itself?' His English was perfect but the French accent was unmistakable and by the amused expression on his face, he found her gauche admiration of the splendour of the house entertaining.

Hattie blushed and then raised her head with a regal lift. She wasn't going to be intimidated by anyone. She was Hattie Carter-Jones and she was here to do a job.

Then she blushed some more as her heart literally stopped in her mouth. Oh my goodness, what on earth did they put in the water here? The man had the most amazing blue eyes with the thickest, darkest lashes she'd ever seen and a head of swept-back curly hair. He wore dusky pink shorts which revealed long, muscled legs. Her mouth opened but nothing came out.

'Can I help you? Are you lost?'

The man raised an eyebrow and she knew without a doubt he knew exactly the effect he was having on her. She must look a right lemon standing there staring at him.

'Hi,' Hattie said. But in trying to control her voice, it came out an octave lower than her usual voice. '*Bonjour*. I'm Hattie.'

'Hattie?' A smirk crossed his face as he dropped the H making it sound adorably sexy and sending a shiver through her. 'Cute.'

Did he mean her name or her? It flustered her even more.

'Well, it's really Harriet, but most people call me Hattie which I much prefer because ... I don't know, don't you think Harriet sounds a bit like a maiden aunt or something quite stuffy? I do.' Now she was babbling and he wasn't even trying to hide his amusement at her verbal outpouring. Then she realised she was probably talking far too quickly and about something that didn't translate terribly well.

She strode forward and held out her hand.

He took it and she gave his hand a firm, no-nonsense shake, trying to claw back some dignity, which was a bit hopeless given his hand completely dwarfed hers. That bloody smile of his deepened as if he knew exactly what she was doing. She felt a bit like a small flea being swatted by a newspaper.

'Luc Brémont.'

God, just his voice, saying his name in that divine accent, made her go mushy inside.

Once again she stood there looking like a gormless idiot. She really did need to pull herself together. It was as if she hadn't been out in the real world for a long time and was adjusting from captivity. Which actually was quite a good analogy.

'Can I help you?' he asked again.

'I'm working here … I'm the wedding planner.'

'The wedding planner!' He stared at her with a mystified look.

Didn't they have such things in France? '*L'organisateur de mariage*?'

'I do know what a wedding planner is,' he said with a look, making it clear that he wasn't a halfwit. 'I would have expected to be given some notice that you were arriving.'

'I phoned.'

'When?'

What did it matter when? Didn't he believe her? She lifted her chin. 'Two days ago.'

He raised an eyebrow.

'I spoke to someone. A woman.' In hindsight, the woman had been quite curt, despite Hattie's self-conscious fumbling through her pre-prepared Google translation of *Je suis l'organisateur de mariage. J'arriverai dans deux jours.* 'I said I was coming. And in French,' she added indignantly, not wanting him to think she was one of those high-handed people who expected everyone to speak English.

'Hmm,' said Luc, his handsome face was marred by the briefest of frowns as if he wasn't convinced.

'I did honestly. I wouldn't just turn up,' she said at pains to reassure him that she wasn't that sort of person.

'The wedding isn't for two months.'

'No, it isn't but they do take a bit of planning,' she said crisply, not wanting to admit she might have acted precipitately. When Chris had given the ultimatum, him or France, she jumped right into the escape hatch with both feet. She smiled at Luc in what she hoped was a winning fashion. 'I hope it's not a problem but I understood the château has been reserved for the next two months.' She certainly wasn't going to admit that she'd booked the Eurotunnel as soon as she could. Business had been light at Bliss, the wedding planning agency she worked at, and she'd surmised correctly that they'd be happy to let her go.

'You have a beautiful…' Could she call it a home? Did people really live in places like this? '… a beautiful place.' And how lucky was she that she was going to be living here for the next few months?

'Yes, it is a *beautiful* place,' he agreed, those beautiful eyes darkening, 'although I'm not sure if you've been made aware –' he paused '– this is a working vineyard. And it is our family home. My father has only agreed to let out the château because Monsieur Carter-Jones is an old and trusted friend.'

This very polite reminder made Hattie pause. Having a whole load of partygoers descending on his house when he was trying to work probably wasn't his idea of fun but the actual wedding was only one day and the guests staying the week would all be staying at a hotel. Her uncle had even booked several Eurostar carriages so that some guests could come just for the day. 'No expense spared' didn't begin to describe his approach to this wedding. She picked up the holdall at her feet.

'Are you just here for the weekend?' he asked with a quick hopeful look at the holdall in her hand.

'No.' She bit back a smile.

'You pack light.'

Hattie laughed, relieved to think about something else. 'I wish.' She looked back to her car where another suitcase was nestled in the boot.

'Ah.' He caught on quickly. 'Would you like a hand?'

'No. No, it's fine,' said Hattie, hoping he didn't think she was expecting him to play doorman – she was far too self-sufficient for that. 'I'm sorry you weren't expecting me. I don't need to be waited on or anything.'

'Just as well,' he observed, dryly.

She frowned, suddenly sick of pussyfooting around fragile male egos. She'd had enough of that to last a lifetime. 'That,' she said with a sharp bite in her voice, 'was supposed to be an olive branch. I apologise for not giving more notice that I was coming but I'm here now.' And he was just going to have to suck it up.

He paused and to her surprise gave her a charming, and somewhat blinding, smile that had her nerve endings lighting up in response. He strode over to her car, opened the boot and hauled out her case as if it were no more than a feather pillow. Muscles bunched in his sinewy arms and she was aware of an odd tightening low in her belly.

'It's not a problem,' he said tossing another smile over his shoulder at her. 'I too should apologise. We've never done anything like this before. So I guess we'll all be feeling our way. Why don't you come in?'

She followed him into the wide airy hall, full of sunshine and light that gave the soft yellow walls a golden glow. The scent of flowers in a huge vase on an elegant console table perfumed the air with the fragrance of summer and what she thought of as happiness. For a moment she paused, the smell evoking sudden light-heartedness. A grand pure white marble staircase, fenced on one side with intricate iron tracery in black and gilt, swept down into the hall, the rounded and smoothed-off lower steps pouring and pooling at the bottom like the train of a wedding dress. Although sparsely furnished, everything was of exquisite quality, including the slender-legged wooden tables etched with gilt that were dotted around the walls, and elegant art deco bronze statuettes of willowy-limbed women arranged to draw the eye to their delicate beauty.

'This is…' Lost for words, she simply stared. Her eyes were probably popping out of her head. This was a full-on stately home. It was difficult to imagine real people actually living here.

'Nice, isn't it,' Luc said with a wink, and strode swiftly towards the back of the house. She upped her pace to follow him, admiring the fit of the fabric of his shorts that moulded his bottom rather nicely, which was totally inappropriate, but seriously he was a hottie. Totally out of her league, of course. She thought of her ex-boyfriend, Chris, with his ratty heavy metal concert T-shirts and perennial jogging pants. She gave a small internal sigh of regret. He hadn't always been so attached to the same clothes. When they were at university, he'd loved his button-down-collared shirts. Could she have done more to encourage him to smarten himself up? The decline in his dress standards mirrored the decline of his zest for life. But you could only badger someone about things so much. She'd felt such a nag all the time. The break-up still felt raw and unfinished. Although it was what she wanted, she couldn't help feeling guilty.

Luc turned onto a long corridor which seemed to run the length of the house, parallel to the front elevation. He led her into a huge kitchen and immediately it was obvious this was the heart of the house. Several tastefully distressed wooden beams criss-crossed the ceiling from which three large antique glass lamps were suspended. Everything else, including the two dressers, the long breakfast bar and the twelve-seater dining table, was in beautifully co-ordinated shades of white and grey, apart from the bright splashes of copper pans hanging from a rack above the big stainless-steel graphite-grey range. Despite the tasteful styling, there was a homely warmth to the room that invited you to take a seat and stay a while. Hattie couldn't help the smile that spread across her face as she stood in the full beam of sunshine streaming in through double French doors that led out to a pretty patio.

'This is gorgeous,' she said.

'Good, I'd hate you not to like it when you're going to be here for so long.'

Gosh, were all French people so direct? Although his words were diluted by the teasing smile on his face.

'Would you like a coffee or is it tea you drink?'

'Not everyone in Britain drinks tea all the time, you know,' she said feeling a bit of her usual spirit fizzle into life. It wasn't like her to be intimidated or flustered by anyone. Perhaps it was because she was a bit of a fish out of water and completely out of her comfort zone.

'I lived in London for a while. All the students in my flat drank that horrible instant coffee stuff.' He shuddered, still smiling. 'It was torture.'

'Some of us like proper coffee,' she replied with a beam. 'And I never touch tea, much to my family's disgust – they all seem to run on the stuff. Give me a decent cup of coffee, any day.'

'I like you already.'

Even though she knew his words were flippant and inconsequential, her heart did a funny flutter.

'It's kept here. Please help yourself anytime.' He opened a cupboard and pointed out a large glass jar of beans. 'Grinder over there. Cafetières in here. Milk in the fridge and the cups are all in that dresser over there.

'Brilliant,' said Hattie with a blithe smile. He was making it quite clear that she wasn't to be waited on. She lunged forward to grab the jar. She hadn't stopped since Calais and she could murder a coffee. Unfortunately, she'd misjudged him because he stepped forward to reach for the coffee jar at the same moment and she found herself planting her nose straight into his chin.

'Ow,' she squeaked, sudden tears filling her eyes at the sudden shock of the pain. Why did noses always hurt so much?

'I'm so sorry,' he said, his hands coming up in flustered alarm, his French accent suddenly much stronger.

'No, id wad my fauld,' she managed to mumble, pressing her nose gently as if that might push the pain back where it had come from.

'Here, sit down.' He grabbed her arm to guide her towards one of the ladderback chairs.

'Id fine,' she said, nursing her nose, feeling a hot trickle dribbling from one nostril. In a panic, she pulled out of his grasp and veered towards the sink, stepping hard on his foot. The last thing she wanted was to drip blood everywhere.

'Dorry,' she said horribly aware of the increasing flood running into her cupped hand. She barged past him and just made it to the large white butler sink in time.

Brilliant scarlet drops fell on the white porcelain, blooming like dystopian flowers in the faint sheen of water on the surface.

Nausea rolled in her belly and she tensed her stomach muscles, fighting against the white hot rush of panic.

'Here.' He thrust a piece of kitchen paper under her nose. In haste, she grabbed it, clamping his hand to her face in the process and elbowing him in the ribs.

'Dorry,' she said again. God, could this get any worse? She looked down, realising immediately it was a mistake. She heard a high-pitched whine in her head. The scarlet blooms flowered and burst like peonies. Please, please, don't let her faint.

Uh oh. Her head felt floaty and not quite there and then nothing was quite there and…

Coming to, cradled in the arms of a handsome Frenchman, had to be right up there in the top ten of fantasies, unless you were covered in blood and had made a complete tit of yourself in the process.

She blinked up at him, a little dreamily, and smiled because how could she not? He was gorgeous. With looks like that he probably dated supermodels or super-successful women who made their first profit of the day before they'd even applied their make-up in the morning.

'You are back with us?' he asked, looking very concerned. Maybe she should faint more often. It was quite nice being the one who was looked after for a change.

'I think so,' she said in a pathetic little voice and then began scrambling to get out of his arms because, seriously, she didn't do being looked after. As soon as she did, she realised her mistake because her head didn't seem to be attached to her body properly and she went all floppy again.

'Stay still. I've got you.'

He most certainly did. His voice, with that divine French accent, was so, so soothing but could this be any more embarrassing – lying on the floor, her head and shoulders on his lap, while he held a wad of tissue to her nose? Thankfully, after that first violent flood, her nose bleed seemed to have stopped. Oh God, she winced. Lying in this position there was only one place to look and that was up at him. It was all a bit too up close and personal and she seemed to have incubated a flutter of light-headed butterflies in her stomach which took off every time he looked down at her with those vivid blue eyes, assessing her.

'Do you think you might be able to stand up?'

'Can you give me a moment?' She felt like she'd been flung into a washing machine put on a high spin and spat out, leaving her like a stranded, disorientated beetle.

'Your English is very good,' she said. Had she already said that?

'Thank you.'

'It's very, very good,' she observed, aware that she was saying it for the sake of saying something and not blurting out anything stupid.

'I lived in London. After university there, I worked in my father's London business. Are you starting to feel better?'

'Mm. Yes. Sorry.' He probably had better things to do than be sitting on the kitchen floor with a damsel in distress.

'Let's get you up off this floor,' he said and helped her to a sitting position before hauling her to her feet. She swayed a second, light-headed again, and then Luc scooped her up in his arms and carried her over to one of the kitchen chairs, where he gently deposited her. Was it wrong to rather enjoy being carried?

'I'll make you a coffee and then I'd better let Solange, our housekeeper, know you're here. She'll be mortified that she's not had a chance to get a room ready for you.'

'Oh. Sorry.' Hattie felt obliged to apologise once again.

'You say that a lot,' he said and she found herself fascinated by his lopsided smile.

'Sor—' She smiled back at him as his eyes twinkled and she felt a funny rush inside her chest.

'And will you need me to move out?'

'Er … I …' She had no idea. It hadn't occurred to her. 'I don't think so. Not until the actual wedding maybe. I hadn't even thought that far ahead. I don't want to kick you out of your own home. I've no idea what was agreed. It's not like there's a contract or anything, is there?' she asked, realising that perhaps she'd been a little precipitate in diving headfirst into this venture.

When she'd heard that the wedding planner for her cousin Gabby's wedding had fallen through mid-arrangements, asking her Uncle Alexander if she could step in had been a long shot. She'd been so desperate to find a way out of a rut deeper than the Mariana Trench.

Luc gave a twisted smile. 'Not as far as I'm aware. It's an agreement between Alexander and my father. As my father says, they have been in business together for the last twenty years, why should it be a problem? We shall have to learn as we go. I would prefer not to move out of my own home.'

'Of course,' she said. It was a big house, there would be plenty of room. She was surprised the bridal party wasn't staying here but her uncle had told her that the original wedding planner had said it would be too much to organise from England when she hadn't seen the château for herself. Hattie got the impression the wedding planner hadn't been terribly impressed by the change of venue from a Surrey mansion to a French château. 'And what about the housekeeper? Does she live here too?'

'Solange. She has her own living quarters. A renovated annexe in the old stable block. My father didn't see fit to tell her of these arrangements or what is to be expected of her. I haven't yet informed her of the wedding.' He pursed his lips, clearly not relishing the idea. 'And I would suggest that you don't expect too much of her. She already has enough to do looking after the house, which she does on her own.'

'Okay,' said Hattie, immediately imagining a Mrs Danvers type who would kick off if asked to do any extra work.

'I'm afraid … I'm not sure what the protocol is. I can give you a key.' He turned and rummaged in a drawer in the big white-painted dresser before handing over a long black iron key. Not exactly purse-sized. She stared at it for a minute. That certainly wouldn't fit in the back pocket of her jeans.

Luc interpreted her expression correctly, 'It's okay, we rarely lock the front door unless we're leaving for a protracted length of time. It's more symbolic. Giving you the run of the house and your own space.'

'It's not like there isn't enough room. I don't think we'll be tripping over each other.'

'Are you sure?' he asked with a sudden teasing lift of one eyebrow, picking up his foot and rubbing at it with a grimace.

'Sorry, I'm not normally this clumsy. It's just you … you … d-d …distracted me.' She looked appalled realising how close she'd come to saying dazzled me.

'I don't usually have women falling at my feet, Hattie.' She wished he wouldn't say her name, not in that super-sexy way. Every time he dropped the H, she could barely think straight.

'Don't you?' she asked and realised that she shouldn't have said that out loud.

'Not usually, no. Are you feeling better now? It's just that I was on my way down to the vineyard.' He looked at the watch on his wrist. 'I was due there half an hour ago.'

She nodded. She wasn't going to say sorry again. The constant apologies were starting to annoy her – she sounded completely wet, when normally she was much more on it.

'I don't have time to show you around. Perhaps you can choose a room for yourself and…' He shrugged. 'My room is on the top floor, under the eaves. If you want me for anything.'

Hattie narrowed her eyes but his guileless, friendly smile gave nothing away. Was he aware of what he was saying or was it a mismatch between English and French? She couldn't be sure. The charming Frenchman had her completely flustered.

Chapter Two

Luc strode down towards the vineyard, his feet pounding the hard-packed ground beneath him with a mix of fury and irritation. He was going to kill his father, a slow, painful death. After all these years, he'd finally persuaded the old bastard to let him take over here and then he dumped a circus on him.

What he hadn't told Hattie, the would-be wedding planner, was that he'd only arrived a few scant hours before her and hadn't even had a chance to unpack his own bag. He was disconcerted by her. By those bright brown eyes and the humour in her ready smile. It was as if he knew her already.

Cute as she was, and she was very cute, he didn't need any of the additional stress of a wedding on site. How could the old bastard do this to him? Well, one thing was for sure, he was not going to be sucked in to help. Cute Hattie was on her own. He thought of Solange. Yup, Hattie was definitely on her own. On his last visit Solange had still been grieving the death of her husband– a difficult character – but it seemed as if he'd taken her spirit with him, leaving her more like a ghost these days, drifting in and around the château. Luc shook his head, not liking the direction his thoughts were headed.

Heaven forbid his father thought weddings were a good revenue stream and opened the château up for more such events. What if he decided to let out the bedrooms too? Luc paused outside the front of the brick-built cellar. He still remembered the very first time he'd been here, brought as a young boy by his formidable Great-Aunt Marthe, the driving force behind St Martin champagne. Like many of the pioneering female champagne makers, including the legendary Madam Clicquot, his aunt had continued her husband's legacy after he had died in a labour camp during the war. She'd only stopped fifteen years ago after a stroke at eighty.

Even at a young age she'd instilled within him a sense of awe at the importance of the building and the history of the caves below, dug by Roman slaves mining for chalk, centuries before. The caves were the perfect place to store fermenting champagne, providing a constant cool temperature, with exactly the right humidity.

'Luc!'

He turned towards the delighted cry and saw his friend Alphonse rushing towards him.

As the current *vigneron* of the vineyard, Alphonse was responsible for growing the grapes. He burst into a stream of excitable French. 'Luc, it's so good to see you.' He clapped both hands on Luc's shoulders. 'You're here at last.'

'At last?' replied Luc. 'I only texted you this morning to tell you I was coming!'

'Yes, another one of your flying visits to see Marthe. Have you been to visit her?'

'Not yet. She's demanding her brandy.'

'That one will outlive us all, her organs will be well

preserved. And how long are you here for?' Alphonse tilted his head to one side.

Luc gave him a broad grin, excited to tell him the news. 'A while.'

'That's good. How long this time?'

Luc paused before making his announcement. 'Time enough to make wine. We're going to make the best champagne St Martin has ever tasted.' Since Marthe had retired, the grapes had been sold to a local co-operative each year, but all that was about to change.

Alphonse stared at him, blinking as if registering each word one by one.

'You're kidding! Seriously! No way!' Alphonse's face lit up and he enveloped Luc in a bear hug, almost squeezing the life out of him. With a broad barrel chest and Herculean brawny arms, Alphonse was almost double the size of Luc. 'You finally persuaded the old man!'

'We came to an agreement.' Luc decided not to tell Alphonse that the future of champagne production rested on one vintage so instead he blurred over the conditions. 'There are a few considerations but nothing that will bother us.' And he'd tell Alphonse about the interruption of the wedding later. For now they could celebrate bringing the plans they'd talked about since they were in their early twenties to fruition, quite literally.

'We need to celebrate. I have just the bottle. Come. Does *Maman* know you're here?'

'Not yet. I didn't see her at the house. How is she?'

Alphonse's mouth tightened and he lifted his shoulders in an indifferent shrug. 'Much the same.'

Luc didn't say any more. They both worried about Solange and the way she'd been since her husband, Alphonse's father, had died. Luc didn't want to pry. Alphonse had never got on with his father, even though they had worked side by side in the St Martin vineyards. Perhaps that was why he and Luc, so different in background, had bonded. Neither of them had much of a father figure. Not that men put voice to such things, but they both had that common link.

Alphonse clapped him on the back. 'You'll want to take a look around then.' He ushered Luc towards the building. 'Come on, nothing's changed,' he said leading the way. The big hall had an empty, deserted feel about it, although it stored a mass of grape picking, pruning and tending equipment. There were large green crates stacked high like Lego towers, rows of secateurs, scissors, leather gloves and tool belts neatly arranged on the walls. Wine might not have been made here for a while but Alphonse had kept the vineyard and the cellars in tip-top condition.

'Want to see the caves?' he asked.

'How did you guess?' asked Luc.

'I can see the eagerness, you're like a hound on the scent. Wait until we have our first bottles, you'll be sleeping down there like a nursing mother.'

'You know me so well, but it'll be a while before we bottle our first vintage.'

'Yes, but how wonderful will that day be.' Alphonse grinned and led the way to the broad stairs that wound their way down to the caves. 'Will we do tours? This looks very romantic.' He indicated the elegant spiral of the brick-edged steps and large chalk slabs and he sighed. 'I don't suppose there's a budget for an elevator.'

Luc laughed. 'When we're as big as Taittinger, perhaps. Besides, I was thinking, this magnificent staircase is part of our brand identity. I might put it on the labels.'

'On the label!' Alphonse was horrified. 'A picture on the label. No! But it is just not done. Think Taittinger, Moet, Bollinger, Veuve Clicquot.'

'Exactly. They all look very similar. If St Martin is to be a success it needs to have some kind of differentiation. Think about New World wines and their labels.'

Alphonse snorted.

Luc held up his hand, not wanting to start what he knew would be a fruitless argument. He had a tough road ahead of him, trying to introduce new methods and processes. He needed to pick his battles and this was not one he wanted to fall out with Alphonse about on the very first day.

'It's just an idea. We're a long way from labels and bottles at this stage. We need a good growing season and I know that you have that in hand.'

'Ha! Yes. I can't wait to tell that bastard Gilles Robard that he won't be getting his hands on our crop this year.' He rubbed his hands together with glee. 'Does Marthe know?'

'Not yet. I'm going to see her this afternoon and tell her the good news. I want to pick her brains for some of the history of the place. She has plenty of stories. We can write quite a tour guide with her knowledge of the place.' Luc paused and looked back at the steps. 'If there is enough money it would be good to improve the access, and knowing the history will be good for marketing.'

The caves at St Martin had had a chequered history over the years, playing a part in both the First and Second World Wars, providing shelter and a hiding place for the local population and members of the *Maquis*.

'Rumour has it she was in the resistance and killed a man with her bare hands once,' said Alphonse. 'It wouldn't surprise me but she's never denied or admitted it and she certainly doesn't want to talk about it.'

Luc could imagine his tough, wiry great-aunt doing what needed to be done without any fuss. She was nothing if not practical but then again she wasn't one to seek glory or notoriety.

They descended into the dimly lit caves and Luc's skin bubbled up into goosebumps, making him wish he'd had the forethought to bring a fleece with him. The unseasonably warm spring sunshine had tempted him this morning and all he was wearing was a long-sleeved T-shirt.

Ahead of them were row upon row of racks where the bottles were stored for their second fermentation. The dark wooden racks were lined up like soldiers on sentry duty, silent and still in the gloomy light. Despite the austere environment, the dark wood against the white chalk walls and the cool dry humidity, Luc loved it down here. This was where the magic happened, where grape juice became something entirely other. A magical transformation aided by natural science, but one could never predict the outcome precisely. There were so many factors that impacted the final product: the weather, the harvest, the pruning – and that was just the grapes. It was said that wine was born in the vineyard, the terroir – the local environment, the soil, the weather, the direction of the slopes, the position on the slope, well-drained, well-nourished... These were the principles of winemaking that Luc had grown up with, but recent trips to New Zealand and Australia had made him start to think differently. Visiting some of the makers of great wine on the other side of the world had been an eye-opener and taught him that the winemaker could also make a significant impact. Convincing Alphonse, born and bred in the Champagne region, might take some time and he could already guess what Marthe would think of what some might say were radical ideas.

Having inspected the caves and feeling chilled to the bone, the men returned to the surface. Luc tipped his face up to the sun, grateful to feel its warmth on his face and was immediately reminded of his new house guest and the way she'd revelled in the bright sunshine of the foyer of the château as if she'd not seen the sun for months. The way the light reflected the tawny shades in her hair and lit up the faint dusting of freckles on her face. Freckles that just begged to be kissed.

'I have a good feeling about this year,' said Alphonse.

'Good,' said Luc. 'You know I want to make some changes.'

'Excellent.' The other man rubbed his hands together. 'We're going to make great wine together. We have to pray for good weather and an excellent harvest. Come to *Maman's* place now for something to eat and I'll bring the champagne.'

Luc glanced at his watch. It was half-past five. It would be better to go and see his great-aunt in the morning.

'Yvette has some news too.'

'Yvette?' Alphonse's sister had been the bane of his life when he was younger and she had been determined that he take notice of her. Luc hoped that she'd lost interest in him long ago.

'Yes.' Alphonse grinned mischievously. 'She's home again.'

Chapter Three

Feeling a little like Belle in *Beauty and the Beast*, Hattie pushed open the double doors and stepped into an enormous ballroom, with what felt like miles of marble floor tiles opening out in front of her. A row of tall windows shrouded in opaque blinds dimmed the brilliant sunshine outside, casting a shadowy half-light across the room. The quiet almost overwhelmed her and added to the uncomfortable sensation of being an intruder. She needed to shake it off and stop being so diffident but it didn't seem quite right, prowling about someone else's home on her own.

Encouraging herself to take charge and treat this like work, she crossed to the windows and tugged at the cord on the blind. As light flooded into the room, the bright beams lit up the fine mist of dust motes released from the fabric. Her nose tickled, a sneeze threatening to burst out at any second. Like a torch beam, the shaft of sunshine cut through the gloom, revealing grubby rugs, the matt surfaces of furniture in need of a good polish, and a general air of tired decay. Any moment Hattie expected a Miss Havisham figure to rise from the sun-damaged chaise longue in front of her, where colour had leached out of the deep green velvet in one broad stripe across the seat and back. Hattie frowned. The elegant chaise, with its curved wood legs and intricately carved edges, had once been a beautiful piece. When she brushed her hand over the fabric another puff of dust billowed into the air and this time she did sneeze. Taking a very quick inventory, she decided to move on and come back later. Obviously a room this size was rarely used these days, hence its neglect. With a bit – okay a lot – of TLC, it could be quite something. This would be perfect for the wedding reception and she could imagine it filled with dozens of round tables which could be cleared back for dancing later. As she left the room, leaving the blind as it was, she pressed the light switch on the wall by the door and looked up at the four magnificent chandeliers. A few desultory bulbs came on but the number of dead ones easily outnumbered the few that lit up – and even those, thick with yet more dust, cast a half-hearted wattage.

Next, she came to what had once been a magnificent dining room. At the sight of it, her heart dropped a little. Surely the whole house wasn't going to be like this? What did the housekeeper do? Although perhaps, in a house this size, only a few rooms were used most of the time. She couldn't imagine that Luc and his family ate formally in here very often, not when they had that fabulous kitchen. Through narrowed eyes Hattie studied the enormous mahogany table, its gloss diminished by yet another coat of dust, while half its length was hidden by piles of yellowing table linen, stacked haphazardly. On a set of equally shabby-looking sideboards were dozens of sets of china: stack after stack of dinner and tea plates, saucers, soup bowls, as well as columns of cups leaning like the Tower of Pisa, clusters of elaborate serving dishes and tureens, all in a variety of colours and intricate patterns. Deep petrol blues, lush greens, intricately painted flowers and elaborate gilt edging. Hattie picked up a delicate dinner plate from the stack nearest her and blew lightly on it, her finger tracing the dirty surface to reveal a lacy gold design around the edge and intertwining pale pink flowers around the centre. She turned it over. Limoges. Picking up another she looked at the stamp on the back – Meissen this time. She whistled. Anyone who'd watched enough *Antiques Roadshow* would know that this was quite a collection. There were at least a dozen matching sets here with place settings for twenty or more people. And it looked as if it had just been dumped on the side.

Hattie shook her head, her sense of anticipation and happiness dimming. If the whole house was like this, she was really going to have her work cut out. It would need an army of cleaners to get it ready. And then she gave herself a talking-to. It couldn't all be like this. These were the unused rooms. The family must use the smaller rooms.

Walking to the other side of the house, she came to an elegant little salon where a pale blue, silk-upholstered sofa was positioned in front of an open fireplace and blue floral wallpaper lined the walls. It was very feminine and chic and she could imagine sipping afternoon tea in here. A mirror hung above the fireplace and on the white, carved mantelpiece was a selection of dust-free ornaments. Hanging on the wall in a corner of the room above a pretty little painted table was a very small pen and ink sketch of a young boy. Hattie breathed a sigh of relief. This was more like it. Perhaps Gabby could use this as an anteroom to gather with her bridesmaids and mother before the wedding ceremony and enjoy a glass of champagne.

That happy picture was quickly shattered. She surveyed

several beautiful reception rooms, each of which required a thorough deep clean, as well as a stunning library with dark wooden floor-to-ceiling shelves harbouring centuries' worth of books, the most wonderful ornate spiral staircases in dire need of a ton of beeswax polish, and a couple of enormous deep sofas that could have doubled as beds. The last room she came to was a pretty salon with teeny, feminine sofas and chairs, upholstered in watered silk, and fine-legged marquetry tables that looked as if they should be in a stately home or on a Jane Austen film set.

As Hattie took the first step on the staircase, she had to force herself to keep moving, almost too scared to find what awaited her on the next three floors. By the time she reached the attic rooms on the top floor, she was ready to weep. The place was awash with beautiful furniture, sumptuous but faded fabrics and the most elaborate cobwebs she'd ever seen in her life. However, she was inordinately grateful that she didn't have to get these rooms ready for guests. That would have been a Herculean task.

Luc had said his room was up here and for a moment she wondered at his choice. These would have been servants' quarters, and must have had far less money spent on them. Surely they'd be even more dilapidated. There were two more rooms to see at the far end of the eaves. Opening the door to one she was pleasantly surprised: it had plain white walls, with a couple of posters on them, and dormer windows opening onto a little balcony. The wide, wooden floorboards had been sanded and polished, and the room was comfortably furnished with a king-size bed tucked under the sloping roof and several shelves lining the wall with books, a few model cars and a Lego model of a *Star Wars* spacecraft – from memory she thought it might be the *Millennium Falcon* – along with a couple of familiar figures. This was obviously Luc's room and from the look of the contents of the shelves it had always been his. She smiled at the childhood books, recognising St-Exupéry's *Little Prince*, a couple of *Babar the Elephant* titles and one that thanks to the Netflix series *Lupin* she knew – *Arsène Lupin, Gentleman Cambrioleur*. There were more recent titles too – thrillers, she presumed, as she picked out the words *mort* and *noir* in some of the titles.

Luc was tidy. There were no clothes in sight apart from a pale blue sweatshirt draped over the chair in the bay of the dormer. On the desk, a simple affair with an Anglepoise lamp, were several large hardback books, a couple open showing pictures of grapes and vines. They looked like reference books. Hattie realised as she stared down at the glossy pages that she was invading Luc's privacy and hastily retreated, going to the room next door.

As soon as she walked in, she knew this was where she would stay. It was a mirror image of Luc's room and she was immediately drawn to the balcony and the view out over the valley. She stepped outside skirting the little patio table and chairs, leant on the white stone balustrade and looked down over the formal gardens. The flash of azure blue caught her eye and she turned. She could just see the end of a swimming pool and a couple of sun loungers on one of the terraces below the gardens built into the hill. She would be checking that out at some point. An early-morning swim would be a lovely start to the day. Which reminded her, she needed to bring her luggage up here.

Although the balcony was the main selling point, she was equally charmed by the simple white wrought-iron bed, the white-painted wooden bedside tables on spindly legs and the cosy armchair. The sloping ceilings were dappled with sunlight and from the bed she could see the lush green of the countryside on the horizon. The bonus was the en suite shower room with a walk-in shower tucked into the sharp angle of the ceiling. She liked the simplicity of the room and the easy access to the balcony and the fresh air. She let out a long breath, feeling something loosen inside her. For too long she'd felt cooped up, like a battery hen unable to stretch her wings. Here she'd be able to spread out and grow. For the first time in a long time, she was looking forward, outwards and not inwards. If nothing else, she'd be perfecting her cleaning skills.

After dragging her luggage upstairs, she unpacked quickly and decided to set up her laptop and notebook in the library. It seemed a fitting place to work and if it was okay with Luc, she'd make this her office. This was his home and she didn't want to overstep the mark and make him feel as if she were taking over.

When Luc pushed open the door to the kitchen in the stable block annexe, he spotted Solange immediately, sitting at the table staring out of the window. She'd lost weight and looked paler than ever but the minute she saw him, her face lit up. 'Luc! What a wonderful surprise. Does Alphonse know you're here?'

Luc laughed. 'He just asked me the same question. I have news.'

'What?' Solange was half the size of her son, but since he'd known her Luc would swear that she hadn't aged. She must be in her early fifties now but her olive skin was line-free, her dark hair not touched by grey, although her bright brown eyes were shadowed where once they'd danced with merriment.

'Alphonse has gone to get a special bottle to celebrate.'

'It must be very good news indeed,' she said, more soberly now. 'He is like a miser with that wine.' She let out a weary sigh and, with what looked like great effort, hauled herself to her feet. 'Have you eaten? I was at the market this morning.'

'No, there wasn't time,' he said, immediately feeling guilty. He should have been more evasive. Solange looked as if finding food was the last thing she needed at the moment. 'When he gets here, I'll tell you all about … everything.'

She nodded. 'Have you seen Marthe?'

'No, I'll go tomorrow morning.'

'There's brandy in the cellar.'

She exchanged a weak smile with him.

'I think the only reason she tolerates visitors is because we bring her illicit goods,' joked Luc.

'But of course,' replied Solange. 'Would you like something to eat?' She waved a vague hand at the fridge.'

'No, it's fine,' he said and was immediately outed by his stomach grumbling in protest.

With another one of her weary sighs, she shook her head. 'Take a seat out in the courtyard.'

'I don't want to put you to any trouble…'

Her mouth pursed and she straightened, an unexpected spark of steel in her eyes. 'The day I can't put a plate of food together, Luc Brémont…' With more animation than she'd shown since he'd arrived, she waved him outside.

A few minutes later she emerged with a tray bearing a plate of cheese, a basket of rustic white bread, a dish of olives and some slices of richly coloured saucisson, along with four champagne coupe glasses, which she put on the bistro table in the shade of a wisteria that was just about to bloom.

'And before you say anything, I like these glasses. No doubt, like Alphonse, you look down on them.' These traditional glasses had long fallen out of fashion. 'The champagne will not be in them long enough. Sometimes,' she said wistfully, her eyes going dreamy, 'there is joy in using beautiful things instead of practical things.'

Luc smiled. She'd always been very particular about presentation and appearances.

'Yvette is on her way,' said Solange. 'Alphonse texted her to say you were here.'

Luc smiled dutifully, although not without a frisson of alarm.

'Luc!' He rose to greet her a few minutes later, as she hurled herself into his arms, making him grateful that she had her mother's build rather than her brother's.

'Yvette.'

She cupped his face with a tanned hand. 'You're still so handsome.'

'Thank you,' he said, relieved to see the twinkle in her eye and one from the diamond on her finger. This was obviously her news.

'Who's the lucky man?'

She held up her hand to admire the sparkling engagement ring. 'Bernard. I'm not sure you would remember him. He was always away for the summers and was in the year above me in school.'

Luc shook his head. Although he'd spent his summers here, he didn't know many of the local children apart from Alphonse and Yvette.

'You'll meet him soon. He's in Brittany this week. Me and Maman are going down to join him tomorrow for a week. You'll have to fend for yourself.'

'I'm so sorry, Luc,' said Solange apologetically. 'If I'd known you were coming...'

Guilt pinched at him. He really should have let Solange know he was coming. 'I shall be fine. You do remember it was you and Marthe who taught me to cook.'

'See, *Maman*. He's a big boy now. And what news from you, Luc? How long are you staying this time?' There was a slight mocking inflection in her voice, reminding him that she'd once had feelings for him and that he'd always disappeared at the end of the summer.

He looked up to acknowledge Alphonse's approach. The other man was clutching a dark green bottle with the tenderness of a mother with her firstborn.

'I'm staying for a while.' He paused before making the announcement, 'My father has finally agreed that we can produce champagne.'

Yvette squealed and clapped her hands. 'Oh Luc, that's fantastic news. Marthe is going to be so pleased. It breaks her heart to know that the grapes are being sold to Gilles Roban. I wish I could be there when you tell him that he won't be getting this year's harvest. He cheated Marthe last year, paying such a low rate per tonne.'

'I'm looking forward to being there too,' said Alphonse. 'He's been pestering me to meet him to discuss terms. He said if we agreed a good rate early, he would take more grapes.'

'Yes, and we know what sort of rate that would be,' spat Yvette. 'He's a crook.'

Alphonse shook his head. 'He's a businessman.'

'Who takes advantage. I wouldn't waste my spit on him.'

Luc laughed. 'Still making friends wherever you go then?' he teased.

Yvette tossed her rich red curls, which matched her fiery personality. 'He is a brute. It will be so wonderful to have a Brémont here producing champagne again.'

'And let's get this champagne open, it's the 2014.' Alphonse waggled his eyebrows. 'I've been saving it for a special occasion. And I think a St Martin champagne is the very best reason.'

Luc straightened in anticipation. The year 2014 had been a very good vintage with a long growing season. He was keen to try it.

Alphonse shot his mother a quick glance as he popped the cork but knew better than to say anything about the glasses.

With the crisp golden wine poured into the delicate coupe glasses, which Luc knew had been in the family for over a hundred years, he reached forward and picked up a glass, taking a good sniff before tasting. He let the liquid swill over his tongue, savouring the sharp tang of bubbles and the biscuity flavour with underlying notes of lemon and honeydew melon.

'Very nice,' he said.

'It's exquisite,' said Yvette. 'Although I notice you didn't open this for my engagement.'

'Luc coming home is more important,' teased Alphonse. As Yvette bristled, Luc decided that a change of direction was called for.

'How is Marthe?'

'I saw her yesterday. She's very well,' said Solange. 'Ruling the roost, of course. She has all the carers running around doing her bidding.'

'I can't believe she's happy there,' said Yvette. She spread expansive hands. 'This is her home. She should be here.'

It wasn't actually – the château had been inherited by Luc's father but he'd let Marthe, his aunt by marriage, continue to live there, although he'd stopped the champagne production when she had her stroke because he didn't want to spread himself too thin in too many different areas.

Solange sank into herself as if it was an argument they'd had many times and Luc realised he was in danger of causing another. The good Bernard must be a saint to put up with Yvette's volatile nature.

'Marthe never wanted to be a burden,' Solange started to say.

'She wouldn't have been. We could have turned one of the downstairs rooms into a bedroom and we'd have all helped.'

Solange shrugged, which luckily Yvette didn't see. Luc knew without a shadow of a doubt that the burden would have fallen on Solange, who would never have complained, but it would have been an unfair responsibility. She was employed as housekeeper to the château, not as a carer.

So what ideas do you have for the champagne?' asked Alphonse, a past master at defusing arguments. 'A brut, a demi-sec, a blanc de blancs, a blanc de noirs, a cuvée?'

'So many questions,' said Solange. 'He's only just arrived. Let him eat and drink.'

'Don't worry, Alphonse,' said Luc, patting his friend on the shoulder. 'There's plenty of time for us to make our plans. We need to hope for the right weather conditions and a good harvest. Competition is going to be stiff. Other countries are producing good sparkling wines, even the British.' He laughed as Alphonse sniffed disdainfully.

'It's not champagne,' he said, sticking his nose in the air.

'No, it's not but we need to make sure whatever we produce is better.'

'We will.' Alphonse lifted his glass. 'To a magical summer.'

'Ah,' replied Luc. 'There is one small problem.'

All three heads turned his way. 'To recoup the costs of not

producing anything this year and not selling the grapes on, my father has decided to rent out the château on an exclusive basis for a wedding party.'

'When?' asked Yvette with a decided snap in her voice as she lifted her chin and gave Luc a direct look.

'The wedding is the last week of July.' He didn't miss the quick worried glance that Solange and Alphonse exchanged.

'July! What day in July?' Yvette gasped. Her eyes blazed with quick fury but he was used to her mercurial moods. 'And so close to harvest.'

'I'm not sure of the exact date.'

'Impossible,' cried Yvette. 'You have a vineyard to run. How will that work? By magic? *Maman* will be too busy to organise a wedding. After all, she's too busy to help look after Marthe.' Yvette shot her mother a surly smirk.

'There's no need to worry. The wedding planner arrived today.'

'She has?' Alphonse perked up. 'How old is she?'

Luc laughed at Alphonse's sudden interest, although at the same time he felt an oddly proprietorial feeling, suddenly remembering the unexpected nudge of attraction when he'd first seen her on the doorstep.

Solange and Yvette looked at each other in horror. 'I would not want a wedding planner,' said Yvette wrinkling her nose.

'You couldn't afford a wedding planner,' said Alphonse.

'I don't need one. I just want my friends and family gathered around me. It's about love. What does a big show-off affair mean? Nothing. Although of course,' she added with a brilliant smile, 'I want to be the centre of attention all day.'

They all laughed at her candid admission.

'There'll be no doubt of that,' said Solange with a gentle smile. 'You'll be a beautiful bride.'

'And you will cry.'

'Of course I will.'

'While inside she'll be cheering that she's finally got you off her hands,' added Alphonse.

Yvette sniffed. 'At least one of us will be off her hands. You don't even have a girlfriend.'

'Now, now,' admonished Solange.

'There's no one good enough,' replied Alphonse with a good-natured grin, despite his sister's barb.

Did Hattie have a boyfriend? Luc wondered, and suddenly he wanted to know rather desperately. There was a part of him that certainly hoped she didn't.

Chapter Four

Hattie woke up to her stomach performing a series of gymnastics. She was starving. She closed her eyes again, wishing she could go back to sleep and ignore the sense of doom which had hit her. What had she taken on? Last night, she'd been so dispirited she'd gone to bed because there was nothing else to do. All she'd eaten was a baguette at a service station en route and half a pack of *palmiers* – the only thing she'd found in the cupboards in the kitchen.

The first sip of strong black coffee and the reassuring hit of caffeine quelled her initial frustration at finding only thimble-sized espresso cups before she remembered that the French drank coffee from bowls rather than mugs. As she nursed the bowl between both hands, taking tiny sips, she began to compile a mental shopping list. Milk was definitely top of the list along with *croissant*, *confiture* and *beurre*. She spoke the French words out loud – they were the principal part of her limited vocabulary – rolling the syllables on her tongue: '*Paté, fromage, saucisson.*'

She didn't even know where the nearest bloody shop was.

Come on now, Hattie. Stay positive, she told herself. Think about why you've come here. For example, over next few months she could eat *when* she liked and *what* she liked. She was going to be the main character in her own life for once.

Her French was basic but being here was an excellent opportunity to try and improve it, although languages had never been her strong point; she found all that grammar stuff tedious in the extreme.

'*Je m'appelle Hattie. Je suis ici* to have some fun,' she said out loud firmly.

'Excellent. I'm glad to hear it. Fun is always good.'

She whirled round to find Luc.

'Hi,' she said over-brightly, the flush of embarrassment staining her cheeks. Amusement lit his eyes as he surveyed her.

'Just practising my French,' she said.

'So I see.' His lips twitched, and damn him, she could tell he was trying to hold back a smirk.

'Yes.' She lifted her chin. She didn't care.

'And are you having fun?' he asked. There it was again, that little lopsided lift at one side of his mouth. Was he teasing her?

'I plan to.' She lifted her chin. 'I've been stuck –' she wasn't going to explain about Chris '– in a … a situation I wasn't very happy in and I'm just happy to be here. Looking forward to an adventure. Something different.'

'I see,' he said gravely. She was babbling again but there was something about him that made her feel all fizzy inside.

Amusement danced in his eyes as they focused on her and his smile was positively fiendish. He leaned back against one of the kitchen counters, lazily folding his arms. Her heart jumped into her throat and a flush of heat washed over her.

Would she ever get used to the sight of him? Hopefully regular exposure would stop her being reduced to a blithering idiot.

'Not *fun* fun. Just, you know, just enjoying the moment.' *Hattie, shut up, just shut up. Close your mouth and stop the words coming out.* Suddenly she found herself unable to stop her gaze dropping to his lips and that movie-star square jaw. What would it be like to be kissed by him? Held against that broad chest, against the soft chambray of his shirt? Oh God, she'd got wedding fever. Too much time thinking about those happy brides and grooms … but then it was so long since she'd kissed anyone but Chris, and in the last few years that had felt nothing more than platonic. Her hormones had been in deep hibernation for longer than was good for them and suddenly they were fighting their way out with spring enthusiasm.

She bet Luc knew what he was doing when he kissed a woman. Suddenly she longed to be kissed again by someone who wasn't worried that his mum might walk in at any second or that the lights weren't dim enough. Someone who had sex with the lights on. During the day. Someone who couldn't wait to rip her clothes off. Someone who would make her feel alive again.

'Hattie?'

Oh, shit, he'd asked her a question and she had no idea what he'd just said. She was still staring at his lips. She might as well have been shouting, *Come kiss me*.

Before she could drop her gaze, his mouth curved into a smile. He was dazzling and it was like receiving a socking great punch to the heart. For the ninety-nine millionth time, she acknowledged he was flipping gorgeous.

'Sorry, what did you say?' she said, knocked off balance by this ridiculous crush.

'I asked the date of the wedding and also if you needed anything?'

She wondered what he'd say if she said, 'Hot, sweaty, mindless, meaningless sex.'

Instead, she managed to put that thought to the back of her mind.

She cleared her throat. 'It's on the twenty-fifth of July and the only thing I need right now is food.'

Concern filled his eyes, which for some reason was rather gratifying. 'I'm sorry. I … didn't think. I had breakfast with Alphonse this morning. I'm afraid Solange, the housekeeper, is about to go away for a week and I haven't had a chance to go shopping yet.'

'So where's the best place to get some food?'

'A hypermarket. That's usually a good place to start.' His eyes twinkled.

She waved a hand to excuse her vagueness, her tone a little prim. 'I mean, would you be able to tell me where the nearest supermarket is.'

'But of course. There's an E. Leclerc in Hautvillers. A fifteen-minute drive away. I'm going to visit my aunt this morning, I could give you a lift if you'd like?'

She wrinkled her nose and rolled her shoulders, which still ached from yesterday's marathon drive. 'That's very kind of you but I'm not sure I can face the thought of getting in a car again or doing a big shop. I only wanted a few things to start with.' Plus she was worried that sitting in close proximity might reduce her to a jellied mess.

'There's a shop in the village, it has most things.'

'Can I walk there?'

'Hmm, it's a bit of a walk. There's a bicycle you can use. It belonged to my aunt, but Solange sometimes uses it, so it should be in working order.'

'That would be great.' The idea of cycling through the French countryside immediately appealed to her.

'Would you like me to go and bring it round for you? I'll check the tyres are okay.'

'That's very kind of you,' she said.

'No problem,' he murmured in French, which even she could understand. Unfortunately, when he spoke in French, it was even sexier.

'By the way.' He paused in the doorway. 'I think I could show you how to have fun.'

Luc drove down the lane from the château in his open-topped vintage Alpine sports car, the breeze raking his hair, and passed Hattie leisurely pedalling along. Guilt made an unwelcome bid for his attention. While he was tucking into bread and cheese with the others last night, he hadn't so much as given poor Hattie a second thought or even wondered what she might do for food. He should have remembered that there was unlikely to be much in the cupboards because Solange still wasn't up to speed and she hadn't been expecting either of them. Given she must have been starving, Hattie had taken it with surprisingly good grace. He couldn't imagine Celeste, his ex, putting up with treatment like that. She'd have raised merry hell and certainly wouldn't have been happy to go off on a bicycle to do her own shopping.

Hattie looked as if she were thoroughly enjoying herself, her head bobbing about taking in the view. Despite himself he smiled at the picture she made and the memory of her appalling French. He put his hand up and waved as he passed and watched her in his rear-view mirror.

He was still smiling to himself when he pulled up outside the residential home on the outskirts of Hautvillers. Pushing thoughts of the Englishwoman aside, he tucked the bottle of brandy in his inside pocket and strode through the doors to reception. The nurse at the front desk had been there several years and immediately recognised him and waved him through.

'She's on the terrace,' she said, pointing through the restaurant area to the wide balcony that overlooked the valley. Overgrown with vines that needed a good trim, it provided a lovely shady spot in the afternoon. He half-laughed to himself; he was surprised that his great-aunt hadn't taken to pruning them herself.

Marthe's tall, spare frame was tucked into her wheelchair with a big blue blanket which brought out the blue of her still bird-bright eyes.

'About time too. Did you bring my brandy?' she asked.

'I did. How are you?'

'I'm the same as I was the last time you were here. Old, irritated and bored.'

'You once told me only boring people got bored.'

Her mouth wrinkled in displeasure. 'I've changed my mind and at my age I'm allowed to. I'm surrounded by boring people and now you're here.' She huffed out an exasperated sigh.

'I'll endeavour to be more interesting,' said Luc slapping a hand over his chest as if wounded by her words.

'You can try,' said Marthe and then her face relaxed into a mischievous grin. 'It's good to see you. How are you? And how is that hopeless mother of yours? And your father.' She shook her head in familiar disapproval.

'The same,' said Luc, catching her eye, his mouth turning down. Only with Marthe could he be honest about his feelings. She'd known him since he was seven, the first time they'd dumped him on her, a spoilt, indulged yet neglected young boy.

Marthe leaned forward with her good arm and patted him on the knee. 'Good job you've got me then, isn't it?'

'It is,' he agreed solemnly but they both knew she was speaking the truth. Since he'd been to stay with her all those years ago, she'd been the constant in his life. The person he could rely on to be there. His parents, easily bored, never liked to stay put anywhere too long. Before he was seven it had been much easier to leave him with au pairs but he'd lost count of the number of times he'd woken up to find they'd left without any notice. It was only later he realised they'd been dismissed by his mother because his father had paid them too much attention.

'You said you had news. Please tell me you're not marrying one of those Parisienne girls.'

'I have no plans to get married.' His parents' example of marriage was enough to put anyone off. He wanted someone he could rely on who wouldn't want to go flying off at short notice or disappear overnight.

'I didn't say I didn't want you to get married, just that I wanted you to find a nice girl, perhaps from around here. You know Yvette is getting married. Thank goodness.'

'Yes and I'm pleased for her.' And rather relieved.

'You would never have suited, despite what she thought. Bernard is a good man, placid. He'll put up with her volcano of a temperament.'

'God help him.'

'He'll need more than divine intervention. So what is this news of yours? Is this another one of your flying visits?' she asked tartly.

Luc smiled as he looked at her, knowing her sharp words hid her feelings. She'd become a surrogate mother to him – not that she'd ever admit to tenderness for him.

'Actually, no. I'm staying for a while.' He'd wanted to tell her in person. 'I have finally persuaded my father to let me take over the château and produce wine.'

He was pleased to see her mouth drop open and then her eyes light up, a slight sheen of tears in them. 'Oh my boy. A Brémont back at the château making St Martin champagne.' This was a rare show of emotion, which was quickly staunched when she asked, 'You will be making champagne, won't you?' Although Luc knew it wasn't so much a question as a command.

'But of course,' he said, smiling at her.

'Hmph,' she sniffed. 'That is very good news.' She paused before adding. 'I hope you're not going to get all modern and innovative and reinvent all the old ways.'

'Not all of them,' he said equably. 'But I'd like to try some new things.' He knew Marthe, while a stickler for quality, was not one to follow tradition for tradition's sake. 'But I'd like to discuss my ideas with you and Alphonse.'

Her mouth tightened. 'What sort of ideas? There's too much throwing out of systems and processes that have worked perfectly well for hundreds of years. This area has been making the best wine in the world for decades. There is no need to change things.'

'There are always different ways of doing things,' he said gently. 'But it is the wine that is the most important.'

'What sort of changes do you envisage?' For a moment Luc glimpsed a hint of worry in her face but he couldn't lie to her.

'Marthe, we have to move forward. There are lots of modern techniques.' He knew that his ideas on wine making went against her fiercely traditional views. Her generation believed that wine was all about the grapes and the *terroir* whereas he believed that wine was made by the winemaker.

He was going to have to tread very carefully.

'What about the winery?' she snapped.

'Don't worry, I have no plans to make any immediate changes to the building.' He didn't have the money but as soon as he did...

'Make sure you don't. Not in my lifetime anyway. Once I'm gone I don't care what you do.'

'You're not going anywhere,' said Luc, deliberately seizing on the change of subject.

'Not in this damned chair I'm not. Too many bloody steps everywhere. But as you're here you can take me to the wedding.'

'Yvette and Bernard's?' he asked.

'Yes,' she said irritably. 'Who else's would I be talking about?'

'You mean you don't know?' Luc was genuinely surprised that she hadn't heard the news about the château. 'My father's business partner in London has hired the château for the summer for a wedding at the end of July.'

Marthe raised her grey, rather wild eyebrows and frowned. 'Ah, now I see. That is what has set the fox to mind the geese. Yvette popped by first thing this morning and was in one of her wild moods.' Her mouth wrinkled. 'That explains everything.'

'It does?' asked Luc.

'Yvette has her heart set on celebrating her wedding in the vineyard. Let's hope the dates don't clash.'

'When is Yvette's wedding?'

'The twenty-fifth of July.'

Luc's vision went black for a second and then he spat an expletive out.

Marthe rose a reproving eyebrow.

'It's the same day as the wedding at the château.'

'Oh dear,' said Marthe, with a sudden malicious twinkle in her eye. 'That is very bad timing. Someone is going to be very unpopular.'

Luc closed his eyes and shook his head, tension pinching with spiteful fingers at his shoulders.

'I'm glad I'm not walking in your shoes,' said Marthe with a wry smile. 'I'd be more worried about Yvette and what she'll do when she finds out. I predict trouble ahead.'

Luc gave a grim smile. It didn't take a crystal ball to tell him she was bang on the money.

Chapter Five

'No!' shrieked Yvette. 'No! No! No!' She picked up the coffee bowl from the draining board and hurled it across the kitchen.

Solange's hands fluttered in distress as it crashed onto the floor and shards of china ricocheted across the floor.

Then Yvette burst into noisy sobs and her mother put her arms around her, giving Luc a helpless look. He sighed and exchanged a quick glance with Alphonse, who for once was being uncharacteristically diplomatic and not winding his sister up. That had gone well then. Thank goodness there was no sign of Hattie. She'd settled in well over the last week, or at least he assumed she had; he'd barely seen her as he'd been out with Alphonse every evening. He'd caught sight of her cycling into the village a few times. Luc hoped she was out and not somewhere in the château to witness Yvette and Solange's dramatic homecoming from Brittany.

'I'm sorry, Yvette.'

'Sorry!' she screamed. 'Sorry! You're going to ruin my wedding day.'

He felt that was a bit harsh as he wasn't personally responsible but now was not the time to argue that particular point.

'Maybe you can change the date,' he suggested and as soon as the words left his mouth he knew he'd stepped into shark-infested water and was about to lose a foot. Even Alphonse stiffened.

'Change the date!' Her voice pitched to a note he wasn't sure he'd ever heard a human make before and he glanced up anxiously at the glass pendants, worried for their safety. 'Change the date!' Her eyes burned furiously. 'Me! This is my home! Me change the date! I have dreamed of getting married here, all my life.' She took a step towards him and Luc felt like he was facing one of the three Furies. She poked him in the chest, hard, not once but twice. 'You,' she said the word with such menace, the hairs on the back of his neck stood up, 'Want. Me. To. Change. My. Wedding. Day.'

Luc shifted on the spot like a schoolboy outside the principal's office but held her gaze. '*I* don't *want* you to but it's a possible solution.'

'What about them finding somewhere else to hold their wedding?' She gave him a wild-eyed stare.

Luc had to be honest with her. 'We need the money from the wedding to make up for the loss of income from not selling the grapes this year. Apparently my father made the agreement with Monsieur Carter-Jones in January. They are good friends as well as business partners. He won't let him down. Besides the invitations have already been sent out.' He'd only just discovered that fact in the car on the way back from Marthe's, when his father had called him.

'My invitations have gone out. The whole village is coming for the *vin d'honneur*.'

'The whole village?'

'Yes. It is tradition. Like *Maman* and Papa. It is their anniversary. The date is very special.' Tears shone in Yvette's eyes now and his gut twisted in joint sympathy and guilt, even though none of this was his fault. 'We cannot change it.' Her face hardened. 'You have to do something, Luc.'

Even Solange was now looking at him with a pleading expression.

He had to be honest about this. 'I'm not sure what I can do. Couldn't both weddings happen on the same day?'

'Idiot!' Yvette tossed her head. 'How?'

'It would be difficult,' said Solange, her hand sweeping around the kitchen, rather ineffectually. 'The food, the cooking.'

'It is impossible.' Yvette glared at her mother and Luc. 'They are the ones that have to find somewhere else to hold their wedding.' With that she tossed her hair and marched out of the kitchen, barging into Hattie, who was coming through the doorway.

It was the worst possible timing, thought Luc as Yvette paused, glaring at Hattie, who was rubbing her arm where she'd collided with the door jamb. Then, without apology, she stomped off shouting a string of insults about entitled foreigners, spoilt bitch brides and interlopers, leaving Luc glad that Hattie's French vocabulary was extremely limited.

'You okay?' asked Luc, a note of apology in his voice, wanting to cross the floor and rub her arm for her.

Hattie looked a little bemused and stared down the corridor after Yvette. 'Someone's not very happy. Is everything all right? Can I do anything to help?'

Yvette did not deserve Hattie's immediate and gentle

sympathy. Luc felt an odd sense of protectiveness towards her. She obviously didn't hold grudges.

He grimaced. 'I'm sorry about that. Yvette's a bit upset about something and we were having a small difference of opinion.' He glanced at Solange.

'Hattie, this is Solange Ferrier and this is Alphonse, her son, and that was Yvette, her daughter.'

'Hello, pleased to meet you,' said Hattie, striding in with a wicker basket of goodies looped over her arm. Luc was impressed by her cheery attitude and friendliness despite the somewhat awkward atmosphere. It was as if she was determined to set everyone at ease.

'*Bonjour*,' said Alphonse, a little awkwardly. 'I apologise for my sister.' Then to Luc's annoyance, he flashed a charming grin at Hattie. 'Not all of us are savages. Welcome to St Martin. If you need someone to show you around, I'll be happy to do that.' Luc watched as Alphonse turned on the charm, his soft brown eyes filling with warmth directed at Hattie. 'Have you been to the village yet? There's an excellent bar there.'

'She's been to the village,' snapped Luc, narrowing his eyes.

'Ah, but I know it better than you. And you'll be busy building your new empire.' Luc's jaw tightened at Alphonse's theatrical wink. 'Perhaps I could show you some proper French hospitality.'

Hattie smiled. 'That sounds lovely. Maybe when I've found my feet and settled in a bit.'

Alphonse nodded. 'But of course. If there's anything you need, you can always ask. I've lived here all my life. If you will excuse me, I must get to work.' And with that he left.

'Pretty flowers,' said Solange in English, pointing to the bunches of blue and pink stocks.

Hattie gave the bunch of flowers an enthusiastic sniff.

'I couldn't resist the smell and life is too short not to buy things that give you pleasure.'

Luc felt an odd twinge in his chest at the picture she made, as her tawny ponytail bounced and she smiled with innocent happiness at her flowers.

'Although they're not as grand as the ones in the hallway,' she added, immediately winning the housekeeper over, as a rare smiled brightened Solange's solemn face. 'Did you arrange those? They're beautiful.'

'I did. We're very fortunate. Pierre, the gardener, keeps us well stocked with cut flowers. I find working with flowers … peaceful.'

'Me too,' said Hattie with chatty friendliness. 'My granny is a big flower arranger. They just brighten up a room, don't they?'

To Luc's amazement, Solange's face brightened even more. 'They do.' She looked at Hattie's basket. 'You have been shopping,' she said before giving Luc an accusing glare as if he should have taken her.

Good God, the Ferrier women had it in for him today. He wanted to hold his hands up in surrender, which he might have done with Yvette – she could more than stand up for herself – but Solange, since her husband's death, bruised easily.

'Yes, I got a bit carried away by all the wonderful cheese.'

'You should go to the market. They have an even better selection.'

'I'd love that.'

'If you like I will take you one day. The flowers there are quite wonderful, although don't tell Pierre I said that.'

'I won't,' said Hattie.

'If you like I can ask my son to bring you fresh croissants in the mornings from the boulangerie.'

'I wouldn't want him to go to any trouble. I've been cycling to the village every day for a coffee and just to sit and enjoy being in France but I'm starting to get a bit busier now.'

'No, now that I'm back he will bringing them for me and this is on his way to work.'

Luc folded his arms. No one had offered him freshly baked croissants. As if reading his mind, Solange gave him a gentle smile. 'You live here. Hattie is a guest.'

'A working guest,' interjected Hattie. 'And I have a lot to do, so if you'll excuse me. I'll just put this lot away and get to work. Nice to meet you, Solange.'

Solange nodded and turned to Luc, speaking in French again. 'She seems very nice.' She sighed, wringing her hands. 'What are we going to do?'

'I don't know,' replied Luc because it was the truth. He watched as Hattie began unloading her shopping and he turned on the kettle for something to do. He didn't have a damn clue what to do.

When he turned round Solange had drifted out of the patio doors.

'Is everything all right?' asked Hattie.

'Mm. Would you like a coffee?' Luc stretched up to retrieve the coffee beans and was grateful for their loud clatter in the electric grinder which prevented conversation, if only briefly.

'Yes please, that would be lovely. That all sounded very dramatic.'

'Yvette is … volatile.'

'So I saw,' said Hattie rubbing her arm again. 'I don't want to pry but if that was a small difference of opinion, I'd hate to see what a big one would be like.'

'Sorry about that. She's a little upset about … some news she's had.' Should he tell Hattie about the date clash?

Hattie nodded and continued putting her shopping away.

It seemed natural for the pair of them to gravitate to the breakfast bar and sit side by side, drinking their coffee.

'Can I ask about something?' Hattie put her coffee down and gave him a direct look.

'Yes,' he said, in the sort of clipped voice which actually meant to anyone that chose to hear that he really meant 'No'.

'You said Solange is the housekeeper. What does she do? I mean, for example, she doesn't do the shopping – you said you stocked the fridge. I'd have thought that would have been something she would do.'

'She does lots of things,' said Luc a little desperately, not wanting to be disloyal to Solange. She'd been with the family for the whole of her working life. In fact, she *was* family.

Hattie raised her eyebrows in obvious disbelief.

'Is there a problem?' he asked, knowing and regretting that he sounded defensive.

'Look, I don't want to be rude but … this place is filthy. Everything needs a good clean. A deep clean. Upholstery, curtains, carpets. I can tell you now that this is not what my uncle or my cousin was expecting. They're going to be very disappointed.'

Luc hardened his heart, seeing a potential glimmer of hope. 'Then you should let them know that the château isn't suitable. There's still time to call off the wedding. Find a more fitting venue.' Despite the terse words, he wasn't stupid enough to believe that anywhere would be available at such short notice.

At the look of hurt surprise in her eyes, he felt like he'd just kicked a kitten, but needs must. 'I'm sorry the château isn't up to scratch but better for them to know sooner rather than later.'

. . .

And just when she was starting to like Luc Brémont, he went and said something like that. Worse still, before she could say anything, like a big arrogant château owner, he got up, left his half-drunk coffee and walked out as if the whole matter was over and done with.

With hunched shoulders Hattie sat and drank the rest of her coffee in moody slurps. There was absolutely no way on earth she was telling her uncle or her cousin that the wedding had to be called off. She needed to get this one under her belt – her career relied upon it. She had to get some truly fantastic pictures to create an eye-catching portfolio for the website she was planning to help her get her business off the ground. This was her big chance. And it was exactly the sort of thing a wedding planner had to be resourceful about. Unplanned obstacles were always cropping up. How many times had she had to swing into action to come up with an acceptable compromise when something had gone wrong? The job was always stressful but that was also part of the fun. You never knew what would be thrown at you and she was a great believer in 'where there's a will there's a way'.

She would hire a team of cleaners, that's what she'd do, as Gabby was already pressing her for pictures of the interiors.

She was going to prove that she could handle anything. With Luc Bremont's help or not.

Chapter Six

The next morning, Hattie reviewed her plans as she drank her coffee and ate one of the big buttery croissants that had appeared in the kitchen as promised by Solange. In the mornings she would carry on with wedding planning admin, liaising with the caterers, the florist, the printers and the celebrant, and supervise the cleaning of the main reception rooms that she thought should be used, so that she could send Gabby pictures. Until she could get a cleaning team on board, she'd make a start herself in the afternoons. It wasn't as if she hadn't had plenty of practice. Somehow she'd fallen into the role of managing the house for Chris and his mother.

There was no sign of Luc although she'd heard the shower in the room next door earlier on. She sighed and told herself she was not feeling lonely. It was just that she wasn't used to being on her own. Her phone rang and she glanced at the caller ID. Chris. She caught her lip between her teeth. For the last couple of days, she'd been ignoring his calls and he'd left a few desperate messages on her voicemail. Guilt gnawed at her as the shrill ringtone sounded again. Paralysed by indecision, she let it ring.

'Your phone's ringing,' Luc pointed out unhelpfully, of course sauntering into the kitchen at that very moment, with still damp hair, rubbing at it with a towel, and wearing a white waffle robe which accentuated the golden tan of his chest exposed by the V in the fabric.

He looked mouth-wateringly gorgeous but she managed to level a hard Paddington-worthy stare at him, while in her head she was telling herself, 'Don't look at his chest, don't look at his chest, don't look at his chest.' To her relief the phone rang off.

'It's not now,' she said, childishly.

He smirked at her. 'Ah, croissants.' He helped himself to one and a coffee from the cafetière that she'd made earlier and sat down.

'Help yourself,' she said calmly.

'Thanks,' he said with a grin and then took a generous spoonful of jam and dipped the end of his croissant in it.

He closed his eyes with evident enjoyment and munched on his first mouthful of the flaky, buttery pastry. She was surprised by the quick rush of pleasure she found in watching him.

Disconcerted, she brought things back to the practical. 'I thought perhaps to save Solange extra work, as she wasn't expecting me –' and she was clearly struggling with the house '– I'd do a food shop … perhaps for both of us.'

'There's hardly any point, is there?' said Luc finally swallowing his mouthful.

She frowned. 'Why not?'

'Well, you'll be leaving soon, won't you? Have you spoken to your uncle yet?'

She huffed out a mirthless laugh. 'I don't give up that easily. Don't worry I shall sort everything out. That's what we wedding planners do,' she said with more confidence than she felt. How hard could it be to find a team of cleaners? Surely she could find a way of asking Solange what the cleaning arrangements were without insinuating that she hadn't been doing a very good job managing them.

Her phone rang again. Luc raised an eyebrow. The moment was pure Mexican standoff.

She certainly wasn't going to talk to Chris for the first time in days with Luc listening in. She hadn't spoken to him since they'd broken up but wasn't that the point of breaking up with someone – you didn't have to talk to them anymore? After all it had been his decision, although maybe that was unfair. He'd never expected her to take his knee-jerk ultimatum at face value. Perhaps she did owe it to him to talk to him.

'Someone really wants to speak to you.'

Her jaw tightened and tension pinged at the muscles in her shoulders. For a second she was back in the kitchen in Chris's house. She could feel the same old tight bands around her temples and that dulling sense of resignation and responsibility. It was like being dragged back under again.

Then, to her surprise, Luc's face softened. 'Are you okay?'

Tears blurred her vision for a second and she had to swallow hard a couple of times but she still couldn't speak.

Luc's hand, warm and comforting wrapped around hers. She glanced up at his face and saw empathy and understanding.

'My father does the same. Keeps ringing until I answer.' Luc smiled at her, his mouth curving with such gentle sympathy it made her want to cry. 'It's a form of control, trying to make me do what he wants. I always remember that when I choose to answer.' He carried on in a conversational tone. 'He didn't want to me to come here. For the last few years, I've been troubleshooting for the family business. We own a lot of vineyards all over the country, so I'm always being sent here, there and everywhere. This year I put my foot down. Said I wanted to make champagne here. This is my home.' This was said with added ferocity before he continued in the previous calm tone. 'It wasn't until I resigned my position as director with a formal letter to the board that he finally took me seriously.' Luc's smile was rueful now. 'I didn't answer a lot of calls that week.'

Her breath evened out – she hadn't realised she'd been holding on to it so tightly. Suddenly she wanted to confide in him. 'I'm running away.' That sounded cowardly so she added, to make her feel a little better, 'For an adventure.'

Luc nodded. 'That's always a good reason.'

Hattie glanced down at her phone and the missed call notification. 'I had the opportunity of this job and I—' Now it was her turn to smile ruefully. 'I grabbed it with both hands even though I knew it would upset my boyfriend – my ex, I mean – because he didn't want me to come.'

'But it's only for two months. That is not so long. He could have come and visit.'

Hattie looked Luc in the eye. 'He knew I wanted to escape.'

At Luc's perturbed frown, she shook her head. 'He's not a bad person … It's just…' How could she say this without sounding full of herself? 'He's very reliant on me. We live … I lived with him and his mother. She has health issues and Chris has too, he hasn't worked for a while, so he stays home and looks after her.

'When I said I'd been offered the job in France, he said it

was him or France.' She closed her eyes remembering the look on Chris's face when she'd answered.

'Ah,' said Luc.

'I said France. I knew he didn't mean it...' Again, she looked Luc in the eye, hoping he wouldn't judge her too harshly. 'But it gave me the easy way out. While he was still sulking, I packed my stuff and then I spoke to him, reminded him that things hadn't been right for a while. He agreed and suggested we have some time apart. Thinking time. I knew if I said yes to that I wasn't being honest with him. So I broke up with him and went home to my parents.'

'And now you're regretting it?' He withdrew his hand.

She felt the metaphorical retreat and missed the warm comfort of his touch. Quick to deny it, her head shot up. 'God no! Not at all. It's the right thing. No, I'm feeling horribly guilty because I know he'll be upset and I've hurt him. And I'm worried he won't be able to cope and that he'll … he'll end up being depressed again and that … I've been a cow. Leaving him when he needs me.' She dropped her face into her hands, kneading her temples. It was all such a mess.

'Hattie, I don't know you very well but you don't seem like a cow to me. No horns or udders.' He gave her hand another one of those reassuring squeezes. 'Maybe you do need to speak to him, to let him know it is over, but no one should be dependent on someone else for their happiness. You have to be happy for yourself. And if someone else is making you unhappy, then you have to look after yourself. You can't be happy for other people.'

She huffed out a breath. 'Thank you. It doesn't stop me feeling guilty.'

'You know, in the aeroplane, when they say, "Put your oxygen mask on before you help others"? Think of it like that.'

She gave him a wan smile. 'Sorry to dump on you. That's all a bit heavy for this time of the morning.'

Luc looked down at his watch and swore. 'I'm supposed to be meeting someone at the cellar in five minutes.' He tugged at the gaping neck of his robe and pushed a hand through his unbrushed hair. 'I have to go. Will you be all right? Why don't we have dinner this evening? I'm used to eating out or on my own. It will be good to have some company.'

Luc, she realised, was very self-sufficient; he didn't seem to need anyone. She wondered what made someone like that, and thought how different he was from Chris. She was somewhere in the middle and sometimes she worried that maybe she needed to be needed by someone. A secret part of her acknowledged that at first she'd enjoyed rescuing Chris. Had she been as much at fault as he was?

Oh God, Luc was looking at her, as if waiting for an answer. She'd tuned out.

He took her hand again as if to anchor her back to the here and now. 'We could go to the market at lunchtime and buy some food together?'

A warm wave of gratitude overwhelmed her. When was the last time someone had comforted her? Even taken the time to look out for her? 'That sounds like a good idea.' Although her words were brisk inside she was touched by his thoughtfulness. 'Thank you, Luc. You'd better go, you're going to be late.'

He shrugged, releasing her hands. 'I'll see you later. And,' he paused, kindness glowing in his face, 'don't be so hard on yourself.'

Her heart fluttered in her chest, triggered by his compassion. Good-looking *and* lovely. She found herself a little embarrassed by the way she'd first judged him, on looks alone, assuming he'd be arrogant. Already she could tell he was a genuinely good person.

Hattie sat at the table for a while longer gazing into her coffee cup. It had been good to say everything out loud. Just being here in the light and space of this wonderful house gave her room to breathe and to take the time to focus on the little things. The buttery taste of a croissant, the rich flavour of the coffee, the beautiful morning sunshine. Being here allowed her to put life back into perspective. She already felt better.

Sitting at the desk in the library, having cleaned the dusty surface, Hattie checked one of the many emails she had been sent by her cousin. First things first. There was no mention of a wedding cake. Gabby hated dried fruit and had once said she would never want a traditional wedding cake. Hattie considered some of the wedding cakes she'd seen recently: St Clements with alternate layers of orange and lemon, rose petal, cranberry and prosecco or perhaps lemon and elderflower. This was what she loved about her job, matching the perfect elements of the wedding to the couple. She'd come up with some suggestions to wow her cousin. However, Gabby was quite clear on what she wanted regarding food. A three-course meal. NO BUFFET. The capitals shouted at her from the notes. Which reminded her she ought to touch base with caterers and introduce herself.

'*Bonjour, puis-je parler avec –*' she referred to her notes '– *Madame Garnier?*'

'Yes, who's calling?' demanded the voice in English on the other end of the telephone. Hattie wrinkled her nose. So much for her best French and the list of phrases she'd copied down from Google.

'Hattie Carter-Jones, I'm calling on behalf of Gabriella Carter-Jones to discuss the arrangements for the wedding at Château St Martin on the twenty-fifth of July.'

'I'll put you through.' Hattie frowned wondering if she'd imagined something in the tone of the receptionist.

'Hello, Mademoiselle Carter-Jones. This is Juliet Garnier.'

'Hello, I thought I'd ring and introduce myself. I'm making the final arrangements here in France for my cousin's wedding.'

'I regret to inform you that we are no longer able to provide the services for the wedding.'

'Sorry?' Hattie spoke automatically, thinking that maybe she'd misheard or that something had gone wrong in translation.

'We are no longer available on the twenty-fifth. I'm afraid we have another wedding that day.'

'So you can't do the catering.'

'That is what I said.'

'But...' Hattie was a little lost for words at the woman's matter-of-fact tone. 'What do you mean? It's been booked for ages.'

'I am sorry but these things happen. We have had no instruction. We thought perhaps the wedding might not go ahead. We did not realise that it was at Château St Martin.'

'That's ridiculous,' said Hattie. 'My uncle... A deposit was paid.'

'Which we will, of course, return.'

'But the wedding is only two months away.'

There was a resounding not-my-problem silence.

'Can't you do something?'

'I'm afraid not. Goodbye.'

Hattie stared at the phone in her hand. This was a

catastrophe. Would she be able to find another caterer in time that could do the job? Thankfully the great god Google provided the details of a number of nearby caterers. Hattie visited various websites and narrowed them down to a list of six and decided the best thing was to work her way through them.

By the sixth one, she already had a good idea of how the call would go but she picked up the phone and dialled anyway.

'*Bonjour. Parlez-vous anglaise?*'

'*Anglais?*'

Hattie winced at her mistake being pointed out and blurted out, '*Yes, that's what I meant.*'

'*Oui.*'

'Bon. I'm calling from the Château St Martin and wondering if you would be available to do the catering for a wedding on the twenty-fifth of July.'

There it was again – or was she being paranoid – that brief pause. A slight indrawn breath.

'*Non*, we are fully booked.' With that, like the five previous suppliers, they put the phone down, without further discussion. Was she being paranoid, or did it seem they knew their calendars rather well? Or was it the Château St Martin name that made them so sure they were unable to help?

Without much hope she made another couple of calls before officially giving up for the morning and wandering back through to the kitchen to seek solace in coffee.

The housekeeper was there, gazing out of the window.

'*Bonjour*, Solange.'

She turned. '*Bonjour*, Hattie. How are you? Did you sleep well?' She frowned. 'I hope the bed was okay. No one apart from Luc has been to stay for a very long time. Luc's parents never come here and no one has been to visit since Marthe went into the home two years ago. When Marthe was here we used to have lots of grand parties.' Her mouth twisted.

Hattie gave a serene smile, determined not to let it show how rattled she was this morning. 'I slept well. Thank you for the pastries. They were still warm and delicious.'

'Bien.'

'I do have a bit of a problem though. I don't suppose you could recommend or have any contacts with local caterers?'

'Are the caterers not booked? It is very late.'

'I know but the ones that were booked have cancelled.'

'The only person I know is Juliet Garnier. She is the best in the area. She was at school with Yvette.'

'That's who has cancelled.'

'Juliet? She's very…' Solange's mouth crimped into a straight line. 'That's unfortunate. But I'm afraid I cannot help you.' With that she drifted out of the room.

Hattie huffed out a sigh. 'Can't or won't?' she muttered to herself.

Chapter Seven

Luc rubbed the neck of his T-shirt, pulling off another stray leaf. His skin itched like crazy since he had been out working on the vines all morning with Alphonse, pruning and cutting back some of the fruit to ensure a better crop. As a result, he could feel small pieces of greenery and probably the odd bug that had worked their way under the fabric.

Out of habit he strode towards the stairs, already pulling his T-shirt over his head, desperate to relieve the horrible scratchy sensation, in readiness for his shower. He was just shaking it out and taking the first step up the staircase, when he heard a crash and the Englishwoman's voice uttering a curse.

He tossed the T-shirt over the banister and jogged towards the noise coming from the dining room. Hattie was wrestling with a stack of plates, trying to remove them from the sideboard without tripping over an upended box on the floor from which knives, forks and spoons spilled.

'Do you need a hand?'

'God, yes, please,' she said, turning around. 'This is heavier than I...' Her voice trailed off as she stared at his bare chest, her mouth open. 'Than I expected. I knocked that box of silver off. Good job it's full of cutlery and not china.' Her words came quick and fast. 'This stuff is valuable. It would be awful if I'd bro—' Clearly realising she was rambling and still staring she deliberately moved her gaze up to his face and he saw her swallow. '...broken anything.'

He grinned at her. His muscles were hard won at the gym, he liked to box, and her shocked appreciation ignited a sudden dart of interest.

She shut her mouth quickly, her eyes widening, and she thrust the stack of plates towards him, a faint pink blush tinting her cheeks. He took the weight easily, amused by her discomfort. He wondered what it would be like to kiss Hattie Carter-Jones. She wasn't his usual type, much gentler and a lot less sophisticated but also a lot kinder.

'Where do you want them?' he asked, grinning at her.

'The kitchen. What?' She narrowed her eyes.

'I like the outfit.' She raised a self-conscious hand to the scarf around her head and glanced down at the denim dungarees, the legs rolled up to reveal bright yellow socks which clashed beautifully with her purple Converse. She looked very cute in a pixie pop-star sort of way.

'Are you making fun of me?'

'No, not at all. I like it, it's quite charming.'

She snorted. 'It's practical,' she said. 'This place is filthy. I thought I'd make a start in here. I've been dusting the surfaces, washing these beautiful dishes. Have you seen them? Course you have, you live here. They're too lovely to be left out like this. I can't believe how much stuff there is. The plus is that there are enough place settings for the whole wedding.'

'Won't the caterers supply that sort of thing?' he asked,

carrying the plates towards the kitchen, looking back over his shoulder.

'Ah,' she sighed heavily. 'That is a whole other story.'

He put the plates on the side and scratched at his neck and caught a whiff of himself.

'I really need a shower. Why don't you tell me in the car on the way to the market? Can you give me half an hour to freshen up.'

'I could probably do with a shower too…'

'You're very welcome,' he said with a teasing lift of one eyebrow, watching her blush again.

'I didn't mean together, I meant … I need one as well. At the same time. Not with you. In the shower with you.' She closed her eyes and put her hand to her forehead.

When she opened them he grinned at her again.

'Go,' she said pointing to the doorway.

'Yes, boss,' he said and walked out wondering what it would be like to take a shower with her and what her soft pale skin would feel like up against his body under a cool stream of water.

'Dear God,' said Hattie bashing her head lightly against the glass shower screen fifteen minutes later. Life just wasn't fair. It wasn't enough that Luc Brémont had a face that could launch a thousand after-shave ads, he also had the taut muscled body of an Olympic swimmer. Hattie had always prided herself on being above noticing someone for their looks but seriously, Luc was a little mind-blowing. He was Hot with a capital H and he had the strangest effect on her body, as if every erogenous zone was covered in iron filings that leapt to attention to Luc's magnetic force.

She had a crush on him, that was all. She was a normal healthy young woman with sexual urges that had been neglected for … she couldn't actually remember the last time she and Chris had had sex. Talking about their lack of sex life had affected his self-esteem, the counsellor had said, so Hattie had given up trying to do anything about their increasingly loveless relationship.

'You're acting like a flipping born-again virgin. You've seen a man's body before, for God's sake.' She paused and glared at herself in the mirror 'What is wrong with you?'

Yes, the voice in her head said, before pointing out with a fair amount of glee, *but not one like that*.

'Get a grip,' she told herself.

After a quick, cool shower, something made her choose to put a dress on and she brushed her hair and left it loose before applying a quick layer of tinted moisturiser and a dash of lipstick.

'You're only going to the market,' she told her reflection and resisted the urge to wipe off the lipstick. If she wanted to look nice, that was up to her. Grabbing her phone and her purse, she left her room and ran lightly down the stairs to meet Luc.

He'd beaten her to it and had brought his car round. At the sight of it, her mouth curved into a delighted smile. 'I've never been in a convertible before.'

'She's seen a few years. My parents disapprove heartily but she's fun to drive.' Leaning over from the driver's seat, he opened the passenger door and Hattie stepped in, gathering her skirts as she did, hoping that she looked a bit more elegant now.

As they drove down the drive, the wind whipping her hair and the sun beating down on them, she pulled on a pair of large sunglasses and relaxed into her seat. This was rather glamorous. She could be a chic character in a European film.

'So what's the problem with the caterer?'

Luc's question brought her problems back and shattered the happy movie star illusion.

'The catering company that had been booked are now saying they can't do the wedding.' Her shoulders drooped with the reminder that she needed to sort it out and quickly.

'They can't do it? That's not very good. Why not?'

'The woman at Garnier's said they'd double-booked and wouldn't budge. And I've spent all morning on the phone trying to find someone else, to no avail.'

'Garnier's? Juliet Garnier.'

'Yes. Do you know her? Damn, you could have put a good word in for me.'

'I don't know her but the name's familiar. I'm pretty sure she's a friend of Yvette's.'

She glanced at him alerted by something in the tone of his voice and saw his brows draw together.

'Yes, Solange said they were at school together.'

'That would be it,' he murmured almost as if he were speaking to himself. 'What are you going to do? Could you self-cater?'

Hattie laughed with a touch of mild hysteria. 'You are joking. There's no way I would have the confidence to attempt to cook for a hundred-odd people and I couldn't do it on my own. Besides Gabby's going to expect something fancy. Proper cooks do all the fancy presentation which I don't have a clue about. At the place, a castle, I stayed in at Christmas I had the most amazing soup but what made it even more special was the garnish of pickled fennel. I'd never think to do anything like that.'

'Juliet might not be able to help but there will be another solution,' he said before adding, with reassuring pragmatism, 'I find that the best way to solve a problem is to relax. Preferably with a long lunch. Let your subconscious do the work and something will come to you.'

Easy for him to say that but worrying about it now wasn't going to help, so she took his advice and enjoyed the whip of the wind through her hair and the sight of the tight green lines of vines fanning out over the hills around them.

As they drew into the town, driving between stone houses with wooden shutters, the something niggling at the back of her head blossomed into a full-blown idea. It was worth a try. She dug her phone out of her bag and began to type a text, stopping to edit it constantly and then add more bits.

'Are you writing *War and Peace*?'

'No, I'm trying to persuade someone.' She pressed send. 'But it's a very long shot.'

'If you like I could speak to Juliet Garnier? Maybe tell her that she's letting the St Martin family down as well.'

'That's really kind of you but she sounded fairly adamant. Actually, not that. She was indifferent. As if she couldn't care less.'

Luc grunted under his breath. 'I can imagine.'

'I'm not sure I want to deal with someone like that, to be honest.' Although beggars couldn't be choosers.

'Let me see what I can do,' said Luc, a grim set to his jaw. 'It might just be a communication problem.'

'Mm,' said Hattie doubtfully. Juliet Garnier's English had sounded pretty good to her.

'Put her number into my phone. I'll call her now.'

The call went through and Hattie heard Juliet's voice again. Though the French was too quick for her to try and translate, it was quickly obvious as the conversation degenerated from polite chat to curt short terse sentences that Luc wasn't having any success.

His jaw jutted out as he finished the call.

'No joy?'

'Sorry. She was adamant she couldn't help.' There was an angry tic in his cheek.

'Hey, Luc, it's not your problem.' Hattie touched him on the arm. 'I really appreciate that you tried.'

When they began to stroll through the market a little while later, Hattie quickly forgot her problems. Everywhere she looked, stalls burst with colour and texture, the rich red of tomatoes tumbling over each other in wooden boxes, piles of green beans like spindly fingers in big baskets, and sacks of golden potatoes still spattered with dark mud. The smell of crepes filled the air from a busy stand with a ten-deep queue of shopping-laden women. She was finding it difficult to concentrate on any one thing, like the display of fresh herbs or the table of shelled and unshelled nuts. Her eyes were constantly drawn to the sharp, bright discovery of a new stall. Just as she picked up a bottle of rosemary vinegar her phone began to ring. She closed her eyes. Seriously. Not again. She looked down at her phone and was pleasantly surprised to see it was someone else.

'Oh! Will you excuse me a minute?'

'Sure, why don't you catch me up.'

Watching him go, she turned and took a few steps back towards the much-depleted boulangerie stall, answering the phone excitedly.

. . .

English people didn't tend to eat well in his experience, thought Luc, selecting some shiny red onions, lush deep red peppers and some *mache* lettuce, the small green leaves quivering when he picked up the bunch. He handed them to the stallholder, an elderly woman he recognised. She'd been a regular fixture here since he was a boy. What if Hattie lived on baked beans and bacon and only ate that horrible sliced white bread that seemed so ubiquitous in English supermarkets? He never minded spending time cooking because he loved food. Marthe and Solange had taught him a lot when he was in his teens. The kitchen at the château had always smelled good. On Sundays there'd be the rich fragrance of the beef in the *pot au feu* bubbling on the range; during the week there'd be a potage of whatever vegetables were in season simmering away; and always, always a large rustic loaf on the table, the scent of wheat and yeast permeating the air and a sharp knife at the ready to cut through the crisp crust.

It had been a long time since the château kitchen had been alive with that sense of warmth and hospitality. Anyone could have turned up and they would always have been fed.

Tonight he'd make a simple *matafan* with bacon and fresh chives. There were still, he'd noticed, an abundance of potted herbs on the patio outside the kitchen and there was a basket of eggs in the kitchen.

When Hattie caught up with him as he was at the cheese stall, trying to decide which to choose, her face fizzed with smug delight that made her hazel eyes glow.

'Hi Luc. Strange question—'

'Hattie, come try this cheese.'

The woman behind the stall was already slicing a piece and

holding it out to Hattie. He wanted to laugh at her wary expression when she took the cheese.

'This is a local sheep's cheese,' said Luc. 'It's one of my favourites. It's very mild. What do you think? Or do you prefer a stronger cheese?'

'Luc, I—'

'Cheese first,' he said. Anything else could wait. For the next few minutes, he insisted she tasted several different types. Food came first in France. These Brits were too impatient, they didn't know how to savour things and to take time to enjoy the good things in life.

It was fun watching her expression as she tried each one, tilting her head this way and that as she examined the flavours. He found himself looking at her mouth, his gaze drawn to her lips.

'Mmm, I like that one, but Luc, I need to—' He shook his head again and popped another slice into her mouth. As his fingers grazed her lips and her eyes widened instantly, a rush of heat flashed through him and for a brief moment, his gaze locked with hers.

He shifted it quickly to the woman behind the counter. 'We'll take that one and this one too, Hattie?'

She nodded, looking a little dazed.

Seconds later he took possession of a bag containing a crinkled, creamy and rather smelly Langres, an oval creamy Caprice des Dieux and a Cendre de Champagne, with a dusty grey ash rind.

'Happy now?' asked Hattie a little impatiently.

'Yes, of course. We have cheese.'

'Excellent,' she said.

'It's important.'

She laughed. 'So is this. Is there anywhere at the château to land a helicopter?'

'A helicopter?' It was quite possibly the very last thing he'd expected her to ask.

'Yes.' She grinned at his surprised question. 'Big flying thing with blades.' She circled with her index finger to illustrate.

'I know what a helicopter is,' he said, laughing back at her. 'You really want to land one at St Martin?'

'Well, not me personally but yes.'

'We don't have an official helipad but there's an old paddock which I think would work perfectly.'

'Brilliant. And we'd need to mark it so the pilot can see it from the air.'

'What about fluorescent orange paint? We use it to mark trees that have to come down, or stray roots that are potential trip hazards. If we sprayed a big H for helipad, a pilot would be able to see it.' He would not be mentioning this to his father; it would put ideas into his head and he'd be dropping in every five minutes.

'Perfect.' Hattie rubbed her hands together, beaming. 'I've solved our catering problem.'

Our? Luc didn't bother to correct her. He didn't want to burst her happy bubble but he was amused by the fact that she now assumed he was part of her team. He was in a very difficult position. If the wedding was a success, his father might want to do more – and being honest he could do with the capital that this one would raise.

'I know someone who is a brilliant cook. She's going to come and she's cadged a lift with her brother who is taking a group of people to the races at Chantilly.'

'You have interesting friends,' said Luc, raising an eyebrow.

'I know,' said Hattie with another grin, 'I thought it was a stroke of genius.'

'When does this friend arrive in her helicopter?'

'In two weeks' time. She's going to confirm the date.'

'Is she a chef or something?'

'No, but she's a very good cook and I remembered her saying that one day she wanted to set up her own catering business. I've eaten her food and seen her in action. She's a real perfectionist and super-efficient. I'm starting to get excited again.' Hattie was almost dancing on the spot, her enthusiasm contagious. He couldn't help grinning at her. He wanted to sweep her up and dance with her and share that sunshine beam of joy radiating from her. Spending time with her was rapidly becoming addictive.

Chapter Eight

'I suggest we take it in turns to cook, when we are here,' said Luc, as they unpacked the shopping bags. 'I'll cook this evening.'

'That would be great,' said Hattie and meant it. It was a pleasant change for someone other than her to take the lead. She filled the fridge with the little wax-paper-wrapped packets of cheese that she and Luc had selected at the fromagerie stall. It had been fun picking them and tasting the slivers of cheese that Luc had insisted she try before they bought.

They'd bought far more than she thought they needed but Luc was adamant. None of it would go to waste, he said, especially not when he made his famous three-cheese tart.

That he cooked wasn't a big surprise, Chris had always done the cooking during the week at home by default because she was out at work. That Luc was prepared to make something that sounded less like weekday food intrigued her. At home, to limit the anxiety of shopping and decision-making, Chris had instigated a weekly rota of cottage pie on Mondays, fish fingers, chips and beans on Tuesday, sausage and mash on Wednesday, takeaway pizza on Thursday and fish and chips on Friday. It was a far cry from when they'd been at university and loved going to Grub, the big street food market in Manchester. A sharp, unexpected stab of sadness hijacked her thoughts. She missed Chris. That Chris. They had been so happy then. Everyone had said they were the perfect couple.

'Hattie?'

She glanced up as Luc repeated the question. 'Would you like a glass of wine?'

'Yes. That would be lovely.'

'I'm making *matafan* this evening, so I think a white burgundy.' He was already pulling a bottle from the fridge.

'Can I do anything to help?'

'Yes, you could make the salad and lay the table.'

'You don't want to eat at the breakfast bar?'

'Non! In France we sit and eat, to enjoy our food.' He turned. 'How can you relax properly, perched like a bird?'

She giggled at his mock-horrified expression.

'There are tablecloths and napkins in the dresser. The silver is in the drawers.' He pointed with the corkscrew. She had a feeling that suggesting forgoing the tablecloth and using kitchen roll instead of napkins would not go down well, even though it was only the two of them.

The heavy linen tablecloth and matching hemstitched napkins were of the finest quality and it really was silver in the drawers, the knives and forks nestled in a velvet-lined wooden canteen. Hattie spread the cloth over the table, taking pleasure in the crisp, pressed fabric. Deciding that she might as well go the whole hog, even though it was only the two of them, and do things properly, she found a couple of raffia placemats and some pretty coloured wooden napkin rings along with a couple of votive glasses with tea lights.

In the meantime, Luc had poured their wine into two beautiful crystal glasses. 'Wow, these are gorgeous.' She said pinging the glass with a finger and listening to the chime.

'They were a wedding present to Marthe's grandmother.'

Hattie's eyes widened and she put the glass down gingerly. 'God, I'd hate to break one.' She felt slightly nervous.

Luc shrugged and took a healthy sip of his wine. 'What is the point of drinking good wine in inferior glasses? It is part of the enjoyment, to appreciate good things. 'Mmm, taste this. Full-bodied, buttery and honeyed.'

It seemed quite decadent to Hattie to drink from something so fine, although she had to admit, picking the glass up, her fingers grazing the long stem, that the glass was one of the most beautiful she'd ever seen. And the wine wasn't bad either. She took another sip, her lips touching the delicate glass rim of the glass, feeling the weight of the crystal in her hand. Something settled within her, a gentle nudge of happiness in using something lovely and tasting the rather wonderful wine. Maybe there was something to his view.

'What do you think?'

'It's really nice,' said Hattie. 'Although I don't know anything about wine.'

Luc began frying lardons in a cast-iron skillet, cracking eggs and weighing flour, like a one-man tornado. Despite his speed, he seemed supremely organised, moving quickly and methodically as he pointed to a white patterned bowl. 'If you could put the salad leaves in there.'

Again it struck her just how self-sufficient he was.

She selected the three different salad leaves he'd bought, romaine lettuce, some lambs lettuce and curly endive, put them on a chopping board and reached to grab a knife from the block.

'What are you doing?'

'Chopping the lettuce.'

He took the knife from her hand. 'Never use a knife on lettuce.'

'There are rules?'

He grinned. 'In France, there are always rules when it comes to food. You must do it properly. With lettuce, always tear it, into bite-size pieces. You can make a vinaigrette?' he asked with a teasing smile.

'I've always thought so,' said Hattie a little unnerved by this attention to mere lettuce leaves. 'Mustard, vinegar and oil.'

'Two teaspoons Dijon, six large spoons of oil and two of red wine vinegar.'

'Yes boss,' she said in response to the very precise ratios. She normally just chucked it all in a cup and gave it a good stir, which she realised as he handed her a tiny whisk and a little porcelain bowl was obviously not right either.

While she was making the salad and dressing she kept half an eye on Luc, who seemed to be making something that was a cross between a Yorkshire pudding and a pancake. He poured the thick batter into another skillet and left it to fry for a few minutes, lifting the edge periodically to make sure it wasn't sticking. At some point he'd dashed out to collect some herbs from the garden and chopped the bright green chives into small pieces, which he sprinkled over the batter along with the pre-cooked lardons and several grinds of dark black pepper and a twist of salt before he put the pan into the oven to finish it off.

When they sat down at the table, the candles glowing, her wrists grazing the crisp linen and her nose filled with the delicious smell of bacon, egg and herbs, she had to admit it felt good. Very good indeed. Although she couldn't describe it as pressure – that would do the relaxed atmosphere a disservice – there was obvious anticipation around the food. When she took a bite of the simple *matafan*, she closed her eyes and groaned. The salty bite of the lardons contrasted perfectly with the simplicity of the light fluffy batter.

'That is so good. I've never heard of it before.'

'Good, hearty peasant food. Perfect after a hard day in the vines. In some places it's served with apples and cinnamon but I prefer a savoury version like this.'

'And so simple. It took you no time at all to make. I thought French food was always very fancy.'

He shook his head. 'I like food, and if you're going to eat, it should be the best quality, but I don't necessarily like to cook or spend a long time in the kitchen unless it is at the table. I think that is the way with most French people unless you are a chef, then you do fancy.'

'Where did you learn to cook?'

Pausing before he took another mouthful, he lifted his head. 'Right here, with Marthe and Solange. And they learned from their *mamies*.' At her puzzled look he qualified. 'Grandmothers.' He gave a sudden smile. 'I was a very reluctant kitchen assistant at first. I didn't see why I should have to help in the kitchen. But Marthe insisted that I chopped vegetables and helped.' He grimaced. 'I was a spoiled brat. It took me a long time before I even admitted to myself how much I enjoyed the camaraderie of the kitchen and being included as part of the team, especially when Alphonse and Yvette joined us. In the winter months it would be like a cosy party in here. The old range, it used to be there –' he pointed to the alcove, which was now full of shelves with potted plants and recipe books and antique kitchen utensils '– and it heated the room. Alphonse and I would take turns putting the wood in, feeling like we were the men of the house.'

'It sounds idyllic,' said Hattie.

'I guess it was, although I'm not sure I would have agreed at the time. Coming here was very strange at first. I was only seven. Dumped here because my parents had each booked a holiday and had forgotten to tell the other.'

Hattie blinked. 'Didn't they go on holiday together?' she asked wondering if she was terribly naïve and unsophisticated. In her world families holidayed together.

Luc huffed out a laugh. 'Rarely together. But at the same time, frequently.'

'And they didn't take you?'

'I think I might have been in the way. They usually went with other people.'

'Oh,' said Hattie. It said so much about his parents' marriage.

'I hated coming here at the beginning. Especially the first time. No one told me what was happening. I was left in a strange house, in the country, with an old woman I didn't know and I had no idea when or if I might go home. I was terrified.' He gave a sudden grin. 'But I wasn't going to show it so I was a little shit.'

He pronounced it 'sheet' which made her smile.

'I was rude, disrespectful and deliberately naughty but Marthe … she never lost her temper. She never held back from pointing out when I'd behaved badly, but she didn't punish me. Just sat me down and told me my behaviour was not acceptable.' He gave Hattie a smile. 'I always knew where I was with her. She never lied to me and after a while this became home. Here I always knew what to expect.'

'It sounds tough.'

Luc laughed. 'Yeah, really tough. All this to run around in. With friends my own age. Being fed and looked after. This saved me – otherwise I might have turned out like my parents.'

'Do you not get on with them?'

'I get on fine with them but they drive me insane. I've lost count of my father's mistresses, although my mother at least has a long-term boyfriend. They're restless. Always on the move looking for the next thing that will entertain them, make them happy. It's exhausting and for a long time I played by that tune. But now I want to stay put, build something here. This is my home and I'm staying. Unlike my parents, I've found my place in the world.'

The conviction in his voice made her a little sad. 'I envy you. I'm not sure I have.' She wasn't sure she even had a home anymore. She could always go back to her parents but she hadn't lived there since she'd gone to university. It seemed a terrible admission of failure. Originally she'd stayed in Manchester and got a job for an events company in the city, sharing a house with some uni friends, but then Chris had a breakdown and she'd changed jobs to go and live with him. In hindsight that hadn't been the best thing but what else could she have done at the time? He needed help. He'd had to give up his job and could barely get out of bed. So she'd left a job she'd loved, taken a demotion and moved in with Chris and his mum.

Luc offered her a gentle smile. 'There's no hurry. There's nothing wrong with having an adventure.' He topped up her wine glass. 'What do you think?' He lifted his own glass and held it up to the light.

'It's good,' Hattie said, vague again because, while grateful for the change of subject, she didn't want to show her ignorance. She didn't have the first clue about wine.

'It's a hundred per cent semillon,' he said, swirling the wine around in his glass.

'Really,' said Hattie, taking a quick sip to avoid saying any more. It could have been a hundred per cent turnip peelings for all she knew. 'So you make champagne here.'

'Not yet but we will. For the last few years, we've been selling the grapes. This year, after the harvest, we will make the first wine at St Martin for fifteen years.'

'So champagne and prosecco, what's the difference. Is one French and the other Italian?'

For a moment there was shocked silence as Luc looked at her with the most appalled expression on his face and then he smiled. 'You're teasing me. I can see I am going to have to take you in hand while you're here. You don't know anything about champagne, do you?'

'No,' said Hattie, deciding she'd go along with him. As far as she was concerned, one was a lot more expensive than the other but they were in essence the same. 'But I'm willing to learn.'

'I shall take you on a champagne tour in Reims. That will only scratch the surface but it's a start.' He shook his head again. 'But never use the words prosecco and champagne in the same sentence again. For that you can do the washing up.'

She grinned at him. 'I was planning to anyway.'

Chapter Nine

H er cousin was growing impatient. Gabby kept pestering for pictures of the interior of the château, even though over the last week Hattie had sorted out the order of service, found local printers, liaised with the new caterer, sourced the pale green and white table linen that her cousin had decided upon, ordered a dozen polaroid cameras for guests to take pictures during the wedding, and arranged for a huge cork board to be made to display the polaroid pictures during the reception.

Hattie had been able to oblige with lots of exterior shots but she couldn't put it off any longer. It seemed Solange was *still* trying to contact her usual cleaning crew, so Hattie had decided to make a start, hoping it might prompt the other woman to pull her finger out. She'd been working her socks off to try and bring the château up to scratch and had barely seen a soul. Luc seemed to go out with the lark and hadn't been home for dinner once since that first night, and Solange occasionally drifted within sight in the distance but rarely came close enough for Hattie to talk to, probably because she was sick of Hattie asking if she'd heard from the cleaners yet.

With a sigh, she told herself that this was what she'd chosen and dipped her sponge into the bucket of warm soapy water to wash one of the many panes of grimy glass in the first of the ballrooms' twelve floor-to-ceiling windows. It was going to take her all day just to clean the windows. Yesterday she'd hauled all the rugs, along with a huge roll of carpet which seemed to be surplus to requirements, outside to try and beat them before attempting to go over them with an antique version of a hoover, which she wasn't convinced had made any difference.

She'd hoped making a start on the windows would brighten up the room but now she wasn't convinced. Instead it sharpened the focus on the faded upholstery and the shattered silk of the drapes around the windows. But she'd started now and she was determined to keep going.

'What are you doing?' asked a sharp voice, a little while later. Hattie jumped and almost toppled off the chair she was perched on. Yvette stood in the doorway with a sulky expression on her face, which was a shame because it marred her classically beautiful features. Dressed in a smart navy shift dress that finished just above the knee, showcasing spectacular legs, further enhanced by fuchsia pink suede heels, she looked as if she probably worked as some swish executive in the heart of Paris. She made a striking contrast to her mother, who lurked in the background just behind her in her usual loose-fitting black dress.

Hattie wondered if Yvette had ever cleaned a window in her life and how good the other woman's English was and how well sarcasm would translate.

'Cleaning windows, believe it or not.'

Yvette's eyes sharpened. 'Why?'

Hattie stared at her.

'I heard that the caterer had double-booked.'

'News travels fast,' observed Hattie coolly.

'It's a small place.' Yvette squinted up at Hattie and then slowly perused the long line of windows. 'You have a lot to do. It's going to take a long time.' She tilted her head consideringly. 'You know, it would be much better if you went to a hotel. Perhaps one in Reims. I could help you find one, you know. It would be much easier for you.'

'It would,' agreed Hattie. 'But them's the breaks.'

'*Pardon.*' Yvette frowned. 'There are some beautiful hotels in Reims – or maybe one of the champagne houses. I could contact some of them for you. I would be happy to help.'

'That's very kind.' Hattie dredged up a smile. This was a bit of an about-turn after the other evening. Why would this young woman be 'happy to help'?

'Excellent. How many people are coming to the wedding? I can start to make some calls right away. There's very little time.'

'Thank you but I have found an alternative caterer.'

'You have! Who?' Yvette didn't sound very pleased.

'I have someone coming from England who will be doing the catering.'

'England but … there is a lot to do for one person.'

'Oh, she's top-notch,' said Hattie with airy confidence and couldn't resist adding, 'She's flying in by helicopter.'

'Helicopter?' Yvette's brow furrowed in disbelief. 'Where? There is nowhere.'

'Luc's going to mark out the paddock. It will land there.'

Yvette pursed her mouth, clearly not very happy, but Hattie couldn't see how it affected her. With that she stalked off on her killer heels with staccato steps that would stab anything in her way and very nearly tripped over the roll of carpet that Hattie couldn't decide what to do with.

Hattie turned back to her windows, feeling the ache across her shoulders. She'd been at this all morning and still was only a quarter of the way through. Just as she soaked the sponge, a shrill scream rent the air. She whirled round.

'Did you see that?' cried Yvette, holding her hands up in horror, her eyes darting around studying the floor.

'See what?'

'*Une souris*. A mouse. It ran right across my foot.' She shook her shoe, giving Hattie an intense stare. '*Maman* was worried there was another mouses infestation. Like last summer.'

'Mouse infestation.'

'Yes. They were everywhere. You could even see them running up the walls.'

'What, here in the château?' Hattie glanced back at the building, unable to believe it. She'd not seen anything since she'd been here.

'Oh, yes. *Maman* had a cat which helped to get rid of them but the cat died a couple of weeks ago, didn't it, *Maman*?'

Solange nodded reluctantly. Of course she did, it didn't say much about her management of the house.

'Have you seen any yet?' asked Yvette, her eyes boring into Hattie's with fervent insistence.

'Mice.'

'Yes, *les souris*. It was dreadful. Luckily no one was staying here, they ran over the beds, up the curtains. In every room.'

'I've not seen any,' said Hattie. Oh God, that sounded hideous.

'You're more likely to hear them, at night. Scratching, scuffling in the walls.'

'Thanks.' Now she was going to be listening constantly.

'If you do, you need to call in the exterminator. They breed every twenty days. They say if you see one mouse, it means there are at least another five or six nearby because they live in nests together.'

Yvette wasn't exactly trying to reassure her.

'I'll keep my eyes open for any.'

'Do.' She turned to her mother. 'Didn't you say you saw one in the kitchen and one in the main salon last week? You know they are a health risk. They spread *salmonelle*. You have this in England?'

Hattie nodded grimly, not needing a translation. No wonder Solange was keeping quiet. That must be worrying, but why hadn't she done anything about it? Or was Yvette exaggerating for her own reasons?

'Don't tell Luc I told you. He is desperate for the money the wedding will make, even though the house is completely unsuitable but –' she turned guileless green eyes towards Hattie '– I would feel terrible if the wedding were spoilt.'

Hattie grimaced. Gabby would do her nut if she thought there were rodents anywhere near the place.

'Thanks for letting me know.'

'It's no problem,' said Yvette with a big smile. 'What is it they say? We girls must stick together.' With that she sauntered out looking as neat and tidy as if she'd stepped from the pages of *Vogue*, leaving Hattie hot, bothered and very fed up. With a sigh Hattie wiped her sweaty forehead and looked at the row of windows still to do. What had she done to deserve the tasks of Hercules? And now there were mice to contend with.

. . .

Hattie screwed up her nose and glared at the windows. They were considerably cleaner but unfortunately they were also considerably smeary. Oh God, they looked terrible.

'Here,' said Solange, appearing at her elbow carrying a large bucket of steaming water along with two spray bottles and a stack of newspapers tucked under her other arm. 'Vinegar, rubbing alcohol and hot water is best, if you want a streak-free finish. And then dry it off with scrunched-up newspaper. I'll redo the ones you've done and you can carry on.'

'You don't have to,' protested Hattie, feeling like she'd guilted Solange into helping.

'Nonsense, this is long overdue. If I'd had more notice I could have made a start.'

'No news on the cleaning crew?'

Solange's mouth tightened as she said a trifle grimly. 'Not yet.'

Hattie hid a smile. It sounded as if Solange hadn't given up; there was a touch of pure tungsten in her words.

'How long have you worked here?' asked Hattie, deciding to make conversation. She liked Solange and genuinely wanted to get to know her a little better.

'My mother worked for Marthe – they were both widows – and then my mother remarried and moved away. I'd been living in London for two years as an au pair. So I came home and took over. I was only twenty-one but Marthe knew I was capable, I'd learned to cook with my mother. In those days we had grand parties. Have you seen the silverware?'

Hattie shook her head.

'The table used to look magnificent. Marthe never spared any expense on the house. We had some parties. See, the painting above the fireplace. No, look at the fireplace. The plasterwork is incredible. The craftsman came from Lille to complete it back in 1848. Marthe and I worked on it to restore it one winter.'

Hattie looked at the huge ornate white fireplace, with its carvings of elaborate, stylised oak leaves, sumptuous curves and delicate details, and watched Solange walk over to it. Her slim fingers reached out and she ran her fingertips over the surface with all the care of a lover. Intrigued, Hattie joined her and, to her surprise, realised that unlike the rest of the room the mantel was immaculately clean although it showed signs of age.

'This was a labour of love.'

'It's beautiful,' said Hattie, now that she was looking at it properly.

Solange poked at a slight stain on one end. 'That's where Marthe spilled her Châteauneuf du Pape one Christmas. She was so cross at first, we'd only finished the work the week before. And this –' she pointed to a chip '– was from Luc playing football in here. But then we decided they were the scars of life and that this is a home, not a palace. Those imperfections should be celebrated and loved as much for those memories.'

'And the picture?' asked Hattie, realising that the gilt frame of the large watercolour was dust free.

'It's my favourite in the whole house, although the one in the little salon in the alcove is also very special. I'll take you to see it. This one Marthe bought not long after Luc came to stay the first time.' Solange smiled. 'She said it was to remind her that life could still be civilised, even with a young boy turning the place upside down. Then later it was a different reminder, that love could find roots in the most unlikely places. Those first few visits were difficult, for both of them. But,' finished

Solange softly, 'they found each other eventually. This painting symbolises hope.'

Hattie remembered Luc telling her he had been left in a strange house, with an old woman he didn't know, and how terrified he'd been. Now that she had studied the picture in more detail, rather than seeing it as a pretty scene of the riverbank and the vineyards in the background, she could see the most important focus of the picture was of a boy and a woman happily picnicking together by the water's edge.

'Come.' Solange tugged at her sleeve and took her to the little picture in the salon. It was the one she'd seen before, the pen and ink sketch of a boy with a fistful of drooping flowers. 'Luc, when he was ten. He picked wildflowers for Marthe for her birthday because he wanted to give her something. He would never ask for any help. Always sorted things out for himself.'

'That's adorable,' said Hattie, looking at young Luc.

Solange laughed. 'Hmm, sometimes. Although he could also be a little devil. There's one plain pane in the stained glass in one of the doors where Luc smashed it, practising with a catapult.' Solange shook her head, 'Alphonse had given it to him. Each of them was always leading the other into trouble. But Marthe refused to have it replaced. She was so pleased that Luc was acting like a small boy should, instead of the closed-off child he'd been when he first came.'

Cleaning was abandoned as Solange took her on a tour of the treasures of the house: an antique bookcase that had taken four men to carry in and could never be moved, an art deco bronze lamp that Marthe had bought for herself on her sixtieth birthday, pictures that held a wealth of history about the inhabitants of the house. She showed Hattie the velvet-lined boxes of silverware, the glass epergne collection which might have been priceless if it weren't for cracks and chips, and the hand-painted tureen and underplate sets.

It was obvious that these things were given care and attention and Hattie realised that she'd underestimated Solange's capabilities. The woman looked after the important things. Hattie found herself looking at her with a lot more understanding.

'It's all so...' Hattie waved a hand unable to sum up her feelings. 'Thank you so much for...' she was going to say, 'showing me', but instead said, 'sharing your treasures with me.'

'It's lovely to revisit them with someone who appreciates them. But now those windows are calling. At least you look a little rested. You mustn't work too hard. I will try again to talk to the cleaning company.'

At four o'clock Hattie had only one destination in mind as she left the château by the wide door at the back and hurried along the first terrace through an avenue of bright yellow laburnum trees dripping with blooms, past beds full of daisies and wallflowers. She gave them no more than a cursory glance she was so focused on her mission. She couldn't wait to immerse her overheated and work-worn body in the pool.

Arriving on the wooden deck, she ignored the cabin that looked like a changing room, dropped her towel on one of the sun beds and crossed to the pool edge. The cool blue looked so inviting and the depth was clearly marked as two metres, so, holding her nose, she threw herself in before she could chicken out. The shock of the cold made her gasp as her head surfaced and she began to swim quickly. As soon as she stretched her muscles with the first smooth strokes, she felt the instant release of the day's tensions as she slid through the water. With a lazy grin, she watched the sun dapple the surface, glinting and dancing across the ripples. The only sound apart from the lapping of the water was the sweet high song of a blackbird.

She flipped onto her back and closed her eyes to float alone with her thoughts. She'd forgotten how soothing this weightless sensation could be. Hattie could already feel the sense of peace stealing over her like a blanket being tucked into place. After a while she forced her eyes open, squinting in the bright sunshine, and swam to the side.

Relaxed and a little dreamy, she flopped onto her towel on the sun lounger in the corner of the patio, slipping her sunglasses on to protect her eyes from the glare bouncing off the white stone terrace. There was nothing quite like the warmth of the sun on your skin, she thought, looking down at her toes, wriggling them just because she could. She was so absorbed in her own thoughts, she didn't see Luc until he strode to the far edge of the pool. It was obvious that he hadn't seen her. Not wanting to startle him, she kept quiet … nothing to do with the fact that she could ogle him without being seen.

She gulped as she watched him strip off his T-shirt. Those abs. A six-pack instead of a six-pound bag of potatoes. Behind her sunglasses she could take a proper look this time, not like in the dining room when she'd looked anywhere but. He looked like a flipping male model in all his six-foot-three gorgeous glory.

Thank goodness for sunglasses. She suspected her eyes were out on stalks like a snail's.

With one quick fluid movement he dived into the cool blue water, arrowing beneath the surface, like a sleek seal, for a good half-length before surfacing with a shake of his head. Should she acknowledge him, she wondered? The last thing she wanted was to engage in conversation with him when she was sitting here in her matronly, baggy Marks & Spencer swimming costume. She looked down and tugged at the faded orange and pink pattern with a slight sense of shame. When had she stopped caring?

She indulged in a little heartfelt sigh as she watched his easy front crawl, his biceps bunching with each stroke. He really was an absolute Adonis and he probably knew it. What's more, she could bet that his girlfriends would sport nearly all-over-body golden tans and wear fabulous tiny bikinis, not manky old swimsuits like this where the Lycra had given up the ghost in strategic regions.

She closed her eyes and tried to block out the vision of Luc, which worked just fine until everything went quiet. When she opened her eyes, he was hauling himself out of the pool, lifting that awesome body up over the edge in a definite show of very masculine strength.

With water running off him, the droplets glistening in the sunshine like crystals, he walked straight towards her, with that confident easy swagger and roll of the hips that made her think of cowboys.

'Bonjour, Hattie.' As usual he dropped the H from her name, which was charming without him even trying.

'Hi,' she said, trying to be cool, but there was a giveaway squeak in her voice. God, she'd turned into a guinea pig overnight.

'Nice costume,' he said with a lift of one decidedly rakish brow. If they were still looking for a new James Bond, he'd got that look nailed.

'Do you think so?' she asked brightly, wanting to cover herself up as he sat down on the sun lounger right next to hers.

'No, it's hideous.' He gave her a wicked smile. 'Why bother? No one's here.'

'Apart from you.'

'I won't mind, if you don't.'

She blushed and picked up her book. How did he manage to make her feel so very gauche and inexperienced? It was bloody irritating because she was a grown woman and she'd had sex plenty of times, thank you very much. Although, looking at him, she suspected his sort of sex was very different from the type she was used to – or rather not used to anymore. Chris hadn't been that interested for the last eighteen months.

'What are your plans this evening? Do you want me to cook?' she asked in a desperate attempt to hold a normal conversation.

He shrugged, a proper Gallic, lazy shrug. He had very nice broad shoulders … and there she went again. But she'd be lying if she said she wasn't attracted to him.

'I have no plans this evening. I finished early. I thought perhaps –' he paused and his eyes rested on her face '– I might seduce you.'

Pardon! Hattie managed out a strangled gasp, even more grateful for the sunglasses that protected her outraged stare. What on earth did she say to that?

Apart from 'Yes please, for God's sake get on with it'?

What would he do if she said, 'Go right ahead'?

Then he leaned forward and removed her sunglasses. The deliberate intent of the move made her freeze, her mouth opening slightly. There was a subtle change in the atmosphere and her nipples hardened in response. His careful gaze roved over her face and the twinkle in his eyes darkened to something a little more dangerous.

'Do you want to?' she asked in a whisper, hardly daring to believe she'd actually ask the question.

He stared at her, considering and studying her before a slow smile spread across his face that sent spirals of heat coursing through her.

He leaned forward, a gentle finger tracing her collarbone. 'I think I do,' he whispered back, 'very much.'

She swallowed.

'Luc!'

They both jumped at the curt shout followed by the tap, tap of heels down the stone steps above them.

'I need to speak to you,' called Yvette from the other side of the pool.

Luc groaned but he stood up. 'I'll see you at dinner time.' His mouth quirked with mischief and she felt her cheeks grow pink but, feeling oddly daring, she replied in a sultry, unHattie-like tone, 'You will.'

She liked the quick jolt of surprise in his eyes and felt quite proud of herself as without a word he pulled on a shirt, slipped his feet into flipflops and walked across the deck towards Yvette.

Chapter Ten

'What do you want, Yvette?' asked Luc.

'Hello to you too,' she said with an arch look. 'You looked like you were getting very cosy with the enemy there.'

'She's not the enemy.' He wasn't going to give away any more than that to Yvette.

'Do I detect you're a little smitten with our English invader?' She arched an eyebrow.

'She's easy to spend time with,' said Luc, trying to sound nonchalant. Actually he'd only meant to flirt a little with Hattie and tease her but that shy smile of hers had turned his insides out and when she'd turned the tables on him, he couldn't think of anything he'd like to do more than kiss her.

'Planning another Brémont conquest?'

'What do you want, Yvette?' It came out more sharply than he'd intended, irked by her insistence on tagging him with the wholly inaccurate playboy label. Was there a slight bitterness there because he'd never responded to her teenage crush? She always liked to insinuate he was the love-them-and-leave-them type but he really wasn't. His parents' glib attitude to relationships had left him with a desire to find something more meaningful. Much as he'd flirt with Hattie, that was as far as it would go. He was here to make wine. And if he met someone now, it would only be someone he could settle and build a future with, not someone who would be leaving in a few weeks' time.

'Did you know *she* has hired another caterer? She's not even using someone local. Taking business away from the area.'

Luc almost laughed at her audacity. 'And here's me thinking that you had something to do with that.'

'I don't know what you mean.' Yvette drew herself up.

'Juliet's an old friend of yours, isn't she? How come she cancelled? I spoke to her. She didn't give a good answer.'

Yvette gave him a cool stare and shrugged. 'It's not just me that should be worried about this wedding. You do realise that if it's a success, your father will turn the château into a wedding business. It's easy money, he wouldn't need to make champagne to make money here, and then he could have you back at his beck and call. He could sell the grapes again without the costs of making wine and still have the St Martin Château money coming in. He's not interested in champagne – that's you.'

Luc flinched; she'd hit his weak spot. He didn't want to have to travel all the time, he wanted to set down his roots, right here, in the place he considered home.

'Just think of all the disruption weddings all summer would cause. People roaming around everywhere. You might have to give up some of the vines for more parking, for an outdoor marquee. Some people want the romance of getting married among the vines. Someone will have to manage it all.

If you're here your father will expect you to do it. You know what he's like.'

The logic of her argument hit hard. Although he knew she was exaggerating, there was the danger that she was right and his father might prefer the easy way of making money from the château rather than from the vines. Making champagne was going to take a while to become profitable. He knew he needed more than one year but it had been all he'd been able to bargain with his father.

'I can't stop the wedding,' he said.

'No, but you don't have to make it too easy for them, do you? I hear there's a problem with mice. I did tell the English girl. You might want to mention it again.'

Yvette was a piece of work, that was for sure. 'I won't tell any lies.'

She pursed her mouth in a tight, disapproving line. 'Fine. It will be your loss.'

He watched her sashay back up the steps. He turned and glanced towards Hattie. She wasn't the enemy but Yvette had a point – he didn't want things to go too smoothly, no matter how much he liked her. And he did, he realised. He liked Hattie rather a lot. Perhaps he ought to back off a little.

Disappointment warred with relief when Luc didn't return. At least she could regain her composure, thought Hattie as she dried off in the sunshine. Now the problem was what was she going to cook for dinner this evening. Luc had made it look so effortless and she found herself wanting to impress him.

She had her head in the fridge and was making disconsolate huffing noises as she studied various ingredients, when she realised that she wasn't alone.

'Is everything all right?' asked Solange with one of her gentle smiles, materialising in her quiet way like a ghost. She stood by the sink, absently deadheading the little pot of African violets on the windowsill.

'Yes. Just thinking about what I might cook for dinner,' said Hattie, with a vague smile as if she were in total command of the situation. 'Something simple.' She glanced at the cookery books on the shelf. 'I just need a bit of inspiration.' Walking over to the shelf, she plucked one of the books, opened it and flicked through the pages. Everything was in bloody French. Of course it was. She was in France.

With an internal groan of despair, she put the book down, admitting to herself that she wanted to impress Luc this evening.

'Do you have some onions?'

'Yes.'

'And you have butter and flour.'

Hattie nodded.

'And there will be anchovies and olives in the cupboard.'

'Will there?' asked Hattie doubtfully.

Solange came over and patted her hand. 'Always.' She crossed to one of the tall larder cupboards and produced a short squat jar of anchovies and a tall thin jar of black olives. 'You can make a *pissaladière*.'

Her airy tone made Hattie laugh. 'I could if I knew what one was, or how to cook it.'

Solange hesitated a moment. 'I could … I could show you, if you would like me to, but, of course, I don't want to interfere.'

Hattie was about to refuse because she didn't want to trouble the other woman – there were eggs, she could always make an omelette with salad – hand-torn of course – but

Solange's diffidence made her stop. There was something in Solange's stance, almost akin to a deer about to bolt, that made her want to accept the shy overture. That and desperation.

'I would love it. If you don't mind.'

'I don't mind. I used to love to cook but –' she shrugged rather hopelessly '– not anymore.'

'That's a shame.'

Solange didn't say anything, just picked at the cuff of her long-sleeved black dress, suddenly shy again.

'So, pissalade.'

'*Pissaladière*,' corrected Solange.

'Yes. That. What is it?'

Solange's eyes crinkled. 'It's the most delicious tart made with caramelised onions. Their soft sweet flavour contrasts with the saltiness of the anchovies and black olives. And the wonderful thing is that it's very easy to make.' Solange was already rolling up her sleeves and for the first time Hattie saw real animation in the other woman's face.

'Okay, that sounds wonderful.'

'It is.' Solange's eyes brightened with a rare twinkle. 'First of all, we have to make the pastry. Puff pastry.'

'Make it!' Hattie took a step back. 'That sounds difficult.' Didn't puff pastry come ready-made in packs from the supermarket? She'd made it once, a million years ago, in a home economics class, which, she vaguely remembered, involved a lot of faff with complicated folding and turning.

'*Mais oui. C'est simple.*' With a touch of mischief on her face, Solange handed Hattie an apron, led her over to the long cool marble counter and began assembling the ingredients. Her posture changed subtly as she directed Hattie to collect butter from the fridge. Now she was more like a general commanding her troops. There was a glimpse there of a more formidable character that had once been in charge of this large and beautiful home.

'You can make a yeast dough as the base but I prefer pastry and that would involve more time,' said Solange, deciding they would both make a quantity of pastry each. 'Then you can have some in the freezer for another time.'

She taught Hattie to rub the flour between the tips of her fingers, to keep the butter as cool as possible and used iced water to bind the resultant crumbs together. Her movements were quick and deft and she made Hattie feel like a lumbering carthorse in comparison. However, she was also very patient and an excellent teacher.

'That didn't take any time at all,' said Hattie, when they put the wrapped blocks of pale pastry in the fridge to chill.

'It's just a question of being organised and focusing on one thing at a time. Now we will do the onions.'

Hattie, slightly nervous in the presence of someone who was so adept, waited to see how Solange chopped her onions. The other woman, seeing her hesitation, paused and showed her the best method.

Solange held up one of the brown onions, running a knife over the skin. 'I always think that there is magic in an onion. The dried skin is so smooth on the inside, that unique paper texture, almost like luxury wrapping paper. Then the flesh is so moist, you can hear the juice as you cut. And then it folds itself into perfect pieces when you chop it like this. There's more sorcery in the flavour, so different raw to the rich depth when it is cooked.' Solange closed her eyes, almost in prayer.

They sautéed the onions very gently in butter in a cast-iron pan, adding pinches of tiny fragrant thyme leaves from the herb garden on the patio. 'Always use a good heavy pan like this,' explained Solange. 'We want to cook them very, very slowly so that every last bit of goodness oozes out.'

An hour later, Hattie was extremely proud of her *pissaladière*, with its lattice of anchovies and dotted with black olives – thank you, Solange. Hattie wasn't sure she could have made it look quite that professional. She was also rather proud of the quiet bond they'd built today, working side by side both in the ball room and the kitchen, as well as Solange sharing her memories of the château. Hattie was grateful for Solange's motherly guidance. While dinner was cooking in the oven, she managed a lightning-quick shower, washed her hair and put on a pale pink cotton dress that was quite worn now and a little shapeless. She pulled a face at herself in the mirror. She'd really let herself go. When had she stopped caring what she looked like? Maybe she should put her jeans back on. At least they showed off her shape, which was more than this dress did. Her only other dress was red and she was worried it would look like she was obviously dressing up. With the soft fabric of the skirt swishing around her knees, she returned to the kitchen keenly aware of the flutter of anticipation in her stomach.

Flirting with Luc had been the touchpaper to memories of being feminine and attractive. It had been a long time since she'd felt desirable or even bothered to dress to show off any of her assets. She wasn't even sure she had any these days. She brushed away that annoying little buzz of disloyalty. Officially she was single and there was nothing to stop her sleeping with someone else if she wanted. Sleeping with… She was jumping ahead a little. But why not? If she wanted to. She could. The idea bounced around her head like a snowball increasing in size. She did want to. She wanted Luc Brémont. Wanted the touch of his skin and the muscle of that gorgeous body against hers. She wanted to know what it would be like to feel again.

He might have teased her about seducing her but there was nothing to stop her from seducing him. She surveyed the kitchen and decided she needed to set the scene. Decision made, she nipped along to the dining room to retrieve some of the newly washed china and snipped a couple of extra sprigs of thyme from the pots, which she tucked between the napkins and napkin rings. Raiding the dresser she selected fine wine and water glasses for each place setting. Last but not least, she found some more tealights as the previous ones had burned away, put them into a couple of small bright red earthenware bowls and set them on the table.

'*Très confortable*,' drawled a husky voice from the French doors.

Hattie jumped. What was it with people in this place creeping up on her?

'Hello,' she said. And took in the full glory of the woman in front of her, who was even more glamorous than Yvette if that was possible.

'You're the English girl,' she said and walked in, pushing outsize glasses onto the top of her head, holding back a cloud of glossy brunette hair as she tucked a Chanel clutch bag under her arm. 'I'm Marine, a friend of Luc's. Is he around?'

'Er, yes. I think he's still upstairs changing. Would you like me to—'

Before she could finish, with a sure-of-herself smile, Marine sauntered past Hattie in a swirl of bright designer silk that put her cheap dress to shame. 'It's okay, I know my way to Luc's bedroom. He'll be pleased to see me.'

Chapter Eleven

Hattie couldn't have been more mortified when Luc came into the kitchen, a smear of bright pink lipstick on his lips, with Marine's hand tucked through his arm.

'Marine is staying for dinner, is that okay?'

'Sure,' said Hattie in that overbright tone that meant what-the-hell-else-am-I-meant-to-say. 'Let me just lay an extra place setting.'

Marine stood there, light amusement touching her lips, while Hattie gathered the extra plates and cutlery and Luc opened a bottle of wine.

'It all looks very romantic,' said Marine with a sly smile directed towards Hattie, before sitting herself down at the head of the table directly between the other two places and pushing her chair back to hold out her wine glass for Luc to fill.

The subtle power play was not lost on Hattie. With ease Marine had claimed the top spot as Luc's guest and Hattie, much to her annoyance, had somehow been relegated to skivvy. It felt horribly familiar, as if she were back in Chris and his mother's kitchen again, looking after them.

As he moved around the kitchen, Marine talked to Luc in fast-flowing French. Hattie clenched her fists inside the oven gloves as she went to remove the onion tart from the oven. So much for impressing Luc. He and Marine were so deep in conversation, she might as well have been a fly on the wall. What on earth had she been thinking? That Luc might be interested in someone like her?

She slid the plates in front of Luc and Marine, who barely stopped talking to acknowledge the food. Bringing over her own plate, she sat down. '*Bon appétit*,' she said and Luc did look her way then.

'*Merci*, Hattie.' He said something else in French and Marine responded as she poked at the tart with her fork.

'Would you mind speaking in English?' Luc might not be interested in her but she wasn't going to put up with rudeness when she'd cooked dinner.

'I'm so sorry,' said Luc. 'Forgive me, it's been a while since we've seen each other. This looks absolutely delicious. It's one of my favourites. Solange always used to make it for me whenever I came back. It was my special treat. Don't tell her –' he put a finger to his lips, which unfortunately drew Hattie's attention back to the slick of lipstick '– but I think it's as good as hers.'

'I won't,' said Hattie, being terribly gracious while wondering if there'd been any agenda behind Solange's choice of recipe.

Marine narrowed her eyes but didn't say anything, perhaps because she was still busy poking at the pastry, as if it might be harbouring something unpleasant. It was like watching a child convinced that a stray spider was lurking under there.

On previous occasions Hattie had found it easy to talk to Luc but now her tongue was securely tied and she felt horribly self-conscious in front of the effortlessly glamorous Marine. She couldn't think of a single thing to say, so when Marine launched into a flood of French, it was a bit of relief as the silence was starting to make her feel stupid and cloddish.

'English, Marine,' said Luc with a laugh. 'She's asking me what I think of the new mayor.'

Hattie gave a polite nod and, determined not to be excluded or give Marine reason to think she was stupid, she asked, 'How is a mayor appointed in France? I'm wondering if it's the same as in England. Our neighbour when I was younger was the local mayor. It was mainly a ceremonial role. I think in France a mayor is more important.'

Oh God, she sounded incredibly dull.

Marine looked down her nose and lifted her shoulders. 'I'm not that interested but I just wonder if his mistress will be his lady mayor or will it be his wife.'

'The mayor is appointed by secret ballot by the councillors and holds the position for six years,' said Luc, obviously taking pity on Hattie.

'Top marks, Monsieur Brémont. I had no idea you were so interested in local politics,' said Marine in flawless English. 'And how is darling Marthe? Have you met Luc's aunt, Hattie?'

When Marine said her name it was without the charm of Luc dropping the H and it jarred a little.

Luc let out a shout of laughter. 'Marine, no one calls Marthe "darling". She's a martinet and you know it. And no, I haven't inflicted her on Hattie yet.'

'So it's not just me she doesn't like,' said Marine, her lips tightening and making unattractive walnut-like wrinkles around her mouth, which the bitchy side of Hattie was rather pleased to see.

'Marthe doesn't like anyone or so she claims,' said Luc.

'Hmmph. And have you seen Etienne or Elaine since you've been back?'

'No, not yet.'

'Etienne has a new job at Pommery, he's very important now. They moved house this year to a lovely place the other side of Epernay. You must go there. They have the most delightful swimming pool…'

Luc's eyes met Hattie's and for a second they held each other's gaze as Marine continued to talk. 'And of course there's the most fantastic view. And do you remember Etienne's brother…'

Hattie felt a quick fizz in her chest at the soft look on Luc's face. Maybe she wasn't imagining things after all. Unfortunately, Marine proceeded to hold court for the next twenty minutes, filling Luc in on all the news of various local people, friends and their relatives. Whenever Luc tried to steer the conversation back to more general topics, Marine found something new to talk about.

Hattie was actually starting to find it amusing until Marine turned her focus her way.

'Yvette tells me you are a wedding planner.' The slight sneer of her lips suggested that this was rather unsavoury.

'Yes.'

'I find it strange that a bride would want to get married in someone else's home. It's really not designed for a wedding. And Solange already has so much to do,' said Marine with a sad shake of her head.

'Does she?' asked Hattie, feeling a little disloyal after Solange had helped her cook Luc's favourite dinner, but Marine ignored her and continued, 'I'm really surprised at your father, Luc, creating more pressure for her. She's still grieving. A wedding here is the last thing the poor woman needs.'

Luc raised a very unsubtle eyebrow at Marine. Clearly he was aware of how little Solange did around the house.

Marine rounded on Hattie with a sugar-sweet smile. 'I think you're being very selfish. Have you considered going to the Hotel du Ville? It would be much fairer. And it would be easier for you. Yvette said you were washing windows today. In France wedding planners have much more important duties.'

'I have a caterer arriving to discuss the wedding this week. If she feels that it would be better to hold the event at an alternative venue, I'll certainly consider it,' said Hattie sharply.

Marine smiled. 'That's very sensible. You're very young to be a wedding planner. How long have you been working in this role?'

'Six years,' said Hattie without batting an eyelid. Marine didn't need to know that this was the very first wedding she'd be organising on her own. Although, at this rate, it might be her last. Maybe she should toss in the towel and go for the easy option of a local hotel. Even with an in-house caterer, would they be able to cook for a hundred and forty people?

'Which reminds me, Luc, I mustn't forget to spray the landing spot for the helicopter.' There! What do you think of that, Marine?

'Helicopter?' she asked right on cue.

'Oh yes,' said Hattie with blasé aplomb. 'My caterer is flying in for an initial consultation.' With that she picked up the plates and carried them over to the sink to load the dishwasher.

'I should do that,' said Luc.

'No, it's fine. You catch up with … with your friend.'

Hattie decided she'd had the last word and retired upstairs, leaving them to it. Of course, Luc was popular with the ladies, she'd always known he was way out of her league.

She sat out on the balcony in the dark with only the hoot of an owl and a couple of dogs barking in the distance for company. It struck her how far away she was from everyone she knew and how alone she was. When her phone began to ring, it caught her at just the right moment. Chris again. Feeling resigned, she answered the call.

'Hi, Chris.' She deliberately put her usual upbeat chivvying-Chris-along tone.

'Hattie. How are you?'

'I'm good. How are you?'

'I miss you.'

The quiet words pierced her like a knife between ribs. She sighed very quietly. She missed the old him. When it had been 'us'. But she didn't miss what they'd had in the last two years.

'I didn't mean it, you know. I'm sorry.'

'I know,' she said in a low voice.

'I've been thinking.'

She swallowed, knowing what was coming didn't make it any easier. 'Maybe when you come back from France we could try again. I've got a job interview. Things will be different.'

Her stomach twisted. Different. Would they? A knot of tension tightened in her shoulders. 'A job interview. That sounds good.' She chose to ignore the subtext.

'It is. It's time I got back to work, although … well, I didn't want to say. Mum's not well. Really not well, this time.'

Ah and there it was. 'Oh dear,' said Hattie instead of what she really wanted to say which was *What's wrong with her this time?* Which she knew was heartless and possibly selfish but Chris's mother had been the main character in their lives in the latter years of their relationship.

'Yes, I've had to call the doctor out a couple of times. She's been having chest pains.'

Audrey Whittaker's chests pains, along with her bad back, her anxiety and agoraphobia, had been bothering her for the last five years, ever since Hattie and Chris had graduated from university. They bothered her more whenever she didn't get her own way.

'That's not good,' said Hattie.

'No, I'm worried about her.'

'I know.'

'You don't sound very sympathetic.'

'Sorry,' said Hattie automatically, falling back into the same old cycle of accusation, recrimination and apology. 'What does the doctor say?'

'Same as always. There's nothing wrong with her. He's not seen her doubled over in pain. That can't possibly be in her head. He just gave her some stronger painkillers. How's that going to help? We're going to have to go private. That's partly why I need to get a job. They offer flexible working and it's local so I'll be able pop back at lunchtime every day to check on her.'

'That's brilliant,' said Hattie, weary now because the job was about his mother, not about his own self-esteem or finding a purpose in life.

'It is. So … I was thinking. Well when you come back. We could maybe move. Get a place of our own.'

'Chris…'

'No, don't say it, Hats. Think about it. Please. There's no need to make any final decisions. Maybe a break is what you need. It's been tough on you as well. But when I have a job, things will change, you know they will. At least say you'll think about it. Please, Hats.'

How could she say no? They'd had nearly seven years together. It hadn't always been like this. 'I don't know, Chris ... you have to give me some time. Stop calling me all the time.' She couldn't believe she was actually going to say it. 'Give me some space.'

'I'll give you all the space you need. Just let me know when you want to talk again. This has been good. Take care of yourself.'

'You too.' She felt the familiar fondness towards him and as she cut the call off, the sensation of being totally alone here returned.

It was only as she was cleaning her teeth later that she realised Chris hadn't asked a single question about her and how she was.

Chapter Twelve

'**M**arine!' Hattie hadn't expected to see her this morning sitting at the breakfast bar with a coffee and a huge smile. Even in last night's clothes, which weren't the least bit crumpled, she looked bright and fresh while Hattie just felt tired and worn out and her head throbbed. She'd woken several times in the night and had gone rooting through her toilet bag in a desperate quest for some paracetamol, which had eluded her.

'*Bonjour*. Did you not sleep well? You look tired,' said Marine as she stretched, pushing her long slender arms above her head. 'I slept very well.' Her smile was as satisfied as a cat that had spent the night in an aviary and eaten every last resident.

The stab of sudden jealousy, insidious and unexpected, caught Hattie off-guard. The pain was so sharp it took her breath away but she covered it well. Swallowing, she moved quickly over to the half-full cafetière and with a shaky hand she poured herself a cup. She had no right to be jealous. Obviously, Luc had been flirting with her the day before and, poor sex-starved sap that she was, she'd made more of it. Now she felt foolish and absurd, as well as ridiculously naïve.

'Interesting outfit. Are you going to repair the boiler?' Marine giggled as if that robbed the words of insult.

Hattie tightened the scarf on her head and hitched up her dungaree straps like she meant business. 'You never know. I'm a woman of infinite talents.' She might be feeling rubbish this morning, but it didn't mean she was going to take any crap from this … this clothes-horse. Her muzzy brain struggled to find a better insult but had to settle.

'She is,' said Luc, leaning past her to snag the coffee, and she caught a whiff of his freshly washed skin. The fresh tang of lemon and pine smelled so good, she wanted to press her nose to his neck, to the smooth tanned skin above his navy T-shirt. 'Thank you for a lovely meal last night.'

'My pleasure,' she said distantly, tying hard to distract herself from the tantalising scent.

He gave her a look. 'Are you okay?'

'Yes, I've got a really nasty headache.' And so much to do. She was determined to finish the windows in the ballroom today and after that she needed to round up all the dust bunnies lurking in the corners and find a long pole and duster to remove the wispy grey cobwebs that were strewn everywhere like funereal streamers.

'Did you drink too much?' asked Marine.

'Hattie had less than we did,' said Luc, adding, with a teasing wag of his finger, 'You were the one who couldn't drive home, remember.'

'I didn't have too much, I was just being sensible,' said Marine. 'But in my experience, English people are never very good at drinking wine.'

'You're probably right,' said Hattie, not wanting to engage

but disappointed at being so spineless in the face of Marine's sly malice.

'Well, some of us have a lot to do,' said Marine, springing to her feet and looping her arms around Luc's neck. 'Thank you for a lovely evening.' She pressed her lips to his.

'It was good to see you and catch up,' said Luc.

'Of course it was,' Marine replied with a light, breezy laugh. 'Don't forget the *Comité Champagne* dinner. I've put in a good word for you with Papa,' she said, tapping his face gently before striding out of the room, her heels tap-tap-tapping across the marble floor in the foyer. He watched her go with an amused shake of his head.

Hattie needed something to do, so she picked up Marine's abandoned coffee cup and put it in the dishwasher.

'You don't need to do that,' said Luc, laying a hand on hers.

'It's no trouble,' said Hattie, stiffening under his touch. He gave her an odd look and removed his hand. 'Marine's an old friend.'

'She's very glamorous,' said Hattie, swinging away from him.

'She likes the good things in life, that's for sure,' said Luc. 'And she's good fun.'

'I'm sure she is.' Hattie looked at her watch. She sounded horribly prim but she couldn't help herself.

'I hope you don't mind that she stayed over. She—'

'Of course not.' Hattie jumped in quickly. 'Don't be silly. It's your house. Why would I mind?' She flapped one hand which struck her as probably looking really odd but she just did not want to talk about this and she was trying to move the conversation on. 'We are all adults.' Hattie's briskness made her sound like Mary Poppins.

'Yes.' Luc looked a little uncertain. 'Right. I'll see you later.

There's … breakfast.' He nodded towards the paper bags on the counter. 'I'll go.'

Hattie turned and began to soak a cloth to wipe down the surfaces to make herself look busy. When she glanced up, thankfully he'd gone. She sagged back against the sink. Way to go, Hattie. Make a complete tit of yourself by being so awkward just because he'd had a woman over to stay. If only she could have been more blasé about it.

Sitting down she checked her phone. A text from Chris.

Good to talk. Xxx

But nothing from Gabby since Hattie had sent some very soft-focus pictures of the ballroom yesterday. Typical – after badgering her for pictures, her cousin had now gone very quiet and she still hadn't updated Hattie on numbers. Was she disappointed with the room? Or maybe she was just busy with other wedding plans at the moment.

Over the next week, Hattie buried herself in the minutiae of wedding favours, order-of-service cards, provisional seating plans, working out the possible layout of the top table in the ballroom, ordering the champagne and the top achievement of finding a local furniture hire company. With that in place, she could start to relax, even though there was still no sign of the cleaning team that Solange had promised would come. In between updating her spreadsheet and making endless calls, she managed to do some more cleaning of the ballroom but there was still a lot to do. Despite this and the added annoyance of a summer cold, not helped by the dust – her nose ran constantly – things were starting to come together, and along with them she was gaining that quiet confidence that she had everything under control. Better still, she'd yet to see a mouse and was starting to think that maybe Yvette had exaggerated or perhaps even invented the problem.

On Wednesday morning she woke with a stuffy nose and also to a text.

We're on our way. Be with you in an hour and a half.

'No!' She threw down the phone, flung herself out of bed, grabbed a robe and ran to the room next door.

'Luc,' she called, knocking on his door urgently.

'Hattie.' His face softened as his gaze fell on her face. 'Are you okay? You look a little pale.'

'I'm fine. The helicopter. It's coming today and I completely forgot...' Even feeling below par, she'd have to have been dead not to notice the loose drawstring cotton trousers draped low over his hips or the mesmerising sight of the shadowed hollows of his stomach and the dark hair around his belly button that ran down below the fabric. Something inside her loosened and she had to force her gaze up to his face. Amusement danced in his eyes. Bugger him.

Focus, she told herself sternly. 'I forgot about marking the landing spot. They're arriving in an hour and a half. And it's not ready. And—'

He put steadying hands on her upper arms to halt her babbling flow. 'It's fine. I did it yesterday evening.'

'You did.' She sagged a little, grateful for the support of his hands.

'I did.'

'Thank you. How could I have forgotten that?' She gave an inelegant sniff, realising she'd didn't have a tissue.

'You've been working too hard. Why are you still cleaning? I thought Solange was arranging her team to come in and do a deep clean.'

Hattie sniffed again. 'They've been busy, apparently.'

He shook his head. 'I think you're overdoing it. You don't look so well.'

She shook her head. 'I'm fine. Just a cold.'

Luc studied her face and then smiled, his gorgeous face lighting up, and she felt her heart do one of those really annoying little flips, like a just-landed fish.

'It's going to be a gorgeous day and there's a great view from the landing place.' Enthusiasm shone in his eyes. 'Why don't we play hooky for a little while and take breakfast up there? We could have a leisurely picnic while we wait for the chopper to arrive?'

'What a wonderful idea.' The words spilled out of Hattie's mouth before she could stop herself. It sounded utterly idyllic and just the thought of it made her beam at him. The fresh air would blow away the incipient sinus headache that had been making itself felt since she'd woken up.

By the time she was dressed and came down to the kitchen, Luc had assembled a picnic in a gorgeous old-fashioned wicker picnic basket, complete with a half-bottle of champagne and two tulip glasses, held in place with neat little straps.

'Ready?' he asked. The woven strands of wicker squeaked as he closed the lid and buckled it into place.

'Champagne for breakfast?' she asked.

'Why not? You're not planning to fly the helicopter, are you?'

'No.' She laughed. 'It just seems a bit self-indulgent.'

'If we're having a picnic, we shall do it properly,' he said seriously, although a smile lurked at the corners of his lips. 'In

France food is a pleasure; you should never feel guilty. There is always time to enjoy a meal.'

'Okay,' she said, smiling back at him, charmed by this philosophy and the seriousness with which he delivered the words.

He picked up the basket and she took the picnic blanket and they set off, cutting through the gardens and then veering right up the hill. Luc led her through the vines up to the top of the hill, to a wide flat plateau, enclosed by a solid wooden fence.

As he opened the gate he stopped dead. 'I don't believe it.'

He dropped the picnic basket and stared around at the churned-up grass, his hands on his hips as he turned a full circle surveying the centre of the paddock. Hattie felt an urge to soothe away the deep lines of uncertain, is-this-for-real confusion that marred his forehead.

'I sprayed the H yesterday evening and I checked the weather forecast.'

He turned another 360 degrees as if hoping that things would miraculously be back the way he'd left them. Hattie studied the ground. There were isolated flecks of luminous orange paint caught in blades of grass but a large irregular patch had been raked away, leaving the surface scrubby and bare. Even she could see there was no way this would be obvious from the air.

'Okay, we've got less than an hour. What can we do?' she asked. 'Do you have any more paint? Could we spray it on the ground?'

'We could try but … I don't know.' He scuffed a foot over the uneven surface. 'It might not take that well. I'd cut the grass to make it easier to spray.'

Hattie caught her lip between her teeth. Where there was a

will there was a way. She glanced at her phone. No response to her earlier text so presumably no phones in flight. Then it came to her.

'I know. That roll of carpet in the ballroom. What if we brought it up here and sprayed the underside?'

Luc looked at her and then grabbed her shoulders and kissed her on the cheek. 'Genius! Hattie, you're amazing. Come on.' He grabbed her hand and took off at a run, back the way they'd just come, pelting through the vineyards at full speed.

'Who –' Hattie panted, trying to speak and breathe at the same time '– do … you … think … did that?'

Luc just ran faster in response and she had to force herself to keep up with him.

'Why would … they … the…' Out of breath, she gave up asking questions and focused on breathing.

'Here you go.' Luc handed Hattie a glass of champagne. 'To teamwork.'

'Cheers,' she said, lifting the glass and watching the bubbles fizz up to the surface in the bright morning sunshine. 'Teamwork.' She glanced over at the big piece of rubber-backed carpet now spread in the middle of the field, the large orange H glowing on the dark surface. 'It looks quite professional.'

'So it should,' said Luc. 'We deserve this.'

Carrying the rug had been a two-man job but they'd managed it with half an hour to spare.

He lifted his glass. 'To your brilliant thinking.'

They tapped glasses and each took a sip.

'That is lovely,' said Hattie with an appreciative sigh, letting the bubbles settle on her tongue.

They were sitting on the picnic rug and she took a moment to savour the wine and the spectacular view. 'And this is lovely.' She gazed out across the valley, striped with the green vines which marched like determined soldiers over and across the contours of the land. Swathes of woodland crowned the distant hills with a broccoli-purple hue, bringing to mind an Impressionist painting. Sunbeams cut through the clouds, creating dappled pockets of light and shade across the patchwork of greens.

Luc took a red and white checked napkin from the basket, shook it out and laid it across her lap before handing her a delicate white plate adorned with a tiny strawberry motif. Then he produced a breadbasket containing a couple of plump brioches, a small dish of almost white butter and a cloth-capped jar of homemade jam, all of which he laid in the centre of the picnic blanket.

'Breakfast is served, *Mademoiselle*.'

With a light breeze blowing through her hair and the early morning sun warming her face, Hattie couldn't imagine being anywhere better. Suddenly her heart felt so much lighter, almost as if spring had blossomed inside her. She grinned at Luc. 'Thank you, this is gorgeous.'

'My pleasure,' he said and there it was again, that little spark of something as their eyes met. Or was it just her pulse that beat faster? It was so long since she'd felt any interest in another man, she wasn't sure if he might reciprocate.

She took a brioche and, copying Luc, carefully slathered it with the creamy unsalted butter that she'd already become used to, before adding a generous splash of the jam. At first bite the combination of butter, sweet soft brioche and the tangy sweetness of strawberry jam made her moan with sheer sybaritic pleasure. Luc watched her and then nodded his approval as he tucked into his own brioche. They ate in companionable silence and Hattie breathed in the fresh air as contentment stole over her like a soft cashmere blanket. It was almost as if she'd been trussed up in a tight corset for the last few years and now she could breathe properly, feeling her ribcage lift and expand with freedom.

'There it is,' said Luc, jumping to his feet, and she felt his excitement because there was always something rather glamorous about a helicopter. The dull insistent buzz grew louder and became a more discernible *wap, wap, wap* of the rotor blades. Looking up, their hands shielding their eyes from the sun, they watched the helicopter come into view, directly above them. It flew in a large loop, circling the whole valley, before coming back again and gradually lowering, the tail and body swaying as it hovered above them. The whir of the rotors cut the air, silencing the birds and sending puffs of dust clouding up around the helicopter.

When the skids touched the ground with a gentle thud, Hattie and Luc both had to duck as dust and hot air billowed into their faces. Gradually the engine noise died away and the spin of the rotors subsided, the long blades drooping slightly as if dejected because their fun had been taken away. Only when they had completely stilled did the doors on either side of the squat body open and three figures jump out, one pulling a helmet off, another with a long telephoto lens camera in his hand and the third unloading a rucksack and a very big holdall, tossing long blonde hair over her shoulder.

'Fliss!' called Hattie, excitement overcoming her weariness. The other woman held up her hand in a cool wave that was so typical of her. Fliss took a bit of getting to know. On the outside she was reserved and a touch superior but on the inside she had the proverbial heart of gold and for those people she liked, she would do anything.

Fliss waited for the other two men and the three of them walked towards Hattie and Luc.

Hattie beamed and Fliss's patrician face broke into a broad smile. 'Good to see you,' she said.

'It's so good to see you,' said Hattie, kissing her on each cheek and refraining from giving her the exuberant hug she wanted to, as she knew Fliss, being the only girl in a family of four brothers, was not given to demonstrative exchanges.

'You remember my brother and personal helicopter chauffeur, Eddie.'

'Oh yes, you gave me a lift to Scotland at Christmas.' That was when she'd first met Fliss. Hattie recalled that Eddie was the explorer in the family and had been to both Poles and climbed Everest, which explained his rugged looks and weather-beaten face. He had the same aquiline nose and wide mouth as Fliss.

'Ah yes, the damsel in distress,' replied Eddie cheerfully.

'Mm,' said Hattie, a touch embarrassed by his recollection. She had been quite desperate at the time, having made the rather fraught last-minute decision to join her family, which had not gone down well with Chris.

'And this is Colin. A friend of Eddie's. He takes photographs.' Fliss gave him a sour look. 'He's just along for the ride.'

Colin held up his hand in a cheery wave.

'Don't buy anything from him,' warned Fliss. He simply grinned, making the freckles on his sunny face dance.

'Okay,' said Hattie, none the wiser

'Nice to see you again,' said Eddie, stepping forward and holding out a hand. 'Bit warmer this time.'

'Just a bit. This is Luc, he's the owner of the Château St Martin.'

'Hi, Luc.' Eddie held out his hand and shook Luc's. 'Do you mind if we take a quick pitstop and have a drink before we head off?'

'No, not all.'

Fliss tutted. 'You're so obvious, Eddie.' She turned to Hattie. 'He's checking the place out to make sure it's all above board because I'm a poor helpless woman who has no judgement of her own.'

'Hey, Luc,' said Colin, diving between the siblings and holding out his hand. 'Nice place you've got here. Don't suppose you fancy some aerial shots?'

Fliss nudged him hard in the ribs. 'Colin!'

'What? It's what I do! And cheap at the price.' He turned to Luc. 'I took a few on the way down. I'll just load 'em up on my laptop and you can take a look. What have you got to lose?'

Luc laughed. 'Sure I'll take a look. They might actually be useful for marketing material.'

'See,' said Colin to Fliss.

She rolled her eyes and hefted her rucksack onto her back.

'Do you want a hand?' asked Hattie.

'No, I'm good –' she patted her rucksack protectively '– and my brother can make himself useful for once and take my other bag.'

'Sure thing, sis.' Eddie picked up the other large bag with a good-natured grin. 'Notice you're not trusting me with your precious knives.'

Fliss shuddered. 'I don't trust anyone with my knives, least of all you. You'd probably use them to skin a bear, hack down tree branches to make a bivouac or something equally hideous.'

'Probably,' replied Eddie, cheerfully.

'It's at times like this I'm glad I have no siblings,' remarked Luc quietly to Hattie.

'Me too,' she whispered back as they led the way down the hill towar.ds the château that nestled into the top of the hill on the opposite side of the valley.

'Why don't I take Eddie and Colin onto the patio for a coffee while you show Fliss up to her room?' suggested Luc as they walked up through the garden at the front of the château. He led Eddie off to the right around the outside of the building, while she took Fliss through the front door.

'Lovely,' sighed Fliss, easing the rucksack from her back onto the floor and looking around at the grand entrance hall. 'This is beautiful. And thanks for inviting Eddie to stay for a bit. He can reassure himself and the rest of the family that I've not signed up to some weird cult or been sold off to human traffickers.' She shook her head. 'I almost regret asking him for a bloody lift but Chantilly is so close it would have been cutting my nose off to spite my face, not that I wouldn't be happy to chop the damn thing off.' She stabbed at her long nose with her fingers.

Hattie laughed. 'What's wrong with it?'

'It's too long and it makes me look even more snobby than I really am – and I'm bad enough as it is.'

Hattie smiled wryly but didn't like to contradict her. Well-spoken Fliss, with her tendency to speak as she found, could come across as aloof and distant. But even as the thought filled her head, Fliss whirled around and grasped both of her arms.

'Thank you so much for giving me this chance. You don't know how much it means to me. I've been fannying about for months now, trying to decide whether to go for it and set up a catering business and go it alone. Your call was just the nudge I needed. I can't wait to get started. And what a place.'

'It's pretty nice, isn't it?'

'Even nicer than Kinlochleven Castle, although don't tell Izzy, who sends her love by the way, and it's a damn sight warmer. I went up to Scotland at Easter and thought I'd freeze my nuts off.'

'No danger of that here,' said Hattie. 'Do you want to see your room?'

'Yes, please.'

'Actually, you've got a choice, if you don't mind moving out to something smaller during the week of the wedding. I may have to let some of the wedding party use the best rooms to get ready on the day of the wedding.'

'Huh! You're kidding me. I'm used to being in the servants' quarters in the attic at home. Being the youngest, the four best rooms had been taken by my brothers by the time I arrived.'

Hattie figured that even the attic, in a house where there were enough rooms for four brothers and her parents, probably wasn't that shabby.

'You know, I've got so many ideas and I've been doing some research into local food and suppliers. I can't wait to get cracking and start planning the menu. And of course cooking for that many we're going to have to do a lot of prep in advance, but I reckon between us we can do it. If there's any chance of getting any additional help that would make a big difference. I bet you could hire some local people.'

'Mmm,' said Hattie. 'That might be a problem.' She didn't want to tell Fliss straightaway about the resistance to the wedding. She had no proof, just a suspicion that no one really wanted this wedding to take place.

'Nothing's insurmountable,' said Fliss with a cheerful flick of her hair over her shoulder. 'Where there's a will, there's a way and all that.'

Fliss was easily pleased and took the first bedroom she was shown, with the comment 'I don't plan to spend much time in here.' She dropped her rucksack on the bed, opened the top pocket and removed a shallow black case which she tucked under her arm. 'Now show me the kitchen.'

'You don't want to unpack?'

Fliss shot her a 'puhlease' look. 'Kitchen.'

'This way,' said Hattie and led her back to the stairs and down to the kitchen.

Fliss slinked in like a panther assessing its prey, running a hand over the white marble counter tops before standing in front of the big range cooker. She reached out and touched the shiny chrome tap-like knobs and sighed before saying reverently, 'Lacanache. Brilliant.' Her head tilted upwards to take in the row of pans hanging on the rack above. 'Copper.' She turned and beamed at Hattie. 'I'm in chef heaven. Oh look, Sabatier knives as well.' She put down the black case next to the incumbent knife block. 'OMG this is heavenly. Just perfect. I might never leave.' She sighed and leaned back against the range, her arms spread wide, and stood there for a minute just smiling to herself.

'Phew, that's a relief,' said Hattie, sinking into a chair, not having thought about any of this. As far as she was concerned, a kitchen was just a kitchen.

'It's bloody wonderful. Izzy's place didn't have a decent knife in sight and her mother killed off the only decent pan cremating the risotto in it.' Fliss opened both doors of the big American-style fridge, nodding her head in approval.

Solange appeared at that moment.

'Ah, Solange, this is my friend Fliss who's come to do the catering. Fliss, this is Solange, the housekeeper, who looks after the château.'

'Hello.' Fliss's usually serene face was alive with enthusiasm. 'This kitchen is wonderful. It's going to be a joy to work in. And what a range. It's beautiful. And the layout, so well designed.'

'Thank you,' said Solange, one of her rare smiles lighting up her face. 'Marthe and I spent a long time on the arrangement. We wanted somewhere that would be a pleasure to work in.'

'You designed it?' Fliss beamed at her. 'I think I might be in love with you. It's going to be a dream to work in. Would you mind me asking what sort of equipment you have? Depending on what menu we decide upon, I may have to go shopping.'

'I don't think that will be necessary,' replied Solange. 'Come.' She led Fliss over to one of the tall units and opened the doors to reveal various utensils.

'Terrine moulds. And a ricer. A blowtorch too!' Fliss turned to Hattie. 'This is kitchen heaven.'

Solange showed her another drawer full of kitchen implements and Hattie listened to Fliss's sighs of appreciation and awe.

'Oh my God. Seriously.' Fliss fanned her face.

Solange stopped, stared at Fliss and then said slowly, almost as if she were coming out of a daze, 'It's a while since I looked at many of these things.'

She touched a few items in the cupboard, her long, slender fingers stroking the stainless-steel and earthenware surfaces.

'I once cooked for the French President,' she said wistfully. 'And for Catherine Deneuve, Serge Gainsborough and Jane Birkin. Lots of others. Politicians, military men, sportspeople. Marthe loved to throw a party.'

Fliss looked at the woman with renewed respect.

'What did you cook for the President?'

Solange looked reflective for a moment and then her face lit up. 'Turbot. It was turbot. With clams, fennel and potatoes. And the starter, now that was very good, a two-mushroom *velouté* which went down very well. And the dessert was baked Alaska, because I recall it was the President's wife's favourite.'

'*Velouté*, that sounds nice. Thickened with cream?

'Yes.'

'And what sort of mushrooms?'

And the two of them were off. They might as well have been speaking another language. Swapping tips and suggestions with each other. Hattie could have sworn she'd witnessed the instant click of soulmates and they were oblivious to her, which was just as well because she was so tired she could have quite happily crawled under the table and gone to sleep.

'Come see the larder,' urged Solange.

'Ooh yes, please,' said Fliss, already following her like an eager puppy. Hattie could hear her exclaiming over things as Solange talked to her.

Hattie stared down at the wood grain of the table, rubbing at her forehead with the back of her hand, trying to ease the biting headache. When they came back into the kitchen, they were speaking fast, fluent, French, each talking volubly, interrupting each other and breaking off as the other spoke. Hattie had never seen Fliss, or Solange for that matter, quite so animated. Both of them had come alive and both spoke with their hands, fingers flying energetically as Solange pointed to yet more utensils and opened every drawer and cupboard in the kitchen for inspection while Fliss responded with yet more delight.

Fliss's command of French was impressive and she spoke so fast that there was no way Hattie could have kept up.

Suddenly Hattie remembered she was supposed to be organising drinks and dragged herself to her feet. Suddenly spooning coffee into the cafetière seemed an effort. Her cold was really starting to get the better of her.

'Are you going to join us?' Hattie asked Solange, as she assembled a tray to carry outside to Luc, Eddie and Colin.

'Thank you but no. I was just calling in to see if you needed anything from the supermarket. Alphonse is taking me.'

'I can't wait to visit some French shops,' gushed Fliss, still bubbling with enthusiasm. 'When is the nearest market? I must go to that. I adore a French market.'

'There is one in the central square in Hautvillers on Thursday. I could take you if you like.'

'I'd love that,' said Fliss rubbing her hands together. 'It's a date. In the meantime I'd better go and see my brother and make sure Colin isn't fleecing Luc.'

They joined the men out on the gravelled terrace under one of the parasols, where Luc was examining the screen of Colin's laptop.

'Hey, Hattie, this is really interesting. Airborne shots of the château and the vineyard.'

'Don't tell me,' said Fliss dryly. 'Colin's going to do you an amazing deal.'

'To be fair,' said Luc. 'It would cost a fortune to hire someone to take these photos, so it's a bit of a bonus.'

'And that's exactly how he makes his money. Being an opportunist.'

Luc wasn't paying attention; instead he was looking back at the screen, tracing the outline of the picture with his index finger.

'There's the boundary of the vineyard, and there ...' He squinted, studying the terrain. 'See those odd squares, they're shafts down into the caves, which were originally chalk mines.' He frowned and sat back. 'Would you mind if I bought this one and printed it off?'

'Sure,' said Colin. 'You can buy as many as you like.'

'I'd just like to print this one. Something isn't right. It looks odd.'

'What?' asked Hattie, coming to stand behind him and having to hold on to the back of his chair.

'Are you okay?' he asked turning to look at her.

'Mm,' she said not meeting his eyes. 'Just a bit of a sniffle, probably set off by all the dusting I've been doing. What are we looking at?' She couldn't quite make out the picture. It just looked like lots of green, more green and yet more green.

'You get a different perspective from this angle. The shafts are in different places in relation to where I'd imagined them from below ground. They're covered these days now that there's electricity in the caves but originally they were used to let light down.' His face changed, and Hattie could see he was caught up in a memory. 'Once Marthe found me and Alphonse standing on top of the shaft covers. We'd been forbidden to go near them, but boys being boys ... she was furious. I've never seen her that angry. It wasn't like her. Usually she'd give me the silent and disappointed treatment, which would make me feel so guilty, I'd blurt out a confession.

'Funny. You see things differently from the air.' He scrolled onto the next shot and the overhead view of the quaint toytown village, with its terracotta tiled roofs and its stone buildings that crowded around the narrow, twisty lanes spread along the banks of the River Marne. Then onto a dramatic one of the château from the south, which was stunning.

'I have to buy that one,' said Luc. 'I could definitely use that in marketing brochures. It really shows the château off.'

It certainly did, thought Hattie. The picture summed up all the romance of the building, while showcasing the beautiful scenery around it. If that were to go on a website, she wouldn't be surprised if Luc was inundated with requests from people wanting to hold a wedding here. With a smile, she realised that while she'd only been here a little while, she'd already fallen under the spell of the château. It would be a hard place to leave.

Chapter Thirteen

Hattie heard the buzz of the helicopter leaving when she was back in the ballroom. It matched the dull buzz in her head. She blew her nose again. Each sweep of the broom seemed to unleash yet another explosive sneeze as the dust swirled around her. Who knew that sneezing could be so exhausting?

'No!' The broom hit a trail of small brown pellets. 'Shit!' Literally. She stopped to examine them and then scanned the rest of the floor. Bloody hell! There really were mice. And judging by the size of these droppings, they were either monster mice or rats.

Luckily the mice seemed to have stuck to the perimeter of the room. Considerate of them, she thought, and only on one side, thank goodness. Although now she was going to have to inspect the rest of the château for signs of rodents. She raised her eyes heavenwards and caught sight of the chandeliers.

'Damn,' she said out loud. She really should have started those before the floor. Each piece of glass would need cleaning.

Hattie manoeuvred the tall ladder into place and after a bit of a struggle managed to open it. She stared up to the apex of the ladder, not far short of the ceiling. It was like the beanstalk in the fairytale, and looked a very long way up. Almost on autopilot, she put one foot after the other on the rungs. Step. Step. Step. Keeping a tight grip, she climbed, her head swimming.

She blinked and felt herself sway a little. This had not been her smartest idea. The bottom of the ladder seemed a very long way down and now she was up here, she had no idea what she was supposed to be doing. She closed her eyes and clung to the ladder, praying that the energy that had deserted her would come back.

'Hattie?'

'Mmm,' she mumbled, not wanting to open her eyes.

'Hattie? Are you all right?'

'Yeah. Just peachy. I'm…' Her voice trailed off as she opened her eyes and the room began to spin around her, the floor undulating like snakes and the windows swimming in out and out of focus. Her fingers tightened on the ladder, fighting the urge to simply give in and let go. Light-headed and slightly nauseous, she closed her eyes again but this time it made things worse.

'Hattie!' Luc's urgent voice sounded closer. 'Hattie, you need to come down.'

She nodded still gripping the ladder, frozen in place.

'One foot at a time. Come on.'

She shifted one foot, lowering it to the next rung, grateful to feel the solid metal beneath the ball of her foot.

'And another,' urged Luc. 'Now your hand. Slide it down.'

She realised she was holding so tightly to the ladder that her knuckles were bone-white, almost bursting out of the skin.

Cautiously she loosened her hold and slid her hands down a few inches.

Bit by bit, she worked her way down the ladder, completely in thrall to Luc's calm, patient voice, but somehow, with a third of the way to go, her co-ordination deserted her and she missed a step. Thrown by this she inexplicably let go of the ladder.

Her stomach went one way, her body the other and she tensed in anticipation of hitting the floor. Instead, Luc plucked her out of the air with a confident 'I've got you.'

Relief flooded her and with her knees like jelly, her body went limp, trusting the security of Luc's arms.

It could have been a wonderful moment if she hadn't had an attack of sneezing, so violent she couldn't stop, with snot erupting from her nose and running down one cheek. Half-heartedly she tried to wipe her face with her sleeve, which just smeared more embarrassing gunk across her face.

'Hattie, you're burning up,' he said, laying a cool hand on her forehead, then putting an arm around her. 'I think you have a fever.'

'Just a cold,' she said, so weary now that she could barely keep her eyes open, which was just as well. She was far too mortified to look at Luc. 'But I do feel terrible.'

'You need to go to bed.'

'Can't. Too much to do.'

'Hattie, you can't keep going. Come on. You're not well. I'm taking you up to bed.'

'That'll be nice,' she said and then realised to her horror she'd said it out loud.

• • •

He hugged her soft body closer to his chest as he carried her up the stairs and tried to straighten out his thoughts, some of which were too busy thinking about her pert bottom nestled just below his right arm, while blood was being diverted to a certain part of his anatomy it had no place going at this moment.

It was a relief to arrive at her bedroom door and shoulder his way through into the mirror image of his own room. He laid her on the bed and turned away immediately to pull the drapes, surprised at how bereft he felt letting her go. He went into the bathroom, dampened a face cloth with warm water and came back to gently wash her face.

Her hand gripped his wrist and an electric frisson raced up his arm. 'You don't need to do that, Luc.'

'Shh, lie back. Let someone else look after you for a change.' He suspected it didn't happen very often. It struck him that she was very self-sufficient. She didn't demand much from anyone but always seemed to be doing things for other people.

'That feels lovely, thank you. I'm not used to anyone looking after me.' She gave a derisory half-laugh. 'I'm always doing the looking after. Sometimes I feel more like a nursemaid than a girlfriend.' He noticed she used the present tense, as if she hadn't yet let go. It bothered him, not for himself but for her. That she still felt responsible.

He had the urge to lie down next to her and take her in his arms and tell her he'd look after her.

He hesitated, wondering whether to leave her to sleep, and then realised that her eyes were wide open.

'Do you need anything?'

'No. I don't know why I thought I could do this.'

'Do what?' he asked sitting down, worried by the defeat in her voice.

'The wedding. I'm not really a proper wedding planner. I was the assistant to the wedding planner. This was supposed to be my big break. Me setting up on my own. Something for my portfolio. But now, I'm not sure I do know what I'm doing.'

'I bet as an assistant you were very involved. Besides, lots of people have weddings without wedding planners. Isn't it just common sense?'

Hattie shrugged listlessly. 'I thought so but nothing seems to be going right. The house is never going to be ready on time and although I've got Fliss here now. I'm not sure whether we can cater for a hundred and fifty people.'

'Why don't you leave her to worry about that? She's the caterer.'

'That's just it. She's like me. This is her chance to prove herself too. We're both amateurs. Am I expecting too much from her?' Hattie caught her lip between her teeth. 'I haven't even thought about, linen and all that stuff. And then there are the flowers and favours and table decorations. And my cousin hasn't let me know what she wants.' She huffed out an exasperated sigh. 'And sorry, it's not your problem.' She sounded so stoic all of a sudden, his heart went out to her. 'And there are mice. Loads of them by the looks of things. What's the word for exterminator in French?'

'I don't think there are any mice,' he said. That was one thing he could reassure her on.

'There are. There's enough mouse poo down there to sink the *Titanic*.' She paused, lowering her voice. 'In fact, I've got a horrible feeling that Yvette got it wrong. It's not mice, it's rats.' He felt her shudder. 'Which is really bad news. I've been trying not to think about it.'

He had a pretty good idea that Yvette had been

exaggerating the problem but this was concerning to hear. No wonder Hattie was worried.

Wanting to reassure her, he lay down next to her, slid an arm beneath her and drew her towards him. She stiffened at first and then went limp.

'Hattie. It's all going to be fine. I'll take a look and get an exterminator in if we need one.' Which he doubted very much. 'You're not feeling very well. You need to stay in bed for a day.'

'I'm okay. Just tired and headachey. Maybe a bit stressed.'

He looked at her pale, drawn face. 'When was the last time you had a proper day off and did nothing?'

Her expression went noticeably blank. Interesting. Why did he get the impression she'd been chasing her own tail for a long time? As she started to protest he shook his head. 'Have a proper rest and then we'll sit down with Fliss and Solange and make a plan. One step at a time. Like eating an elephant. Bit by bit.' And he would have to speak to Yvette about her sabotage tactics. It really wasn't fair on Hattie – she was only trying to do a job and make a fresh start for herself. He could relate to that. How would he feel if someone was trying to stop him making champagne?

'But I can't.'

'Hattie, you can. I'll tie you to the bed if you're not careful.'

'Kinky.'

His eyes met hers. 'I can be,' he said and felt a satisfying hitch in his pulse when her eyes widened slightly. They stared at each other for too long a moment before she said, 'God, you must think I'm such a wuss.'

'A wuss? What is that?'

'An idiot. Someone who is pathetic.'

He pulled her against him and rested his forehead against

hers. 'I don't think that you are an idiot or pathetic. I think you're brave, determined and stubborn. Every problem so far, you've found a solution. You've just got on and done things. Marthe would like you a lot. I must take you to see her when you're feeling better.'

'I'd like that. She sounds quite a character.'

'Hmm, that's one way of putting it.'

There was silence for a little while and then Hattie gave him a gentle squeeze. 'Thanks, Luc.'

'No problem.' He was going to have to talk to Yvette. There had to be some sort of compromise.

'God, I don't want to give you my cold,' she said, pulling back in sudden alarm.

'It might be too late for that,' he said, giving her a gentle kiss on the forehead, because it felt completely natural.

Chapter Fourteen

When she woke she was tucked up in bed, her dungarees neatly hung across the back of the chair opposite. Puzzlement had her checking beneath the covers. Knickers, T-shirt, bra and socks, all present. No one had seen her naked then. She couldn't decide whether she was relieved or disappointed. It took her a few seconds to sift through her memories and piece everything together. Luc carrying her. Luc kissing her – okay, on the forehead, but it was still worth registering. She tucked the memory of his lips brushing softly across her skin safely away while at the same time peeling back the misery of spilling her guts about her inexperience. Her having a complete self-pity party. She closed her eyes and groaned. Really?

Scrabbling around for her phone, she checked the time. Half-past five. She'd been asleep for most of the day. The sharp, pinching headache she'd been battling had changed tack and was now a dull throb across the back of her skull, her nose felt as if it were stuffed with a whole damn pillow, and her skin was coated with a clammy sheen of sweat. Grim didn't begin to describe it. And she still had so much to do. And Fliss! Oh God, Fliss, she'd abandoned her on her first day.

'I can see you worrying from here.'

She looked up to see Luc edging through the doorway with a tray in his hands.

'Hi.' It took all her effort to huff out the word. He looked good, as always.

'I brought you some food and a special St Martin tisane.' He put the tray down on the bedside table and perched on the bed.

She examined the steaming cup and inhaled a mix of liquorice and peppermint. 'Tisane? What's in it?'

'It's a herbal tea that's supposed to do everything from warding off a cold and boosting your immune system to soothing a sore throat and helping with toothache, if I remember correctly.' He grinned at her. 'Marthe used to make it for me whenever I was poorly. I had to ring the home to speak to her to get the recipe. All I know is that it tastes good and most of the time helped.' He paused, giving her a self-deprecating grin. 'Or maybe Marthe insisted it did. I didn't dare argue with her back then. Here.' He handed it to her and she took it with both hands.

'Thank you,' She took a tentative sip. Not too bad at all.

'How are you feeling?'

'Better,' she lied and then spoiled it with a sudden burst of sneezes.

He raised an eyebrow.

'Okay, I feel crap.' Her voice was horribly nasal. 'And embarrassed that you had to put me to bed. Happy now?' She knew she was being grumpy but she couldn't help it. Here she was, at her skanky worst, and he was sitting there on the edge of her bed, exuding gorgeous, good-looking, healthy pheromones. Life just wasn't fair.

He grinned at her. 'Solange has made you her special chicken potage. You're very honoured.'

'That was kind of her. Tell her thanks.'

'Actually, it's nice to see her doing something,' said Luc and then he caught himself as if he'd been disloyal. 'That sounds unkind. I don't mean it like that ... I'm not complaining about her. We've all been worried about her. For the last year, she's been drifting, never really settling to anything. Today is the first time that she has actually volunteered to cook.'

'How long ago did her husband die?'

'Two years ago.'

Hattie was surprised. 'I thought it was ... you know, more recent.' She screwed up her face in quick reflection. 'Not that anyone should judge or decide that there's a prescribed amount of time for grieving but I...'

'It's all right. Alphonse and Yvette are worried too. Since Georges died she hasn't got her va-va-voom back.'

'That's a shame.' She sniffed and scrabbled for a tissue and realised she'd run out. Luc handed her a fresh box that he'd brought up with the tray.

'Thank you.' She shot him a grateful if rueful smile. He thought of everything, which made her even grumpier. She really wasn't enjoying him seeing her like this – all snotty, flushed and braindead.

'Yes, although today I saw a glimpse of the old Solange. You should have seen her, giving Fliss orders like a field marshal. And she says you mustn't worry about anything. Just rest and eat her soup, which I promise is excellent.'

All very well for Solange to say, thought Hattie

uncharitably as she wrinkled her nose at the thought of food. 'I'm not really very hungry.'

'Try it. She made it specially and she'll be very offended if you don't eat it.'

Hattie picked up a spoon. Despite her bunged-up nose she could just make out the smell, but when she took a spoonful of the rich golden soup, she couldn't help an involuntary sigh. The vibrant taste packed a powerful punch, smashing through her dulled senses. With a surprised half-laugh, she said, 'That's lovely. Just what I didn't know I needed.' Even with her taste impaired, the tarragon and chicken danced over her tongue in a delicious samba of flavours, partnering each other perfectly.

'That's the magic of Solange's potage.' Luc twisted and leaned back on the bed against the pillow, crossing his legs at the ankle, making himself comfortable. 'She always used to make it when anyone in the village was sick. She'd put it in the front basket of her bicycle and Alphonse and I would cycle with her.' He paused, his eyes crinkling with his usual ready smile. 'I seem to recall our altruism had a motive. We usually got some sort of treat for the trouble.'

Hattie laughed, imagining Luc as a boy. He was probably as adorable then as he was now.

To her surprise she finished the soup, enjoying every last drop.

She lay back against the pillow, exhausted just by eating, as Luc chatted about his memories of Solange, Alphonse, Yvette and Marthe. When her eyes started to drift shut, he got to his feet.

'Do you need anything?' he asked, gathering up the tray again.

'No, I'm fine, but can you make sure Fliss is okay?'

'I wouldn't worry about her. She's in her element. Last I

saw she had every recipe book out on the table and was poring through them. You should probably stay in bed tomorrow.'

'I can't.' She sat upright. 'There's…'

He held up a stern hand. 'If you take a proper day of rest, it will be better in the long run.'

She sank back down into the pillows, not convinced he was right.

'Just one day,' he said.

'All right,' she grumbled, closing her eyes. She could always sneak downstairs when he went to the vineyard.

'I'll be back later,' he murmured and she felt his lips brush her forehead. Again!

She kept her eyes firmly closed while her brain took off at a thousand miles an hour, trying to figure out whether a kiss on the forehead was significant or not. It seemed quietly intimate at the same time as dispassionately brotherly, and for the life of her, she had no bloody idea which was his intent.

The next day he reappeared, cheerful and forthright, bringing her a breakfast tray, complete with a warm croissant and jam, as well as a small vase filled with brightly coloured flowers arranged in a pretty hand-tied posy.

'They're beautiful. Thank you, Luc,' she exclaimed, touched by the gesture.

'I can't take the credit, they're from Pierre the gardener. He heard from Solange that you were unwell.'

'That was very nice of him,' she replied over-brightly. Of course they weren't from Luc. 'Especially when I've never met him.' She had seen the gardener a couple of times early in the mornings but always at a distance.

'He likes to keep himself to himself. He's Solange's cousin

and a bit of a recluse. He would far rather be with his beloved plants than people. Officially he works here two days a week, but I suspect he's here more often than that. He's the unofficial gardener of the whole village. Now and then window boxes will appear, or planters outside someone's home, and he'll plant seeds in verges. He has a huge greenhouse at the back of his cottage and is always taking cuttings or sharing bulbs. People often find seeds or bulbs on their doorsteps.'

'How lovely,' said Hattie, charmed by the idea of a phantom gardener. 'Is that a local thing?'

'No, it's just Pierre. In return the local widows leave pots of cassoulet on his doorstep.'

'I hope he likes cassoulet,' said Hattie.

'I think there's probably more on offer but he prefers his own company.'

A sudden burst of laughter rose from outside. 'You have visitors,' said Hattie, looking towards the open balcony window.

'Friends of Solange,' said Luc with vague indifference.

'Sounds like they're having fun.' Hattie could make out several different voices talking in rapid French.

'Mmm,' Luc didn't seem interested. 'And you don't need to worry about Fliss. She said to tell you that she's as happy as a pig in muck and that the kitchen is perfect. She seems very easy to please.'

'Mm, not sure about that. She has exacting standards but she's thrilled with the kitchen.'

But Hattie was pleased to hear that Fliss was okay. Tomorrow she'd make up for her absence and they could sit down and talk menus and what could realistically be achieved between the two of them. Which reminded Hattie, she needed to check her emails. When Luc had gone she'd get out her laptop and catch up on some of the admin she'd neglected while she was cleaning. She'd been waiting on her cousin for final numbers for the last couple of days. Last time she'd checked there'd been no response to her most recent email or to the pictures of the ballroom or Hattie's proposal that they hold the reception in the ballroom and the service with the celebrant in the larger salon, with drinks served in between the two out on the terrace, weather permitting. It wasn't like her cousin to be so reticent all of a sudden.

'I can see that look, Hattie.' Luc reached up with his hand and traced the spot between her eyebrows. At the touch of his finger her eyes caught his and for a full second their gaze held. Blue, blue eyes, she thought. And those tiny darker flecks around the iris.

'What look?' she asked, all innocence, having already decided that the minute he left, she'd get up and dress.

He paused before smoothing the line that habitually formed on her forehead whenever she was worried, then dragging his finger down her cheek and studying her with a gentle smile on his face, which sent her heartbeat into overdrive.

'Stop worrying. Everything will still be there tomorrow. Just rest now. Take a day.'

He pulled away making her feel a little bereft. What had she been hoping? That he'd kiss her?

'I'll come back later and check on you. If you need anything, text me.'

'Yes, boss.'

Despite everything he'd said, as soon as Luc left, she picked up her phone. Phew. An email from Gabby.

Ballroom looks epic! Great work. Numbers tbc. And I'd really like the ceremony outside. Agree the terrace for drinks. Busy here. Call soon. Gxxx

Still no numbers. Even a ballpark would be helpful. Were they looking at a hundred? A hundred and fifty? A hundred and twenty? And where outside were they going to hold the ceremony? Another problem for her to address tomorrow.

She eyed the text notification, betting it was from Chris. She hadn't replied to the last one.

I know you want some space and I'm giving you space but just wanted you to know I'm thinking about you. I still love you, even though you probably don't want to hear that but I can't help the way I feel and I think we should always be honest with each other and ourselves. Cx

What on earth was she supposed to make of that? She slumped back against the pillows, her shoulders tight with tension, weighed down with guilt, and spent a frustrating half-hour going over and over old ground in her head, still trying to work out if she was doing the right thing.

Eventually she put it aside and was able to focus a little on her spreadsheet. Now that Fliss was here, she could start ticking a lot of things off.

At a knock on the door, she hastily shoved the laptop under the covers. 'Hello. Come in,' she called.

The door opened and Fliss popped her head around. 'You up for a visitor? I've brought some more of Luc's special tisane. Smells vile. But he was quite insistent it would do you good. I'm glad it's for you, not me. I like proper put-hairs-on-your-chest builders' tea.'

Hattie laughed, pleased to see a friendly face. The four walls were starting to get on her nerves. She wasn't used to not doing anything.

'How you doing?'

'I'm bored now. I hate staying in bed with nothing to do.'

'If I dared cross Luc, I'd have brought my notebook up and we could start talking recipes and menu planning.'

'It's all right. I've got my laptop.' She withdrew it from under the covers and Fliss smiled approvingly.

'Just don't let him catch you. He's very territorial, isn't he?'

'Is he?'

'Yes. He was quite clear that he didn't want anyone disturbing you.' Fliss raised her eyebrows. 'Is there anything going on I should know about?'

Hattie swallowed and lifted her chin. 'No,' she said, her voice shaking just a little.

Fliss smirked.

'I just have a stupid crush on him. That's all. You have seen him? But I think he has a girlfriend, or a friend with benefits. Marine. She's very glamorous. She stayed over the other night.'

'That's a shame. I was only allowed up because I made these.' Fliss as always was more interested in talking about food. 'Try one?' She offered Hattie a plate of still warm cheese straws. 'I thought I'd practise a few little appetisers –' she grinned '– and I wanted to play in the kitchen. It really is wonderful and I think I'm going to learn so much from Solange.'

'I wouldn't count on that, she's not around that often,' said Hattie before lowering her voice. 'I'm not really sure what she does. But I don't want to cause trouble. She's supposed to be the housekeeper but, well, if you have a good look around, you'll see there's not been much keeping going on.'

Fliss nodded. 'I guess she's like an old family retainer. And I take it that Monsieur Grumpy Vigneron who tramped mud all across the floor this morning is her son.'

'Who? Alphonse? He's not grumpy, he's a sweetie.'

Fliss pulled a face. 'Hmm, he'll be a dead sweetie if he doesn't take his boots off before stepping into *my* kitchen.'

'Oh dear.'

Fliss gave a satisfied smirk, her eyes twinkling. 'He didn't take kindly to me telling him off. Seemed to think that because he'd been walking across the floor quite happily for the last twenty years, he would carry on, and he wasn't going to pay any attention to some Englishwoman who will only be here for five minutes.'

'What did you say?'

'That, five minutes or not, I had high standards and I wasn't going to let some inelegant oaf, in need of house training, in my kitchen if he didn't know how to behave like a gentleman.'

Hattie winced. 'Ouch. How did he take that?'

'He turned very red in the face and stomped off like a big bad bull.' Fliss looked very pleased with herself.

'Have you met his sister yet?'

'Not in person. I saw her outside through the window. The redhead.'

'That's her.'

'She was having a very sulky conversation with Luc.'

'Sounds like her. She's a bit like an unexploded bomb, always cross about something, and you worry how easy it is to trigger her.'

'I can see that. Solange is so sweet. How did she end up with a pair like that?'

Hattie shook her head. 'They're okay. Although Yvette's a

bit prickly. For some reason, she's dead against having a wedding here.'

'I wonder why?' mused Fliss.

'You and me both. You'd think it might be a potential boost for the local economy. We'll source as much as we can locally and we're going to have to employ some local serving staff. Maybe we could pay Solange to help?'

'That's a good idea.'

'Although maybe that's why Yvette is against it, because she feels it might be too much work for her mother.'

'Funny. Luc was complaining to Yvette about *her* making extra work.'

'Really?'

'Yeah, I didn't quite catch the gist of it, especially as half of it sounded nonsense. If my French is correct Luc seemed to be talking about rabbit poo.'

'Rabbit poo?' Hattie frowned.

'Yes. I'm sure he said something like *Are you pleased you made extra work? Next time you'd do well to remember that rabbit poo is a lot bigger.*

Hattie sifted through the words and something struck a chord. She whipped out her phone.

'What?' asked Fliss.

'Google.' She typed in a quick question, 'What does mouse poo look like?' and studied the answer and resulting images. 'Of course. I am so stupid and she is a sneaky cow. She only filled the ballroom with flipping rabbit poo to try and convince me we had a mouse infestation.'

'Eeuw,' said Fliss, scrunching her eyes up in disgust. 'That's disgusting. Talk about taking things to extremes. Why the hell would she do that?'

Hattie shook her head.

'What about Luc?'

'He tried to tell me the other day that it's something to do with tradition but he didn't really seem to know either.'

Fliss's eyes gleamed with sudden devilry. 'Why don't we ask Solange? A pincer movement. I bet the two of us could break her.'

Chapter Fifteen

'You're up, excellent,' said Luc, striding towards Hattie as she hit the bottom step, almost as if he'd been lying in wait for her. The sight of him in a crisp white cotton button-down shirt and navy shorts, with that big smile on his face, made her heart dance.

'How are you feeling?'

There it was, that ability to make her think she was the only person in the world worth his interest.

'Much better for having a day in bed, thank you.'

He gave her shirt, cropped jeans and white trainers a quick approving once-over, which for some reason struck her as odd.

'I thought you liked my dungarees,' she said.

'I do. But that outfit is perfect for what I have in mind for today. It's a glorious morning.'

Before she could ask any questions, he'd tucked his hand into her arm and steered her across the marble floor and through the front door.

He was quite right, it was indeed a glorious morning. There were a few translucent candy-floss clouds in the brilliant blue sky and the bright sun already felt warm on her face. It was the sort of day that made you want to play hooky.

'Why don't we go for a drive?'

'A drive?' She felt like she was in the wrong scene in a play.

He was already ushering her towards the car.

'But I've got a ton of stuff to do and I've just taken a whole day off.'

'Humour me,' he said.

Fliss appeared on the doorstep with Hattie's handbag and a sweater. 'You might want these.'

'What's going on?' asked Hattie, looking from one to the other.

'Go,' said Fliss, shooing her with both hands. 'Have a nice time.'

Feeling a little bemused, Hattie did as she was told, strapping herself into the passenger seat. 'Are you going to tell me where we're going?'

'Not yet. First we'll stop in the village for coffee and croissants. I'm starving.'

As they drove down the drive they passed a group of women walking up towards the château.

'Is it busy on the vines at the moment?' Hattie asked assuming they must be working on the vineyard.

'So-so. There's always something to do. But it's quiet at the moment. It gets busier at the end of July when we have to manage the crop. There's a fine balance between having a high yield with lots of grapes and fewer grapes but much better quality. We have to measure the sugar levels in the grapes to determine when we'll harvest.'

'There's so much more to growing grapes and making champagne than I realised.'

Luc turned and grinned at her as they sped along the road. 'And that's what today is all about.'

Twenty minutes later, they pulled up outside an elaborate set of wrought-iron gates through which Hattie could see fairy tale castle towers painted in an elegant grey blue, topped with darker slate turrets and elaborate weathervanes. Hattie thought it looked very pretty and a little like a mini-Disneyland set in the middle of the city of Reims. She almost expected to see, at any moment, knights on horseback jousting with each other on the pristine green lawns.

'This is the Pommery Champagne House,' said Luc. 'It's one of my favourite tours. I thought you might enjoy it. You haven't been anywhere since you arrived. I thought you deserved an adventure.'

He was right. Apart from that one brief visit to the village, she'd not actually been anywhere. So much for her fresh start and expanding her horizons. She shot him a grateful smile. 'Thanks, Luc.'

He grinned at her, his face boyish and bright. 'My pleasure.'

The tour guide, a pretty young Canadian girl who swapped from English to French with amazing fluency, paused before a set of double gothic style doors and waited until she had everyone's attention, giving the young couple busy snapping selfies a sharp look until, chastened, they put their phones away.

'Now we are going into the famous Pommery caves. In 1868 Madame Pommery employed French and Belgian miners to turn the ancient caves into a series of interconnected galleries which stretch for eighteen kilometres, thirty metres below the surface.'

Hattie frowned and looked over at a nearby tree. Thirty metres? She couldn't imagine what that looked like.

'We are now going to see the caves.'

With that she threw open the double wooden doors and on cue everyone gasped. Hattie had to admit it was a dramatic sight and thirty metres was a very long way down. A long flight of steep stairs unfolded, neat parallel concertinaed pleats tumbling down, down, down, and above them a curved ceiling of mottled chalk, stained with dark patches. For a moment everyone was silent. Then the phones came out and everyone started taking photos. Hattie preferred to stare up at the ceiling and take in her surroundings. It felt a little creepy and, as they descended the shallow steps, it was like entering another world. Hollow voices from around and below them bounced and echoed off the walls. Hattie shivered a little, as much from the gloomy atmosphere as from the temperature, and she was grateful for the sweater that Fliss had shoved into her hand.

'You okay?' asked Luc, and she felt warm fingers interlace with hers.

She glanced at him and he smiled as if his holding her hand was completely natural. Smiling back she gave his hand a little experimental squeeze. It felt good. Comforting and something else. She didn't feel like she was on her own.

'Yes, just a bit … daunted. I had no idea it would be so deep,' Hattie whispered, overawed by the huge cavern and hanging onto the handrail on her other side. If you fell down these steps it was a very long way down. She cursed herself. That was such a Chris thought. Always expecting the worst. What had happened to the sunny optimism she'd always greeted the world with?

'I never thought to ask – you're not claustrophobic or anything? We can stay upstairs if you'd rather.'

She squeezed his hand. 'I'm just being an idiot. I've spent too long doing things in my comfort zone. I'm supposed to be having an adventure, remember.' Instead she'd spent the last few days worrying and stressing too much.

'It is quite spectacular, *non*?' he answered.

'It is,' said Hattie resolving to be awed and interested and not be negative.

It wasn't that hard to be awed and interested, there was so much to see and marvel over – from the brick-built barrel vaults that held up the vast ceilings to the huge bas-reliefs carved into the walls, not to mention the wooden racks of champagne and piles of dusty bottles tucked into different niches. As their guide led them through the tunnels they stopped in front of one of the reliefs which she told them was fifteen metres across and six metres high. The image of drunken debauchery was cleverly lit by the beams of daylight that filtered down through a square tunnel high above them, enhancing the shadows and the depth of the sculpture. It was entitled *Silene* and dated 1884. 'Alas, poor Gustave Navlet carved all of the reliefs by candlelight and it took him over two years. In 1889 Madame Pommery had electricity installed.' Everyone laughed at the irony as the guide turned to lead them onto the next section of the caves, but Luc stayed put, staring thoughtfully upwards towards the light.

'Are you okay?' asked Hattie.

'Mm,' he said, a look of concentration etched into his face. 'It's reminded me of something I was going to do but I can't remember what it was.' He looked down at her and laughed. 'And that doesn't make any sense, does it?'

'Not really,' replied Hattie, laughing at his confused face as they hurried to catch up with the rest of the tour party.

The guide stopped by a wall where words, messages and images were etched into the soft chalk. 'During the Great War, the city of Reims was constantly shelled. So many of the inhabitants of the city moved underground to live in the caves. They left their mark on the walls. There were classrooms, hospitals, dormitories and even gymnasiums for the children, who never went above ground for years.'

Hattie looked around at the walls and shivered. Although it was majestic, she couldn't imagine living down here in the constant chilly air with no natural daylight, but she supposed it was better than the alternative. God, she was grateful she'd been born in the dying embers of the twentieth century.

'Makes us count our blessings,' she said.

The group moved on into a new set of caves.

'Now here—' The voice of the guide provided a welcome interruption. 'What do you think these signs would have meant?'

Like everyone else in the group, apart from Luc, who had a distinct know-it-all grin on his face, she stared puzzled at a large sign which read 'Manchester'. What on earth could the connection be between here and a distant British northern city? Then she saw another sign for Zurich.

'Okay, Mr Smart-arse, spill,' she whispered to Luc but he just put his fingers to his lips as the perky tour guide began to explain.

'Back in the day, they would blend the champagne for the palates of specific markets and this is where they would store them. In fact Madame Pommery was one of the first to make Brut champagne, which she did for the British market. Before then champagne was always sweet. She had gone to school in

England and knew that the preference there was for dry wines. She produced a champagne specifically for the British market and then later on went a step further, as you see here.'

'That is customer service,' murmured Hattie.

With the underground part of the tour completed, they came back to the flight of stairs. Then, when they stepped through the double doors back into daylight, she experienced a Narnia moment as she stood blinking in the sunshine. She felt like that first morning when she'd arrived at the château, escaping the cold and dark confinement of her relationship with Chris.

'That was really interesting but I'm not built for cave dwelling.'

Luc laughed. 'Good to know.'

'I'm ready for a sit-down and some of this fizz I've been promised. Considering I'm living in Champagne I don't think I'm drinking enough of the stuff.'

'An oversight we must rectify,' said Luc. 'Maybe we should open a bottle to celebrate...'

Hattie waited.

'Things,' said Luc, evasively, and Hattie wondered what he'd really been about to say.

The tasting room was beautifully laid out but, best of all, they were finally served a glass of champagne.

'This is the Pommery Brut Royale.' The sommelier held a glass up to the light. 'See the colour. It is pale yellow with faint highlights of green.'

'If you say so,' muttered the young man next to Hattie.

Next they were urged to take a sip.

'Tastes like wine to me,' Hattie's neighbour muttered again. 'Don't know what all the fuss is about?'

'Shh, Leigh,' said his girlfriend, swatting his arm.

Hattie took a sip and swirled the wine around her mouth.

'This wine,' announced the sommelier, 'is elegant and lively.'

Hattie focused on the taste. Nope, it just tasted fizzy to her. Nice, but wine.

The sommelier continued. 'You can taste the assertive notes of red fruits. It's a well-balanced wine.'

Hattie nodded, wondering what an unbalanced wine would taste like and why were they serving the wine in these tiddly glasses.

'Why don't they serve it in flutes?' she asked Luc in a whisper, not wanting to look stupid in front of everyone.

'These are tulips. Much better for tasting as they allow the aroma to fill the glass. They capture it in the bulb shape. Flutes are better for drinking rather than tasting, as the narrow neck stops too many bubbles escaping.'

'So what, those pretty coupe-shaped glasses are no good?'

'Sorry, they look very elegant but they allow the bubbles to escape and let the champagne go flat much quicker.'

'And is it true the shape was modelled on Marie Antoinette's breast? My dad always claimed that.' Hattie remembered her dad declaring this fact with much relish. She realised with a sudden pang that she missed both of her parents and felt guilty she'd neglected them in recent years. Yet they'd never nagged her to come see them more, they'd let her be her own person.

'Sorry, that's one of those urban myths. It's complete rubbish. Although,' his face lit up, 'it is true that about fifteen years ago, Karl Lagerfeld and Dom Perignon partnered to create a drinking bowl based on Claudia Schiffer's breast.'

'Funny you should remember that,' said Hattie with amusement.

'And then there was Kate Moss. A coupe glass was created on the shape and size of her left breast by London's 34 Restaurant to celebrate her twenty-five years in the industry as a model.'

'Nice work, if you can get it,' said Hattie with a laugh, thinking that she wouldn't want her boobs immortalised in that way.

'For the model –' he paused '– or the glass maker?'

She nudged him in the ribs. 'You're terrible. I'm beginning to think you have a one-track mind.'

He leaned in and whispered in her ear. 'Only around you, Hattie.'

They emerged into the bright sunshine again and Luc insisted on taking her to lunch.

'I know a place that does an excellent *plat du jour*. Three courses.'

'For lunch?' It seemed such a decadent thing to do. 'I'd be quite happy with a baguette on a park bench or a quick sandwich.'

'That isn't lunch.' He sounded mildly outraged.

'Are you sure?' Hattie asked.

'I'm French. I'm sure. Lunch is the most important meal of the day.'

'Really? What about dinner?'

'That's equally important. But we're not in a hurry. We will have time to digest properly and then we can visit Notre Dame.'

'I thought that was in Paris.'

'Notre Dame is Our Lady – there are lots of Notre Dames

all over France. The cathedral here is officially Notre Dame de Reims. The one in Paris is Notre Dame de Paris.'

Luc led her through the streets to a tiny restaurant that had fewer than ten tables inside and some crammed onto the pavement.

'This looks lovely.'

'It is. The food is excellent.'

'It's very busy.'

'That's because everyone stops for lunch in France.'

Hattie, a great one for sandwiches at her desk, raised a sceptical eyebrow.

'It's true. Did you know UNESCO declared French gastronomic meals a part of the Intangible Cultural Heritage of Humanity?'

'You're having me on,' said Hattie, not believing a word of it.

'I promise you. Look it up.' He tapped at his phone screen and then held it up. 'It is important for togetherness, pleasure and the balance between people and the bounty of nature. Do you want to sit inside or out?'

'Can we sit outside?' replied Hattie immediately. 'I love being able to eat outside. It always feels terribly decadent and as if I'm on holiday.'

Once seated at a table with crisp white napkins and a blue and white checked tablecloth, and with a leather-bound menu in her hand, Hattie struggled with a few words that were beyond her schoolgirl vocabulary.

'What's a *ballotine*?' she asked, having worked out that *purée fumée* was smoked mash, although smoked mash of what, she wasn't quite sure.

'It's a boned thigh that is stuffed and rolled and served in slices.'

'And what is *maroilles*?'

'It's a type of cheese.'

'Okay. What do you recommend?'

'Everything,' said Luc. 'It's all good here.'

'You're no help.' She laughed and went back to the set menu. 'I'm not sure I can eat three courses for lunch.'

'Don't worry. Here the focus is on quality rather than quantity. French people don't tend to snack between meals.'

In the end she chose the home-made terrine of pork, chicken, and pistachio with grape must and a mustard and mesclun salad. Of course, she had to ask what mesclun was – it turned out it was a blend of salad leaves. For her main course she chose the pollack with Noilly Prat sauce on a bed of garden herbs, which sounded delicious.

'And the most important thing is the wine,' said Luc. 'What would you like?'

'You are officially in charge of my wine education,' said Hattie. 'You choose.'

He spent some time perusing the wine list and Hattie studied him. The more time she spent with him, actually getting to know the man, the more she liked him. At first she hadn't really taken him seriously; she'd thought he was a light-hearted flirt who was interested in some fun, but now she was starting to realise that there was a lot more to Luc. He was very loyal to his friends, passionate about his goals and had a strong sense of who he was and what he wanted. He didn't need to rely or lean on anyone else and he didn't expect anyone to rely or lean on him. It was an extremely attractive trait.

'You look lost in thought,' he said, his words penetrating her quiet contemplation.

'I've got a lot to think about,' she said.

'Do you want to talk about it?' he asked.

She scrunched up her face. Did she?

'No,' she said with finality and flashed him a bright smile. She was with a gorgeous man having what was set to be a delicious meal. Life was good; now was not the time to think about the future. She had the summer to enjoy herself and she was damn well going to.

The terrine when it arrived was a perfect striped square of layers of chicken and pork drizzled with grape must, which reminded her of a rich syrupy balsamic vinegar, and topped with a light crunch of pistachio. The bite of the mustard, rocket, frisée and endive leaves was the perfect accompaniment to the coarse texture of the meat. Hattie sighed when she finished the last mouthful.

'That was delicious and just the right amount.'

'Told you,' said Luc, with a quick superior smirk.

'Although I might need a rest before the next course.' She turned her wrist to check the time.

Luc put his hand over her watch. 'Where's the fire, hotpants?'

She laughed.

'You should slow down, enjoy life, savour things, enjoy lunch … the French way. You take things too seriously. You need to slow down and have some fun.' He poured her another glass of wine. 'What do you think of the wine?'

'It's very…' She paused and then took another sip, determined to not just say it was nice. She swilled the golden liquid around her mouth, taking the time to assess the feel of it in her mouth and thinking about what the wine reminded her of. 'Summer sunshine, honey and hay,' she announced.

Luc beamed at her. 'Very good. It's a Chenin Blanc from the Loire Valley.'

She felt a quick kick of delight as if she'd got the right answer in a difficult exam.

They sat and drank wine in the sunshine, watching passers-by including a group of very tipsy pensioners, who were clearly having a very lovely time. Luc caught Hattie's eye and they exchanged wry smiles as they watched two elderly ladies trying to prop up a third between them.

Now that she wasn't worrying about the time, Hattie allowed herself to relax, enjoy her wine and the golden sunshine. Maybe she did need to have some fun.

It was almost a shame when the next course arrived, since it meant she had to do something, but the first taste of the perfectly cooked, fragrant fillet of fish made it more than worthwhile. The large white flakes had absorbed some of the flavours of the lemon thyme, fennel leaves, parsley and tarragon.

'Sorry,' she said apologising for her earthy groan of pleasure. 'That is … something else.' She reached for her glass of wine.

'Don't apologise.' He paused before adding wickedly, 'There's a certain pleasure, watching a woman enjoying herself.'

Hattie choked, spluttering slightly as the wine almost went down the wrong way, her eyes widening, but she wasn't about to let Luc get away with his outrageously risqué comment.

'I wouldn't know,' she said, which was the best she could come up with, after the sudden hitch in her pulse.

'Of course, there's even more pleasure in making sure a woman enjoys herself.'

'Is there?' Hattie couldn't believe the question had popped out but she felt brave and bold.

Luc's eyes darkened and he gave her face a slow thoughtful perusal.

'Oh, yes,' he said, and his voice turned husky, intensifying the flare of attraction she felt for him.

For some reason she was unable to tear her gaze away from his lips. She wanted to kiss him, be kissed by him. Know what it was to feel that gorgeous body against hers. The words 'Show me' hovered on her lips. What would he say? It would be embarrassing if she'd read him wrong. What if he were just flirting with her? This was the problem with having only slept with one man. One you'd known for months before finally one drunken night out you ended up in his bed. She felt so out of her depth.

'This fish is so well-cooked. I'm always nervous about cooking fish. It's easy to overdo it, isn't it. I'm guessing this has been pan-fried. I like the crispy skin. I don't normally like skin.' She was talking utter rubbish, determined to change the subject. 'How's your pork blanquette?'

'Excellent. Try some.' Luc didn't seem fazed or was perhaps kind enough to overlook her turning into a babbling idiot. He forked up a piece of pork loin in a creamy sauce and held it out to her.

Grateful for his sang-froid, she took it. 'Oh, that is really good. I might have food envy, except mine is just as good.'

'Just as well, this is my favourite here. You're very honoured I shared even that little bit,' he teased and Hattie relaxed a little, grateful that the buzz of sexual tension had been dialled down. Luc discomfited her. He was so sophisticated, with that enviable, effortless savoir-faire, that next to him she felt like a gauche schoolgirl. But he had said she took life too seriously and she should have some fun. Maybe she should just throw caution to the wind and go for the adventure she said she was looking for.

'I think I might just burst out of these jeans,' complained Hattie as they wandered after lunch along the ancient streets of the city. She laughed. 'Sorry, that's too much information.' Hardly the thing you said to someone you wanted to fancy you. 'Oh my.' She stopped dead, all thoughts of her waistband scattered, when she saw the façade of Notre Dame Cathedral. With the tiny carvings and elaborate details, it was like a highly decorated wedding cake. Three huge gothic arches, layered with traceries of carved stone, dwarfed the enormous wooden doors. The gigantic scale of everything made Hattie's mind spin. How on earth had men built this?

'It's breathtaking,' she whispered to Luc, a little overawed.

'It never gets old,' he said, taking her hand, just as he had in the cellars at Pommery. 'Come on, let's go inside. You must see the stained-glass windows.'

They wandered into the cool serene space and Hattie wondered anew what it was in humans that had the capacity, against the odds, to build something so spectacular in the name of something they believed in. This had been built before cranes and mechanical engineering, although much of it, she learned, had had to be rebuilt after the First World War.

For the next forty-five minutes, they walked through the dappled stained-glass reflections on the floor, hand in hand, absorbing the still atmosphere, without saying a word to each other. Every now and then they would look up at something, catch each other's eyes and smile. Luc was so easy to be with. It was one of the most restful, peaceful afternoons Hattie had experienced in a very long time. Now she understood what

Luc meant about slowing down and taking the time to savour things. When they moved back outside into the heat of the day, it was as if she'd stepped out of time for a while and all her problems had melted away.

She turned to Luc to thank him and as she looked up at him, he took her other hand and pulled her towards him. Their gazes met. Her breath caught in her chest and she couldn't help herself. She leaned up and kissed him.

As soon as her lips touched his a burst of sunshine lit up inside her, the slow warmth of his kiss powering up every cell with a battery charge of its own. Her pulse fizzed in her veins and her breath stuck in her chest and she never wanted to let go of him, ever.

Wow, Luc could kiss. What had she been missing all her life? Was this a French thing?

However, when he pulled back he looked every bit as dazed as she felt.

'Uh,' he said, staring at her.

'Uh, back at you,' she said, reeling a little but also feeling a delicious thrill of feminine power. No. This was just… Kisses weren't that electric, that heart-squeezingly tumultuous. A kiss was just a kiss. Yeah, poems and songs were written about them but it wasn't real.

Luc was still staring at her. Maybe it was real.

'Do you want to try that again?' she murmured.

He pressed his own lips together and nodded.

This time this kiss didn't take them quite as much by surprise. The sparks had dulled but there was still that delicious slow slide into each other, a sense of ease and a heart-stopping something. Unable to help herself, she wrapped her arms around him, pressing herself closer to him even as he pulled her to his body. She could feel … she could feel definite signs of mutual attraction.

It was only the over-excited cheers of a group of schoolchildren that broke them apart.

Luc's eyes were filled with wonderment and Hattie felt sure hers looked exactly the same.

'That was…'

'It was,' she agreed.

He took her hand and by unspoken agreement they began to walk, their fingers interlinked. The street was busy, which, Hattie decided, was just as well, because all she could think about was kissing Luc again. Judging by the sidelong glances he kept giving her, he wanted to do the same.

As they squashed together against a wall to accommodate a coachload of tourists following a man with an umbrella held aloft, Luc whispered in her ear, 'I want to kiss you again.'

'Me too.'

He grinned. 'Fancy going home?'

'*Absolutement.*' She grinned shyly back at him, even though she wasn't sure if she'd just made up a French word.

Chapter Sixteen

I t was probably just as well that Luc's car was an open-top model, thought Hattie, as they drove back from Reims. An ordinary car wouldn't have contained the charged atmosphere. They kept sneaking looks at each other and then catching each other at it and smiling. Luc's hand held hers nearly all the way, apart from when it was imperative that he changed gear. The feelings were new and wonderful and a thousand butterflies careered around Hattie's stomach the whole way home. She thought she might just take flight herself.

It was a relief when the château came into view and Luc turned off the main road. They looked at each other. Hattie knew the minute they stopped the car, they would burst through the front doors and race up the stairs. As they drove at quite a pace up the drive, they passed the same crowd of women they'd seen earlier, laughing and chattering among themselves.

Luc slammed on the brakes and they both leapt out of the car, grinning at each other. The same intent in their minds. Luc took the stairs to the front door two at a time and then waited at the top to grab Hattie's hand. They were two strides across the foyer when Solange came scurrying into view with an unfamiliar urgency.

'Luc! Hattie! You're just in time.' She clapped her hands together in delight and Fliss appeared behind her.

Their hands fell away from each other, although, judging from the excited looks that Solange and Fliss were sharing, neither had noticed.

'Come, see,' said Solange, bustling forwards with uncharacteristic bossiness to grab Hattie's arm. She led her down the hallway and along the corridor to the ballroom and threw open the doors.

The room shone. Everything seemed to have been dialled up several notches. The faded curtains had been replaced, the chaise had been reupholstered, the paintwork gleamed and light sparkled from the immaculate, fully lit chandeliers.

'Oh my goodness,' said Hattie drinking it all in, from the doorway. 'It looks beautiful.'

Solange nodded and then lifted her chin. 'I apologise, it should have been done before.' Tears glistened in her eyes. 'I… I lost my way since Georges died, thinking the house didn't matter anymore, especially with Marthe gone, but Luc coming home and having you here has given me back my purpose. And it's wonderful to be able to share the treasures of the house.'

Fliss put her arm around her shoulders. 'That's a lovely thing to say.'

Hattie stepped forward into the ballroom and gasped.

'Solange! *C'est magnifique!*' She hoped her pidgin French would convey her delight. 'Did you do all this today?' she asked, slightly overcome by the scale of what had been achieved as she wandered around the room, touching the plush new velvet upholstery. Even the gilt paint had been touched up to hide any knocks and bumps. Dozens of silk cushions had also appeared and there were filmy cream-coloured drapes at the windows. It was quite the transformation.

'Non. We had a team of cleaners in yesterday and today. And I know someone in the village who does upholstery. She and her father also came for two days.'

'It looks…' Hattie's face crinkled into a big smile. 'Just amazing. I can't believe you've done all this. Thank you.'

Solange shook her head. 'You don't need to thank me. It was long overdue.'

'And it all looks fabulous,' interjected Fliss as if sensing there was about to be a lot of recrimination and self-reproach. 'I think you should have a rest this evening. Why don't I cook dinner for everyone? I'm starting to feel a bit like a spare part.'

'That sounds an excellent plan,' said Luc.

'I'm supposed to be cooking dinner for my children tonight,' said Solange looking rather regretful.

Fliss took her arm and put her own through it. 'Well, we've all got to eat tonight, why don't we combine forces?'

Confusion crossed Solange's face.

'Cook together,' said Fliss before lapsing into French.

Solange brightened and the two of them held a quick conversation before Fliss turned to Hattie. 'All sorted. Potluck supper tonight and then I'm going to cook something special later in the week when we've been to the market.' She rubbed her palms together. 'That's a much better plan because I can really go to town.' She nudged Hattie. 'And show off a bit.'

'You're so kind, Fliss,' said Solange, looking at her grubby sleeves. She'd clearly played her part within the cleaning team. 'I'll come back later and bring the *boudin blanc* and we will cook together.' There was almost a skip in her step as she headed off to her own home.

'Excellent,' said Fliss, clearly pleased with herself.

'I think I'll just go upstairs and—'

'Oh no you don't, Hattie, you've been skiving today. I want to talk to you about my ideas. I'm really excited and I think you're going to love them.'

'But—' Hattie cast a look at Luc.

'What else are you going to do?' asked Fliss. 'The cleaning is all done. Don't tell me you've got any plans.'

This time Hattie didn't dare look at Luc as she said, inwardly cursing, 'Of course I can.'

'I think I'll pop down to the vineyard to see Alphonse and persuade him to release a bottle of champagne for us this evening,' said Luc.

'And perhaps you could remind him not to traipse mud into my kitchen.'

Hattie sneaked a quick look at Luc. He winked at her and turned and left, leaving her stirred-up hormones on a low simmer.

'So,' said Fliss as she steered Hattie back into the kitchen, almost as if she knew that given a choice Hattie would bolt straight off in Luc's direction. 'I've got a final menu suggestion. What do you think about an asparagus, assorted peppers and new potato salad for the starter? Followed by lemon sorbet and then, as a main course, either a filet mignon with potato, onion and smoked mozzarella pavé and asparagus bundle or herb-crusted wild salmon with lemon-scented mash potato, green beans and parsley sauce.'

'All sounds delicious to me.'

'Good, I'm going to write it all down and then you can see what your cousin thinks. And you'll need to ask her again about the wedding cake. I'm surprised she's not come back about that yet. You don't think she might call off the wedding, do you?'

'No! Definitely not. She and Hugo are perfect for each other and … the family all love him.'

'Right. Well, I'm going to start cooking for dinner tonight and you can help.'

An hour later, exhausted by Fliss's demands, Hattie asked, 'Can I do anything else?' her gaze inadvertently drifting to the doorway for the ninety gazillionth time in the last hour. She'd grated cheese, washed up and laid the table, so she hadn't been entirely useless.

Fliss tilted her head on one side and levelled an exasperated look at her, before marching over to the fridge, grabbing a bottle of wine and pouring a glass.

'Here. Take this. Go have a shower or whatever you need to do and get out from under my feet. This is just a simple meal and Solange will be here soon.'

'I was helping,' Hattie said indignantly, trying to pretend that she wasn't hanging around hoping Luc might materialise.

'Course you were. Vamoose.' She flicked one hand, shooing Hattie to the door. 'You're like a mooning teenager.'

'I don't know what you mean,' said Hattie..

'Course you don't.' Fliss made a big deal out of rolling her eyes. 'Now bugger off and leave me to cook in peace. You're useless to me like this.'

It was a relief to give up and go up to her room. She'd been fidgety and distracted all afternoon. She'd see Luc soon enough. After a refreshing shower, she bundled her hair up, turban style, wrapped one of the large bath sheets around her chest and stepped out onto the balcony to enjoy the early evening sunshine with her glass of wine and to give Gabby a call.

She hung over the wrought-iron balustrade taking in the view as she phoned her cousin's number. It rang a couple of times and then annoyingly went to voicemail.

'Gabby, it's Hattie. Good news, we've got some menu ideas for you. Perhaps you could take a look and let me know what you think. With a sigh, she put the phone on the small metal table and took a seat at the little patio table, raising her face to enjoy the sensation of warm sun on her skin.

She could hear the peep of small birds flitting in and out of the clematis climbing up the wall below and the distant chug of a tractor on the small road that wound down through the valley. A pattern of greens spread before her, colouring the soft, undulating landscape, bisected by the immaculate lines of the vines. She loved this view from high up with its wide panorama and the sensation of somehow being part of the scene but distant at the same time. There was a feeling of peace and having some time to herself. No sooner had the thought popped into her head than a message beeped on her phone.

Hi Hattie. Hope you're having a great time. Haven't heard from you this week so I hope everything is okay. Always here for you. Would be great to hear how it's going? Cx

Reluctantly, she typed:

All good here. Busy but making progress. Hope all good with you. H

She paused. Should she put in a kiss or not? That bloody x

should be deleted from the alphabet; it served no main purpose unless you were having an x-ray. She regretted not being honest when he asked to try again instead of vaguely avoiding answering. Worse, she knew that if she missed the x it would bring a torrent of worry and anxiety that they weren't still friends.

'You look deep in thought.'

Hattie jumped and inadvertently pressed send before she was ready, without the kiss, which was going to cause consternation. She looked up to find Luc with a towel around his waist, the white fabric enhancing his deep tan. Her simmering hormones almost burst into flames as her gaze strayed over the low-slung towel and the hairline below his belly button, bringing with it an instant and insistent tug of lust.

'Twins,' said Luc, nodding to her towel, coming to stand at his balcony's edge, a scant metre from hers.

'Mm,' she said, nonplussed by the sight of his bare chest. He grinned as she automatically tucked her towel in tighter around her chest.

Should she stay or go? He clearly didn't feel the least bit awkward.

'Lovely view,' she said, for want of anything better to say, and then immediately could have bitten her tongue off.

'It is,' he said, a smile tugging at the corner of his mouth.

She gave him a severe look and then burst out laughing. Rising, she went to stand opposite him. He was so close and yet so far. That earlier kiss sizzled between the divide and the small hairs on her arms rose as she wondered what would happen right now if it weren't for that small but enormous gap.

'I walked into that.'

'Sadly, not literally,' said Luc, eyeing the gap between the two balconies before giving a mock wistful sigh. 'How's your afternoon been? I missed you.'

Her heart did a funny salmon leap.

'Okay. How about you?'

'I'd rather have been with you. Alphonse isn't anywhere near as pretty as you to look at.'

Unused to compliments, Hattie laughed. 'I hope you didn't tell him that, you might have hurt his feelings.'

Luc's face softened. 'I think he might have guessed from my goofy face that I spent most of my time imagining kissing a certain cute Englishwoman.'

Her heart had surely just turned to mush. Any moment now her knees were going to give up on her. 'I ought to go and get ready for dinner,' she said, her eyes inadvertently straying to his chest again. She was a coward but if she had to look at half-naked Luc any longer she might spontaneously combust. She rose clutching the towel tightly. She thought she'd done quite well to have a conversation without once checking it was still secure.

'See you soon,' said Luc, and his eyes twinkled, full of wicked promise. She couldn't wait.

Chapter Seventeen

Hattie walked into the kitchen wearing her best dress, enjoying the feeling of the fabric floating about her legs. Fliss had also changed and was wearing white linen trousers and a neat navy T-shirt.

'Nice frock,' said Fliss topping up the empty wine glass Hattie carried before filling her own.

'Ta. You look nice, too.'

'I thought we'd eat outside on the patio this evening. There's a lovely big wooden table out there and it's been such a lovely day.'

'Good plan.'

'So you can go lay the table.'

'Yes, boss,' said Hattie.

They grinned and toasted each other. Hattie realised it was actually rather nice having another woman around – someone who already felt like a friend. She'd lost touch with most of hers in the last few years and while she hadn't had time to acknowledge it, she had been lonely.

Taking a handful of cutlery, she exited through the wide

French doors onto the pale stone patio, coloured with patches of yellow lacey lichen. As she brushed past the needle fingers of a rosemary plant, so vigorous it seemed to be climbing out of its terracotta pot, the pungent woody scent perfumed the air. She paused for a moment. Sunlight crept through a vine-covered pergola, dappling the stone. Herbs – basil, oregano, thyme, chives and many more she didn't recognise – were arranged around the corners of the patio in curving sweeps of varying sized terracotta pots. Just off centre the wooden table was beneath the pergola, perfectly positioned to take in the view over the valley.

This would be the ideal place for the bridal party to assemble before the ceremony. It was hidden behind a wing of the château, so small and private. Pleased that another piece of her jigsaw had fallen into place, Hattie laid the table, humming under her breath.

She returned to the kitchen just as Alphonse swaggered in. She watched him in surprise. Although a big man, when she'd met him before, although definitely masculine, he'd been a lot more understated. The swagger was new and exaggerated.

'Something smells good. What are we having?' he asked, starting to tug open one of the oven doors to find out.

'No! You idiot,' screamed Fliss from the patio doorway. 'What are you doing?'

She rushed over and pushed his bulk out of the way.

The two of them stood glaring at each other, practically snarling, as Hattie involuntarily stepped forward as if to intervene.

'God save me from interfering fools like this who think it's okay to go around opening ovens willy nilly. What were you thinking?'

Alphonse, had he had a better day, Hattie suspected might

not have reacted in quite the way he did, but at her words, he puffed himself up like a wood pigeon. 'What was I thinking? This is my mother's kitchen. She's never had a problem with me in here before.'

'I don't have a problem with you being in here, per se. I have a problem with you opening the oven.'

Alphonse responded with a short, terse comment in French. Unfortunately, he'd underestimated Fliss's command of his native tongue.

'Who are you calling a spoilt princess?' she spat in response.

Alphonse, to be fair, had the grace to look a little shame-faced and might have even apologised, if Fliss hadn't stuck her nose in the air and tossed her hair over her shoulder. 'It's true the peasants are revolting.'

Hattie would have said they were one-all, at that stage, except that Alphonse had to have the last word. 'It's better than being a stuck-up bitch.' Even the heavily accented pronunciation of 'beetch' didn't soften the insult. Solange entered the kitchen at that moment and gave her son a sharp clip around the ear.

'Alphonse, apologise to her, this minute.'

He gave his mother a mutinous glare and then turned to Fliss. 'I beg your pardon.'

Fliss, who wasn't the least bit magnanimous, tilted her nose again and with a gloating smile said, 'Apology accepted,' before adding darkly, 'Although if you've ruined my soufflé I might have to kill you.' She looked at her watch. 'I hope Yvette will be on time. Those soufflés need to come out in five minutes, although I can't guarantee they won't have deflated, thanks to our friend here.' Her mouth twisted in distaste and Alphonse glared back at her. Hattie wanted to laugh at them, although she had noticed that he seemed fascinated by Fliss because every time she looked away he covertly watched her.

Right on cue, Yvette came bursting through the patio doors.

'You're new,' she said, catching sight of Fliss.

'Yvette!' her mother chided gently. 'This is Fliss, she is here to help Hattie.'

'Great, another one,' muttered Yvette in French, and although it took Hattie a second to translate, her displeasure was obvious.

However, quick as a flash, Fliss retorted, 'Great, another rude one,' before turning to Solange and saying more kindly, 'Your children did not inherit your manners.'

'No,' snapped Solange, 'it would appear they did not.' She cast both Yvette and Alphonse the classic I'm-so-disappointed look. Alphonse kissed his mother on the cheek, apologising. Then he turned to Fliss and took her hand, dwarfing her slim white fingers between his huge hands. 'I am sorry, *mademoiselle*. I've had a terrible day but I should not have taken it out on you and been rude.' He bowed his head and it was utterly charming. Fliss, clearly taken aback, blinked up at him and didn't say a word. It was the first time Hattie had seen her struck dumb.

'Ah, happy families,' said a familiar voice. Hattie turned to find Marine dressed in another stunning dress, this one a little more formal than its predecessor. 'Good evening, everyone.'

'Hi, Marine. You look ravishing,' said Yvette, rising to give her a kiss on each cheek. 'I'm not sure Luc is ready yet. He must still be doing his hair.'

Hattie frowned and couldn't stop the 'Luc?' that escaped from her mouth.

'Yes,' said Yvette giving her a brilliant smile. 'It's the *Comité Champagne* annual dinner. A very important date on the calendar, especially for Luc this year when he is representing the St Martin house for the first time. Marine's father is on the executive board.'

A movement in the doorway caught Hattie's attention. Luc looked utterly breathtaking, dressed in a smart black suit, a crisp white shirt and a black bow tie. The butterflies that initially soared at the sight of him promptly shrivelled and plummeted.

She felt a complete idiot.

'Ah, there you are,' said Marine, immediately snaking an arm round his waist and posing slightly as if she knew the picture the pair of them made – possibly the best-looking couple on the planet. 'Shall we go? Our driver is waiting.'

Luc nodded and Hattie could see he was trying to catch her eye but she wasn't having any of it. She was embarrassed. Now she understood exactly what he meant by not taking life too seriously and having some fun.

'Have fun,' said Yvette, almost as if she'd read Hattie's mind. Hattie dredged up a smile and directed it his way without actually looking at him. She felt sick.

'*Au revoir*,' chorused Alphonse, Solange and Fliss.

The glamorous pair departed and Hattie took a large sip of wine, not quite draining the glass, although she wanted to.

Chapter Eighteen

'**M**y soufflés!' Fliss jumped up and disappeared into the kitchen. Alphonse watched her go. 'I'll see if she needs any help,' he said before ambling after her.

From the kitchen door they heard her say, 'If I needed help, I'd ask for it.'

'Poor Alphonse, I don't think she likes him very much,' said Yvette with a snarky grin.

Solange put her hand on her daughter's arm, shaking her head gently.

Hattie, who'd been doing her best to join in the conversation and pretend everything was fine ever since they'd come out to sit on the patio, lifted her glass. 'Thank you, Solange. The ballroom looks absolutely wonderful. I shall take lots of photos tomorrow morning to send to my cousin.'

There was the subtlest of changes in the atmosphere, as Yvette's head swivelled sharply to look at her mother. Solange withdrew her hand, folding her arms across her chest.

'*Quoi!*' Her hazel eyes flashed. '*Maman?*'

Solange shrank a little in her seat, before answering. At first her words were a little hesitant, especially as Yvette kept interrupting her. Then Yvette slammed her hand on the table, shouting. Her mother shook her head and tried to reason with her. Hattie looked at Alphonse, who'd returned to see what the commotion was; she was hoping for some enlightenment but he was earnestly reassuring Solange, who looked close to tears.

'Pah!' spat Yvette, rising to her feet and thrusting her chair out behind her. With angry, jerky movements, she gesticulated at her mother and then Alphonse, her hand catching one of the champagne glasses. It crashed to the floor and Solange's eyes suddenly turned furious. 'Yvette!' she snapped and jumped to her feet, remonstrating with her daughter. Even though Hattie couldn't understand a word, she was pleased to see Solange standing up for herself.

Her daughter snarled at her and then marched off into the gardens, her head held high.

Hattie sat there, her heart pounding, not knowing what to do, as tears filled Solange's eyes and Alphonse went to comfort her. A sense of dread filled her. She'd never been good with disagreements, part of the reason she'd stayed with Chris for so long. This had been loud and angry and even though she'd not been directly involved, she felt a little shaky. Poor Solange's face was pale but she kept her chin up and was talking to Alphonse, calmly.

'I want to ask if everything is all right, but clearly it isn't.' The language barrier frustrated her.

'A family dispute,' said Alphonse, his mouth tightening. 'I'm sorry. Yvette is a bit displeased with *Maman*.'

'So I gathered.' She turned to Solange and gave her a gentle smile. 'Are you okay?'

Solange wiped away the tears, her mouth firming into a

straight line. 'Sadly, I am used to Yvette's tantrums. She takes after her father. He was a difficult man to live with sometimes. I am sorry she has disturbed our meal but no matter.' She rose. 'I shall go and see if Fliss would like any help or would like me to remove my son.'

'What was all that about?' asked Hattie watching the other woman's straight-backed retreat, tension knotting her stomach.

'A difference of opinion,' said Alphonse sitting down heavily.

'Quite an extreme reaction,' she observed, something in her gut telling her that it wasn't the whole truth.

'Yvette's always been volatile,' said Alphonse. 'Once –' he paused with a noticeable shudder '– when me and Luc wouldn't let her go fishing with us, she filled our shoes with worms.'

'Urgh!' said Hattie imagining it all too clearly. 'Poor worms. That's horrible.' He was clearly trying to lighten the mood.

'Not as bad as leaving a grass snake in my bed.'

Solange, who was bringing out a dustpan and brush, raised her eyebrows at him. 'And what did you do to deserve that?'

Alphonse attempted to look innocent, failing miserably, and Hattie surprised herself by laughing. 'Now the truth comes out.'

'The boys pushed her off a log into the river,' explained Solange.

'Marthe made us peel potatoes for a week for that one,' he said, his lips drooping mournfully, 'and I think she probably helped Yvette catch the snake.'

'It was her idea,' said Solange with a wry smile and both she and Hattie giggled, the earlier mood lifting.

'Sorry, *Maman*, I will have a word with Yvette,' said Alphonse.

'She's stressed about the we—' Solange broke off as Fliss appeared carrying a large white soufflé dish. A golden, crisp cheese crust rose above the sides. Hattie's mouth watered, even though she was still feeling nauseous about Luc's earlier disappearance.

'That smells divine,' she said, glad of the diversion, knowing she was a coward but she really did hate any kind of conflict.

Conviviality soon returned as everyone praised Fliss's soufflé and Solange's *boudin blanc* – local sausages, served with greens and dauphinoise potatoes.

'These are lovely.' Fliss dissected one of the white sausages. 'What's in it?' she demanded, waving a piece on her fork.

'It's a white sausage,' explained Alphonse, suddenly enthusiastic as if he were pleased to be able to help. 'A Champagne Ardenne speciality made from minced pork, breadcrumbs, cream, marjoram and sage. I take *Maman* to the butchers in the town of Rethel specially to buy it.'

'It has always been Alphonse's favourite,' said Solange, with a fond smile at her son.

By the time they finished dinner, the temperature had cooled. Alphonse had gallantly been in to load the dishwasher and tidy up. 'Would anyone like another glass of wine? he asked when he returned. He turned to Fliss. 'I think you'll like the bottle I brought with me.'

'I've had enough for this evening. I shall leave you young people to it,' said Solange and, kissing everyone on both cheeks, melted away into the dusk.

'I wouldn't mind another glass, although shall we go inside? It's getting a bit chilly,' suggested Fliss.

'I think I'll head up to bed,' said Hattie. 'I'm still quite tired after my cold.'

Limp and dispirited, she climbed the stairs. She couldn't decide who she was angrier with, herself for falling for Luc's oh-so-smooth lines – he was good, she'd give him that – or at him for being so careless in his treatment of her. It stung more than it should.

Chapter Nineteen

'Just look at that cheese,' said Fliss with a heartfelt groan of delight, immediately flitting over to the busy market stall. Solange exchanged a pleased glance with Hattie.

Hattie nodded with a bland smile, wondering where she'd acquired her newly found acting skills. Fliss, oblivious to her mood, had jumped at her suggestion to go out this morning after her first coffee, although Hattie wasn't sure even a vat of coffee would have quelled her simmering fury with Luc bloody Brémont. Sleeping on it had just fanned her indignation. How dare he treat her like that?

'She likes cheese, *non*?' asked Solange, who had insisted on joining them.

'She likes everything. Just watch – she'll want to try everything too,' said Hattie, familiar with Fliss's passion for food. She'd once been to a farm shop in Scotland with her and it had been over an hour before she could winkle her out again.

'And why not?' asked Solange, her face lighting up. 'It is good for your food education.' Her mouth lifted in a half-smile. 'You should always try everything once.'

Hmm thought Hattie sourly. Did that include kissing a French playboy?

'Hattie, Hattie. You've got to try this Brie de Meaux, it's delicious.' Fliss held out a piece of pale cream cheese with a white rind, oozing over a small cracker. 'You know that would make an amazing starter. A round of baked brie on each table with rustic French bread. Have you heard back from your cousin?'

'Not yet, and I think that would be a bit messy, perhaps,' said Hattie, pointing to a dab of cheese on Fliss's chin. 'You wouldn't want it all over the bridesmaids' dresses.'

'Spoilsport.'

'Sorry.' She had to stop being negative this morning and save her bad mood for someone who deserved it.

'Do you know I saw a wedding cake made out of rounds of cheese at one wedding I went to? Do you think your cousin might like that idea?'

'No!' said Hattie, lightening her quick vehemence with a laugh. 'Gabby is not exactly making up her mind about things at the moment. We don't want to give her more choices.'

'Ah, good point.' Fliss had already whirled away and was busy examining the abundant fruit and vegetable stall, stacked high with baskets and boxes, spilling over with several different types of lettuce leaves, vibrant tomatoes piled high next to bundles of asparagus. It must have taken the stallholders hours to set up, as everything was displayed to advantage.

'Asparagus with a drizzle of hollandaise would be a nice starter for everyone. Very simple to do and it would look lovely and colourful. Or I could do a tomato salad with chicory with fine slices of jambon.'

For the next twenty minutes, Fliss moved from stall to stall, taking lots of pictures and writing notes on her phone.

'I just want to cook,' she said. 'Thank you so much for inviting me, Hattie.' She clasped both of Hattie's hands in hers. 'It's so inspiring.'

'I need a coffee,' said Hattie half an hour later. She'd noticed that Solange was starting to flag and it was hardly any wonder – Fliss had been bouncing recipe ideas off them non-stop.

'There's a good place, just across the road. It's run by a friend of Yvette's.'

'How is she?' asked Hattie. 'Is she speaking to you now?'

Solange lifted her shoulders in a half-shrug. 'She stayed with Bernard last night. I've told her she's not welcome until she apologises.'

Hattie was coming to realise there was a lot more strength to Solange than her faded appearance had first suggested.

The small café was buzzing with people, all of whom had baskets or bags bulging with fruit and vegetables, fresh from the market. People were chatting from table to table, greeting each other as they arrived or left. Everyone seemed to know everyone else and Solange was greeted with several cries.

'*Bonjour*, Solange,' called the large lady from behind the counter at the front.

'*Bonjour*, Marie. How are you?'

A quick conversation erupted between the two and once again Hattie marvelled at how fast French people spoke. Solange's hands were gesticulating almost as quickly as her words tumbled out.

Fliss was already studying the cakes on display.

'What are those?' she asked, pointing to a plate of pale pink rectangular biscuits, coated with sugar glaze. 'They look interesting.'

'Roses de Reims,' said Marie. 'They are a local speciality and perfect with coffee. Would you like to try some?'

'Yes,' chorused Hattie and Solange before Fliss could answer.

A minute later Marie brought over a small plate filled with the delicate biscuits, along with three cafés au lait.

'These are so pretty,' said Fliss. 'They would be gorgeous served at the end of the meal.'

'Originally they were made in Reims as an accompaniment to champagne,' explained Marie. 'You can dip them in your glass. The flavours complement each other well.'

'I wonder if I could make heart-shaped ones for the wedding,' said Fliss.

Solange clapped her hands together. 'What a wonderful idea.'

'Oh yes, they would be perfect for the *vin d'honneur*,' said Marie, beaming at Solange. 'Yvette will love that.'

'Yvette?' Fliss looked confused.

'Solange's daughter,' said Marie. 'The bride. We're all looking forward to it. Only three weeks now. It will be so beautiful for her to have her celebration in the vineyard, where she's grown up. And with the whole village. It's going to be so much fun.'

Solange seemed to shrink into her seat, her eyes closing.

'Enjoy,' said Marie and sailed off back to her kitchen.

'Yvette's getting married,' said Hattie, slowly piecing new jigsaw pieces together.

'Yes,' said Solange in a monotone, her fingers plucking nervously at the hem of her skirt.

'On the same day as Gabby?'

'Mm.' Solange looked positively stricken, staring down at her plate.

'Oh my god, poor Yvette. No wonder she's so upset,' said Hattie, immediately stretching out a hand and laying it on Solange's arm.

'I'm sorry I didn't tell you. I didn't know what to do,' she said rubbing at her eyes, which had dark shadows underneath them. 'She was furious that I'd had the rooms cleaned. She's been trying to persuade you to hold it somewhere else. I was worried about what she might do. But you were so nice and I felt so bad that you were making yourself ill.' Solange covered her face with her hands. 'She's determined to hold the party at the vineyard but I've told her there are other vineyards.'

'But it is her home,' said Hattie.

Solange nodded wretchedly. 'But your uncle has given you exclusive use of the grounds and the château. What would he say? Yvette is so stubborn. I've tried to talk to her but she's adamant she has the party at St Martin.'

'You should have said something. I'm sure we can find a solution.'

'She wouldn't let me. And if Monsieur Brémont heard he might ban her from using the château grounds altogether. She never asked permission, just assumed it would be all right because the Brémonts never come. But then Luc turned up and then you.

'She's determined to go ahead and hold the *vin d'honneur* and not tell you, but I've no idea how I'm supposed to make, store and have the canapés served on the day. I think you'd also spot the food as well as the two young girls we're hiring to serve them.'

'How long does this *vin d'honneur* last?' asked Fliss. 'And what exactly is it?'

'It's a traditional celebration held after the service at the town hall. Usually all the local people come to wish the bride and groom well and a glass of wine is drunk in their honour. A few canapés are served and then after an hour or two the wedding party move on to a restaurant or somewhere for a meal.'

'Two hours,' said Fliss glancing meaningfully at Hattie. 'That's nothing.'

'Depending on the two hours,' she replied, 'but we don't have a timetable yet. What time would Yvette want the *vin d'honneur* to take place?'

'I… I'm not sure,' said Solange, her eyes widening with hope.

'I'm sure we could make it work,' said Hattie. 'We could help with canapés. Annnnd maybe you could help us cook for Gabby's wedding.' She looked at Fliss to ensure she was in agreement.

'That would be ace,' said Fliss. 'You're in charge, Hats.'

'You would do that?' asked Solange with a shell-shocked expression.

Hattie nodded.

'But you don't know us.'

'It's your home.' Hattie patted her arm. 'And if I'm honest, it feels that Yvette has more right to have her wedding party there than anyone else.' Then she smiled. 'Also I have an ulterior motive.'

'You do?'

'We will need some staff for Gabby's wedding, to serve the food, to set up the tables, lay them. If you can help us find the right people to do that, we can help you. I can always order an extra fridge.'

'Seriously?' Solange gazed at her with starstruck adoration. 'You would do that.'

'It would help,' said Fliss. 'We could hire everything together and … I assume Juliet Garnier might be a little amenable to helping us.'

Solange dropped her head. 'Sorry.'

'No matter,' said Hattie. It wasn't Solange's fault. 'It's much easier doing two events together than two separately.'

'This is such a weight off my mind,' said Solange, tears welling up in her eyes, as she clasped the hands of both Fliss and Hattie. 'I've been so worried about what will happen. Yvette has always been strong-willed and normally I handle her, but at the moment she's also very emotional because her father won't be at her wedding. They were always very close. She and Alphonse have been fighting like lions and tigers. And I've been caught in the middle. Of course, I want my daughter to have the wedding she wants but I don't want Alphonse to have to lie to Luc or possibly lose his job. Monsieur Brémont, Luc's father, still owns the château. He is the one who rented the house to this wedding party. If he is displeased, he might not let Luc stay to make champagne.'

'Between us, we'll make sure both wedding parties have the weddings they want without impinging on anyone else,' said Hattie perhaps more boldly than she felt, especially as Gabby hadn't responded to any of her emails or texts this week. It would be a bit of a juggling act but with everyone onside, surely they could manage it. In the meantime, she would be having serious words with a certain Luc Brémont. It was just one more reason to be angry with him. He'd obviously known about Yvette's wedding all along. Is that why he'd been so *nice* to her?

Chapter Twenty

Hattie stomped down to the vineyard, marching through the vines in search of her prey. Her original intention had been to play it cool with Luc when she next saw him, ignore what had happened with Marine and pretend she was *au fait* with casual relationships, but now she had a good reason to pick a fight with him.

He and Alphonse were standing at the end of one of the rows in earnest discussion, examining the vine leaves and peering underneath the canopy. They both looked up at her angry Amazonian approach.

'Hattie,' said Alphonse, with an I-know-we're-in-trouble-but-let's-see-if-we-can-front-it-out smile. 'How are you today?'

She glared at him and was glad to see a glimmer of alarm on his face. Nice girl Hattie had left the building. No one would be charming her today.

'Luc, can I have a word?' she snapped.

Alphonse smirked and murmured something in French to Luc, before picking his hat up from the top of one of the fence posts, putting it on and sauntering off, whistling.

'Hattie.' He threw down the secateurs he was holding and strode forward to grasp her arms. 'Where have you been? I've been looking for you everywhere, to explain and to apologise.' How dare he sound so cross?

Damn, it was annoying. He'd caught her out; she'd deliberately gone to the market to avoid speaking to him. She folded her arms and then immediately unfolded them because it looked defensive, which it was even though she wasn't in the wrong here, and then folded them again because she didn't know what else to do. She must have looked an even bigger idiot than she felt.

'Hattie, last night. It must have looked so terrible. And there was no time to explain. I promise you it was a business engagement. I completely forgot that I agreed to accompany Marine to the *Comité* dinner. It's an important networking event and I'd promised Alphonse I'd go – he hates things like that. It was only when I saw the car coming up the drive that I remembered and changed into my tux. You must have thought I was a complete bastard.'

'I did,' said Hattie, now a little wary as she studied his face.

He had an honest face, damn him.

'Would it help if I told you that my brain was so scrambled by that kiss, everything had gone out of my mind?'

Whaat!

'Nice try, Luc,' she said, determined not to be swayed by the smooth words.

'But true.' He sighed, reached forward and brushed a strand of hair from her face. 'I can't seem to think straight around you.'

'I'm sure you can.' She swallowed. Don't give in, Hattie.

'I'm sure I can't,' he said and cupped her face, leaning in to kiss her.

She could have moved, ducked away, but then again, it appeared she couldn't. Her mouth softened as soon as his lips touched hers, that frantic fizz of excitement reigniting in her chest.

It seemed where Luc was concerned she had sod-all willpower.

He pulled back. 'Forgive me.'

'I'll think about it. Although you haven't mentioned Yvette's wedding.' She gave him a snarky smile.

'You know about Yvette's wedding.' Luc screwed up his face, a touch of disgust and shame marring his features. It surprised and pleased her.

'I know.' Her voice held a crisp bite. She wasn't about to forgive him immediately despite his obvious embarrassment, although he had pleaded her case with Juliet Garnier.

'Thank goodness. I've been trying to get her to talk to you. She's so pig-headed. Alphonse and she have been fighting constantly about it. I need Gabby's wedding to happen as much as you do. I need the money for new equipment. It was me that persuaded Solange's cleaning team to come back. Have you spoken to Yvette?'

'Not yet.' Hattie considered him for a few minutes and then sighed. It wasn't his fault. What was the point of holding a grudge? She needed to move forward and make this wedding happen and she needed everyone onside.

'I presume she was the one that destroyed the helipad, put the caterer off and –' Hattie began to smirk '– doesn't know the difference between mouse and rabbit droppings.'

'What's so funny?'

'I-imagining Yvette c-collecting rabbit…' It was no good, she couldn't stop the gale of giggles. 'R-rabbit p-poo. I would like to have seen that.'

Luc smiled.

'I really am sorry, Hattie.'

'Hmm. Now how many hectares is the vineyard?'

'Forty,' said Luc, clearly taken aback by her sudden change of gear.

'Within that, there must be a way of managing two weddings.' Hattie narrowed her eyes at him, not quite growling but close. 'It just takes planning and organisation. And if people trusted the wedding planner to do just that … perhaps playing to her strengths, it might not have become such a big issue.'

'Point taken,' said Luc, before adding with a flirty grin, 'I like it when you're fierce.'

'Don't try and flatter me, Luc Brémont. I haven't decided if I've completely forgiven you or not yet.'

'Okay.' Then he flashed an unrepentant smile, his voice lowering 'Can I take you out to dinner this evening to help you decide?'

Chapter Twenty-One

A s soon as they were seated in the restaurant, they were served a glass of Kir Royale and Luc toasted her. '*Santé.*'

'*Santé,*' responded Hattie taking a tentative sip of the elegant-looking drink. 'I assume that means "cheers".'

'Originally it was *à ta santé*, to your health. To your good health.'

'It's very nice. I could get used to this,' she said, taking a second sip as she perused the menu, trying not to be intimidated by the limited selection. Once again there were words that she had absolutely no clue about. A bit like this situation. It was well-nigh impossible to stop sneaking looks at Luc's mouth. Every time he caught her eye, her heart rate rocketed and she kept taking steadying sips of wine, which probably wasn't helping at all. Her thoughts had meandered off-piste and were now on the edge of a precipice thinking about the possibility of sex.

God, she was so out of practice, and she'd only ever slept with one man, who hadn't exactly been demanding or adventurous. What if Luc knew tricks and things? Weren't French men supposed to be great lovers?

'You look worried,' said Luc, taking her hand across the table, which didn't exactly help. At his touch, her pulse did an excited little hiccup.

God, did it show that much? She was so out of her depth, maybe she should just come clean and admit that she had no idea what the rules for *this* were. What even was *this*? A fling? An affair? A holiday romance? And would it be gauche and show her inexperience to ask?

'It's just food,' said Luc with an encouraging smile.

Food. Think of the food. She could do that instead of worrying about sex and fidgeting in her seat.

'What's French for Brussel sprouts?' she asked suddenly, realising that Luc was watching her and waiting for a response. She almost giggled, wondering what he'd say if she asked him if it were true that French men were better lovers.

'*Les choux de Bruxelles. Pourquoi?*' He raised an eyebrow almost as if he knew that her thoughts were a million miles away from Brussels sprouts. God, she needed to get her mind back in the game. 'Not a fan?'

She shuddered. 'No, not my favourite thing at all.'

'That's because the English murder them, death by boiling. A softer touch is always preferable.' His eyes met hers and she wondered if the almost-there double entendre was deliberate or not. A small frisson of excitement danced along her skin. 'They are delicious fried up with onions, garlic and lardons.' Delicious indeed! How could a man make something sound so delicious just by lowering the tone of his voice and maintaining eye contact?

She eyed him cautiously trying to sound normal although

inside she was feeling increasingly antsy. 'I'll take your word for it. What's *poulpe*?'

'Octopus.'

Hattie wrinkled her nose. 'What do you recommend?'

'The *cacasse à cul nu* is a local speciality and it is particularly good here.' A mischievous quirk lifted one corner of his mouth. 'The literal translation is bare ass.'

She raised her eyebrows and took a hasty sip of her drink, unable to quash the image of his half-naked body. Of course, she choked, because sod's law was having a field day this evening.

'Bare ass,' he continued, a wicked light in those blue eyes, 'as in without meat. Originally it was a working man's dish. Although, these days it's served with bacon and pork sausages. It's cooked in a cast-iron lidded dish with potatoes, onions, garlic, thyme and bay leaf.'

She managed to get her equilibrium back and sound relatively normal when she replied, 'That sounds delicious, I'll try that.'

'And wine, what colour would you like to drink?'

'I'm definitely leaving that up to you, you're the ex … pert.'

'In that case I would suggest a white Burgundy. It's a nice full-bodied wine with buttery and honey flavours that complement the potato element of the dish.'

'Okay,' said Hattie, feeling that the conversation was back on a more even footing. 'Although as I've told you, I don't know anything about wine.'

'White Burgundy comes from Eastern France and is made from the grape variety chardonnay.'

'And this is why French wine is so complicated. How am I supposed to know that? Why not just call it chardonnay and have done with it? I know I like chardonnay.'

He gave her a naughty grin. 'Your education has been sadly lacking.'

'Are you going to be my teacher?' The words popped out before she could stop them.

His Adam's apple dipped before he said, holding her gaze, 'What do you want to learn?'

It was one of those now or never moments. Jump in or bail.

'Everything,' she said, meeting his gaze head on.

She almost laughed out loud when she saw the fingers on his wine glass tighten.

'Everything?' he murmured. 'That's a lot.'

'Worried you might not be up to the task?' She flashed him a mischievous grin and he burst out laughing.

'I think France is having an effect on you, Hattie,' he said, his thumb stroking the palm of her hand.

Hattie was pretty sure it was Luc that was having an effect on her. Her body felt as if it were fully charged with static electricity, every move she made sparked another tingle.

Thankfully, a young waiter glided over to the table and took their orders and Hattie sat back while Luc discussed the wine choices and breathed an internal sigh of relief. All that seductive, smoky interplay had died down and she could relax.

'Luc, *cherie*.' Hattie looked up. Dear God, not again. Marine and a woman, who could only be her mother, were bearing down on them.

'Marine.' He stood and accepted her kisses on each cheek before accepting another set of kisses and bestowing a charming smile on the older woman. While he was doing that, Marine turned her attention to Hattie.

'Oh, the wedding planner. You're still here then.'

'Still here,' said Hattie brightly, although all the warm

happy Mexican jumping bean feelings in her stomach had withered and died. 'It's full steam ahead for the wedding.'

Marine's mouth shut with a crooked line, reminding Hattie of a closed Venus fly trap.

'Luc, *cherie. Maman* hasn't seen you for ages. Perhaps we could join you,' suggested Marine, with a winsome smile.

Hattie's fingers closed around one of the knives in front of her and she sat totally still.

'I'm sorry.' Luc lifted Hattie's hand, the one he'd been caressing with slow circles of this thumb, and lifted it to his lips, kissing it. Without looking at Marine he gave Hattie a warm smile. 'We're on a date this evening.' There was a brief silence and Marine stiffened before turning to Hattie and saying with a charming smile, 'That explains why you're hanging about.' She paused and then added, 'When no one wants this wedding held here.' Her smile widened, her red lips reminding Hattie of the Joker. Marine would not have liked the comparison.

'You don't have to worry about that, those problems have all been solved,' said Hattie with a guileless smile. 'It's going to be a lovely day for everyone.'

She saw Luc's shoulders shake. Marine tossed her hair, said something in very polite French to Luc and towed her mother away.

Hattie watched her go, a little pink in the cheeks at Luc's very public declaration.

Luckily the food arrived just then, served with a flourish by the waiter. Hattie had ordered the starter of *asperges blanches habillées*, white asparagus wrapped with crepe and Bayonne ham.

'Oh that is seriously good,' she said, closing her eyes and savouring the flavours, licking the butter from her fingers.

When she opened them Luc was staring at her, disconcerting appreciation written all over his face, and it didn't take a genius to guess what he was thinking, especially not with that slow smile of his.

'Don't say it,' she said, remembering his comment in the restaurant.

'Why not, if it's true? I like watching you take pleasure.' The softly spoken word vibrated through her.

'Do you?' she asked, provocatively lowering her voice and looking at his lips.

There was a long pause as he gave her words careful consideration.

'Yes,' he said, with a very direct gaze and there was no mistaking what he meant. A fierce blush heated Hattie's cheeks but she managed to hold her own, looking back at him.

'Will you come to bed with me, Hattie?' he asked softly.

Chapter Twenty-Two

'Shall we take a glass of wine up to my balcony?' asked Luc as they entered the château on their return from the restaurant. He gave her an easy smile. Hattie nodded, too full of nerves to speak.

She watched as he opened the bottle, the coil of tension in her stomach twisting tighter. When she took the glass from him, her hand shook. She gave him a stricken look.

He leaned down and kissed her. 'There's no hurry. Let's drink our wine and enjoy the night air.'

She closed her eyes. 'Sorry, Luc. I'm rubbish at this. I've only slept with one person and not for a long time. I'm not really the sort of girl men want to sleep with. I help people plan dream weddings but really, I'm very boring and I'm not sure I believe in romance anymore.'

'I definitely want to sleep with you … and more. I think I have since the moment I opened the door and found you there.'

She almost melted on the spot.

'There is no pressure. If not tonight then perhaps another night.' He took her hand and led her up the stairs.

Entering Luc's bedroom, despite the rapid pumping of her heart, she managed to smile at him. Apart from a few discarded clothes on the chair near the balcony and the pile of change and keys on the bedside table, it was still very tidy, although it had a comfortable, lived-in feel to it. She remembered the first time she'd been in here. Hattie smiled at the sight of his childhood books, making a mental note to ask about them later ... much later.

Luc who was also examining the room, sprang forward and with one hand hastily tugged at the white broderie anglaise duvet cover on the bed, which was already quite neat. 'Sorry, I wasn't planning ...'

His honesty was endearing and just the reassurance she needed. She took the wine glass she realised he was in danger of spilling – evidently he wasn't quite as sure of himself as she'd assumed. When she placed it along with hers on the dressing table, she caught sight of her bright, flushed eyes in the mirror. She smiled back at herself, pleased that she didn't look like some inexperienced girl. She looked like a woman who was desirable and attractive. She wanted Luc Brémont, wanted to have the touch of his skin and muscle against her body and to know what it would be like to feel again.

She moved into his arms and their mouths fused into a kiss. When they came up for air, he murmured against her hair. 'Are you sure about this?'

'Yes,' she whispered, her voice fierce in the quiet of the room.

He undid the top button of her dress and stroked her collarbone, ducking his head to kiss the sensitive skin there. She sighed with pleasure, as he trailed kisses back up to her mouth. It had been so long since she'd been kissed properly. She was going to enjoy every minute of this. She tipped her head back, giving him access to her neck, her knees almost buckling at the delicious sensations that his roaming lips were evoking. Suddenly it wasn't enough, and she tugged him closer and opened her mouth, kissing him more deeply. He responded immediately, his mouth opening, his tongue stroking and tangling with hers. Sensing her growing desire, his fingers undid another button and he slid a hand into her bra and cupped her breast. The sensation almost felled her. It was like being on a runaway train and she was sticking with it, for the ride of her life.

'Luc,' she whispered, pulling back and looking up at his glittering eyes.

'*Oui*,' he said, his chest heaving.

'Don't stop,' she said. 'Don't stop.'

Hattie lay curled in the crook of Luc's arm, a dreamy smile on her face. The bedside light was on, a first for her, and Luc was idly stroking her shoulder. She felt soft all over and well-loved. Sex with Luc was still a revelation. Who knew that sex could be so much fun? And … the orgasms. Two! That had never happened before. She was rather embarrassed because she might have let out a few too many enthusiastic squeaks of pleasure but seriously he knew what he was doing. He'd taken so much tender care with her, kissing every inch of her – and it really had been every inch. She was getting a little hot just remembering what he'd done to her. Lying in his arms, she could honestly say she felt cossetted but, at the same time, well-used.

'That was lovely,' she sighed turning to look at his face.

'Lovely. You English, the masters of the understatement.'

She laughed. 'Okay, it was bloody lovely.'

'Bloody lovely,' he teased, copying her English accent. '*Magnifique*, I think you'll find.' He kissed the soft spot just under her ear, his hand drifting south, to toy with her inner thigh.

'You can't … you know … want to do it again.'

'I can't?' His eyes twinkled wickedly. 'I think I probably can.' He skimmed his hand higher and she wriggled in his arms, as her nerve endings leapt to attention. 'I love touching you. You're so responsive and those little cries you make. You like it when I do this.' He demonstrated and she sucked in a sharp breath. She and Chris had never talked about sex. Never discussed what they liked. She pushed Chris to the back of her mind. It wasn't fair to compare.

Her mouth dropped open. She'd wanted to ask if it had been all right. She was so out of practice, although once Luc had gently peeled off her clothes and she'd felt his naked body up against hers, she'd forgotten to be self-conscious. He had a way of making her feel that she was the centre of his attention.

She remembered waking at some point in the night, realising where she was, feeling the weight of Luc's arm draped across her – and then the next thing it was morning and the sun was streaming in through the long French windows. She stretched, feeling very pleased with herself. Her supine and softened body popped with pleasure.

'Good morning,' Luc's voice drawled from next to her and she turned to find him propped up against his pillows, his tanned skin emphasised by the crisp white cotton.

'Good morning. What time is it?'

He hauled her up to him and kissed her on the mouth. 'Time to say good morning properly.'

Her body melted against his and just like that she wanted him all over again.

'Define properly,' she said with a giggle.

'Making sure every last bit of you is wide awake.'

'And which bits do you propose to wake up first?'

He dropped his head and kissed her breast, his tongue flicking over one nipple, making her gasp. 'That one.' He moved onto the other breast and did the same again. 'That one.'

His hand moved down to her thigh. 'This one.'

He didn't need to elaborate and, before long, every last bit of her was wide awake and raring to go.

Half an hour later he rolled onto his side and gave her a guileless, happy smile. 'That is how you say good morning properly.'

'You might have to remind me again.'

'It will be my pleasure to remind you as often as you like. Unfortunately, I have promised Alphonse that I would help him in the vineyard this morning.' Luc kissed her on the nose and unselfconsciously got out of bed. 'I must get in the shower.' Hattie averted her gaze, although not until she'd had an eyeful of long lean legs and a very white, perfect bum.

'Me too.' She sat up and, not as comfortable as he was, perched on the edge of the bed looking for her dress. It had been puddled around her ankles the last time she had it.

'Here.' Luc tossed her one of his shirts. She pulled on the soft chambray which came down to her thighs. Even though it was a cliché from so many romcoms, she was touched by his understanding.

'I ought to go.' She rose and crossed the room picking up her discarded clothes.

'Are you sure? You could join me in the shower.'

Hattie blushed. Despite last night she wasn't quite ready for that. Her confidence was evaporating fast. 'I'll take a rain check.'

'Anytime,' said Luc, crossing to her, still naked, to kiss her softly on the lips. 'But I hope we can do this again.' He looked into her eyes, a gentle smile on his face.

Her knees turned weak. *Do this again.* Gosh, there was a whole lot of meaning in 'again'. Now the consequences she'd blithely ignored last night roared back to bite her. What happened next? Should it happen again? Was that a casual 'again'? Or an I'll-leave-it-with-you 'again'? Hattie cursed herself and her stupid brain, which had gone into analytical overdrive. That was the problem when you'd been stuck in one relationship for years, you didn't know the rules anymore.

Luc placed a finger on her forehead between her eyebrows. 'You're frowning. It's easy.' God that French accent, it made her toes curl. 'I'd very much like to take you to bed again. There are lots of things I'd like to do but there is no pressure. I'd like to get to know you some more –' he grinned, a wicked glint shining in his eyes – 'all of you, and spend some time with you. Would that be okay?'

She gave him a tremulous smile and nodded. 'That would be … okay.' More than okay but she felt perhaps she ought to play it cool. After all, Luc probably did this sort of thing all the time.

Luc whistled as he helped to prune the vines and cut back some of the vigorous canopy. Today he could take on the world even though at this time of year, the job was never-ending. The prospect of a good harvest was very promising as was the rest of the day. He couldn't wait to see Hattie again even though he'd only left her warm naked body a couple of hours before.

He smiled as he thought of her and her unabashed enjoyment in bed last night. There were no sides to her, her responses were genuine and honest. Describing her as sweet would make her sound insubstantial and sickly when she was anything but. If he had to describe her like a wine, he'd choose a Chablis, light and elegant with a honeyed warmth about her. She was so different from the brittle sophisticates he'd dated in the city and he couldn't stop thinking about her.

'Do you have to whistle so loudly?' complained Alphonse as he came off a call, putting his mobile in his pocket. 'That bastard Robard is playing games. He's suggesting they might not have the capacity to press our grapes separately.'

Luc grinned. 'What if we had our own press?' Alphonse's eyes widened comically.

'Yes, the money from the wedding will pay for our own. I'm going to see a distributor in Paris to buy one.'

'No one is that happy just about a wine press.' He narrowed his eyes and studied Luc's face. 'Did you sleep with the English girl?'

'What, Fliss?' Luc focused on reaching up to a particularly long tendril of vine, hiding a smile.

'No! Not her,' said Alphonse in a strangled voice. 'She's a harridan.'

'Oh, you mean Hattie,' teased Luc.

'You know exactly who I mean. She's nice,' said Alphonse and when Luc turned to him, added with a sly smile, 'Far too good for you.'

'I think she might be,' acknowledged Luc gravely, realising

that his friend spoke the truth. But he did wonder about Alphonse's extreme reaction to Fliss.

'You like her.' Alphonse stilled and stared at his friend in disbelief. 'You really like her.'

There was a short silence before Luc said with a touch of wonderment, 'I do.' After a second short pause, following a series of mini explosions between the synapses in his brain, he added slowly because he was still coming to terms with it, 'I think she might be the one.'

'Really?' Alphonse gave him a bug-eyed look of alarm, studying him as if hoping that at any moment Luc might turn round and say, 'Only joking.'

Except Luc wasn't going to do that.

'Yes.' He sighed, equally disconcerted by the rogue feelings that had not so much crept up on him but leapt on him and pinned him down with a ferociousness of emotion that had blindsided him.

'Are you sure?'

Luc nodded. 'Do I sound crazy?'

'No. Yes. No.' Alphonse shook his head in bewilderment. 'But Luc, my friend, you barely know her. She's only been here for a month.' He frowned, lines of genuine concern creasing his forehead.

Luc sighed again. Alphonse was his oldest friend. He knew Luc better than anyone except possibly Marthe. 'That's what makes it so crazy … but since she arrived I haven't been able to stop thinking about her. When I'm with her … I feel like I do know her.' He paused but he had to say it. Alphonse was his best friend. They didn't lie to each other. 'She's like coming home.' Saying it out loud made it sound fanciful and overly sentimental, even more so when Alphonse's mouth opened in horror.

'I know.' Luc held his hands up in mock surrender. 'It's mad.'

'No, I was going to say it sounds very dull. No fireworks? No electrical surges? No tsunamis?'

Luc shook his head, a sudden smile breaking out across his face at the memory of the previous night. 'I didn't say that. I promise you she makes my heart beat faster.'

Alphonse's expression was sceptical. 'Are you sure it's not just a rush of blood to –' he nodded towards Luc's groin '– robbing you of your ability to think straight? Can't you shag your way out it and come out on the other side to regain your senses.'

Luc pursed his lips, wishing he hadn't said anything. 'No, I don't think I can,' he said ducking his head into the nearest vine, wielding his pruning shears with sudden enthusiasm.

'Someone looks like the cat that ate a full pint of cream,' drawled Fliss when Hattie came into the kitchen that morning.

'Wouldn't they drink it?' Hattie asked, hoping to change the subject with this quick, if pedantic, reply.

'So how was dinner with the lovely Luc?' Fliss wasn't about to let her off the hook. 'Here, have some breakfast, fresh out of the oven.' She pushed a plate of warm cinnamon buns towards her.

'Dinner was very nice.' Hattie took one of the flaky pastries and pulled off a coil, popping it into her mouth.

'And dessert?' Fliss teased.

'Mmm,' she mumbled around the pastry, commending herself for not blushing. She was quite proud of her attempt to sound nonchalant when there was a fizz of happiness bounding like bubbles through her bloodstream.

'I saw Luc. He looked very chirpy,' said Fliss. 'He was just off to the vineyard. He had quite a spring in his step.'

'Did he?' Hattie tried to keep the smirk from her face but failed miserably and her face burst into a big grin.

'He did. I take it you're responsible for putting it there.'

'Mmm,' responded Hattie again, busy dissecting the rest of her bun. She didn't know Fliss well enough to be divulging details, even if she'd been that sort of person. She hadn't had the mental bandwidth for a girlfriend or confidante in recent years.

Fliss took pity on her. 'Good for you. Life's too short not to be happy. I wasted far too long before deciding what I really wanted. I could tell the two of you fancied the pants off each other, I just wasn't sure *you* would do anything about it.'

'Am I that sensible and boring?' asked Hattie, a little stung.

'God, no. Wary, I would have said. Or even cautious, and perhaps because ... oh God, I'm talking my mouth off ... sorry.'

'Don't apologise. It's a bit of a relief to talk to someone.' Hattie glanced over her shoulder as if someone might overhear them. 'I'm not sure I'm doing the right thing but ... how could I not? Look at him.' After their conversation last night she wasn't going to think about whether it was right or not, she was just going to enjoy it.

Fliss pulled a face. 'I suppose, if you like that type.'

Hattie stared at her. Surely she had eyes.

'Sorry. He's a bit too clean-cut and tidy for me. I guess too much like my brothers. I mean I don't like Alphonse, not at all, but he is all man.' Fliss's face took on a slightly wistful expression which made Hattie stare even harder at her. She thought Alphonse was more attractive than Luc – *Alphonse*?

'And I don't see why you think you're not doing the right thing. You're both single, aren't you?'

'Yes,' said Hattie, 'but I've just come out of a long-term relationship, the last thing I want to do is dive into another one. I just want … a bit of fun.'

'Well, why not? No one's going to judge you.'

'It just feels a bit weird. I was with Chris, my boyfriend, for so long.' Hattie couldn't help worrying that it might be disloyal to move on so quickly. Chris would be so hurt.

'Sometimes when you've been dumped, the best thing is to get back in the saddle.'

'I sort of finished it,' said Hattie, and with the words came the weight of guilt.

'You did? So, what's the problem? As they say, you're a free agent. It's not like you signed a non-compete clause that forbids you to have carnal relations with another man.'

Hattie shook her head.

'And you like Luc, don't you?'

'Mmm.' After a night like that she liked him a whole lot more this morning. It was ridiculous how much she liked him. You couldn't fall in love with someone when you barely knew them, could you? This buoyant effervescence was just the lightness of being after spending so long in the dark – that was all.

'Mm, as he's all right, or mm, as in I'd like to cover every delectable inch of him in honey and lick it right off?'

Hattie burst out laughing at Fliss's totally deadpan and unexpected words and said through her gentle snorts, 'I thought you didn't think that much of him.'

'I didn't say that, just not in comparison to a man like Alphonse.' She paused before observing with a slight smile, 'Now there's a man deserving of a whole barrel of honey.'

'Who deserves a barrel of honey?' asked Solange coming into the kitchen. 'Is this an English saying?'

Fliss's eyes widened. 'Mm,' she muttered.

'I have eggs,' said Solange indicating the basket on her arm.

'You do,' said Hattie. 'That's a lot of eggs.'

'I thought we could start some preparation for one of the weddings. There are lots of things we can make in advance for canapés. Choux buns. Macarons. Pastry cases.' Solange plonked the basket down and rolled up her sleeves.

'I'll leave you two to it. I'm going to look at some timings and make some plans. Remind me what time Yvette's service is at the *Mairie*.'

'She's getting married at ten o'clock. Then the *vin d'honneur* and the restaurant is booked for twelve-thirty.'

'So people will be here between ten forty-five and twelve-fifteen.' Hattie scribbled down the times in her notebook.

'*Oui*.' Solange nodded.

'Excellent. Leave it with me.' Taking a cup of coffee with her, Hattie strode off to her makeshift office in the library feeling more confident than she had in weeks. She knew exactly what she needed to do. Phone the celebrant, Juliet Garnier, the florist and Gabby, again.

Chapter Twenty-Three

When Hattie walked back into the kitchen several hours later, it was like walking into a rainbow factory. An explosion of colour lined the whole of one counter, which was filled with cooling racks of different coloured macarons from the palest blue to almost midnight, along with sunshine yellow, orange and russet through to baby pink and shocking fuchsia. Piled up by the sink were the bowls that had been used to mix the food colourings to achieve the huge variety of shades.

'Someone's been busy,' she said. 'These look gorgeous. Where's Solange?'

'She's taking down curtains in some of the bedrooms to be dry cleaned. She's really got the bit between her teeth and, my goodness, the woman can cook. Taste one of these babies. I made these ones and she made the ones over there.' Fliss pointed to another cooling rack full of cream and chocolate macarons. 'She's got such a delicate touch with flavour.'

Hattie took the proffered pale pink macaron and bit into the soft sugary texture. A burst of raspberry hit her tastebuds, followed by the nuttiness of the pistachio cream sandwich in the middle. 'Oh my. That is divine.'

'She's a genius.'

'Afternoon.' Alphonse walked into the kitchen bearing a thermos mug of coffee. 'Have you seen Luc?'

'He's gone into Hautvillers,' said Hattie. 'He said he'd be back by four.'

Alphonse was already examining the nearest macarons. 'These look good. Did you make them?'

'Don't sound so surprised,' snapped Fliss. 'And don't let your filthy hands near them.'

Alphonse shrugged and then deliberately poked one. 'Oops.' He sent her a challenging smirk. 'I'd better eat that one.' And before she could protest he'd picked it up and popped it into his mouth, crunching it happily.

Fliss's mouth opened in outrage and she marched over and pushed him away. 'Leave them alone. Those are for your sister's wedding.'

'Not all of them surely.' Deliberately he snaked a hand out and grabbed another one, popping it into his mouth.

'*Arrête!*' she spat, following it up with a stream of French, and Hattie was pretty sure she heard the word *cochon* as Fliss put herself between him and the macarons, glaring belligerently at him.

'Mmm,' he said right into her face. 'They're really quite good.'

'Quite good.' Fliss put her hands on her hips. 'They're excellent, which you would know if you knew anything about food. Now out of my kitchen.'

He gave her a defiant grin and ambled out of the room, giving Hattie a wink behind Fliss's back. She had a feeling he enjoyed winding Fliss up – they were total opposites.

'God, he drives me mad,' said Fliss. 'Wandering in, in his dirty overalls, as if he owns the place, always commenting on my cooking. Who the hell does he think he is?'

'He does work here…'

'In the vineyard, which is where he should stay and not under my feet,' snapped Fliss. 'I need to go and have a shower. I've been cooking all morning. Yvette is coming to dinner in a couple of days' time; her mother has told her she has news about the wedding. Let's hope we can placate her.'

'Don't you think we should tell her before?' suggested Hattie.

Fliss gave an evil grin. 'No, she's given Solange a hard time, I think she should suffer a little longer.'

'Remind me not to get on the wrong side of you. I've worked out a potential schedule which will accommodate both weddings,' said Hattie, rubbing at her temples, rather pleased with herself.

'You life saver, thank you,' said Hattie when Luc walked into the library with a tray of drinks in his hand. As always her heart did a little skip at the sight of him. It was like hitting a big bump in the road and leaving her stomach behind.

'I could do with a break. Today my cousin has now decided she doesn't want any bridesmaids, just a best woman. The good news is she has approved the final menu. But you don't want to hear about that.'

'Only because I don't like to see you worrying. Fliss made some *citron pressé*.' He put the tray on her desk. 'I thought it was safer to have it in here.'

Hattie gave him a quizzical look.

'She and Alphonse are in the kitchen arguing again. He seems to delight in tormenting her.'

'I wouldn't worry, she's quite able to give as good as she gets. Even my French is good enough to know she called him a pig this morning.'

'I know, he was most indignant when I got back to the vineyard earlier. Hasn't stopped cursing her all afternoon.' Luc said with a laugh. 'And then in the kitchen, just now he foolishly suggested that Fliss's soufflé was a fluke. They looked as if they were preparing for a duel. I was worried I'd get caught in the crossfire.'

'Ouch. What did she say to that?'

'Quite a lot but the short version is that she's cooking dinner in two days' time for everyone, and he'll be choking on his words.'

'Ah, there's not much love lost there,' observed Hattie.

'*Au contraire,*' murmured Luc, a sudden impish smile tugging at his lips. 'There's *Much Ado About Nothing*. I think Alphonse likes Fliss very much but he has no idea how to go about telling her and because he's slightly shocked that he's attracted to someone who is so much not his idea of the perfect woman.'

'Really?' Hattie said, although, when she thought about it, Fliss did seem to have quite a swarm of bees in her bonnet about Alphonse. She never missed an opportunity to insult him or complain about him.

'Perhaps we should set them up like Beatrice and Benedick,' he said.

Hattie, recalling the play, grinned. 'You mean I tell Alphonse that Fliss likes him and you tell Fliss that Alphonse likes her?'

'That's it,' said Luc. 'Solange would thank us. Alphonse is

always complaining he can't find a woman he likes. What better than a woman he doesn't like?'

Hattie laughed. 'That sounds like a line Benedick would use.'

'You know what I mean. I've known Alphonse since I was seven. I can promise you he likes Fliss – a lot.'

'Well, I don't know Fliss that well.' Hattie stopped and thought back to Christmas and Fliss's relationship with her best friend Jason, a Cockney who could turn the air blue with his swearing. They couldn't be more dissimilar but they got on like the proverbial house. Honesty compelled her to add, 'Although when I met her before, she and her friend Jason never missed a chance to take the piss out of each other.' She took a thoughtful sip of her drink, welcoming the tart refreshment. 'They do seem to strike sparks whenever they're together. Maybe she does like him. How about I keep an eye on her and let you know?'

'You'll see,' replied Luc. 'How are the wedding plans progressing?'

'Slowly, but I've made good progress today, so I count that as a win.'

'We should celebrate,' said Luc with a teasing smile, coming round to her side of the desk and tugging her to her feet.

'And how do you propose doing that?'

He sat on the edge of the desk, pulling her between his legs. 'Well…' He lifted a hand to trace her lips. 'I could kiss you or … how would you like a trip to Paris next week?'

Chapter Twenty-Four

Hattie craned her neck to get a better view of the city as the train slowed down. Luc had said it was much better to take the train as it was only forty-six minutes on the TGV rather than an hour and forty-six minutes if they drove, and the traffic was 'always crazy in Paris'.

'Where do you want to go?' asked Luc, watching her with an indulgent smile.

'Everywhere,' she said, bouncing in her seat. 'I want to see it all. Or as much as possible. The Eiffel Tower? The Arc de Triomphe? The Seine? Notre Dame? Place du Concord? I don't know. I've never been to Paris before.'

'We've got two days I'm not sure we can do everywhere,' laughed Luc.

And with the wedding just over two weeks away, two days was the absolute maximum she could be away for. Everything was suddenly becoming very last-minute. Gabby was cutting it fine as she hadn't confirmed numbers or decided which flavour sponge she was going to choose for the wedding cake. Fliss, bless her, was completely calm about everything.

'And I know it's horribly girly but I'd like to go shopping at some point. I need a dress for the wedding now that I'm not a bridesmaid.' Hattie sighed happily. Everything was suddenly coming together perfectly. Fliss was in seventh heaven practising the different components of her menu every day, with Solange encouraging her. They were quite the double act all of a sudden and Solange was almost a different person, buzzing with energy and enthusiasm.

'Although I haven't got a clue where I should go but I just have to buy something in Paris, it seems a terrible waste not to.'

'Don't worry, I have arranged for us to meet my friends Nina and Sebastian. I gave Nina a call and she suggested that you go see her tomorrow morning while I meet with the distributor of the wine press I want to buy. You can have a coffee with her and she'll tell you the best place to go.'

'That would be brilliant, if she doesn't mind.' If the worst came to the worst, she knew they had Zara and H&M, but she wanted to treat herself to something a bit posher. After all, she was in France – the home of fashion. 'I was worried I might have to wear my dungarees.'

'They are cute,' said Luc, hugging her and giving her a kiss before taking their bags down from the overhead rack.

'Not sure anyone else would agree with you.'

When the train pulled in and they stepped onto the platform, Hattie's head darted around trying to take in everything. Pigeons skimmed the air overhead while travel announcements, whistles and the hydraulic whine of train brakes echoed together under the huge arched glass roof. Hattie stood for a moment, transfixed by the thought of being *in Paris* until Luc tugged at her hand.

'Come on. I thought you wanted to see *everything*.'

They were both travelling light, with small rucksacks on their backs. Hattie had worn jeans and trainers but had packed her red dress for dinner tonight along with a pair of sandals. She wished she had something a bit more glamorous, like the floaty dress Marine had worn, but her wardrobe reflected the sad state of her social life over the last couple of years. Even her red dress wasn't that exciting.

The Métro was bewildering and she lazily left Luc to navigate as he knew what he was doing. She studied the place names, rolling them around her tongue silently: Château d'Eau, Strasbourg St-Denis. Once they changed onto *Ligne* 1 from *Ligne* 4 some of the names like Palais Royal Musée du Louvre, Tuilleries and Concorde were more familiar.

'The centre of Paris is quite small. We can cover a lot of ground on foot and then maybe get a boat later,' said Luc, getting up at their stop.

They surfaced at the Charles de Gaulle–Etoile Métro station and immediately, looking down the street, Hattie could see her first landmark.

'The Arc de Triomphe!' she cried. 'Gosh, it's huge. So much bigger than I imagined.'

'Didn't you say that last night?' teased Luc.

'Oh dear, men are just so predictable,' said Hattie tapping him lightly on the arm.

As they entered the underpass beneath the busy road, the traffic thudded above them while the chatter of fellow tourists echoed and bounced off the walls.

When they emerged, Luc insisted on buying their entry tickets.

'You don't have to pay for me,' she grumbled half-heartedly, unused to being looked after.

'I want to,' said Luc, before leaning in and whispering against her ear. 'It gives me pleasure.'

She nudged him with her elbow and giggled. 'When you put it like that, how can I refuse?'

Up on the observation deck on the roof, Hattie eagerly drank in her first proper view of Paris. Although the air was filled with the scent of melting tarmac and car fumes, she felt she could also smell the essence of the city. To the south, she could clearly see the Eiffel Tower and away to the west, as Luc told her, the office blocks of La Defénse. The roads radiated around the monument like perfectly even bicycle spokes and the traffic … well, Hattie couldn't figure out how anyone managed to get where they wanted.

'It's mad,' she said staring down, listening to the cacophony of impatient horns tooting, each one trying to outdo the last. Below, the predominantly black shiny tops of the cars reminded her of ungainly beetles, lumbering about the road, stopping and starting, barely missing one another. It was like an insane dodgem ride.

'It is a little crazy but it is the only roundabout in France where drivers give way to the traffic coming onto the roundabout from the other roads.' He pointed to the stream of cars filtering onto the road from a wide boulevard on the left. 'See.'

'How many roads are there?' she asked. It looked utterly bamboozling to her. 'And have you ever driven round it?'

'Twelve and yes, many times. It's not so bad.'

'I'll take your word for it,' she said with a visible shudder.

After they'd had their fill of watching the kamikaze drivers they descended the steps back to ground level.

'Where next, Mr Tour Guide?' asked Hattie.

'Straight down Avenue Kléber to the Trocadero where you

get a really good view of the Eiffel Tower and then we can cross the Seine to see it. It will be busy. I probably should have booked tickets.'

'Don't worry. I'll be happy that I've seen it.'

'It's quite a walk.'

'It's such a gorgeous day I don't mind. We can always stop. We have to have a drink at a pavement café in Paris. It's in the rules.'

'Is it?' Luc took her hand and together they walked at an easy pace, passing through the locals, who all looked busy and in a hurry compared to the army of tourists who smiled, chatted and ate ice creams as they meandered in the same direction.

'It's nice to be a tourist. It's like being on holiday.' Hattie smiled, tipping her face up to the sun, glad of her sunglasses. The last time she'd been on holiday had been to a static caravan in the Lake District with Chris's mum and it had rained every day for a whole week.

'It is nice playing tourist.'

'So where are we staying tonight?'

'At my parents' apartment.'

'Is that where you grew up?'

'No, we had a place out at Chatou which is about fourteen kilometres away but my father kept the apartment for business or if they came into Paris for a show or dinner.'

'Will they be there?' asked Hattie. She hoped not. God knows what the wealthy Brémonts would make of her.

'No.' He gave her hand a squeeze. 'My mother is away in Switzerland and my father is down at the vineyard in Bordeaux.'

Hattie relaxed a little.

The wide tree-lined boulevard, full of grand old apartment

buildings, was characterised by the elaborate wrought-iron balconies that trimmed the upper floors. All along the street imposing wooden doors, with stone surrounds, opened directly onto the pavement. There was a decidedly genteel atmosphere about the neighbourhood, with its café tables beneath red awnings on every corner, along with the tabacs and pharmacies.

They dropped down into the gardens of the Trocadero and Hattie took out her phone to take pictures of the Eiffel Tower, which was every bit as striking and impressive up close as it was at a distance. She wanted to pinch herself to prove that she was really here. Luc must think she was very gauche but when she glanced up at him, he was smiling at her and leaned in to give her a kiss.

'You look so happy,' he teased.

'I am.' She tucked an arm through his. What was not to like? Wandering the streets of Paris on a sunny day with a gorgeous Frenchman. Life didn't get much better.

They covered a lot of ground that day, walking from the Eiffel Tower across the Seine to the Place de Concorde, through the Tuilleries. They took a boat trip along the river past the Ile de la Cité and Notre-Dame before stopping for a glass of wine and a plate of cheese at lunchtime in a pavement café that Luc complained was a tourist trap and ridiculously expensive. She admonished him with a laugh – 'It ticks one of my boxes.' They enjoyed ice cream as they strolled along the banks of the river but at Hattie's quelling glance, Luc refrained from making a comment about the four-euro price tag.

Hattie couldn't remember when she'd been happier.

• • •

'Wow, this is ... something,' said Hattie standing in front of one of the floor-to-ceiling windows in Luc's parents' apartment, peering through full-length voile drapes of pale grey.

Her feet ached but she wasn't about to complain. Paris had been everything she could have wished for, from the stylish women, the extravagant patisserie displays, the manic traffic, astounding parking and the buildings. So many wonderful, elegant stone buildings. It was the most gorgeous city.

She studied the view out over a park, before turning to sigh over the oh-so-elegant and stylish room. The ornaments and furniture must have cost several million arms and legs. Dove grey linen sofas with deep feather-filled cushions that just begged to be sat on faced each other across a wooden table covered with glossy magazines, high-cheeked models staring from the covers. The palest of pale pink watered silk cushions were arranged at either end of the sofa along with an even paler pink cashmere throw.

'It's stunning,' said Hattie.

'Yes, *Maman* has excellent taste, although I prefer living at the château,' said Luc.

She knew what he meant. This apartment was beautiful, with every luxury and no expense spared, but it was all show. The château was equally luxurious with lots of fabulous ornaments and furniture but they had an authenticity. They held memories and history – they were part of a story – and she thought, with a start, she was becoming part of that story.

'I know what you mean,' she replied. 'The château is home...' The thought bought her up sharp. 'I mean homely. More homely. Than this. This is lovely but...' She smiled vaguely at Luc, conscious of the odd slip. It didn't mean anything.

He led her through the double doors back down the

hallway to a heavy wooden door. Inside the room was a big wooden sleigh bed, covered in a puffy white duvet, perfect for snuggling under, and decorated with yellow and grey cushions. By the bed were pretty lamps with yellow silk lampshades on wooden bedside tables, topped with etched glass carafes and water glasses alongside silk-covered boxes of tissues and embroidery-backed hairbrushes. Several books nestled in niches, among little figurines, china trinket boxes and miniature bottles of expensive hand and body lotion.

'Oh, I love the bath,' cried Hattie, exclaiming over the claw-footed bath in the centre of the en-suite bathroom. 'I've always wanted one of these.'

'You know there is one in the master suite at the château. Why didn't you stay in there?'

'Because it felt like a bridal suite and to be honest –' she tried not to smile '– I liked the balcony and the fact that you were next door.'

'Did you now?' Luc came towards her, slipped his arms around her and trailed kisses along her chin. 'Why was that?'

'Don't get too big for your boots,' said Hattie, softening into him. 'I didn't like the idea of being on my own in such a big house. It felt a bit lonely.'

'You mean you didn't have plans for me.' He pouted and she laughed.

'Not then,' she said with a teasing smile. 'But I do now.' She slipped her fingers into his shirt and unfastened the button below his throat, gazing up at him with mischief.

A little while later, spreading her arms on either side of the enamel bath, Hattie said, 'I love this bathtub.'

Luc sitting opposite her raised his glass of wine. 'I do now. Funny –' his gaze dropped to the water line and the bubbles that just about hid her breasts '– it's never held a particular attraction before.'

'I wonder why,' said Hattie with a pert grin.

'You do know we can't stay in here all night. I've booked a very nice restaurant for dinner.'

When he climbed out, she admired the view of his long lean legs and muscular bottom until he caught her looking.

'Out,' he said holding up a bath sheet. She stepped out of the bath into the towel that he wrapped around her, kissing her as he did. Would kissing Luc ever get old, she wondered as her mouth softened under his? She wrapped her arms around his neck and pressed close to him.

She wanted to murmur, 'Maybe we should stay in,' but it occurred to her that it sounded horribly domestic – exactly what she'd been escaping from.

He shook his head. 'I think I have bred a monster. What happened to the shy girl who was rubbish at this sort of thing?'

'You corrupted me?'

He swatted her on the bottom. 'Go and get dressed. I am taking you out to dinner.'

Chapter Twenty-Five

Hattie studied the red candle flickering on the tiny table, her knees wedged up against Luc's as he took her hand. The waiter beside them uncorked the bottle of red wine Luc had selected. With the necessary pomp, he poured a taste for Luc, who swilled and sipped before nodding.

'This is lovely,' she said glancing around at the small low-ceilinged room, filled with other couples. 'Very romantic.'

'Of course,' he said, lifting her hand and kissing her palm, his steady gaze meeting hers, making her shiver a little.

'You're not cold, are you?' The candlelight caught the wicked glint in his eyes.

'No.' She pursed her lips primly. 'We had a hot bath, remember?' She was still overheating after they'd spent nearly an hour in there, topping up the hot water until it ran out.

'How could I forget?'

Feeling yet another surge of heat flooding her face, she studied the menu, handwritten on one sheet of paper. It was simple, with a choice of two starters, two mains and two desserts, but she knew that whatever she chose it would be perfect. It was that sort of place. There were probably no more than twenty covers in the restaurant and the small square tables were crammed together with only just enough room to squeeze between them without knocking someone's wine over – and even then it was advisable to hang on to your glass.

'I've been told the steak frites are the must-have dish, that's what they're known for.'

'Have you been here before?' Hattie asked.

'No, but it was recommended by my friend Sebastian who is a chef. If we could have booked his place, I'd have taken you there but even for a friend and an investor he couldn't squeeze me in today. He's the current darling of the Parisian food critics.'

'How do you know him?'

'I invested in his first restaurant. I met him at a wine tasting when he was a chef and I was working for my father's wine distribution business. He's a cocky sod but he knows what he wants and he's an excellent chef.'

It was such a different world from the one Hattie was used to; her previous existence felt positively humdrum in comparison. She barely went anywhere or did anything. The height of culinary excitement had been occasional fish and chips on a Friday night. Without realising she was doing it, she shrank into her seat.

'Hey, Hattie. Where do you go?' The sudden tender expression on his face made her straighten her shoulders. She was here now, with a gorgeous man who made her feel sexy and desirable, and she was going to enjoy every minute of it. In another month this would be nothing more than a memory.

'I'm right here.' She picked up her glass and took a good

sip, savouring the berry aromas. Hell, yes, she was here in the moment. 'I'm going to have the steak. Rare. I've heard that chefs in France will throw a tantrum if you ask for anything else.'

Luc shrugged. 'That might be an exaggeration but I think they do take exception to ruining a good piece of meat.'

After giving their orders, they handed their menus back to the waiter.

'So tomorrow. You have a meeting at nine-thirty to buy this press.'

'Yes.' Luc leaned forward. She could almost see the excitement fizzing from him. 'It's the first step for the winery and it's very exciting.' He began to explain why the press was so important and then he got his phone out. 'Look.' He showed her a picture. 'It's a pneumatic lateral membrane press, it's completely automated.'

'So it is,' she said deadpan, studying the picture of a big shiny stainless-steel cylinder on a metal box frame.

'Ah, but…' He launched into an enthusiastic explanation about 'vertical juice channels', 'a pressure of less than zero point eight bar' and 'reduced pressing times'.

Hattie listened as he then began to expound his plans for St Martin champagne production. His face shone with enthusiasm and even though she maybe had no right to, she felt proud of him, for that single-minded determination and focus. She took his hand and squeezed, not wanting to stop him. Although she only understood a fraction of what he was talking about, just being in the presence of his energy and passion made her feel as if she were stepping into and sharing a beam of sunlight. It was energising and infectious, making her think about what she wanted to do and how she was going to expand on what she'd started. She had no doubt that wedding and event planning was for her. Being at the château had reinforced that and she was proud of what she'd achieved so far, even if it had been a bit rocky along the way. The real fun and games would start when the wedding guests began to arrive but she was looking forward to that. The hard slog was pretty much done now.

'It's going to … I'm so sorry, Hattie.'

'It's fine. It was interesting.'

He raised sceptical eyebrows. 'I think not.'

'No, it was.' She smiled at him, although inside she was struck by a pang of envy and regret. She probably wouldn't ever see his first bottle of St Martin champagne. By the time production was underway she'd be back in England, living who knew where. The thought depressed her and she took a fortifying sip of wine.

Hattie couldn't believe how easily she and Luc had fallen into sync with each other. There was no awkwardness as they shared the bathroom in the morning or moved around each other in the well-stocked apartment kitchen, making coffee and heating croissants from the freezer, lounging together on the sofa in thick fluffy robes discussing the forthcoming day.

Luc's phone beeped and when he checked the message he scowled.

'Great. My father wants to see me this morning before my meeting with the equipment people. How the hell does he know I'm in Paris?'

He rose regretfully. 'I'm going to have to leave sooner than I planned. Will you be all right finding Nina's?'

'Yes,' she said firmly, tapping her phone. 'I have the directions right here and I'm a big girl.'

'Okay, have fun shopping and give her my love.'

It was that simple, she thought. Being a grown-up and an independent adult, one half of a couple. Talk about refreshing. Chris would have cross-examined, worried and checked and double-checked that she knew where she was going. That she'd be all right. That she'd be safe. And insist on her texting him when she arrived. Luc merely nodded and said, 'Okay, I'll see you there for lunch.'

'Yes. I hope your meeting goes well and you buy your big shiny new toy,' she teased.

He grinned at her and went off to get dressed. When he returned in a smart navy suit with a pale blue shirt she wondered for a moment how she was going to let him out of the door.

'You look...' Her heart jumped up into her throat and she stared at him, sucker-punched by a sudden overwhelming flood of love for him. She made an involuntary sound that caught his attention.

'Are you okay?'

'Mm. Fine,' she said, horrified by the strength of that rush. This wasn't supposed to happen. To steady herself, she put her hands on his broad shoulders, her fingers spreading out on the soft crisp wool of his suit jacket and pecked him on the cheek. 'Good luck.' She backed off. 'I'd better dress. Have a shower.' She scuttled towards the bathroom and, once in there, shut the door and leaned against it, throwing her head back.

She'd only gone and fallen in love with him.

· · ·

Grinning to himself, Luc walked down the street wondering at the summons from his father, though it couldn't dim his happiness. Spending time with Hattie just brought sunshine into his soul. He could have done without this meeting today but he knew from experience it was easier to talk to his father face to face. Since he was relying on him to hand over the rental from the château to pay for the press, it was a small price to pay, especially as he was now in the driving seat.

He had made it quite clear to his father that he would no longer work for the family business and if he hadn't been allowed to take on St Martin, he would have joined another company. He'd been headhunted enough times to know that he could pick and choose his jobs, a fact his father was well aware of. It was a useful bargaining chip.

When he walked into the foyer of the Brémont building the doorman recognised him immediately and waved him through the security barriers. His father's secretary, Caroline, was sitting outside his office, her blonde chignon and perennially pleasant smile in place. She was the most unflappable person he'd ever met and also the most discreet.

'Luc,' she greeted him. 'How lovely to see you. We've missed you. It isn't the same around here without you but –' she lowered her voice, glancing towards his father's door '– I'm so glad you are doing your own thing. How is it going? How is Marthe? I bet she's thrilled with what you're doing.'

'Thanks, Caroline. I'm not sure thrilled is quite the word. She's worried I'm going to go all modern on her, I think. But it's going well. Although there's still a lot to do before we make our first vintage.'

'I'll let Monsieur Brémont know you're here.'

Five minutes later she motioned for him to go in.

His father was seated behind the vast leather-topped desk,

a cigar in one hand, a phone in the other. Luc ignored the chair his father nodded to and walked across the office to look out of the window while his father finished his conversation. He'd lost count of how many times he'd sat in that bloody chair waiting for his father, dancing to his tune, and being told where he was going next. At least his father couldn't do that to him now. He stared down at the trees on the wide avenue below, wishing that he was back at the château.

'Luc!' his father bellowed, and he turned.

'Father. How are you?'

'I'm well. It's good to see you. Marthe phoned me. Told me you were here.' Ah, that was how his father had tracked him down.

Luc nodded, slightly surprised by this. Marthe only interacted with his father when she absolutely had to.

'How are things with the wedding? Alex was on the phone yesterday. Set me thinking, if we renovated the place, we could earn a lot more money renting out the whole place. Bet it's turning the place upside-down.'

Luc smiled, thinking of Fliss, Solange and Hattie and the way that the kitchen had become their hub just like it had been when he was a boy. The château was a home again. 'Something like that.'

'Excellent. If this is a success, I'm considering opening the house up for more. It will keep you busy.'

'I've got enough to do with the vineyard,' said Luc stiffly. This was so typical of his father. A new idea, a new business venture that he would want Luc to set up for him. 'You do remember that I've left the company.'

His father sighed irritably. 'Yes. Which is what I wanted to talk to you about. I've had a discussion with Marthe. She says Gilles Roban has offered an excellent price for the grapes this year and she says I should accept it. That would give some more capital to refurbish the château and then you could make the champagne next year.'

There was a buzzing in Luc's ears, like angry wasps bursting out of a hive.

'Pardon?' It was as if he couldn't quite get his head around the words even though they were quite plain.

His father shrugged. 'There's always next year. If you want to make wine, come down to Bordeaux.'

'Father, I want to make champagne. This year.' Luc hated that he sounded like a spoilt brat but he knew his father. Next year there'd be another reason for the delay – and besides, this year's harvest was shaping up to be a good one. No wonder Roban wanted the grapes.

'I told Marthe that's what you would say.'

'I don't understand. Marthe hasn't said anything to me about accepting an offer from Roban.'

His father puffed on his cigar. 'It isn't her decision but I thought I'd check with you, especially as I heard you're talking to D'Arreau about buying one of their wine presses. Is that a wise investment just yet?'

Luc sat down and went through in great detail exactly why the press was a good investment. Luckily Yves Brémont wasn't a detail man but someone who was easily distracted by new toys, new technology and quick wins.

'The idea of a press is a good one but you should wait until next year. By all means have your meeting but I agree with Marthe, we will sell the grapes this year.'

'But…'

'Your aunt knows her champagne. If she thinks it is a good idea, then so do I. My mind is made up.'

Luc gritted his teeth, knowing that arguing with his father

was counterproductive. He would speak to Marthe, see if he could persuade her to change her mind. What had made her interfere this time? Surely she wasn't scared of change, it wasn't like her to be backward-looking or to duck out of a new challenge. Something wasn't right but he was damned if he knew what.

Chapter Twenty-Six

Hattie walked briskly to Nina's berating herself all the way. She wasn't in love with Luc. All it was was too many endorphins from too much good sex. It was an infatuation. Nothing more. Just a reaction to the attention. The novelty of being desired again. It had gone to her head.

Even to her the words felt like excuses. With a heavy, heartfelt sigh she directed her attention to her phone. Just another street and then she'd be there.

When she walked through the door of Nina's she wasn't sure where to look first: the glass counter with a dazzling display of cakes and pastries, or the under the seascape mural that ran the whole length of one wall? Mermaids, with tails of iridescent greens and blues and streaming hair of red and silver, swam among rippling seaweed, ornate shells and sunken treasure. Tearing her attention away she approached the counter where a rather formidable older man waited.

'*Bonjour.*' She attempted a smile which was rebuffed by his stern expression. 'I'm … I'm here to see Nina. I'm Hattie.'

'She's teaching a class at the moment. Perhaps you'd like to take a seat while you wait.'

'Thank you, that would be lovely.' She didn't dare ask for a coffee in case he thought she was after a freebie. 'I'll just sit and stare at the mural. It's beautiful.'

His face softened with a gratified smile. 'Why don't you take a seat, and I'll make you some coffee and perhaps I can persuade you to have an éclair.'

Hattie looked at the glass counter and the mouth-watering selection of goodies. The names printed on the labels in swirling italics looked somewhat familiar, although the pastries themselves didn't. Jammy dodger, bourbon, millionaire's shortbread: they were English biscuit names but definitely French patisserie. She was intrigued but too bamboozled by the choice. She decided to leave it to her waiter to decide.

He served her a few minutes later with an éclair topped with smooth chocolate and decorated with a couple of flakes of gold leaf, along with a coffee in the most beautiful, almost translucent fine china cup and saucer. It was all so pretty she fished out her camera to take a picture, making sure she captured the mural in the background. The éclair, filled with whipped cream and dotted with tiny flecks of strawberry, tasted every bit as good as it looked.

The elderly woman at the next table smiled at her and said something in French. Hattie smiled, catching the word *bien*.

'Très bien,' she replied, wiping cream from her lips.

'You're English,' said the lady.

'Yes,' said Hattie.

'The chocolate strawberry delight is one of my favourites. Nina is very clever with her flavours.'

'You say the loveliest things, Marguerite,' said a petite, neat girl with a dark bob who appeared carrying an amazing conical tower of what looked like profiteroles. 'What do you think of our salted caramel *croquembouche*?'

'*Magnifique*,' said Marguerite, nodding at the group of people behind her. 'You've all done very well.'

There was a chorus of thanks and lots of thumbs-ups as they began to gather coats and bags.

'See you all tomorrow,' called Nina to their departing backs.

'Another group of happy students,' said Marguerite.

'Yes, they're a lovely group. And they're very proud of this.' She lifted the plate with its tower of choux pastry.

'What is it?' asked Hattie.

'Hi,' said Nina. 'You must be Hattie. And this is a *croquembouche*. A traditional French wedding cake.'

'It looks complicated.'

'Not really, not when you know what you're doing and you've had enough practice. The trick is to make sure your choux isn't soggy.'

'I'll take your word for it.' Hattie glanced at the terrifyingly impressive-looking confection. She made a note to talk to Fliss. Maybe they could add it to the menu, as Gabby was still dithering about the cake.

'Mind you, if it tastes as good as that éclair...' Hattie eyed Nina enviously. In her black capri pants and a shawl-collared cream top with three-quarter-length sleeves teamed with little black ballet flats, she looked very chic. If she was to be Hattie's fashion guru, then Hattie guessed she was in good hands.

Nina beamed. 'Thank you. Marguerite, this is a friend of Luc Brémont. She needs a dress for her cousin's wedding. Marguerite knows all the best shops in Paris.'

'A dress for a wedding. Then you must take her to Galeries

Lafayette. They've just opened a vintage shop as well which I've heard has some lovely secondhand pieces.'

'That's exactly what I was thinking,' said Nina, winking at Hattie. 'Are you ready to go now? I haven't been shopping in ages.'

'I wasn't expecting you to take me.'

'It's not a problem and the perfect excuse to take a day off.'

'You work far too hard,' said Marguerite, tapping her cane on the floor.

'Yes, Marguerite,' said Nina kissing her on her powdery cheek. 'But if I didn't, where would you go for your morning coffee?'

'Hmph,' said Marguerite, picking up her cup and sipping genteelly.

The two young women left the patisserie and Nina wound her way expertly through the streets to the nearest Métro station.

'Have you been here before?' she asked.

'No, it's my first time but hopefully not my last.'

'I'm sure it won't be your last. There's something about Paris that draws people back time and time again. It has its own quintessential essence of Frenchness. There's nowhere quite like it and I'm not saying that because I live here. I felt it the very first time I came.'

'So how does an Englishwoman end up running a patisserie in Paris?' asked Hattie, curious as the other woman seemed as French as anyone else on the street. She seemed to fit in perfectly.

'It's a long story,' said Nina with a quick smile. 'The short version is that my husband broke his leg and needed someone to help him run a patisserie course in the shop. Nick, my brother, volunteered me and despite Sebastian being a grumpy undeserving bastard at the time, I fell in love with him.' She wrinkled her nose before adding. 'He's much better now. He just needed the love of a good woman.'

Hattie frowned. 'But how do you feel about giving everything up to live here?' The thought made her feel anxious. 'Don't you miss home? Don't you get homesick?'

Nina sighed. 'I grew up on the moors in Northumberland. Living in Paris is about as different as you could possibly get. I love it here. The lifestyle. The attitudes to food, to life. But I'll be honest, I miss my family, although they do come and visit. A lot.' She rolled her eyes. 'But Sebastian is my home. We have our own lives, our own goals – I think that's important – but we're also a team. It works because we love each other and so we work at it.' Nina suddenly grinned. 'Although I am, of course, always right.'

Hattie laughed but inside she couldn't help thinking that Nina was romanticising things. Moving for one person was never a good idea. Leaving Manchester, she'd sacrificed a good job, given up her independence and Chris had become totally reliant on her. There was no way she would tie herself to a man again.

Galeries Lafayette was like no other department store Hattie had ever visited. The building itself was a work of art with its magnificent central blue cupola of stained glass. Around the rotunda were three tiers overlooking the main floor below. Each tier held a number of ornate balconies, each decorated with floral wrought-iron motifs picked out in bronze and gold, and with curving balustrades of polished brass railings.

Like every other tourist Hattie stopped dead and gazed

upwards. 'Wow.' It epitomised what she thought shopping in Paris should be.

'Fab, isn't it. I'm not sure there's another shop like it anywhere.'

Hattie was pretty sure she was right.

'Ladies' fashion is on the first floor. Have you any idea what you're looking for?'

The image of Marine flashed into her head.

'I want something smart, glamorous, chic.' Hattie laughed. 'French.'

Nina giggled. 'You've come to the right place for that.'

'To be honest. I want something completely different. Not safe. Not me. Or rather the real me.'

'Ha! I know that feeling. Before I came here, my family – oh God, they used to drive me mad, trying to pigeonhole me as something I wasn't. I get it. I really do. So no preconceptions.'

'None whatsoever. But I think I'd like something bright and patterned.'

'Okay. Got that.'

Nina was fun to shop with. She took Hattie at her word and once they'd established what size clothes she needed she led her to the changing rooms.

'Wait here. You have to try on everything I bring you.'

'Everything?'

'Everything,' said Nina, the naughty glint in her eye at odds with her no-nonsense tone.

'What, even that pink tulle tube on the model at the front?' asked Hattie a touch nervously.

'Even that. But credit me with some taste. Besides, did you see how much it was? Silly money. I'm guessing you're not loaded.'

'Not loaded, no, but I do want something nice. The rest of

my family are loaded. There'll be plenty of designer outfits there, I can guarantee.'

'Leave it with me. Be right back.'

Hattie sat down on one of the velvet cubes in the dressing room wondering what Nina would bring her. She wasn't disappointed when Nina came back just five minutes later with three dresses.

'Try these on. I'm still hunting.'

Hattie examined each dress. Not one of them was what she'd have chosen. The first, a yellow chiffon zebra print with a silk slip dress beneath, was far brighter than she'd normally pick but Nina had met the brief. Hattie stripped off and pulled the dress on, curling her lip when she looked in the mirror at her brown ankle socks. Not quite the look. The dress fitted well but it wasn't right. While she had no idea what she wanted, she knew what she didn't want.

The second dress was a bright green and fuchsia pink print with an empire line and a frilly tier. It was a bit too busy for Hattie's taste and far shorter than she was comfortable with. The third dress was a pale pink and grey print, off the shoulder, and did absolutely nothing for her complexion.

'Ugh no,' said Nina, appearing over her shoulder. 'Definitely not. Try this.' She held up a plain pale blue satin dress. I know it's doesn't quite fit the bright and patterned brief but I think it will suit you.'

As soon as Hattie tried it on, she knew it was the dress. The almost halterneck line showed off her slim shoulders, and the wide sash criss-crossed just under the bust, with the skirt falling away, slightly lower at the back, with a curved hem. It was elegant, classy and she loved it. It was exactly what she was looking for. Even better, it was Ted Baker and in the sale marked down from two hundred and fifty euros to one hundred and twenty-five.

'Perfect,' said Nina.

'I think it is.' Hattie twisted her body in the mirror.

'It's very you.'

'Do you think so?' asked Hattie, delighted by the comment. It was the her that she really felt like deep inside. The her she always aspired to being and had never quite got there.

'Right, next one.'

'But this is the one.'

'I know,' said Nina with a smug grin. 'But there's no reason not to buy more. I brought these. You might as well try them. I also found these amazing palazzo pants. Aren't they gorgeous?' Hattie had to agree, the flowing black silk pants with big blue and pink flowers were striking.

'With a plain black vest and a pashmina they'd look wonderful.'

'I've got a black vest and a pink pashmina that would match.'

'See – even better.'

By the time Nina had finished bullying her into trying everything, even a shaggy lime green jacket with a black bias-cut slip dress, Hattie settled on the blue dress for the wedding, the palazzo pants because she had to have them and, as Nina pointed out, she already had something to go with them, and a pretty summer dress in sunshine yellow that finished just above the knee and swished delightfully around her legs when she walked, making her feel feminine and flirty.

'Do we need shoes?' asked Nina, her dark eyes bright with mischief. 'A handbag?'

'Shoes, yes.'

They found the most perfect gold court shoes with slender

high heels that went with all three outfits and did amazing things to Hattie's legs. She didn't even look at the price but just handed over her credit card.

'That was fun,' said Nina. Her own bag contained a pair of high-heeled suede ankle boots she'd fallen in love with.

'It was, thank you.'

'It really was my pleasure.' Nina swung her rope-handled bag happily. 'I'm so glad you got the perfect dress.'

'So am I,' said Hattie, knowing that she would feel wonderful in the dress and shoes on her cousin's wedding day. She couldn't wait to wear her new clothes.

Chapter Twenty-Seven

'Wow! You look busy,' Hattie said when she walked back into the kitchen after their return from Paris. She watched as Fliss sliced strawberries with manic precision.

'How was gay Paris?'

'Wonderful. I went shopping.' She held up her bags. 'Cinderella has a dress for the wedding. I also met some friends of Luc's, you'd love them.' Before they left the city they'd had a late lunch with Sebastian and Nina. 'They're even more into food than you if that's possible.'

'Where is he?'

'He dropped me off, he's gone straight to see Marthe.'

Hattie wasn't going to tell her that Luc had seemed very preoccupied on the way back. She'd not exactly been chatty herself, she had too much to think about, wondering in the main if she ought to put some distance between them.

'While you've been gallivanting, some of us have been chained to the cooker.'

Hattie laughed. 'And you've enjoyed every minute of it.'

'Might have,' said Fliss but her lips narrowed as she

selected another strawberry, slicing through the rich red flesh. The smell was so good, Hattie risked a finger and snagged a slice.

'Oi.' Fliss gave her hand a quick slap. 'If you're not careful you'll be put on sous chef duty.'

'So, this evening. It's all about a bet, I hear.'

'Luc told you, did he?'

'He mentioned that you'd had words.'

'Hmph. I remember Luc scarpering leaving me with the big oaf, who rather rudely made the assumption that my soufflé was luck and that patisserie is my limit and macarons the sum total of my repertoire. He insinuated that a three-course meal for more than four people would be beyond my capabilities.'

'And?'

'And I bet him he was wrong.'

Hattie bit back a smile. 'And what happens if he loses the bet, which I'm assuming he's going to.'

'Too damn right he is. I will be receiving a bottle of Dom Ruinart Blanc de Blancs 2015,' crowed Fliss in triumph.

'I take it that's a very good one, whatever it is.'

'It's a champagne. Blanc de Blanc is made solely from chardonnay grapes and it's my favourite. And –' she puffed out her chest in triumph '– it's all mine. Every last drop.'

'Would you drink something as expensive as that or would you save it?'

'Normally I'd keep it for a special event but on this occasion I shall enjoy drinking it in front of Alphonse. I might even let him have a glass. And tonight I shall enjoy watching Alphonse eat his words.'

'So what are we having?'

'Remember I bought some scallops the other day at the

market, which I put in the freezer, I'm going to use those. We're having Coquilles St Felicity.'

'Which is?'

'Normally you have Coquilles St-Jacques, which are basically pan-fried scallops in a rich creamy sauce topped with breadcrumbs and gruyere. There are variations on the recipe. I'm doing scallops on lemon, parmesan and white bean puree topped with a lemon and thyme crumb.'

'Yum, I adore scallops,' said Hattie.

'And then I'm doing coq au vin, with whole baby mushrooms, and mixed greens with shallots, garlic and lardons. And for dessert we're having a strawberry tart made with crème anglaise, strawberry coulis and a sweet pastry case.'

'Wow. You're going for it.'

'Of course,' said Fliss with a sniff and a toss of her hair. 'He might think I'm an amateur and that my soufflé was a fluke but he's about to learn differently.'

'What time have you said?'

Fliss glanced at the clock on the chimney breast. 'Seven o'clock, which gives me another two hours to finish up and change. I'm going to have a nice soak in the bath and put a dress on.'

'Do you need any help?' Hattie looked around the immaculate kitchen.

'Yes, you can lay the table and make it look nice. The chicken is all prepared and in the oven, the vegetables are chopped and ready to sauté, the bean mash is done, I'll fry the scallops just before I serve them, and the lemon breadcrumbs are done, so it's just a matter of assembling the starter. And I just need to knock up a strawberry glaze to go over the top of the tarts and I'm done. Easy peasy.'

Hattie raised an eyebrow. 'For you maybe. You don't even look as if you've broken into a sweat.'

Fliss gave her horrified look. 'Of course not.'

Hattie looked at the long kitchen table. 'It would be nicer to eat in here than in the dining room, I think.'

'Mm,' said Fliss doubtfully. 'But that would be smarter.'

'Not when I've finished with this table. Leave it to me.'

Since she'd been here, she'd not put any of her decorating skills to good use. Ransacking the dresser, Hattie found all sorts of bits and pieces she could use, as well as a selection of tablecloths, napkins and placemats.

'Do you know what you're doing?' asked Fliss, eyeing white carboard, raffia and scissors. 'It all looks a bit Blue Peter.'

'Trust me,' said Hattie before disappearing out into the garden to pluck some foliage from the immaculate troughs of flowers at the front of the house.

Half an hour later, having unearthed some pretty blue bowls from one of the sideboards in the dining room and a set of plain white china, Hattie put the finishing touches to the napkins, which she was rather pleased with.

'*Voila*. What do you think?'

Fliss glanced over and then did a double take. 'Wow!' She crossed the room to take a closer look and gently touched the sprigs of dried lavender tied with sage-coloured raffia to rolled white damask napkins. Hattie was rather proud of the handwritten name cards, with more sprigs of lavender like single stitches threaded through the cardboard, that were set in front of each straw placemat on the white damask tablecloth. The simple rustic touches helped to create a welcoming atmosphere.

'This is fantastic! I love the lavender touches. You've got a real flair for this. Simple and elegant.'

'Wait until you see my ideas for the wedding flowers and decorations.' Any day now a ton of stuff would be arriving for her white-love-heart-themed table decorations. Hattie loved doing things like this and having free rein today had reminded her how much she enjoyed it. Chris's mum didn't like fancy but on the odd occasion people had come to dinner, Hattie had spent a lot of time theming the table.

'I think we both deserve a glass of wine and a little toast to ourselves. The dream team. Would you mind opening a bottle? I need a drop for the glaze and then I'll take a glass up to the bath with me.'

'Which one?' asked Hattie when she opened the wine fridge, which had been restocked since this morning.

'Hmm.' Fliss appeared at her shoulder and pulled a bottle from the rack, perusing the label before putting it back and selecting a second. That one was also rejected and she chose a third bottle.

'Ah, this is more like it. Pouilly-Fuissé. Perfect. It's not just the French that can match their wines with food.' She handed the bottle to Hattie and went back to slicing her strawberries, every now and then tossing the rejects into a pan on the hob. It looked painstaking but Fliss worked quickly and methodically.

'Can you pop a dessert spoon of wine into those strawberries in the pan? All I need to do is boil them up with sugar and strain them to make the glaze.' She finished slicing the last strawberries and removed a tray of mini pastry cases from the fridge. 'I've already filled these with crème pat. I just need to arrange the strawberries on the top.'

'Crème pat?'

'*Crème patissière*,' she said as she began to carefully arrange the slices of strawberries, vertically, so that they stuck up like little love hearts. 'It's just a sweet custard but a lot more delicate.'

Hattie had to admire her flair. It wouldn't have occurred to her to put the strawberries in like this. It elevated the tarts to a new level. When the last slice was placed, Fliss stood back and gave them careful scrutiny.

'They look amazing,' Hattie said, unwrapping the foil around the top of the bottle.

'Of course they do,' said Fliss, folding her arms in satisfaction, and stuck her nose in the air. 'And Alphonse is going to choke on them.'

Having opened the bottle – God, she missed screwtops – Hattie poured them each a glass of the pale straw-coloured wine. Fliss swirled the wine before sinking her nose into the top of the glass and Hattie eyed her dubiously.

'Peaches, honey and hazelnuts,' declared Fliss after a taking good slurp which she rolled around her mouth.

Hattie took a tentative sip and swilled it around her mouth too.

'Peaches! I can taste peaches.' Hattie punched the air, almost spilling the contents of her glass. She really could taste the peach flavour. Luc's teaching had rubbed off on her.

'Right,' said Fliss. 'I'm off to go and have a soak. There's the most wonderful jar of Moksa Sel de Guerande and Lavender bath salts which I'm going to help myself to and I might even treat myself to a candle too.'

'Sure there's nothing else I can do?'

'No, see you in a while. Besides, I think you're wanted.' Fliss raised her glass in a quick farewell, nodded to Luc, who was lounging in the doorway, and flitted past him.

How long had he been there? As usual, her body reacted to him with an involuntary warm glow of happiness.

'Hey, Luc,' she said, trying to be cool. So much for the idea of keeping her distance.

'Hey, Hattie.'

'How was Marthe?'

His lips flattened and he shrugged. 'She was sleeping, apparently.'

Hattie guessed at the grand old age of ninety-five she probably slept a lot. At the sight of his unhappy face, her earlier thoughts of putting some distance between them faded. There was something wrong, she could sense it, and it just wasn't in her nature to turn her back on someone in need. She held out her glass to him. How had she thought she could stay away from him?

'Peaches eh?' he asked, his fingers brushing hers as he took it from her.

'Mm,' she said airily, still rather pleased with herself.

He sipped and nodded with approval, a sudden wicked light glinting in his eyes. 'You must have a good teacher.'

'Oh yes,' she said, 'but there's always more to learn.'

Chapter Twenty-Eight

When Luc walked into the kitchen that evening, he felt so much better. There was a hell of a lot to be said for shower sex and for a woman as generous and giving as Hattie. His heart swelled as he sought her out across the room, where she was leaning back against the counter chatting away to Fliss. Even though she'd instinctively known he was worrying about something, she hadn't pressed him or pried for information. Instead she'd applied herself, rather thoroughly he might add, to taking his mind off things. He sighed with pleasure at the memory but it was more than good sex, so much more.

As if she read his thoughts, Hattie looked up, caught his eye and smiled before glancing away. Was she as aware of him as he was of her? He couldn't help his gaze drifting towards her whenever she was around. He should have told her in Paris that he loved her but then his father had thrown a curve ball. Knowing of her previous relationship, he'd been biding his time, but now it was racing away. He didn't want her to leave but would she want to stay?

He swallowed the fear. Knowing her history with her ex had made him wary of telling her how he felt. He needed to choose the right moment. It wasn't now.

He sniffed appreciatively. 'Dinner smells good.' Not just that but there was a cosy atmosphere in here that he wasn't used to. Something was different. For one thing, someone had taken a bulb out of the three pendant lights above the central island, which softened the light, while two fat creamy candles glowing in large hurricane glass vases gave the room a warm, homely golden light. These considered touches created a warm welcome, inviting a body to relax and stay a while. Quite a contrast to when he'd first come here as a boy and those memories of quiet evenings with just him and Marthe. At first, he'd found it intimidating sitting in here, especially with the dim lighting and scary shadows that danced on the high walls before the kitchen was modernised several years ago. Now the room shone with subtle gold light that was reflected by the cream paintwork of the cabinets. It made him breathe more easily, although he still wondered how his parents had abandoned him with so little thought or preparation. He wasn't even sure they'd told him they were leaving him, which in hindsight seemed rather cruel. Now he felt happiest here, but it had been a long time coming. Tonight, for some reason, it felt more like home than ever before. Perhaps because he knew he didn't have to leave.

'*Bonsoir*,' called Solange, entering the kitchen carrying a bunch of hand-tied flowers which she handed over to Fliss. 'This is such a treat. I can't remember the last time someone cooked a whole meal for me. I'm so excited.'

'I'm a terrible daughter,' said Yvette following her. 'I can't cook.'

Luc had been pleased to hear from Alphonse that Yvette

had apologised to her mother and taken her to lunch as well as buying her a large box of chocolates.

'You can, just not as well as *Maman*,' said Alphonse, who loomed behind Solange. As usual he looked like a shaggy bear with his overlong hair in its perpetual unbrushed state. Alphonse had always been his own man and a scruffy one at that, although Luc doubted whether, even if he dressed in a cashmere designer suit, he'd look much better. From day one it had made Luc like him all the more. He was so different from the neat, well-pressed children he was forced to spend time with at his private school or his parents' parties.

Luc watched with amusement as Fliss shot Alphonse a disapproving glance. 'Nice to see you dressed up,' she said.

Luc ducked his head to hide a smirk. Poor Alphonse was wearing his best jeans. For him this was as dressed up as it got.

'*Bonsoir*,' he said, brushing at his trousers with a shrug. 'They're clean.'

'Hmph,' said Fliss, taking the two bottles of wine that he held out.

'I wasn't sure what you were cooking,' said Alphonse, 'So I brought a red and a white.'

'That's very thoughtful of you,' said Fliss, regarding the labels with a nod. 'We're having seafood, but I've already opened a very pleasant Pouilly-Fuissé. Would you like a glass? Or would you prefer one of these?'

Alphonse considered her response. 'That's an excellent choice,' he said and Luc could tell he was reluctantly impressed, not that he would show it. Pig-headed as ever, Alphonse was convinced that this Englishwoman couldn't possibly know anything about wine.

'Dinner will be ready in five minutes. Would you all like to take a seat?' said Fliss, rolling up the sleeves of a dress which accentuated her tall, slender figure. Where she was willowy, Alphonse was stocky, and she topped him by an inch.

Luc sat opposite Hattie as directed by the neat little place cards at each place setting. In comparison to his mother's immaculate formal table, with crystal wine glasses, silver cutlery and starched tablecloths so stiff they could be folded like card, this was charming.

'These are beautiful, Hattie,' said Solange examining one of the place cards, her fingers tracing the sprig of lavender. 'Such a simple, clever idea.'

'So...' Yvette waved her fingers, intimating 'fiddly', as she was obviously unable to find the right word in English. 'I would not have the patience.'

'You don't need to tell us that,' said Alphonse, sitting next to Luc beside the empty seat awaiting Fliss. Luc, noticing the placing, looked over at Hattie and raised an eyebrow. She shrugged as if to say she was giving him the benefit of the doubt. Luc was absolutely convinced that Alphonse was attracted to Fliss. They'd make a good match. He was all bluster and noise, while she cut through the crap and gave as good as she got.

'Are you sure you don't want a hand serving?' asked Hattie, looking over at Fliss, who was darting around the kitchen at speed but in a collected manner that suggested she knew exactly what she was doing.

'No. You'll only get in the way,' she said, not even turning around.

A minute later the first plate was placed in front of Solange bringing with it the smell of lemon and caramelised shellfish. In no time, Fliss had served everyone and sat down in her chair. Luc watched as Alphonse examined the dish, keeping half an eye on Fliss. Three scallops were delicately arranged on a bed of bean mash, sprinkled with a herby mix of cheese and breadcrumbs toasted to a golden brown.

Fliss waited. Alphonse grinned at her and, picking up a fork, prodded one of the scallops and raked the breadcrumb mix. 'Looks good. Nice presentation. Good colours.'

'We're not on bloody *Masterchef*,' she snapped. 'Taste it.'

'It's lovely, thank you for having us,' said Solange from the opposite end of the table. She and Yvette were clearly oblivious to the challenge that had been laid down, although neither had yet picked up their knife and fork.

Like Hattie, Luc was watching Alphonse, who, with deliberate slowness, cut one of the scallops in two. 'Nice texture.'

Fliss drummed a finger on the table.

The tension had now been communicated to the two women at the other end of the table and they too fell silent as everyone watched Alphonse neatly tuck the food onto his fork and slowly put it in his mouth.

He closed his mouth and chewed reflectively. Fliss rolled her eyes but Luc noticed that the whites of her knuckles were showing on the hand in which she held her wine glass.

Luc could have sworn Alphonse was deliberately chewing as slowly as possible.

Finally he swallowed and then picked up his wine and took a long thoughtful sip.

'Very good,' he pronounced with understated calm, as if unaware of the atmosphere around him.

Fliss rolled her eyes again and snapped, 'It's excellent and you know it. You just can't bring yourself to admit it.'

When Alphonse didn't reply, she picked up a forkful of food and began to eat, which was the signal for the rest of them to start eating.

As soon as Luc took a mouthful, he knew that Alphonse had lied. It was more than good. The scallops were perfectly cooked, lightly caramelised in butter, with a very slightly sticky edge and a firm bite, and the texture of the soft creamy bean mash, flavoured with lemon and thyme, was a perfect match. Fliss was an accomplished cook, that was for sure, and Luc knew that Alphonse's response was deliberately grudging.

Hattie caught his eye and gave him an almost imperceptible nod.

'I think it's amazing,' said Yvette, glaring at her brother.

For a moment, Hattie wondered if Solange had maybe already broken the news to Yvette about the joint wedding plans. She seemed uncharacteristically placid.

'For an Englishwoman,' she added, with a tart smile.

Fliss raised an eyebrow and gave a deliberate look at Hattie.

'Actually, Yvette, we have some news.'

Yvette looked alert, like a mouse on the scent of cheese. 'The wedding has been cancelled.'

'No,' said Hattie, 'but we have a plan that will accommodate your wedding too without the other wedding even being aware.'

Yvette shot a quick glare at her mother. 'You told them.'

'No,' said Hattie, for once feeling in total control. 'Your friend Marie in the café told us. But I've worked it all out.' She pulled her notebook out from under the table.

'You will arrive in the orchard at ten forty-five. We will serve canapés and wine from then until twelve-fifteen.' Luc smiled to himself. Hattie was in total command, sure of herself and her organisational skills. It was the first time he'd really seen it. She was good at what she did. Up until now, she'd been diverted by too many other things.

'Meanwhile, up at the château, the guests staying here will have a later breakfast, which will be serve-yourself from ten-thirty, so that Fliss, Solange and I can prepare your canapés and drinks. Gabby's ceremony will take place in the orchard, which will still be decorated from your *vin d'honneur*, and guests will arrive from two for the ceremony at two-thirty. Drinks will be served on the terrace at three-fifteen and the reception will be at four-thirty in the ballroom.' Hattie picked up her glass and raised it. 'That should sort all the problems out.'

Yvette sat there with her mouth open and then to everyone's astonishment burst into tears. Solange's arms closed around her, pulling her into a warm-hearted hug.

'Fliss has agreed to help prepare the canapés and Hattie will decorate the orchard for you. Isn't that kind of them?' said Solange, in that mum-prompting-a-thank-you sort of way.

The conversation flowed, focusing on the weddings, where they might share resources, economies of scale and what crossovers there might be, as Fliss served the next course.

'Luc, would you mind serving the wine, I think it will go well. We're having coq au vin.'

Before Luc could reach for the bottle being handed to him, Alphonse intercepted it and perused the label. 'Beaujolais Village. Interesting choice.'

'I thought the pepper and spice notes would go well with the herbs in the dish,' said Fliss with a quick tilt of her chin. 'Although the chicken is still very much the main flavour.'

Alphonse inclined his head but didn't say anything as he poured Luc a glass and waited for him to taste it.

'Lovely.' Luc swilled the wine around his mouth, seeking out the aroma notes. Cherries, he thought. He'd always been fond of Beaujolais, which was made with gamay noir grapes, producing a light and fruity wine which made a pleasant change sometimes from the heavier reds of the other parts of Burgundy.

This time there was a lot less tension as everyone tucked in, without paying attention to Alphonse's careful contemplation of the chicken in its rich wine sauce. Again it was cooked beautifully, the lardons salty and slightly crisp, the mushrooms firm and the chicken tender.

'Fliss, this is *delicieux*,' said Solange. 'Better than my mother's.'

Yvette gasped. 'High praise. The best.'

Alphonse grunted. '*C'est bon*.'

'Thank you, Solange.' She turned to Alphonse, as if the thought had suddenly struck her. 'Can you cook?'

'*Moi?*' Alphonse shrugged but didn't reply.

'He is what some would call a back-seat chef,' said Yvette, with a malicious smile at her brother. 'He knows all the theory and is an expert on flavours but he doesn't cook. He doesn't need to because his *maman* still feeds him.'

Fliss shot Alphonse a look of pure scorn at which Alphonse shrugged again. Luc wanted to leap to his defence but couldn't because he knew he'd be breaking a confidence. Alphonse was perfectly capable of cooking, in fact, he was quite the chef once he got into the kitchen, but he kept up the pretence that he wasn't interested so that his mother would continue to cook for him. If she hadn't she wouldn't have bothered cooking for herself. As it was she was very thin and Luc knew that Alphonse worried about her not eating properly.

'We must all do what we are good at. I am good at growing grapes,' said Alphonse stoutly. 'What are you good at, Yvette, apart from stirring up trouble?'

She gave him a wide smile. 'Nothing. Just stirring up trouble and dragging you into it whenever I can.'

The two of them laughed and Luc was pleased to see that Hattie was as baffled by their behaviour as he was. One minute brother and sister hated each other, the next they loved each other. It made no sense, although he noticed Fliss joined in the laughter while Solange's face held a look of amused exasperation. He looked over at Hattie and she shrugged.

When they'd finished the course, he joined Hattie in clearing the table as Fliss set up dessert plates for her final pièce de résistance.

'Luc, there's a dessert wine in the fridge, would you mind opening it for me?'

'I can do that,' said Alphonse jumping up from the table. Luc suspected that he felt his job as chief sommelier was being usurped.

'As you wish,' said Fliss, stirring a pan on the stove. 'It's the Sauternes.'

'Has anyone thought about a present for Marthe?' Luc asked, deliberately steering the conversation away to calmer waters. What do you buy for someone turning ninety-six?

'I was going to give her a bottle of brandy,' called Alphonse from the other side of the kitchen.

'You can't do that,' Fliss and Yvette spoke simultaneously, one in English, one in French, but with equal disdain.

'Why not? She likes brandy.'

'It doesn't show any thought,' said Fliss reprovingly from her position at the cooker.

'But...' Alphonse held out his hands in a 'what else?' gesture. Luc sympathised with him, although Marthe would probably end up with enough brandy to open her own liquor store.

'Perhaps we could get something from all of us,' he suggested.

'You're as bad as he is,' said Yvette. 'You just want us to come up with a good idea for you. Well, it's tough because *Maman* and I have already bought Marthe something.'

'And you didn't think to include me,' Alphonse said with a frown.

'Darling, I hardly think a silk dressing gown is something you'd have chosen,' observed Solange.

'What about the picture of the château that Colin took?' Hattie suddenly piped up. 'You could get it framed and it would a nice reminder and it could be from both of you.

'What a brilliant idea,' said Luc, staring at her with delighted admiration. 'The prints are in the library. All I need to do is buy a frame. I want to have another look at them, as well.' He took out his phone. 'I took pictures of them but I'll need to get a proper print done.'

'Here we go,' said Fliss, carrying over a tray of pretty glass dishes. In each one was an immaculate strawberry tart served with a whirl of cream and a drizzle of deep red coulis. A couple of basil leaves tucked in the top gave a hit of contrasting colour to finish off the pretty plate.

Once Fliss was seated, everyone picked up their spoons but Fliss's eyes were on Alphonse. Even Solange and Yvette paused to watch as he dug his spoon in and snapped off a piece of the tart, scooping a little cream and coulis. He popped it into his mouth and then to Luc's surprise he closed his eyes and groaned.

'That,' he said, 'is exquisite. The best strawberry tart I have ever tasted. What is in the crème patissière? The flavour is incredible.'

Fliss gave him a smug smile. 'It's champagne, of course.'

Alphonse rose to his feet and lifted his glass. 'I salute you, Felicity. You win. You are a very fine chef. Thank you for an excellent meal.'

'Thank you for the excellent bottle of champagne that is coming my way,' said Fliss, preening shamelessly.

Solange and Yvette both frowned in confusion. Luc felt he ought to explain. 'Alphonse made a bet with Fliss, and he's just lost.'

Yvette snorted out a laugh. 'Let me guess, he underestimated a woman again.'

Alphonse glowered at her.

Solange tutted. 'I sometimes wonder when the two of you will grow up.' She turned to Fliss. 'It was a lovely meal. Thank you very much. Yvette and I need to talk about wedding arrangements at the restaurant – will you excuse us?'

After they'd left, Alphonse opened more wine and Fliss tracked down the proper balloon glasses she knew she'd seen somewhere. Luc pulled Hattie onto his lap.

'Alone at last,' he whispered into her neck, unable to resist the soft skin there. 'It seems for ever since I kissed you.'

Hattie's breath hitched as his mouth moved over hers and he smiled as she tried to pull him closer – or was it him, trying to get closer to her? When his tongue touched hers, his brain once again turned to mush. He loved the very bones of this woman. She might be wary given her previous history, and he didn't want to frighten her off. He just needed to find the right moment to tell her.

Chapter Twenty-Nine

Fliss was in the kitchen the following morning, her head resting on the table between her arms, which were flat on the wooden surface. She looked like a rag doll that had been draped there.

'Morning,' trilled Hattie, still very much full of the joys of spring and bloody good sex. As she'd said at the outset, *Je suis ici to have some fun*. She was worrying too much about things with Luc. From now on she was going to go with the flow. They were having fun.

'Go away,' groaned Fliss.

'What time did you get to bed last night?' asked Hattie. She and Luc had left Fliss and Alphonse drinking.

'Three. Alphonse opened another bottle of wine. That man can drink.'

'He's a lot bigger than you.'

'Mm,' said Fliss a touch dreamily. 'He's all man.' Hattie hid a smile.

'Why don't you go back to bed?'

Fliss sat bolt upright and then moaned and clutched her

head. 'I'm cooking with Solange this morning. We're going to make choux pastry and freeze a hundred mini éclair cases for Yvette's wedding party.'

'Paracetamol?'

'Good idea.' She rubbed at her bleary eyes. 'You had an early night. I didn't even notice you go.'

'No, you were too busy arguing with Alphonse.'

'We weren't arguing. I was telling him he was wrong. Honestly, the man is so narrow-minded, bull-headed and … and … annoying,' she said, rising to her feet and pouring herself another coffee from the large cafetière on the side.

'Who's annoying?' asked a loud voice. Hattie was convinced it was deliberately so. She turned to find Alphonse standing in the doorway, his hands wrapped in oven gloves, clutching a bright orange Le Creuset casserole pot.

Fliss sipped her coffee with a leisurely sigh. 'A friend of ours,' she said with studied casualness. 'How are you this morning?' and Hattie could see she dredged up every last crumb of acting skill to put on a brave face.

'*Je vais bien – et toi?*' he said with a cheerful, over-bright grin.

Hattie wasn't sure which of them was overdoing their forced nonchalance.

'I brought you some onion soup,' he said. 'Made it this morning. I'll leave it here.' With that he placed the casserole on top of the oven and strolled out with a casual wave.

'Onion soup?' Hattie frowned. 'Were you talking about it last night or something?'

'No,' said Fliss, obviously equally perplexed. Crossing to the oven, she lifted the lid and sniffed. 'It's still warm. He must have made it this morning, but I've no idea why.' Her eyes narrowed with suspicion. 'He's making some point. He doesn't like to lose.'

'Like someone else I know,' observed Hattie dryly, deciding that Luc was right and the two of them were a good match.

Fliss shrugged; she was the first to admit she was competitive. It came with growing up with four older brothers.

'Can I borrow your car? Solange and I are going shopping to buy extra flour and butter, which is going to weigh a ton, so if we take your car that would be brilliant. Yvette is popping by soon, bringing *more* eggs from her neighbour.'

'Yes, of course. Luc and I are going to visit Marthe later this morning. If you're going out, I'll work in here for a while.' These days Hattie preferred working outside or in the kitchen rather than in the library. She enjoyed being in the thick of things with everyone bustling around her.

'Help yourself to croissants.' Fliss pointed to a paper bag on the side by the sink. 'Solange dropped them in earlier. That woman gets up so early. She'd already been to the bakery before I even got up. God, I need some paracetamol.'

Hattie helped herself to a coffee and a croissant and sat at the bar while Fliss downed a couple of tablets and a large glass of water.

'*Bonjour*,' called Yvette, marching in with a small box loaded with eggs of varying colours and sizes. 'Some of them are still warm.'

'Eggscellent,' said Fliss but the pun was wasted on Yvette, who immediately noticed the soup on the stove.

'Onion soup?' she asked with a grin. 'Someone has a sore head?'

'Your brother brought it over,' said Fliss, her mouth thinning again as she added, 'I've no idea why.'

Yvette let out a shout of laughter. 'It's a traditional

hangover cure, for anyone that gets a hangover, of course. I'm glad I didn't stay up with the two of you.'

From the set of Fliss's jaw, Hattie could have bet, with fair odds in her favour, that the other woman was gritting her teeth so hard she could grind peppercorns.

'I must go,' said Yvette. 'See you soon.' With a mile-wide smirk she waltzed out of the kitchen.

Fliss hissed out a breath. 'That man.'

Hattie ducked her head to hide her amusement, already dying to tell Luc about this.

'Are you ready, Hattie?' called Luc from the foyer an hour later.

'Just coming.'

She closed her notebook with a satisfied thunk. Over the last few days, she'd made huge progress. Funnily enough Juliet Garnier had called and offered to help with tables, chairs and linens, which was quite a turnaround.

The wedding was coming together, although Hattie noted that Gabby had ignored her ninety-fifth request for final numbers.

She'd heard a lot about the formidable Marthe and, as they drove to the village, she twisted her hands in her lap, hoping the woman was going to like her. She knew it was important to Luc. From the way he spoke about her, it was obvious he was very close to her.

Unlike the kindly, motherly old lady that Hattie had pictured, even at ninety-five Marthe Brémont was an imposing figure, with her beak-like nose, piercing blue eyes and crown of pure white hair swept back in an elegant style. Her frame was tall and spare and one immediately sensed that she missed nothing.

Luc kissed her on both cheeks, which she accepted with a regal nod, rather than an effusive welcome.

'Marthe, this is my friend Hattie.'

'Girlfriend?' asked Marthe, quick as a cobra striking.

Hattie and Luc exchanged a quick glance; they hadn't given what they had a label yet.

In tandem, Luc said, 'Yes.'

And Hattie said, 'No.'

'We're working on it,' added Luc as Marthe raised both eyebrows and gave them an amused look.

'I hope you'll make up your minds soon,' she said. 'Nice to meet you, Hattie.'

'It's nice to meet you too,' said Hattie rather formally, conscious of Marthe's flawless English. 'Solange sent this.' She handed over the large Tupperware box that the housekeeper had pressed into her hands as they were leaving.

'Ah, she knows me well. Florentines. How wonderful.' Marthe hugged them possessively to her chest. 'But it's a long time since Solange made them for me.' She looked thoughtful.

'She's coming back to life,' said Luc.

'Is she now? About time too. Especially when she makes me Florentines.'

'They're your favourites?' asked Hattie.

'Oh no,' said Marthe with an airy wave of her hand, her eyes suddenly twinkling. 'I like them because I don't have to share them.' With a laugh she lapsed into French, leaving Luc to translate.

'You're a wicked woman, Marthe.' He turned to Hattie. 'She likes them best because no one else can eat them because they get stuck in their dentures.'

Hattie laughed and shook her head.

'However, I quite like the look of you, so you can have one with coffee. Luc, go and sort some coffee out for us. Go see Janine.' She shooed him away. 'I want to talk to your non-girlfriend, without you around to listen.'

Luc rolled his eyes, clearly used to Marthe's forthright honesty. 'Yes, Madame.'

As soon as he'd gone Marthe turned to her. 'So what brings you to the château?'

'I'm here to help organise the wedding for my cousin.'

'How strange? Does your cousin not want to get married?'

Hattie laughed again; she liked the old lady's quick mind and her directness. 'She's very busy. And I was not.'

'Ah, I see,' said Marthe, a mischievous light dancing in her blue eyes. 'You know Luc likes you.'

Hattie's eyes widened, not sure how to respond.

'It's the first time he's ever brought anyone to see me.'

'Oh,' said Hattie, even more unnerved now. What did she say to that?

Marthe studied her, her eyes boring into Hattie's as if she might be able to see right into her head.

'You know he's very rich.'

'So is my uncle,' replied Hattie. After years of putting up with veiled rude comments from Chris's mother, and with him not sticking up for her, she refused to allow herself to be insulted anymore. 'I'm not a gold-digger, if that's what you mean, but even if I were, don't you think Luc is smart enough to work that out? And I thought it was his father that was very rich.'

Marthe leaned over and gave her an approving pat on the hand. 'I'm old enough to spot a woman like that from a thousand metres. But that sort of wealth brings its own problems, I just wondered if you were aware of them. I was warning you that if you care for Luc, you'll need to know that.'

'We really haven't known each other that long,' protested Hattie, slightly alarmed by the feeling that she was being weighed up as a potential niece-in-law or something. 'And I'm going back to England after the wedding.'

Marthe raised those straggly eyebrows again and gave her a kindly, if superior, look. 'Luc would not have brought you to see me, if you weren't important to him.'

The breath whooshed out of Hattie's chest although she hid it well and her smile at the older woman was non-committal.

'I'm not some senile old woman, you know,' said Marthe with a smirk.

Hattie lifted her chin. 'The last thing I think is that you're senile,' she retorted, feeling some of her old fire sneak back into her veins like sluggish lava, slow but persistent. What had happened to her? When had the spark been extinguished? She knew how, but at what point had she surrendered that part of her personality, the real her?

Marthe cackled. 'I think I like you and I don't like that many people these days. Not enough of them say what they really think. Although of course that is easier with age. People excuse my rudeness because I'm old.' Her lips twitched and she looked around as if checking that no one could hear. 'I'm rude because I can get away with it.'

Hattie burst out laughing. 'I like you, even with the rudeness.'

'You two look like you're getting on. Care to share the joke?' asked Luc, with a delighted smile. His genuine pleasure rang a distant alarm bell in her head which at that moment she chose to ignore.

'Marthe was just checking that I'm not a gold-digger after all your money,' said Hattie.

'*Moucharde*,' said Marthe, with an outraged smile and Hattie guessed she'd just been called a snitch.

With an amused snort, Luc put down the tray of coffee he'd procured and sat down to join them.

Over coffee, his aunt carefully allocated them one Florentine each from her precious haul. She seemed quite happy for him to talk in English, so Hattie could join in, not that she had much to add. She was happy to sit back and watch him. The affection the pair felt for each other was obvious. He treated her with respectful deference punctuated with teasing warmth.

Things were going well until Marthe said, 'I'm pleased that your father talked you out of buying the wine press. It would be a waste of money.'

Hattie felt Luc stiffen next to her. 'What do you mean?'

'I spoke to him and he told me you were considering buying a wine press. I didn't think it was a good idea.'

'That's a shame,' said Luc. 'We discussed it and I've bought it.' He'd decided to go ahead and hoped that this show of commitment would help change her mind.

'Bought it. But I told your father that we should sell the grapes.'

'I don't want to sell the grapes. I thought you wanted me to make champagne. What has changed?'

'But where will you put it?' Marthe ignored his question. 'That will be a big upheaval in the cellar.' Marthe's face was flushed and her lips pinched.

'I'm not sure yet but it would be sensible to make sure the floor can support the weight. And the building has never been surveyed.'

'It doesn't need surveying,' snapped Marthe, her fingers fidgeting on her lap. 'And what is wrong with sending the grapes out to be pressed? You are trying to run before you can walk.'

He frowned. She was contradicting herself now.

'But—'

'I don't want to talk about it any more today.'

It was even more frustrating when the very next second an alarm went off and Marthe pulled a phone from the pocket of her cardigan. 'You have to go now.' Right on cue a nurse appeared to wheel her back into the house.

As she was wheeled away, she didn't say goodbye or even look back.

'What was that about?' asked Hattie.

Luc sighed. 'I really don't know.' He scowled with disappointment. 'I think she's finding it hard to adjust to change and no longer being in control of the winery. I'll come and talk to her again. I'm sure she'll come round.' His words didn't match the shadowed expression on his face.

Chapter Thirty

Hattie took a slug of wine and then picked up the phone. It was time for tough talking. The wedding was a week and half away, for God's sake, and everything was in place apart from final numbers. This was done with FaceTime. There was no one else around and she had an hour before dinner, so she slipped into the library. She'd texted her cousin earlier and by some miracle Gabby had agreed to speak to her.

Gabby picked up on the second ring.

'Hi, Hattie, how you doing? What's the weather like there? It's done nothing but rain here for the last week.'

Hattie wasn't about to be sidetracked. 'Gabby. Numbers. I need numbers. We need to finalise the menu and the furniture order.' And a dozen other things, although she'd already bought the wedding favours and was hoping that 150 would be enough. The flowers for the table centrepieces had also been ordered on the basis of fifteen tables of ten.

Gabby swallowed and looked stricken. Then Hattie noticed two things: one, that her cousin wasn't wearing any make-up and looked tired and drawn, and two, she was sitting in front of a very familiar-looking picture.

'You're at Mum and Dad's,' Hattie said a touch indignantly. It seemed wrong that her cousin should be spending time with her own mum, which was completely irrational given that she had been deliberately avoiding them for so long. She hadn't wanted them to know how miserable she'd been.

'Yes. I needed … I just wanted a change of scene.'

'Is everything all right? With you and Hugo.'

'Of course,' said Gabby, her voice a little shrill.

'I know I'm nagging but do you have any idea on numbers? The invitations went out ages ago. Do you need a hand chasing people up?' Hattie crossed her fingers out of sight. She had more than enough to do. 'I know people are all a bit last-minute these days but do you think you ought maybe to phone a few people? It's all getting a bit close and I need to finalise orders.' Hattie paused, unnerved by the blank expression on her cousin's face. 'The invitations did all go out, didn't they?' It was such a stupid question, she couldn't believe she'd asked it.

Gabby's throat moved convulsively and she shot an uncertain look at someone beyond the phone screen.

'Is Mum there?' asked Hattie with sudden suspicion.

'Hello, darling,' her mum trilled a little to cheerfully to be natural. What was going on?

'Hi, Mum.'

'Gabby and I were just having a little chat.' Hattie's mum moved in front of the screen and sat down next to Gabby, taking her hand.

Hattie narrowed her eyes and a sense of unease gripped her. 'What's wrong? Have you and Hugo split up? Has he changed his mind?'

Gabby gave a very weak laugh and shook her head. 'No, nothing like that.'

'But something,' pressed Hattie.

Gabby's face began to crumple.

'It's all right, love,' said Hattie's mum, putting an arm around her niece. 'Come on. This is your wedding. You have to do what you want to do.'

With a small sigh of gratitude, Hattie rubbed at the knot of tension at the back of her neck. Thank God for Mum, she would help get some decisions made.

Gabby nodded and wiped her eyes with the tissue Hattie's mum handed to her.

'Thing is, Hats,' she sighed and looked at her aunt for reassurance, 'I'm just really nervous. I never wanted a big fancy wedding. It's Daddy that wants it. And Mummy. I just wanted family and close friends. He's invited loads of business bigwigs and their smart wives, and Mummy all her charity lunch friends. It's got out of control. Daddy wants it to be the wedding of all weddings, to show everyone that he's made it, and I can't tell him now that I just want a small intimate celebration. That's why Hugo and I decided on the register office wedding in the first place. But then Daddy got hold of things and decided we needed a big party afterwards and another ceremony and it's just snowballed. I'm not sure I even want to get married now.'

Hattie felt sick. How could she have not seen this? Now she felt awful for badgering her cousin and, less charitably, a little bit irritated. Actually, a whole lot irritated.

'Oh my God, Gabby. Why didn't you say anything?'

'Partly because it's impossible to say anything to Daddy because he's so bloody excited about the idea and then he was so pleased with himself for coming up with something for you...' Gabby trailed off.

'Coming up with something for me to do,' Hattie said woodenly.

'Playing to your strengths, darling,' said her mum, in her motherly placating way, which was no consolation whatsoever, and then she disappeared out of view.

'You have been doing a brilliant job, Hats. It's just...'

Hattie slumped in her chair. 'So what do you want to do? Call off the celebration over here?' This gig had always been too good to be true.

'No! No! I can't do that to Daddy. It will be fine. Sorry, pre-wedding jitters, that's all. I'll chase up the numbers tomorrow, I promise.'

'Great,' said Hattie, relieved to hear it.

'I've got something else to tell you.'

What now? Hattie steeled herself, giving her cousin a patient smile although she was about ready to throttle her.

'I've changed my mind about the colour of the flowers. I don't think we need the pink roses as well. Can we just stick with the white ones?'

Hattie laughed; that was a small amendment. The florist would only buy the flowers a day or so before the wedding. They needed advance notice to ensure they had enough people to make the floral arrangements on the day before or on the day of the wedding.

'That's fine. I'm sure I can sort that out.' She'd better not let her cousin know how easy that would be, she'd be changing her mind over and over.

'And I've changed my mind about the wedding cake. I don't think a sponge is going to be special enough.'

'Okay.' Hattie didn't let her dismay show. There was so little time now. Then she thought of the *croquembouche* Nina had made. 'I've got an idea. I'll text you some pictures, see what you think.'

'Hats, you're so much easier to deal with. I wish Daddy was as easy.' Gabby winced. 'You know what he's like. He won't listen. He'll just think I'm worried about him spending too much money. He's so determined to give me a "proper" wedding because he and Mum didn't have two beans to rub together when they got married. And Mummy is so excited.'

Her uncle was a man who killed with kindness and didn't listen. He wasn't a bully, just so jolly and determined to make everyone around him happy that he didn't believe that he couldn't, and wouldn't take no for an answer.

'I'm so worried that he's wasting his money.'

'His money isn't going to waste, I promise you.' To make her cousin feel better, Hattie proceeded to tell her all about Luc's champagne ambitions and how the money was going to help. 'Honestly, he's so driven and determined,' she finished, realising she'd been talking about Luc for a solid five minutes.

'The complete opposite of Chris, then,' said Gabby.

There was a knock at the door and Luc peeped around it holding up a bottle of wine to refresh her glass. Hattie immediately brightened at the sight of him – how could she not? – and then panicked, not wanting him to hear what her mother might say next. But it was too late, he was advancing into the room holding out the bottle.

Then as if all the gods of sod's law had lined up to deliver their very best, Gabby suddenly said out of the blue, 'Oh my God, Hattie! Luc Brémont is fit! I've just looked him up on my laptop.'

'Oh my,' said her mum, peering sideways off screen. 'He's very handsome.'

Hattie focused on the screen with sudden intensity. She was NOT going to look at Luc.

'Are you sleeping with him?' asked Gabby in a high-pitched squeak. 'He's lush.'

Oh God, could this get any worse?

Luc was grinning from ear to ear. Of course he was.

'Er hello. My mother is sitting right beside you. I'm not sure she needs the details of my sex life.'

'Oh darling.' Her mum gave an exasperated sniff.

'So you are,' pressed Gabby. 'Good for you.'

Luc looked at Hattie for a couple of seconds and then he sauntered round the desk to stand beside her. There was time for her to snatch up her phone and turn away but for some reason she sat there and let him hand her the glass and appear on the screen of the phone that was propped up on the desk in front of her.

'Thank you,' he said and lifted his glass in a toast to them.

Part of Hattie wanted to curl up and die, but funnily enough a much larger part wanted to say, 'Hey yes! Isn't he gorgeous? And hell yes, I'm sleeping with him.' But her mum and Gabby's wider than saucer eyes were more than enough for her.

'This is Luc,' she said. 'Luc, meet my mum and my cousin, the bride, Gabby.'

'*Bonsoir*. I'm very pleased to meet you and I shall look forward to meeting you in person. You are both well?'

They both nodded vigorously, like a pair of nodding dogs in the back of a car.

Dear God, Hattie wanted to shut her eyes. Her mum was

positively swooning and, even more inappropriately, Gabby was beaming with unseemly interest.

'Hello, how nice to meet you,' said Hattie's mum, her vowels suddenly a lot richer.

'We're so looking forward to coming to the château. Hattie tells us it's beautiful,' said Gabby, suddenly reverting to her usual self-assured, confident self.

'It is and we're looking forward to having your wedding here. Hattie has some wonderful ideas. She's so talented.'

Hattie glanced round at Luc in surprise and found pride on his face.

'She's going to do a wonderful job for you. There is nothing for you to worry about. You must be very proud of your daughter, Mrs...' Hattie wanted to laugh; they were sleeping together and he had forgotten her surname. If ever that was a sign that they were having a no-strings-attached thing, that was it.

'Carter-Jones,' she whispered under her breath but Luc moved on seamlessly. 'She has a genius for organisation. It will be a wonderful arrangement and I can't wait to meet you properly.'

Hattie's mum and Gabby both smiled beatifically, completely charmed by Luc.

'I'll speak to the florist tomorrow,' said Hattie, interrupting the love-in to break the Brémont spell.

'Thank you, Hattie, you're the best,' said Gabby with a sappy smile.

'Mm,' she replied, anxious to wind the call up and making a mental note to avoid speaking to her mum for a few days. She could do without the Spanish Inquisition. Mum would ask those questions she didn't want to answer. 'Do you like him? How long have you been seeing him? (Hattie didn't think 'every day since I've been here' would cut it – what her mum would want to know was how long they'd been sleeping together and whether it was serious.)

'Lovely to meet you,' said Luc.

'Speak soon,' said Hattie, reaching to terminate the call. She grabbed her wine and took a swig.

'They seem nice,' said Luc.

'How can you possibly say that?' Hattie scoffed. 'On such brief acquaintance.'

Luc shrugged. 'They're like you. You're a close family.'

Hattie was about to deny it. She'd only seen her family a handful of times in the last year but then she realised that keeping her distance hadn't diluted their feelings for her or vice versa and it heightened her guilt about deliberately shutting them out. Had she done it for self-preservation or so they wouldn't see what was going on?

'They care about you.'

Her guilt redoubled because she knew Luc didn't have this from his own family. She rose and put her arms around him. 'I know,' she said softly. 'I'm very lucky.'

'Not lucky. You deserve it.'

She pulled away, appalled. 'And you don't?' She leaned in and kissed his mouth, his cheek, his neck. 'Never think that. Never. They don't deserve to have a son as wonderful as you.'

He raised a hand to her face. 'I'm not sure they would even think that.'

'Their loss, Luc,' she said, reaching up to brush the curl from his forehead. 'Their loss.'

For a moment they stood, knee to knee, toe to toe, in silent contemplation of each other. Like a pair of batteries drawing strength from one another.

Luc cupped her face. 'Thank you, Hattie. Thank you.'

Then he kissed her, a gentle reverent kiss that almost broke her heart. The boy that didn't believe he deserved to be loved.

Unable to help herself, Hattie wrapped her arms around him and kissed him back, pouring her heart and so much more into the kiss, so that he would know he was cherished, he was loved, he was cared for.

When he answered the kiss, his arms coming around her, holding her in a gentle embrace, the sort of embrace that she could either step back from or step deeper into, she knew that she loved this man. This time it didn't strike her like a bolt of lightning; it was more like a bud unfurling in her heart, a bright flower unfolding in sunshine, breathing life into the desert.

They stood there together, arms around each other, soaking in the moment. Hattie closed her eyes. This wasn't sensible, it was very unsensible. The very opposite of sensible. She wasn't supposed to fall in love with Luc Brémont. She never wanted to be trapped again.

Luc kissed her and she looked up into his eyes, her heart flooding with warmth and unspoken joy. This wasn't supposed to happen. But even though the words echoed in her head, a hopeless warning that no part of her was taking any notice of, she melted into the kiss and abandoned all thoughts of being sensible. That could wait until tomorrow. Tonight, she couldn't resist the siren call of his kisses, the heat of his body and the wonder of being with him.

Chapter Thirty-One

'What do you think about making a *croquembouche*?' said Hattie, waltzing into the kitchen the following morning, closely followed by Luc.

'You mean a traditional French wedding cake made from a pyramid of choux pastry buns?' asked Fliss with a pert smile.

'Show-off,' said Hattie.

'Great – and funnily enough, Solange and I were discussing that very thing yesterday. We wondered if she might like a *croquembouche*.'

'Great minds,' said Hattie. 'I texted her and sent a picture of an example.'

'You have, have you? Just as well some of us are ahead of the game.' Fliss cast a conspiratorial smirk towards Solange, who was leaning on the counter. 'We were thinking limoncello-cream-filled choux buns, decorated with sugared roses and stuck together with white chocolate.'

Luc, who had a casual hand on Hattie's shoulder, groaned. 'That sounds marvellous to me.'

'You always did have a sweet tooth. I remember when I

used to make Breton salted sables. You and Alphonse would have eaten a whole batch in one sitting if I'd let you.'

'They were very good,' said Luc, pouring them both a cup of coffee.

'Oh and look. A text from Gabby.' Hattie waved her phone.

'She'd already said yes, hadn't she?' Fliss folded her arms. 'Good job we think can make one.'

'Apparently the secret is to make sure your choux pastry isn't too soggy,' said Hattie archly.

'If you're not careful, you can make it, Miss Smart Arse,' said Fliss.

Hattie snorted. Solange smiled at the pair of them. 'I don't think you'd let her.' Solange's gentle voice held laughter in it. 'You wouldn't want to forgo the treat of making it yourself.'

'You're so right, Solange,' said Fliss, putting an arm around the older woman. 'As long as we do it together.'

'But of course. You're not leaving me out.' Solange put her hands on her slim hips in mock indignation.

Hattie and Lux exchanged a private smile. The transformation in Solange was quite something. The silent ghost that had drifted around the house had long gone.

'It's always a joy when the *croquembouche* comes out, everyone gasps in appreciation.' Solange looked round at the three of them, her face brimming with happiness. 'Your guests are going to have a wonderful day now that the château has come back to life.'

'Our guests,' said Hattie. 'You've done as much as anyone to put the shine back.'

Solange nodded with a touch of satisfaction. 'I can't wait. To see their happy faces. For them to enjoy the hospitality. This house deserves to be full of people, enjoying each other's company. Marthe used to throw the most wonderful parties when her husband was alive.'

'I have to admit,' said Luc, 'I'm getting excited at the prospect. Solange is right, the house needs to be used the way it should be. I've had it to myself for so long, I'd forgotten. It needs to be shown off, enjoyed and shared. It wasn't built to be used by one person or one family. It was built to entertain.'

'And once we have final numbers, it will make things a lot easier,' said Fliss with a glare at Hattie.

'Gabby has promised them today.'

'About bloody time,' grumbled Fliss.

When Hattie disappeared to go and update her spreadsheet and Solange went to collect something from the dining room, Luc deliberately loitered for a minute.

'Do you want a cup of coffee, Fliss?' he asked pouring himself another one.

'Yes, please. Black. I live on the stuff.'

'Like Alphonse. You're well suited,' he said with a laugh, as he handed her a small cup.

'Me and Alphonse?' Her voice peaked in pitch.

'You do know you've turned his head,' said Luc.

'Don't be ridiculous,' said Fliss, giving him a sharp look. 'He never has anything nice to say to me.'

'I've known Alphonse a very long time. He's shy with women.' Luc crossed his fingers in his pocket and hoped that he wouldn't be damned for all time for the outrageous lie.

'He's not shy, he's just rude,' replied Fliss, tossing her hair over her shoulder.

'That's because he doesn't know what to say to you. To be

honest … well, I've never seen him quite like this with anyone.'

Fliss turned, hand on hip. 'Really?' she sneered.

'Oh yes,' said Luc, widening his eyes in what he hoped was earnest reassurance.

'Hmm,' said Fliss, wiping her hands on a tea towel.

'He's been trying to summon up the courage to invite you out for a date.'

'He has?' Fliss did seem faintly interested.

'Yes, even suggested a double date with me and Hattie. We're going to Marc's, one of the village bars, tomorrow night. Of course, I didn't want to upset his feelings and say that someone like you wouldn't find him attractive.'

'Why wouldn't I?' snapped Fliss.

Luc had no answer for this, so just raised his hands, palms up.

'Maybe I will go with you.' She shrugged. 'Make him feel better.'

Luc nodded, feeling that his plan had backfired and all he'd done was confirm that Fliss wasn't interested at all in Alphonse. Maybe, in this case, his friend was destined for unrequited love.

'In the meantime, some of us are busy. I need to go and pick some herbs.' As she left the kitchen by the patio doors, Solange walked in carrying two large platters which he immediately relieved her of. 'Where did you find these?' he asked. 'I haven't seen them since I was a kid.'

'I saw Marthe this morning and she reminded me where to find some of the china we used to use when we were entertaining. These were on the top shelf at the back of the cupboard in the dining room. They will be perfect for both weddings.' She paused and levelled a look at him.

'Hattie is very nice. She suits you.' Clearly she'd overheard his conversation with Fliss.

'She is,' agreed Luc, smiling to himself, deliberately not giving Solange the information she wanted.

'You could do a lot worse.' Solange studied him and he wanted to turn away from her motherly scrutiny.

'I could,' he agreed again, knowing she had something she wanted to say.

Solange huffed and began plucking at the leaves on a plant on the sill with a little more force than was needed. 'Don't get too tied up in the vineyard, Luc. I know you want to prove something to your father but there is more to life than making wine. Marthe will tell you that. After Henri died, she could have married again but instead she chose to dedicate her life to the vines until she finally relinquished control to your father. I know that she regrets it.'

'Does she?' Luc couldn't believe that. 'She's never said.'

'She's proud of what she achieved and wants to set a good example. Don't get me wrong, she still wants Brémont champagne to be made, but not at the expense of happiness. Contrary to what Yvette thinks, Marthe is very happy to have shed the burden of this place. It is a lot for one person to bear and she bore it for a very long time.'

Luc remembered past summers. Marthe up been up at dawn most days and out in the vineyard until dusk. Solange had been as much of a mother to him during those summer days.

'Ah, Fliss, you found the basil,' said Solange, as the other woman returned with a fistful of greenery.

'That herb garden is heaven. I'm so jealous.'

As the little garden beyond the patio was Solange's pride and joy, Fliss had said exactly the right thing.

Luc left them weighing up the benefits of basil over tarragon and popped into see Hattie before he went down to the vineyard.

She was tapping away at her laptop and he very nearly left her to it, but the curve of her neck under her high ponytail was too enticing.

'I know you're standing there,' said Hattie without lifting her fingers from the keys or looking at him.

'Just admiring the view,' he said.

She laughed. 'Are all Frenchmen this smooth?'

'No, just me. I came to tell you that I sowed the seed with Fliss. About Alphonse.' Well, he'd tried. He wasn't sure that the ground was that fertile. 'I'm pretty sure she'll come with us to the bar in the village, once she knows. But it would be helpful if you came down to the cellar tomorrow at lunchtime and invited Alphonse.'

He perched on the little table next to her.

'Okay,' said Hattie. 'I can do that. Tell him Fliss fancies him, which is sort of the truth. She does find him attractive.' Hattie giggled. 'More than you, apparently.'

'More than me? What?'

'She thinks he's more attractive than you.' Hattie cocked her head to look up at him, all innocence. The quick amusement and challenge in her teasing smile made his pulse kick up a notch.

'And what do you think?' he asked, lowering his voice, keeping his gaze on her face.

Her eyes twinkled for a second and then she grinned. 'Don't you know?'

'I might need a touch of reassurance.' He lowered his voice.

She laughed up at him, her brown eyes, full of amber flecks, dancing like leaves in autumn. 'Luc Brémont. You. Do not.

Need any kind of reassurance. You were born with super-power flirting genes.'

He grinned at her. 'But of course.'

It was tempting to tease her some more but he did want to help Alphonse.

'I am being serious. I think Fliss likes him more than she's letting on.'

'I hope you're right. What if it all goes wrong?' Hattie looked genuinely concerned.

'Where's the romance in your soul?' He lifted her chin and kissed her on the mouth.

'I'm too sensible to be romantic,' she said, putting on her best prim face.

He kissed her again, his lips toying with hers before he felt her mouth soften beneath his.

'I don't believe that, Hattie.' His hand skimmed her jaw and he whispered against her mouth, 'I don't think anyone has looked after you properly,' before deepening the kiss and sliding a hand along her collarbone.

When they pulled apart, she looked up at him, pink and a little dazed. Adorable – and he couldn't help a sharp tug of possessive satisfaction. He did enjoy disconcerting her.

He kissed her quickly. 'And I don't think you're sensible. Not at all.'

'Luc Brémont, you're a very bad influence.'

'I know,' he said, touched her lips with his fingers and left the room before she could have the last word.

Chapter Thirty-Two

L ater that afternoon Hattie set off down to the vineyard on her mission and found Alphonse sitting on the wooden bench in front of the cellars, scrolling through his phone. There was no sign of Luc.

'Hi, Alphonse. How are you today?'

'*Bonjour*, Hattie,' called Alphonse. 'Luc has gone into Hautvillers, I'm afraid.'

'No problem.' She knew that because he'd told her just before he left. 'I just wanted to get some fresh air. It's a beautiful day.'

'It is.' Alphonse lapsed into silence and went back to his phone.

'Are you looking forward to the wedding?' she asked, cursing at her inanity.

He shrugged. 'It will be good for *Maman* to get Yvette off her hands.'

'She's enjoying Fliss's company.' Even to her that sounded a lame way of introducing the subject.

'Mm,' said Alphonse. Hattie's heart sank. She was rubbish

at this sort of thing and he wasn't the most talkative of people – unless he was talking to Fliss. It was the lightbulb prod she needed. They were perfect for each other.

'I don't suppose you'd come out for a drink with us this evening.'

Alphonse looked up.

'With me, Luc and Fliss,' she added.

'I could. *Pourquoi?*' He tilted his head to one side, clearly trying to work something out.

She made her sigh theatrically heavy. 'I'm not very good at this.' She stared up at the sky for a moment, hamming it up, as if she were considering things. 'Alphonse, she really likes you – I've never seen her like this before.' Which wasn't really a lie because she didn't know Fliss that well.

It was subtle but she saw it, a slight lift of his shoulders, a straightening of his spine, a tilt of his chin. It wasn't exactly the preen of a peacock, more the puff of a pigeon, but it was enough to make her plough on.

'But –' Hattie put on her sad face '– she's convinced you can't stand her. If you could just perhaps be friendly, it would make her feel so much better.' She was no actress – was she overdoing this?

'But … she…' Alphonse checked himself. 'Has a very sharp tongue.'

Hattie waved his objection away with a waft of her hand. 'That's Fliss. She has four brothers. She's not being rude to you.' Now what did she say? She wished she'd planned this better.

'Actually,' she said suddenly, 'It's a sign of affection.' Hattie beamed at him, wondering at the same time if any second she might descend straight to hell for her outrageous lies. Fliss's tongue was sharper than her favourite knives. It didn't matter who you were.

'We're going to Marc's at six o'clock. Luc is driving us down. See you then?'

'Mm,' said Alphonse, nodding. 'Why not?' He scratched at his bristled chin. 'Six o'clock, you say.' She could almost see the cogs turning in his head.

Hattie nodded. Excitement fluttered in her stomach. She'd done it and he seemed to buy it. Proud of herself, she said, before he could ask her any questions or change his mind, 'See you later, Alphonse.'

She almost skipped back to the château. She couldn't wait to tell Luc it was all set up.

'I think I'm going to wear my new dress this evening,' announced Hattie when Fliss came into the library later that afternoon.

'Sorry? I brought you some new *macarons* to try. What do you think?' Fliss placed a plate of pretty shiny discs in front of her.

'So dainty. Gorgeous,' said Hattie, wondering how to reintroduce the subject of the evening's apparel. Although if Alphonse did like Fliss he wasn't going to care if she was in her usual cargo pants and T-shirt.

'Taste them. Honestly, Solange is a genius. I always thought *macarons* were overrated. But these …' She popped one in her mouth and waited expectantly for Hattie to do the same.

Hattie took one, slightly puzzled because she'd tried Fliss and Solange's *macarons* before. Fliss seemed to be dancing about a bit on the spot. 'Delicious.'

Fliss perched on the edge of the desk, fiddling with one of

the little boxes on the top. She fixed Hattie with an intense stare. 'This place would make a fabulous venue for weddings, anniversaries, special events. Solange barely has anything to do and ... well, I'd love to set up a business here. And you ... you're brilliant at organisation. I was thinking maybe ... well, maybe we could put a proposal together to Luc. For us to run the place. What do you think? Wouldn't you love to stay here?' Fliss's face shone with enthusiasm, her eyes starry with dreams.

Hattie stared at her. Stay here? She'd never even considered it. 'Fliss, I hate to say this but it's Luc's home. He's not interested in people getting married here, he wants to make champagne without the distractions.'

Fliss slapped her hand on the desk. 'Stupid me. That's the exciting bit. I forgot to say. We could make the venue famous for its champagne. There would be so many marketing opportunities. Luc could even consider a special wedding brand that's exclusive to the bridal party...' She bobbed up like a startled meerkat, her ideas running away with her. 'And it would be exclusive to them in the future. Only previous bridal parties who had been to the château can buy it. And only they can buy it in the future. I just thought of that. I bet Luc would go for it. It's not as if it would impact on the vineyard. And it would bring in income that they can invest.'

Hattie stared at Fliss. What had happened to her? Fliss was normally as sensible and practical as she was.

'You want to stay here?' What had brought this on?

'Hell, yes. I'd love to. I suppose this is my way of thinking of a way to make it happen. I love it here. I love working in that kitchen. I feel so inspired and ... I don't know ... it feels like home.'

'But...' This wasn't real life, it was an interlude. A long

holiday. Hattie had never even thought about the possibility of staying. Living abroad was one of those pipe dreams – normal people didn't give up their jobs and everything familiar. It happened in films and books and those *A Place in the Sun* type telly programmes. Yes, it was nice here but it wasn't real life. People had roles, responsibilities – they had ... well, responsibilities. Sensible people did not up and move to another country on a whim.

'Think about it, Hattie. I need to go. I've got another batch in the oven. Laters.' And with that she disappeared, leaving the plate of pale pink *macarons* in her wake.

Hattie shook her head, staring at the closed door. As if she could stay here. What a ludicrous idea.

'Wow! You look nice,' said Hattie when she came downstairs to find Fliss in an expensive-looking white linen sleeveless dress which accentuated her slim boyish figure. The three-inch spiked heels made her tanned legs look endless and several delicate silver bracelets emphasised long, slender arms. She'd arranged her straight blonde hair in an intricate braid down her back, leaving delicate tendrils curling around her face. With her masculine square-jawed face, no one would ever describe Fliss as pretty, but she was extremely striking, especially with the expertly applied make-up that drew attention to her bright blue eyes and her high cheekbones. She looked as if she'd stepped off the cover of *Vogue*.

Fliss shrugged casually, lifting her tanned swimmer's shoulders. 'I like dressing up every now and then, especially if there's a good reason for it.' She gave a wicked grin. 'I wanted to make sure Alphonse knows he's punching. Are we set?'

'Yes, Luc is just bringing the car round.'

At the toot of a horn, they went outside to the front of the château and got into the convertible.

'You look ... nice,' said Luc, his eyes widening in quick appreciation which Hattie didn't feel the least bit jealous of. In fact, she was only surprised his tongue wasn't hanging out. Fliss looked stunning.

Fliss rolled her eyes. 'Honestly, you two. It sounds as if I normally look like the back of a bus. I thought I might as well give Alphonse plenty to think about. I'd planned to take the sofly, softly approach and reel him in slowly but since you two have decided to stick your oar in, I'm moving my agenda forward and I'm going in for the kill.'

Hattie and Luc gave each other a sideways glance and Fliss roared with laughter. 'I know exactly what the pair of you are up to. Luc, you have the subtlety of a dead fish. And Hattie, you couldn't be more transparent if you were made of glass.'

'I don't know what you mean,' said Luc, doing his best to look innocent, giving Hattie's hand a surreptitious squeeze.

'Give me a break, guys. It's the old Beatrice and Benedick set-up. Isn't he "well nigh dead for me"?' She raised one elegantly arched brow and laughed. 'Why do you think I want to stay, Hattie?'

'For Alphonse?'

'He's one of the reasons.'

'You want to stay?' Luc asked Fliss, giving Hattie a questioning glance.

'Yes, I have a proposal but we'll talk about it later. So what was the plan, were you two going to abandon me and Alphonse in the café?'

'There was no plan,' said Hattie. 'We were just giving you a nudge. I didn't realise you knew Alphonse liked you.'

'Of course I knew.' Fliss's scorn couldn't have been more

blatant. 'I was just deciding how to bring him to his knees and when I'd make my move.'

Hattie admired Fliss's confidence.

'I think I might be starting to feel a bit sorry for him,' said Luc, giving Hattie's hand another squeeze.

Fliss just grinned and settled back into her seat in the back, and in the wing mirror, Hattie noted that her smile was smug as a cat's after it had swallowed a dozen canaries.

Luc pulled up outside the café and Hattie decided he couldn't have planned things better. Alphonse was already there, seated at one of the roadside tables, so he got an eyeful of Fliss's shapely legs as she eased herself, with remarkable poise, from the back of the car. From the expression on his face, Hattie guessed he'd come close to swallowing his tongue. He stood up abruptly and knocked over his own chair and stared at Fliss as she sauntered towards him, a deliberate sway in her hips.

'Alphonse, *bonsoir*,' she said and went up to him and kissed him on the lips, before picking up the fallen chair and sitting down.

'And that's how it's done,' murmured Luc in Hattie's ear. 'She's terrifying.'

Alphonse had gone pink and stood quite still, staring at Fliss as she crossed her legs and reached forward to pick up the bottle of wine. She examined the label. 'Chablis?'

'I ... I ... um ... yes ... Chablis.'

Fliss helped herself to one of the four glasses sitting on the table and poured herself some wine.

'Nice, very nice.' She turned to Alphonse after she'd taken a good sniff and sip. 'You have excellent taste.' She crossed her legs again. He seemed mesmerised by them but then he pulled himself together and sat down, although Hattie noticed, with great amusement, that when he picked up his glass he took quite a slug of wine. Poor man didn't know what had hit him.

Luc poured wine for himself and Hattie. 'So, Hattie? What can you taste?'

With a long-suffering sigh, she stuck her nose in the glass and... 'Pear. I can taste pear. And...' No? Really? But what the heck – 'Chalk?'

Luc clapped her on the back. 'Excellent.'

'But,' said Fliss, 'do you like it? That's always the most important thing. Life is too short to drink wine you don't.'

Hattie took another sip of the crisp, dry wine. 'I do like it. I like it a lot.'

'You have expensive taste, but that's no bad thing,' said Alphonse, lifting his glass and holding it up to the light. 'This would taste good with a *poulet à l'estragon*, I think.' He turned to Fliss.

She smiled at him, a genuine smile for once, without sarcasm, impatience or superiority. 'Yes. It would. I adore the flavour of tarragon, especially with chicken.'

'I have a very good recipe at home,' said Alphonse.

'Which you're going to share with me,' observed Fliss.

'But of course.' He grinned.

'They're a perfect match,' murmured Hattie as the two of them began discussing their favourite herbs and the best use of them. The words came with a quick pang of envy. Once upon a time she thought she'd found her perfect match. She and Chris had been the best of friends, they'd shared the same opinions, enjoyed the same things, had so much in common. Where had it all gone wrong?

Surreptitiously she studied Luc. There was no denying she'd fallen for him big time – who wouldn't? – but she wasn't kidding herself. This was just a holiday romance.

Chapter Thirty-Three

Moonlight flooded in through the open shutters, casting long lines of silver between dark shadows. After the bright noise of the day and the lively conversation of the bar earlier in the evening, the quiet stillness of the night resounded in the room. Her body lay draped over Luc, satisfied after making love.

'You could stay, you know,' said Luc, his fingers idly stroking her shoulder.

The words tumbled out like an unexpected starburst lighting up the sky, sending Hattie's emotions scattering in a dozen different directions.

'Stay?' Her stomach tightened and her throat constricted with sudden strain.

'Stay here at the château.'

The offer, request, invitation – she couldn't decide which – held her fast in a grip of utter indecision. What to say? What to do? What to feel? What to respond?

Caught up in a whirl of conflicting emotions, she was

unable to say anything. Her heart thudded so hard that blood hammered at every pulse point.

'If you wanted to,' Luc continued stroking her shoulder, as if he were soothing a frightened animal, as if he knew that 'you could stay' had launched a grenade into her serene denial of the way things were developing.

Luc waited and she felt the silence heavy in the room. The weight of expectation on her.

'I can't stay,' she finally said. 'I have to go back.'

'Why?' He turned and propped himself on his elbow so that he could look at her face in the silver strobe of moonlight.

Because she was scared.

'I love you and I think you might love me.'

The quiet declaration punched her, releasing a flood of emotion. She did love him but was love enough?

'I know you had a bad relationship before but I'm not him.'

'No, you're not.' He really wasn't. But she was still her. That woman tied and trapped with obligations that her conscience wouldn't let her shake off. She couldn't tell him she loved him, it would make it even harder to leave, so instead she asked, 'What would I do?'

The quick flare of pain in Luc's eyes made her feel guilty. But it also strengthened her resolve. She couldn't be responsible for someone's happiness, not again.

'You could set up a wedding business here.'

'Luc, you don't want that. Remember you want to make champagne.'

'Originally, yes, because I thought it would impact me, take me away from my work. But it doesn't and also, I've seen how the house has become a home again. It deserves to shine too and be shared with people.'

He made it sound so simple. But she'd done that once before. Given everything up and then she'd been trapped.

'I … I just can't. I don't live here. This is just temporary. It's not real life.' The excuses came tumbling out, as if forced out by the tight fist gripping her diaphragm.

'Do you want to?' he asked in a soft voice that sent a tiny shiver down her back. The voice of temptation.

The question floored her. Want? What did that have to do with anything? This had been a break, a holiday from real life. She couldn't stay here for ever.

'I mean it would be lovely. But … I –' she shook her head '– I just can't.'

'Not even to try? For me?'

For him. She closed her eyes. It would be so easy to say yes. For him, but what about her? Could she do it again? Invest her whole life in one other person. End up being responsible for another person's happiness. The weight of it was already unbearable – could she do it twice over?

Luc was silent and she knew she'd hurt him. He was offering her so much and she couldn't give him anything back.

'Luc, this … this is lovely but there was always an end— I can't just pack up my life and start again for … for a man.'

'For me, you mean.'

'Not you personally, no, but I've done it before. What if it didn't work out? I'd be stranded in France with nothing.'

'But what if it did work,' he said, stubbornly.

'I can't be reliant on you.'

'I'm not asking you to be reliant on me. You're your own person. We could be a team.'

Something twisted hard and sharp in her stomach. It would be so tempting to stay here. She loved it. She loved Luc.

'Luc,' she said gently. 'I can't.'

. . .

Neither of them slept well and when, at five, Hattie finally faced the fact that she wasn't going back to sleep she carefully pulled back the sheet so as not to disturb Luc.

'I'm awake,' he said.

'Sorry.' She sat on the edge of the bed and turned to look at him. The sheets were pushed down to his waist and her eyes roved over his body, regret punching through her. A longing to run her fingers across his chest and down to his waist spiked through her, a match strike to lust. One thing, for sure, was that she'd never get enough of him.

His lips curved in a slow smile, reading her so well, and he reached for her, catching her hand and tugging her down. He rubbed his nose against hers. 'There's no reason why we can't make the most of the time we have left. I respect your wishes, Hattie. Let's not fall out.'

And that right there was one of the reasons she'd loved him. His generosity of spirit and open, fun-loving attitude to life. This had been a magical interlude, and she should enjoy every second until she finally said goodbye. With a sudden jolt she realised that after the wedding there was no reason for her to be here any longer. The hollow feeling in her stomach floored her. Instead she let herself be distracted, burying herself in his kiss, and when she finally let go, she held on to him tight. While she could, she would hold him close. She needed to bank a lot of memories.

They both fell asleep and when they woke again it was nearly eight, which was a lot more civilised. Luc took a quick shower, pulled on his jersey boxers and sat on the edge of the bed. There were still drops of water on his shoulders and Hattie gave in to the quick temptation to kiss them away, reflecting how easy and confident she felt with her nudity around Luc.

He turned and smiled at her. 'Some of us need to go and do some work.'

'I know,' she said, 'but I couldn't resist.'

'It's a problem I frequently encounter.'

She gave him a teasing nudge. 'Of course you do. You'll be replacing me in no time.' It was supposed to be light-hearted banter, to hide her true feelings. 'I mean, you were sleeping with Marine before me.' It was supposed to be a light dig but as soon as she said it, she realised she was punishing him. She wished she could take it back.

He sat bolt upright, his back suddenly rigid.

'I did not sleep with Marine. I'm not like that.' His eyes flashed with anger. 'I don't go from one woman to the next so easily.'

'Sorry,' said Hattie, realising that she'd given in to her insecurity and jealousy. Luc hadn't deserved that comment.

'She slept in a different bedroom. Why would you assume I slept with her?'

'She seemed very…' Hattie squirmed with mortification.

'She wanted to. She made that clear. But I'm not some dog that eats every plateful put in front of him. I thought you knew that.'

Hattie blushed bright red, realising she'd seriously hurt his feelings. 'I'm sorry. I… I…'

Luc had retreated, folding his arms across his chest. His blue eyes had darkened and his jawline was taut with tension. She didn't dare touch him.

'Luc, I'm sorry.'

'Sex is about quality, not quantity,' he said in a flat voice as if he were talking through clenched teeth. 'And caring that your partner has as good a time as you do. I'm quite choosy about who I go to bed with.'

Hattie wanted to cry. She'd got it so wrong. She huffed out a breath.

'And for your information, Hattie, no one's going to replace you. Not for a very long time. If ever.'

Chapter Thirty-Four

There were walks of shame and then there was Fliss's deliberately cocky barefoot saunter into the kitchen the next morning, carrying her shoes and wearing a bright-eyed smile. The epitome of shameless.

'What they say about Frenchmen being the best lovers – it's all true,' she said, sinking onto one of the bar stools. 'Although I guess I don't need to tell you that.'

'Mmm,' said Hattie, non-committal. This was possibly absolutely the last thing she wanted to talk about this morning. She continued to tie ribbons around the necks of jam-jars, giving them all her attention. Just yesterday she'd been so excited to show Yvette her plans for the decoration of the orchard.

'I had a good night, thanks,' said Fliss, giving Hattie a sharp look.

'Sorry, miles away. How was your night?'

Fliss beamed. 'The best. That man knows his way around a female body and he is all man. Every last inch of him.'

Hattie blushed on her behalf – that was too much

information – but Fliss, oblivious to her discomfort, sat back and sighed, an uncharacteristically dreamy expression on his face. 'I think I'm in love.'

'Already?' said Hattie, a little shocked. Was Fliss still drunk?

'When you know, you know.'

'Mmm.' She gave a brief grunt. Why did she have to remember the first moment she laid eyes on Luc and that instant flutter of interest? That attraction that she'd dismissed as infatuation because she'd been too scared to own it. She was hopelessly in love with Luc and she'd made a complete mess of things.

Fliss buzzed about the kitchen, humming to herself.

'How do you fancy poached eggs with hollandaise sauce for breakfast?'

'Not for me, thanks,' said Hattie helping herself to more coffee. She'd probably overdone the caffeine already this morning but lack of sleep made her feel a little punch-drunk and light-headed.

Fliss paused. 'Are you okay?'

'Fine.' The clipped tone was her mistake and Fliss gave her a sharp look.

'Did Luc talk to you?'

'What about?' asked Hattie, a touch warily, wrapping both hands around the warming body of the cup. For some reason she felt cold down to her bones.

'About running the château as an events business. We'd make an awesome team.'

Hattie pursed her lips.

'Oh no, you didn't. You said no, didn't you? Why?' Fliss put her hands on her hips.

'It's okay.' Hattie said quickly, feeling defensive. 'You can still run the kitchen.'

'But I haven't got your amazing organisational skills. We're a team, Hats. And your decorative ideas complement my cooking perfectly. We could be the dream team.'

The constriction was back in her throat, strangling her words. 'I … I can't. I have to go back.'

With that she burst into tears, surprising herself more than Fliss, who came to her side and put an arm around her shoulder.

'Hey, hey, Hats. It's okay.' She led her to one of the bar stools and they sat down together.

'Sorry,' sniffed Hattie, trying to wipe her eyes, except the minute she did, a fresh flood poured down. God, she was pathetic.

'What's wrong? You don't need to be upset.'

'I don't know,' sobbed Hattie. Her brain felt too full, with thoughts zinging backwards and forwards like demented bluebottles against a kitchen window. 'I'm … I don't know what to do. I'm so torn. I'd love to stay … but I c-can't.'

Fliss regarded her patiently as Hattie fumbled for a tissue in her jeans pocket. Once she'd blown her nose and stopped crying, Fliss leaned forward and took her hand, giving it a little squeeze.

'Okay. You can't stay, but you want to?'

'Yes, but I can't.'

'Why not?' asked Fliss with millpond calm. 'Give me a list of reasons.'

Hattie stared at her for a long moment as Fliss pulled forward the notebook she used around the kitchen and uncapped the pen she kept in the pocket of her apron. Pen poised, Fliss gave her an unflinching I-mean-business look.

Hattie took a deep breath, which steadied her and reduced the sense of panic.

'Because.'

'Because?'

Hattie screwed up her face and sighed. 'It's a bit more complicated than that.'

'It's the ex, isn't it? asked Fliss. 'The one that messages you all the time.'

Hattie swallowed, thinking of last time. 'When I wasn't there, because I wanted to stay and live in Manchester instead of move in with him, he couldn't cope with the long-distance relationship. He had a breakdown. Couldn't even get out of bed. It was awful. It took months for him to get back on his feet.' Hattie closed her eyes. 'His mental health is…'

Fliss took her hand, rubbing it gently before saying very quietly, 'It's not your responsibility, Hattie.'

Logically Hattie knew that, but if anything happened to Chris, she would never forgive herself.

'But he … he needs my help and support. I can't turn my back on him. I have to go back, even though it will be a platonic relationship. I owe it to him.'

Fliss put her pen down. 'You're not going to like what I say here but have you considered that you are part of the problem?'

'Me!' It was as if she'd been punched in the stomach. The unwelcome observation sat there as heavy as undigested dough.

'This sounds harsh –' Fliss held up her hands as if to disown personal responsibility for the words '– but don't you think you might be a crutch for him? You're an enabler. Enabling him to carry on being reliant on you. Maybe you're not doing him any favours.'

Hattie stared at her. 'You're saying it's my fault.' Ouch, that didn't sit well at all. Was Fliss right?

'No. It's not your fault. But things won't change if you don't do things differently.'

Hattie rubbed her face, trying to make sense of the complicated rush of emotions at war with each other. Guilt rubbed up against anger, regret fought with disappointment, while honesty flared up at self-awareness. It was hard to pick her way through the confusion.

Defensive now, she said, 'I'm not trying to make out I'm some kind of saint and the only person that can save him, but there is no one else. He hasn't got anyone else. His mother is completely reliant on him.'

Fliss reached over her and patted her arm. 'He's got himself, Hattie. What if I said Luc needs you?'

Hattie smiled sadly at that one. 'Luc doesn't need me. He's strong enough on his own.' That was one of the reasons she'd fallen in love with him. He knew what he wanted and where he was going. He had a purpose in life. And they would get over each other. Everyone always did.

'So you think he doesn't deserve to be happy.'

'I didn't say that… Please don't make this any harder, Fliss.'

Now Fliss pursed her lips. 'Well, I think you're wrong. I know you're wrong. I hardly know Alphonse, but we're right together and I'm prepared to give it a try because there's nothing worse than not trying.'

'It's different for you, you were looking for a new challenge. This fits with your plans. It completely scuppers mine. I was never meant to be here.'

'I'm being selfish looking out for me and what I want, but sometimes you have to be. Each of us has to be the main character in our own life.'

Chapter Thirty-Five

The next few days Hattie did her best not to show her misery, which was difficult, even though, with the wedding in less than a week, there was a lot to do. Every day she, Fliss and Solange worked in the kitchen preparing as much as could be done in advance. She owed it to the other two to keep up a cheerful front and not let her inner turmoil show. They'd achieved a lot and the two deep chest freezers Hattie had hired were full of profiteroles, canapés, sorbet, frozen mash potato and wild salmon. This morning they were making more canapés.

'Could you pass me the rolling pin?' asked Fliss. 'I'll—'

Her words were drowned by the crash and reverberation of the front door of the château slamming. All three women jumped and Solange dropped the heavy rolling pin on the floor with a clatter.

'What the…' said Fliss.

Hattie, wiping floury hands on her apron – she'd been roped into cutting out the pastry for vol au vents – rushed out into the hall to find Luc sitting on the stairs, trying to tug off his boots and snarling under his breath. He looked sweaty and red-faced. Her heart turned over at the sight of him. Since that last morning she'd left his bedroom, they'd been excessively civil to each other and Hattie hated it. She missed being with him more than she could have thought possible.

She swallowed. 'Are you okay?'

Giving up on his boot, he stamped his foot.

'No, I'm fucking not!' He paused and looked up at her with woebegone eyes. 'Sorry, Hattie – I'm pissed off. Really, really pissed off.'

'What's happened?'

'I went to see Marthe again, I was hoping I might get her to change her mind but she's adamant that we should sell the grapes and I have no idea why. It doesn't make any sense. I've been going over and over it in my head.'

'I'm so sorry, Luc.' Without a second thought, she came to sit down beside him.

'I just don't understand.' He dropped his head into his hands, his elbows propped on his knees.

She had to fight the urge to run her fingers down the tantalising skin on the back of his neck but she couldn't help putting a hand on his arm.

They sat there in silence for a minute until Luc glanced up and gave her a miserable smile.

'Thanks, Hattie.' He sighed heavily.

'I'm really sorry,' she repeated.

'It is what it is.' His mouth twisted. 'But I'm not going to give up. I'm not. I don't know how yet but I will make champagne, even if it's not St Martin champagne. I'll find a—'

He was interrupted by Hattie's phone ringing in her apron pocket. She ignored it, even though she was desperate to answer it. At this stage of wedding planning every call was important.

Luc nudged her. 'Hey, you'd better get that, hadn't you?'

'It's okay.'

'Answer it. I'm fine. Just throwing a tantrum. I'll get over it.' He rubbed a weary hand across his forehead.

Reluctantly she drew out her phone and saw who was calling.

'Hi, Mum.'

'Hattie…' The static silence filled Hattie with foreboding.

'Mum?'

'Oh, Hattie.' Her mum's voice broke on a sob.

'Mum, what is it? What's happened?' Next to her Luc put his hand on hers and at the gesture of solidarity she looked at him. He squeezed her hand, just to let her know he was there. She squeezed it back, surprised by how grateful she was for the reassurance it gave her.

'It's Gabby. She's … she's…'

A chill inside and out settled over Hattie. Saliva gathered in her mouth.

'She's what?'

'She's gone. Her and Hugo, they've gone to Las Vegas. To get married.'

Hattie dropped the phone, her fingers suddenly numb and useless.

Luc picked it up. Hattie's mum's voice was so loud, Hattie could hear her calling her name.

'It's Luc here,' he said. 'Hattie's a bit shocked.'

That was an understatement and a half. Hattie's teeth had started chattering for some bizarre reason.

'Oh, bless her. God, it's awful. My brother-in-law has got his secretary phoning and emailing everyone to cancel the wedding. He's cancelling the train and the flights. Can you tell her?'

Luc looked at Hattie. 'I'll tell her. Perhaps she'll give you a call in a little while.'

'Tell her I love her and how sorry we are. I'll speak to her later.'

'I will,' said Luc.

Hattie closed her eyes as if that might shut out the enormity of the news.

'I think we both could do with a drink,' said Luc. 'Come on. I'll get the brandy out and then shall we let Fliss know?' He pulled her to her feet and put his arm round her, holding her tight. Like a shipwreck survivor finding wreckage, she clung to him, her teeth still chattering, unable to think straight.

As soon as he led her into the kitchen, Solange and Fliss, clearly agog with curiosity, swivelled their heads like a pair of meerkats. He steered her to the table and sat her down, his arm around her.

'Solange, would you get the Hennessy? And four glasses.'

Without questioning him, Solange disappeared. Fliss came over to the table, her face creased with concern and trepidation.

'What's happened?' she asked.

'Take a seat,' said Luc, his voice gentle despite the command.

Solange joined them and Luc poured a cognac for Hattie and pushed it into her hand.

She managed to lift her shaking hand and took a sip. Concentrating on the smooth slide of liquid immediately calmed her and she took a second, bigger sip and then sat back as the warmth stole through her.

'Better?' asked Luc, pouring glasses for the others.

She nodded, now a little embarrassed that she was being so pathetic, but it was a wonderful relief to lean on someone else for a change. Taking a reinforcing breath – she needed to do this – she said, 'I'm afraid the wedding has been cancelled.'

'Your cousin's?' asked Fliss, disbelief etched in the frown lines on her forehead.

Hattie nodded. 'She's run off to Las Vegas.'

'Oh God, not the Elvis chapel. Not when she could have this?' Fliss threw out both hands, narrowly missing her cognac. Then she picked it up and knocked it back in one before saying, 'Well, all I can say is, I hope you like wild salmon and lemon scented mash and sorbet, Luc, because you're going to be eating them for a long time.'

Hattie managed a mirthless laugh at that. There were 150 salmon fillets in the freezer.

'Not to mention the ton of green beans and asparagus that are arriving tomorrow.' Fliss leaned over and squeezed Hattie's arm. 'On the plus side, sorry Solange, but Yvette's going to be very happy.'

Solange smiled dryly. 'You think? She's in such a spin about this wedding. I'm not sure it will register.'

'It is a terrible shame, when you've all worked so hard. I'm really sorry.' Luc's arm tightened around her shoulders and Hattie gave him a watery smile.

'Like you said, it is what it is. I'm sorry about the champagne too.'

Solange cocked her head.

'Marthe has vetoed us making champagne this year,' explained Luc.

'*Non*! But why? Why would she do that? She was devastated at having to retire, giving up the brand. I don't believe it. For what reason?' Solange locked her hands together as if she were praying, except the knuckles were bone white. 'I don't understand.'

'Me neither,' said Luc. 'But it's been agreed that Roban will have the grapes this year.'

'Uh! Alphonse will be furious.'

Luc shrugged. 'I tried to change her mind. She told me to leave.'

'What about your father? Did you speak to him?'

'Yes. He wants to open the château up for events. Looks like you might have a job, Fliss. If you're interested.'

'Oh my God. Yes. Yes and yes. I'd love to stay.'

Hattie couldn't believe she could make such a big decision just like that.

'You should stay too,' said Solange.

Luc stiffened and he slowly withdrew his arm from around her shoulders. Immediately she missed the weight of it, the solid anchor that had kept her moored since the news of Gabby's elopement.

'I can't,' she said and slugged back the rest of her cognac. There was an awkward silence around the table and then Luc rose. 'I'm going to find Alphonse and speak to him.'

As he walked through the door, Hattie jumped up. 'Wait a minute, Luc.'

He paused and she caught up with him and then walked with him into the hall.

'Luc…' She almost chickened out but he'd been so kind to her, she owed him an apology. 'I'm sorry.'

'I know.'

'Can we at least be friends? I'm only here for a few more days.'

His face softened and he touched her cheek. 'I'm sorry. You're right,' and his face lit up with that familiar smile, his eyes crinkling at the corners. 'And I find it really difficult to be cross with you. I'm not going to apologise for it, I love you, but I want you to be happy.'

Oh shit. Why did he have to be so damn lovely?

He walked away out of the front door, leaving her standing a little lost and lovelorn.

'Those vol au vents aren't going to make themselves,' said Fliss when Hattie returned to the kitchen. 'We've still got a *vin d'honneur* to prepare. Do you think Yvette would like us to serve a limoncello cream and white chocolate *croquembouche* in the orchard? I'm damned if all those bloody choux buns we made are going to waste.' She paused and then added with a comical pout. 'And I really wanted to make it.'

Solange laughed and even Hattie managed a smile before saying, 'I'm sure she'd love it.' The situation wasn't perfect but no one had died. Hattie suddenly decided it would be far better to make the best of things. She'd had a wonderful month here. Why not go out on a high and make Yvette's celebrations truly memorable? She could still take lots of pictures of the château, the food and the decorations for her website.

Solange came around the table and kissed Hattie on the cheek. 'You are a very good, kind and generous-hearted girl. Thank you for giving the château a new lease of life.'

Chapter Thirty-Six

On the day of Yvette's wedding, the sky couldn't have been any bluer and the sun any brighter. The sunrise that heralded Fliss and Hattie as they made their first coffees of the morning at silly o'clock was the prelude to a glorious day.

Like them, Solange appeared in her dressing gown, her hair done up in rollers, almost skipping like a child.

Hattie and Fliss had now been invited to the restaurant meal later in the day – and Hattie had decided that it would be a shame not to wear the blue dress she'd bought in Paris. They would dress just before they took everything down to the orchard.

'I thought I'd pop in and see if you needed any help,' said Solange.

'You mean you couldn't keep away,' teased Fliss.

'Or she didn't trust you to do things properly,' added Hattie, laughing when Fliss gave her the evil eye.

'I know you'll both do a brilliant job. I just wanted to share in... Us all being here. It's been such fun working in the kitchen together. I'd forgotten how much I miss being with other people, especially other cooks. When Marthe was still here, she always spent most of her time in the kitchen with me, and before that, I always had additional staff to help when we were entertaining. There's something about being with other people with a shared passion.'

'I know what you mean,' said Fliss, linking her arm through Solange's. 'And lucky for you, you're stuck with me, even if Hattie is buggering off home.'

'I think you are wrong,' said Solange. 'Very wrong. You belong here. You have blossomed since you came.'

'She's right, you know,' said Fliss. 'You were an awful sad sack when I came.'

'Thanks,' said Hattie, mildly affronted.

'No problem,' replied Fliss with a cheerful grin. 'You wouldn't want me to lie to you, would you? You were like you were at Christmas. A candle that had been snuffed out. And now –' she walked over and patted Hattie's cheeks '– you're aglow and it's lovely to see.'

Solange nodded. 'Yes, that's it. All the lights had gone out.'

'I don't think I was that bad. I just needed a holiday.' And now she'd had one, she had to go back.

'No, it's more than that.' Solange, to her surprise, put both hands on her shoulders and steered her towards the kitchen table, pushing her into a chair. 'Sit. Stay there.'

Hattie cast a puzzled look at Fliss, who merely shrugged. Seconds later Solange returned carrying the large bevelled mirror that normally hung in the cloakroom just off the hall. She held it up in front of Hattie. 'What do you see?'

Hattie glanced suspiciously at Solange, feeling self-conscious. She wasn't the sort of person who spent time looking at herself in the mirror. She'd never had any great hankering to change the way she looked – she was what she was. Average-looking with a few nice features. She didn't mind her eyes, her nose was a bit short and stubby and her lips too full. As for her freckles, they were a fact of life and she quite liked them.

'Look,' urged Solange.

Hattie reluctantly looked in the mirror.

'Look properly,' instructed Solange.

What did that even mean? But Hattie, obliging as ever, did as she was told, regarding her own familiar features. Okay, so there was a bit of colour in her cheeks, her freckles had popped out and … admittedly there was a curve to her lips that had replaced the habitual downturn to her mouth. Tiny lines fanned out from her eyes, crinkles from laughter and smiling rather than crow's feet. But what she noticed most of all was the light in her eyes. Happiness became her. The more she looked, the more she could see it, etched on every feature. She was happy here. She'd learned to be happy again. The joy in life had seeped away so gradually before that she hadn't missed it. The subtle differences on her face heralded its return.

She swallowed the huge lump in her throat. 'You think I should stay,' she whispered, fearful of acknowledging what she knew deep down.

'You must do what will make you happy,' said Solange firmly. 'Look into your own heart. You have a good soul, Hattie, looking after other people, but perhaps it's time to stop looking out for everyone else and focus on you for a change.'

Hattie wasn't sure she could do that.

Hattie had dressed the canapés with strings of little white wooden love hearts that curved in and out of the tiny pastries. Now Fliss assembled the trays and stood back to check them over with a chef's discerning eye. There were two types of delicate vol au vents, some filled with mushrooms, cream and thyme and the others with smoked salmon and dill sauce. Fliss had also prepared savoury mini mille-feuilles with sharp gruyere cheese in the pastry sandwiched with goat's cheese, and tiny onion galettes in home-made puff pastry. She'd also insisted on making sausage rolls, even though they were very English. 'Who doesn't love a sausage roll?' she'd said to Hattie.

Waiting in the wings were several trays of chocolate eclairs and raspberry madeleines topped with pistachio icing, and the pièce de resistance, the *croquembouche* tower of white chocolate coated profiteroles, decorated with tiny sugared rosebuds and spun caramel.

The guests for the *vin d'honneur*, comprising most of the village, were due in just half an hour. They would be greeting the wedding party straight from the service at the *Mairie* and following the horse-drawn carriage that would bring Yvette and Bernard from the village centre to the orchard. After that the wedding party would depart to the restaurant for the small reception.

'God, I hope there's enough,' said Fliss for the nineteenth or even twentieth time, as she pulled the last of the tiny quiches from the oven.

'No one is expecting a full meal. It's just canapés to soak up the champagne.'

'But you don't want anyone to leave disappointed.'

'Fliss, these all look gorgeous. And I hate to say it but they're coming to see Yvette and Bernard, not for the food.'

Fliss drew herself up. 'Yes, but I want them to say, *That English girl can cook*.'

'Alphonse won't have it any other way.'

Fliss's face softened in a way that Hattie still wasn't used to. 'He's such a sweetie.'

Hattie had trouble keeping a straight face. 'You've changed your tune.'

'Female prerogative.' Fliss waved away the comment before adding, her eyes glinting with wicked satisfaction, 'Besides, he's something else in bed.'

Regret stabbed Hattie, hard and sharp, as her mind revisited those quiet moments in Luc's arms, the slow seconds when their breaths intermingled and the silent exchanges of driving passion. Hattie wanted to lock the feelings away inside her like precious possessions and never forget them.

Ignoring the tightness in her chest, she busied herself fussing over the flowers, which she'd been out first thing to collect. 'Whose idea was it to hang a hundred jam-jars of flowers from the trees in the orchard?' She'd not even completed half of them yet. Thank goodness, Solange and Fliss didn't need any help in the kitchen.

'Yours.' Fliss dusted her hands together, absolving herself of any involvement. 'And it will look stunning.'

'Hattie, those are so pretty,' said Solange, admiring the jam jars of white posies she'd assembled so far.

Her next job would be to hang them in the orchard. 'Thank you, I'm pleased with them,' she said, patting one of the jars, pleased with how they'd turned out. She hoped they were going to look really effective, along with the satin ribbons that would be tied in big bows around the trunks of the small, stubby apple trees.

'You've got a real eye for this sort of thing, Hattie,' said Fliss with a touch of misplaced belligerence.

Hattie didn't respond. She'd heard it several times already

and it was making her very wobbly. Fliss made no bones about what she thought about her decision to return to England. Instead she asked, 'Do you think people will want water? I thought perhaps we could fill some of those big glass jugs with ice, water and lemon and have them dotted around the orchard.'

'No, Hattie, people will not want water. They're coming for a glass of champagne and to make a toast to the happy couple,' snapped Fliss.

'Right you are,' said Hattie with forced cheerfulness, doing her best to ignore the bite in Fliss's words.

'You all scrub up well,' said Fliss, and Hattie turned to see Alphonse and Luc dressed in their wedding finery.

Luc's broad shoulders and long legs were shown off to great advantage in a well-cut navy suit with the natty addition of a pale pink tie. Her fingers tingled, wanting to smooth her hands down his chest. His blue eyes met hers and, as if he knew what was going through her mind, he gave her a crooked smile. Stupidly she felt a pang of jealousy. All the women would be looking at him today – how could they not? And she had no claim on him, which was her own choice but it was the right thing to do, wasn't it? The doubts that had plagued her in the middle of the night returned with a vengeance.

'Luc, Alphonse, we need to go.' Solange, immaculate in a cerise silk suit, began to check the contents of her handbag as she rounded them up. Hattie marvelled at the difference in Solange since Hattie's arrival at the château. The house wasn't the only thing that had come back to life. 'Tissues, rose petals, lipstick. I'm ready.'

'Good luck,' said Hattie, putting her thoughts aside. 'Hope it all goes well and we'll see you soon.'

'I hope so too,' said Solange. 'At least I know everything here is in good hands.'

'*Maman*,' said Alphonse, taking her arm. 'Stop worrying about Yvette. She's a grown woman and Bernard is a very sensible man – well, aside from his decision to take her on permanently – she won't do anything crazy – well, not too crazy.'

They finally climbed into Alphonse's car and the minute they left, Hattie and Fliss jumped into action. Hattie left Fliss in the kitchen while she went down to the orchard to hang the jam-jars and tie the ribbons. Excitement filled her as she imagined the wedding guests' reaction when they first saw them. It was going to look like a fairy bower, full of romance and magic.

'Okay, action stations,' said Fliss, picking up the last of the foil-covered canapé-laden trays to load into Hattie's car.

'And even though I say so myself, I think we both look gorgeous. That dress looks wonderful on you.'

'Thanks,' said Hattie, smoothing down the pale blue fabric. She had to admit she felt a million dollars in her new dress and shoes.

Even though the orchard was a short distance, taking Hattie's car meant they could carry everything down in one go. Hattie carried out two wicker baskets of white paper napkins decorated with little gold doves, which they planned to carry over the crook of one arm with a tray of canapés in the other hand.

Fliss held up a hand for a high five.

'This is it,' she said and looked proudly at the loaded car.

'And even though I say so myself, I think we've done a brilliant job.'

Hattie nodded, a little choked up by what they'd achieved together. She hadn't expected to feel like this. When she'd come to the château it had been an escape route, something practical and a little different to do that played to her strengths. She hadn't anticipated that she'd feel so at home and so much a part of the fabric of the place.

When they got out of the car at the bottom of the hill, Hattie locked the car.

'For goodness sake, don't let me lose the car keys. I need to put them somewhere safe.'

'Don't fret. You can put them in my go-to basket which I keep all my emergency catering supplies in,' said Fliss. 'I'll put it on our station table.'

Fliss led the way, carrying the first of the trays. She stopped dead.

'Oh, Hattie, this looks fabulous. It's so romantic, like an enchanted glade. Everyone is going to love it.'

Hattie beamed. It was exactly the reaction she wanted and it was a relief to hear someone say so.

'Thank you. That's exactly the look I was going for. I hope Yvette likes it.'

'Hats, everyone is going to love, love, love it. I hope you've taken lots of pictures. All the brides are going to want this. Wait until I set up an Instagram page.'

Hattie smiled, even though inside she felt a tiny pang that she wouldn't be part of it. What if she changed her mind? And just like that, she knew. She wanted to stay. Going home no longer felt like the right thing to do. She wanted to stay here and be part of this. As soon as she could find a quiet moment with Luc she would tell him.

. . .

They heard the wedding party long before they saw the horse-drawn carriage enter the orchard. Shouting and cheering heralded the arrival of the group as it wound down the lane from the village. Hattie wondered at the docile nature of the poor horse, who seemed oblivious to the bells and whistles and general cacophony of the high-spirited crowd.

As the carriage drew to a stop, Bernard hopped down and held up his hand to guide Yvette down. Hattie beamed. Yvette looked as beautiful as every bride. A simple white sleeveless dress emphasised her slender form and contrasted sharply with her bright red hair piled on top of her head. The thread of tiny white orchids winding through her hair and a large spray of crocosmia in her hands completed the picture, making her resemble a wood nymph, perfectly at home among the apple and cherry trees.

As everyone swarmed around the couple, kissing them and offering congratulations, Hattie recognised Patrice from the shop, the grumpy florist, who was actually smiling today, the butcher, Marc from the bar and Pierre the gardener along with lots of other faces that were familiar. It made her smile, thinking of the friendly community that she had become part of.

'Hello, Hattie.' As always Luc dropped the H but it was the mere sound of his voice that sent goosebumps racing over her skin.

'Luc.' She smiled up at him, as always unable to stop her immediate response to him. Would familiarity ever dull that quick jump of delight?

'It all looks wonderful. You've done a beautiful job. Congratulations,' he said with a swift smile. She very nearly blurted out that she'd changed her mind and was going to stay but Alphonse joined them at that moment, munching a vol au vent with great delight.

'I think I might have to marry her, you know,' he said convivially taking a bite and watching Fliss move among the guests. 'Great cook and she's got one gorgeous arse.'

'As good a reason as any to marry someone,' said Luc with a wink at Hattie.

'I think so,' said Alphonse, chewing as if he were seriously considering the idea. 'After all, with Yvette married off now, I've no reason not to.'

'And yet another good reason,' said Luc before adding, 'And they say romance is dead.'

'Exactly,' said Alphonse before marching off towards Fliss to snag another canapé.

Luc shook his head, laughing. 'I despair.'

'I need to take this around,' said Hattie indicating the tray in her hand, even though she'd have far rather stayed with him.

'And I ought to check in with Marthe.' Luc loped away towards his aunt whose wheelchair had been placed under one of the trees.

Hattie began to circulate but it was slow going, especially when she was dying to speak to Luc properly. Everyone was in such a good mood, they wanted to chat and share their views on the wedding.

'Hattie, ah, the wedding it was beautiful,' Pierre the gardener told her in his quiet shy way, speaking in slow careful French. She was quite pleased with her growing fluency.

'The flowers in Yvette's bouquet are gorgeous,' she told him and watched as he flushed with quiet pride before taking an onion galette from her tray.

'It is my honour to see flowers give so much pleasure. They suit her colouring, *non*?'

'They do,' she agreed.

'And these, they are quite beautiful. You have such an eye,' he said indicating the little posies suspended from the branches of the trees. 'A beautiful idea. I would be happy to grow flowers for you all the time, you know.'

'Thank you,' said Hattie, realising that he was bestowing quite an honour upon her. She wondered what the château gardens would be like in spring. Those gorgeous eucalyptus trees would smell divine in the scented wreaths and table centrepieces in the winter months. In December she could create the most marvellous festive decorations… She grinned to herself. 'I must take these round.'

'But of course.'

She moved on to a small crowd gathered around Bernard, who immediately drew her into the circle. 'Do you know Hattie? She is Luc's girlfriend and she did this.' He pointed to the trees.

'It's beautiful,' said Patrice from the village shop. 'Such a pretty idea. You are very clever. So original. I don't think I've seen anything quite like it.'

'Mm,' said Hattie smiling but wondering if there was some sort of conspiracy going on.

'You should stay, you know,' said Bernard, without any preamble and attempt to dress his words up. Maybe she preferred his blunt approach. She gave him a slight smile – after all, you couldn't be rude to the groom on his wedding day – but she was starting to wonder if the whole village hadn't been discussing her affairs and were ganging up on her.

'Ah, Hattie.' Solange greeted her a minute later, kissing her on both cheeks. 'These are my friends Dorothea and Leonora, Yvette's godmothers.'

Hattie greeted the two very elegant woman, both in smart dresses and heels. She asked after the bride and Solange's eyes sparkled with happy tears. 'She did look beautiful.' Dorothea and Leonora nodded and they discussed the dress for a moment before Leonora added with a naughty wink, 'Bet you're glad to get her off your hands.'

'Am I ever,' laughed Solange. 'Now she's Bertrand's firecracker.'

'He's more than man enough,' said Dorothea with a laugh.

'And what about you?' asked Leonora, turning to Hattie, her kind face wreathing into smiles. 'I hear young Luc is very smitten.'

Solange watched her carefully.

Hattie smiled politely. Even her own mother wouldn't have been quite so forward but it was clear that the village felt some kinship towards Luc. He was one of theirs.

'I must say you have done such a wonderful job here. If the château became a wedding venue, it would be marvellous for the local economy, you know.' Leonora looked at Solange as if seeking approval.

'Yes, these flowers are so pretty,' enthused Dorothea.

'Thank you,' said Hattie. She held up the plate of canapés 'Duty calls'.

She moved on to the next group of people, all of whom were so busy chatting, they barely acknowledged her, for which she was grateful. It seemed everyone wanted her to stay except Luc, who, when she came to think of it, hadn't really put up that much of a fight. Which was just downright contrary because his calm acceptance of her reasons had been so preferable to the begging and cajoling she'd have received from Chris. Luc understood that she had to do what was right for her. She stole a glance at him, desperate to talk to him in private. His head was bent, nodding as he talked to Marthe, who was gesticulating with her usual animation towards the vines on the hillside.

'Earth to Hattie.' Fliss nudged her. 'Your tray's empty. And another guest has just snuck in. He polished off the rest of my tray without pausing for breath. Bloody philistine, and he was English.'

'Sorry, boss,' said Hattie. 'Wool-gathering. It's a lovely party, isn't it. Everyone seems so happy.'

'Of course they are. Free food and booze, what's not to like.' Fliss winked. 'And superlative food at that. Even for an Englishwoman. Everyone is very impressed, especially with the flourishes.'

'Oh, don't you start.'

'Start what?' Fliss gave her a doe-eyed look of innocence.

'You know exactly what.' Hattie tossed her head with a smile. It was rather nice to be wanted. Much as she would like to tell Fliss about her change of heart, Luc had to hear it first. 'I have vol au vents to dish out.'

'Dish out!' squeaked Fliss indignantly, only to be interrupted by the arrival of the butcher.

'Madame Fliss,' he said, dropping to one knee with a roguish wink. 'Marry me. I will supply you with the best ingredients this side of Paris. Forget Alphonse. What can he do for you? A mere champagne producer. Together we can make the finest sausage rolls with French saucisson.' Fliss giggled at his pronunciation – 'sossaaage'.

'I'm sorry, Giles, but Alphonse has stolen my heart and I do like champagne.'

'Pfft.' Giles rose to his feet with a bellow of laughter and his friends slapped him on the back. 'Well, I must get back to work.'

'You were right, the sossaaage rolls were a hit,' murmured Hattie, watching the three men wander off in that genial happy state induced by lunchtime drinking.

'They certainly were with that Englishman. Now look at him hoovering up the macarons.' Fliss discreetly pointed to the edge of the orchard.

Hattie glanced over to the figure standing under the tree, a little disconcerted by his watchful stare. He looked familiar and then he lifted his head…

Chapter Thirty-Seven

'Chris?' Hattie's voice came out in a croak and he was probably too far away to hear her. No wonder she hadn't recognised him at first. He'd had a haircut, and the scruffy beard that had made him look like Papa Smurf's long-lost brother had been shaved off. He was even wearing a shirt and smart chinos. Hattie hadn't seen him out of baggy tracky bottoms and torn heavy metal T-shirts for years. She almost swallowed her tongue as the sight of him took her back to her university days.

He walked towards her while Fliss muttered, 'That's him.'

'Hattie?' he asked with a tremulous, slight overawed tone.

'Chris.' She stared at him, feeling the earth slide to one side – or was it her losing her balance? Whatever it was, she didn't feel right. Light-headed, disconcerted, disbelieving.

He smiled at her. 'You look amazing.'

'Er, thank you. W-what are you doing here?'

'I needed to see you. Before you come home.'

The small stone of weight that she'd been aware of in her stomach quadrupled in weight at 'come home', bringing with it a wave of pure panic. She wanted to run, run as fast as she could, up through the vines and far, far away. It was the only time in her life she'd felt this urge to flee without giving a damn about the consequences. There might have been times before when she'd wanted a break from things but never this overwhelming desire for pure flight.

'I've got some bad news, Hats.'

'Bad news?' She still couldn't quite comprehend that he was here.

'Do you want to sit down?'

His face looked so grave, she led him over to one of the benches they'd put out earlier that morning. And then a dozen thoughts began to crowd into her head. What was he doing here? It came to her, like light through a crack in the door, bringing a wonderful sense of hope and relief.

Had he found someone else? She examined his stern expression and sat down. It would be just like him to come all this way to do the right thing and tell her in person. She sagged in her chair as the sudden glimpse of freedom made her hopeful.

'It's okay, Chris,' she said, huffing out a relieved breath. 'I really … well, it's for the best.'

There was a long silence as if she'd spoken in another language and he was taking his time to translate the words. Then he stared at her, horrified, quick tears springing in his eyes.

'F-for the b-best?' he whispered. 'Hattie? I n-never thought you could be so cruel.' Then he began to cry in earnest, proper shuddering sobs so heart-wrenching that she froze. Each pain-racked sob punched into her.

'Chris?' She put her arm around him. 'What? What is it?'

'M-mum. It's M-mum … she's … she's…'

Hattie had never felt so cold inside. Dead? She couldn't be. She was only fifty-five.

Closing her eyes, trying to come to terms with the enormity of such simple words, she cradled Chris to her as he continued to cry. She rubbed his shoulder, unable to think of anything she could possibly say.

When Chris finally raised his blotchy face, Hattie hugged him.

'God, I'm sorry. I just think I might be all right and then it comes back to me. Finding her like that.'

'I'm so sorry, Chris. What happened? When?'

'Last week. She said she had one of her migraines. She went to bed and … I found her…' he began to cry again.

She rocked him in her arms and as she did she looked up to see Luc staring at her with a bleak expression on his face. Chris buried his head in her neck, his tears, hot and wet, sliding down her skin. She lowered her gaze and rubbed Chris's back. He needed her. She had no choice.

When he finally stopped crying again, there was a fragility about him, and Hattie felt the tug of guilt, gossamer-fine but with tensile, energy-sapping strength. She'd left him to deal with this on his own.

'Hattie, please come home. I need you. We could drive back in your car this evening. I came by taxi from the station.'

She looked into his face. How could she say no?

'The good news is, I've got a job and I've smartened up my act. Look at me.'

She did and cursed herself for comparing his soft brown hair with Luc's thick curls. 'God, I let myself go, didn't I? No wonder you gave up on me. I don't blame you for wanting a break. But I've got this job in a warehouse. Manager. Not quite a grad job but the pay's good. Enough for us to get a mortgage between the two of us.'

Hattie nodded, fighting against the sensation of feeling trapped. She was just being selfish. Chris needed her, especially now. She couldn't leave him, not now. And he'd made the changes she'd wanted him to for so long. Maybe things would be different.

She swallowed hard. She had to do the right thing and look after Chris.

'I'll come home with you,' she said.

'You won't regret it,' said Chris fervently, clutching her hand. 'I don't recognise any of the guests. Where are your mum and dad?'

Hattie clapped a hand over her mouth. 'This isn't Gabby's wedding. She cried off. It's a long story.'

'So whose wedding have I gate-crashed?' Chris looked mortified. 'I found the château and just followed the noise. I'd better go. Can you come? If Gabby's not having a wedding we could leave today.'

'I'm working,' said Hattie, as cold fingers of panic gripped her. 'In fact I ought to be serving canapés. Maybe you ought to go back up to the house to wait for me. I'm supposed to be attending the next part of the wedding at the restaurant too.'

'Or I could just wait here. No one has noticed me. And I'm sure no one will miss you at the restaurant.'

Hattie saw Fliss giving her the evil eye. 'Look, I've got to go.' With that she dashed over to replenish her tray and began to circulate again, her eyes involuntarily scanning the crowd for a glimpse of Luc.

People had relaxed into the party, especially since a jazz band had started up. With Gabby's wedding postponed and there being triple the number of canapés available now, Yvette, who had booked the whole restaurant for her wedding lunch had been able to push it back to the evening. So friends of Bertrand had suggested they play some swing music during the afternoon and the whole affair had turned into a mini festival. Quite a few couples danced on the grass, while other people were settling down on the picnic blankets and benches to watch the band and the dancers. Yvette and Bertrand were standing hand in hand, swaying to the music together.

'Hattie,' a slightly tipsy Alphonse bellowed at her and beckoned her over to where he was standing, waving a bottle of wine. 'You haven't got a drink.'

'I'm still on duty,' said Hattie.

'*Non*,' he said taking the tray from her. 'Everyone can help themselves now. Where's Fliss? You should both be enjoying the party now.'

'He's right,' said Fliss. 'I could murder a glass of champagne. We were due to knock off at twelve-forty-five. Yvette's not going to mind now.'

Alphonse pressed glasses of champagne into their hands.

'Has anyone seen Luc?'

Hattie shook her head, remembering his pained look before he'd turned his back on her.

'I saw him heading down to the cellars,' said Fliss. 'But that was a while ago.'

'Do you think we ought to check on him?' asked Hattie, motivated by both guilt and concern and then self-disgust. Surely, if he knew about Chris's mum, he would think better of her. He would understand that she simply had no choice but to go home, even though she now realised she wanted to stay.

'Yes,' said Alphonse. 'There is no reason for him to go to the cellars now. I'll go.'

'I'll go with you,' said Fliss. 'Come on, Hattie, you know you want to.'

Hattie shot her a half-hearted glare but Fliss tucked her arm through hers. 'Sorry. I know you're feeling rubbish about him. But he shouldn't be moping by himself.'

They saw him at the entrance to the cellars.

'Luc!' Alphonse hailed him. 'What are you doing? Come back to the party.'

'I think there's another cellar,' called Luc in an excited voice, waving his phone. The three of them picked up their pace to join him.

'What? Now?' asked Alphonse.

'Well, I think it's been there a while, but I've only just thought of it.' Luc's explanation seemed just as crazy as Alphonse's question and Hattie wondered whether she'd fallen down a rabbit hole into her very own episode of *Alice in Vineland*.

'Look at the photo. That shaft. It shouldn't be there. I think there must be something behind the wall just beyond the stairs.'

'And you want to look now?' asked Alphonse.

'Before I bought the press, Marthe was quite happy. I remember she changed her tune when I mentioned that I'd need to get a surveyor in to survey the building. I think if we find the cellar it might tell us the reason Marthe changed her mind. We're running out of time. My father is going to sign the contract with Roban next week.'

'That would make sense,' said Hattie remembering the taut conversation with the elderly woman.

'Why hide a cellar?' asked Fliss. 'If Marthe knows about it, why keep it a secret?'

Luc and Alphonse exchanged worried glances and then Luc squared his shoulders. 'There's only one way to find out.'

The four of them hurried down the stairs in their wedding finery, Hattie and Fliss in strappy sandals that made incongruous loud tapping noises on the stone flags. She'd wanted an adventure. Well, traipsing into a dark cellar in the middle of a wedding certainly fitted the bill. Once at the bottom, Alphonse suggested he and Fliss examine the walls at the other end of the corridor, leaving them to do the same around the stairwell.

Luc paced a few metres one way and then the next, studying the photo of the original aerial print. Together, with the torches on their phones, they studied the chalky walls stained with water and patches of mould and with the odd name engraved into the soft surface. Even to Hattie's inexpert eye, everything looked normal. Finally, after twenty fruitless minutes, Luc moved to the dead end to study one of the brick vaulted walls that was only partially visible behind a big rack of shelving.

Hattie shivered. It was freezing down here.

'Can you see a lighter patch there?' he asked, shrugging off his jacket and handing it to her. Her heart did its usual lovesick flutter as she huddled into the residual warmth from his body, surrounded by the smell of him. It only confirmed what she'd known all along. She loved him.

She squinted at the wall as he held up his phone to shine the light on the surface.

'I'm not sure.' Was the cement between the bricks slightly

different in places – a little lighter, perhaps? It was difficult to judge in torchlight.

'Hey, guys,' Luc called. 'Come and help me move this,' The three of them began to take down the assortment of old boxes and tools that had gathered on the big wooden shelving unit over the years. It was so old and heavy that Hattie figured it must have been built in situ.

'What do you reckon?' asked Alphonse.

'I'm not sure but we'll have a better idea when we move these shelves out of the way.'

'I was worried you were going to say that.' Alphonse rubbed his hands together. 'Come on then, let's do it.'

With a good deal of effort and a good many grunts, the two men dragged the heavy shelves a few feet away from the wall.

'Think you can squeeze in?' asked Alphonse, even as Luc was already wriggling his way through the heavy wooden uprights. Luc shone his torch on the back wall.

'I think there's a doorway here!' His excited shout made Hattie, Fliss and Alphonse squeeze their way in behind the shelves to join him. 'Look. I've never noticed it before.'

'Bloody hell,' said Fliss. 'Even looking for it, I can only just see it. You're right, there's a doorway.'

Hattie leaned forward, still not convinced. 'Look,' said Luc, using the torch on his phone to trace the outline. Studying it, Hattie thought perhaps the brickwork did seem a tiny bit neater.

'The pointing is ever so slightly different.' Luc's torch wavered back and forth to make his case.

'So now what?' asked Alphonse. 'You need a sledgehammer.'

'I think we can manage a bit more subtlety,' suggested Luc.

'If I take just a few bricks out, we can see if there's anything on the other side.'

'Do you think there'll be anything there?' asked Fliss.

'Who knows?' Alphonse's big shoulders lifted. 'During the war quite a few champagne houses bricked up cellars to hide champagne and stop it being shipped out of France. This area was occupied for most of that period.'

'But wouldn't they have unbricked it after the war?' said Hattie.

'Yeah,' agreed Fliss. 'Surely. No one's going to forget they have a lost fortune of champagne squirrelled away.'

'You'd have thought so,' said Luc, his grin a little maniacal in the torchlight, 'but Bollinger discovered an unknown cellar in 2010 full of pre-war vintages.'

'And no one knew it was there?' asked Fliss, disbelieving. Hattie had to agree, it didn't seem possible.

'Apparently not,' said Alphonse. 'Do you remember, Luc? It went for a fortune at auction. But what a fantastic story. It would be an amazing coup for us if we found lost vintages of the original St Martin champagne.'

'If we were allowed to make it,' grumbled Luc. 'And there might be nothing here.'

'A find like that might make people change their minds. Especially your father. He's going to love it and the papers won't be able to get enough of our handsome faces,' said Alphonse with gleeful delight, already getting carried away.

Fliss rolled her eyes and, ever practical, asked, 'Would it still be drinkable?'

'Very possibly,' said Alphonse. 'Bottles of 1825 Perrier-Jouët were opened in 2009 and it was tasted by the top wine tasters and found to be drinkable.'

Hattie studied the wall again. 'And you think there might be champagne in there?'

'Doubtful.' Luc frowned. 'But I think there's another cellar here. And Marthe knows. She was twenty-one when the war ended and she was heavily involved in the winery and to some extent the resistance movement, although she's very cagey about it.'

'Yeah,' agreed Alphonse. 'My father told me once that the cellars here were used extensively by the resistance.'

'Surely if she knew there was champagne in there she'd have unbricked it before now,' said Fliss. 'Sorry to rain on your parade and all that.'

'True,' agreed Luc, his face falling a little.

'But it's still interesting,' said Hattie, directing a quelling glare at Fliss, not wanting to spoil Luc's excitement. 'There must be a reason for bricking it up.'

'Probably because the roof was unsafe or something.' Luc sounded despondent. 'I ought to ask her.'

'How big do you think it is?' Hattie was determined to rekindle his enthusiasm.

'No idea. The shaft in the picture is as big as the others. If there is a cave here … maybe the same size as the other caves.'

'What are you going to do?'

'Find some tools,' said Alphonse, already squeezing his way back past the shelving. 'Be right back.'

He returned clutching a large lump hammer in one of his meaty hands and a heavy-duty chisel in the other. He shot Luc a smirk. 'This is man's work,' he said, hefting the hammer.

'You can put more weight behind it,' replied Luc. 'I'll give you that. Try not to demolish the whole place. I'd suggest knocking a few bricks out so that we can get a light through and see what's there.'

'Okay.' There wasn't much room in the small space between the wall and the back of the shelves so Alphonse couldn't swing the hammer too far at the chisel that he'd inserted at chest height into the brickwork. He chipped away round the edge of one brick before pausing to try and push the brick through. It didn't budge. He tapped at it with the hammer but it still didn't move.

'Hit it a bit harder,' suggested Fliss.

'I wouldn—' Luc's words were lost as Alphonse swung back the hammer as far as he could in the limited space and landed a mighty blow on the brick. There was a shudder and the brick and four surrounding ones all vanished with a crash.

'See.' Alphonse turned round to face them, grinning. 'That's the way to do it.'

Even as he spoke there was a series of cracking noises like pistol shots and Jacob's-ladder fissures began to appear, running stepwise through the brickwork. A doorway appeared before their eyes.

'Well, that was easy,' said Alphonse, dropping the heavy metal hammer on the floor with a triumphant thud.

There was an ominous creak and a loud groan. The entire wall began to shudder.

'Wha—' said Alphonse.

'Get back,' said Luc, grabbing Alphonse by the sleeve and pushing Hattie through the gap between the shelves. He and Alphonse ducked down and rolled across the shelving as Fliss bumped up against Hattie.

'*Merde!*' yelled Alphonse, stumbling backwards. The four of them, now standing on the other side of the shelving unit, watched as in slow motion the wall began to collapse, bricks tumbling down one after another like unruly dominoes. They all turned and ran as a black cloud of dust enveloped them, small explosions of debris filling the air as the wall crumbled.

Dust scoured Hattie's eyes, the taste of dirt filled her mouth, and she felt a film of fine grit on her face. She blinked rapidly, trying to dispel the tiny particles, and beside her Fliss began to cough.

'*Merde!*' yelled Alphonse again, pulling Fliss into his arms as Luc did exactly the same to Hattie, shielding them from the growing dust cloud. The four of them ran on towards the exit coughing and spluttering, racing up the stairs to ground level. They emerged into the sunlight, doubled over, gasping as they tried to wipe the dirt from their faces.

'What the…' wheezed Alphonse.

'Fuck,' said Fliss, her eyes white and wide in her blackened face.

'Here.' Luc turned on an outside tap and they all reached to dash handfuls of water into their faces. Behind them there was silence but a cloud of dust filled the cellar building.

'Bloody hell,' said Fliss. 'Someone doesn't know their own strength.'

Alphonse grinned at her.

'It wasn't a compliment, you pillock.'

Hattie sniggered.

'Peellock?' Alphonse asked.

'Idiot,' said Fliss, rolling her eyes at him.

He shrugged. 'It worked, didn't it?'

'In the immortal words of Michael Caine, "You were only supposed to blow the bloody doors off,"' she drawled.

'I'm not sure it translates,' said Hattie, seeing Luc looking confused.

'Did you see? Did you see?' Alphonse was practically dancing on the spot.

'I think I did,' said Luc, grinning from ear to ear, his teeth white against his grimy face.

'What?' asked Fliss.

'Bottles. I'm sure I saw bottles,' said Luc, clearly itching to go back.

After an impatient wait of five minutes with Luc and Alphonse pacing up and down outside the cellar like restless expectant fathers, they could wait no longer and, despite the grey dust cloud, insisted that they went back down. Hattie and Fliss weren't going to miss out and insisted on going too, so Alphonse, in a particularly heroic gesture, took off his shirt and ripped it into pieces to create makeshift masks to cover their noses and mouths. Fliss sighed, her eyes going a little dreamy at the sight of his stocky muscular chest and whispered to Hattie. 'Told you, all man.'

Hattie gave the clear blue sky one last reluctant look and followed the others back down the stairs.

What had once been a wall was nothing but a pile of rubble, and the dust was still settling, but as the torch beams cut through the murky gloom, they lit up the ghostly shadows ranked like a battalion of soldiers. Rack upon rack of bottles lay beyond, thick with dust.

'*Mon dieu!*' gasped Alphonse. 'This is amazing. No one has been in here for years.'

Luc stepped forward and touched one of the bottles, leaving a fingerprint in the thick dust. 'There are hundreds of bottles here. Why did no one know? Marthe can't have known. She wouldn't have left them untouched, surely.'

Suddenly the room was flooded with light. Alphonse had found an old switch and most of the lamps studding the walls at regular intervals lit up, except for a few blown bulbs. They must have been made to last, thought Hattie a little irrelevantly.

'She must have known,' replied Luc. 'The only reason to hide champagne would have been during the war, from the occupying forces.'

'But then why has she never said anything?' argued Alphonse.

Luc and Alphonse walked the length of the room, wandering up and down the rows like two schoolboys in a storeroom full of sweets, muttering to each other, 'This is amazing.' '*Incroyable.*' '*Mon dieu.*' 'Look.'

'Do you know how old they are?' asked Hattie stepping forward and gazing around. The room was full of the distinctive riddling racks, each filled with dark green bottles.

'No idea. None of them have labels,' said Luc. 'There must be records somewhere but every vineyard had its own system for storing and recording its stocks.'

The four of them wandered around.

'This will make a brilliant story,' said Alphonse. 'Put St Martin's champagne on the map, reminding people of its proud heritage. Champagne had been made on this site for the last two hundred and fifty years.'

'Someone must have known about this and why it was bricked up,' said Hattie.

'Well, no time like the present. I'm going to ask Marthe now,' said Luc, grabbing one of the bottles. 'I think it would be best if we don't mention this to anyone until I've spoken to her.'

'Er hello!' Hattie said, shaking dust out of her hair and brushing down her dress. 'You don't think people might notice something? And Alphonse is going to need a shirt.'

'Shame,' murmured Fliss.

'Luc and I can change on our way to the restaurant. It will be fine,' said Alphonse, running his fingers through his shaggy hair, which didn't look very different from its usual bird's nest state.

'Eeuw,' said Fliss, wiping her sleeve across her face. 'I'm going to be blowing my nose for a fortnight to get the dust out.'

Chapter Thirty-Eight

M arthe appeared to be dozing in her wheelchair in a shady spot under one of the trees. Luc watched her for a moment, Hattie, Fliss and Alphonse standing a little way behind him like three coal-mining musketeers.

'Are you going to stand there scowling at me all afternoon?' asked Marthe, her milky blue eyes sharp with awareness.

'I thought you were asleep.'

'I was resting my eyes. And don't think because I'm in a good mood and have had two glasses of champagne I'm going to change my mind. You look serious and ... what have you been doing?' Her gaze skirted him and came to rest on the other three. 'You look like you've been...' Her voice trailed off.

He gave her a reluctant smile as he sat down on the bench next to her wheelchair, brushing at the sleeves of his shirt.

'Not serious, exciting. We've found a fourth cellar behind a wall, full of champagne.' He grinned at her, the exhilaration of discovery still coursing through his veins. He held up the bottle of champagne from the hidden cellar.

She blanched, swallowing, her eyes filled with alarm as

they focused on the bottle. He could virtually see the blood draining from her face.

'You found it?' She lifted her veined hand to her throat, accentuating the rapid rise and fall of her breathing. 'Oh God, Luc. I wish you hadn't.' She doubled over, clutching her chest. Her eyes rolled back and she slumped in her chair.

Luc jumped up and reached for her wrist. 'Marthe. Marthe. Alphonse, call an ambulance,' he yelled, feeling her thin, thready pulse. 'I think she's having a heart attack.'

He felt a hand on his shoulder and he glanced up into Hattie's face. She didn't say anything but her eyes signalled steadfast support. Gratitude for her quiet presence flooded him. Suddenly people were crowding around them but he held onto Marthe's hand, the lump in his chest so hard he was finding it difficult to breathe. 'Don't die. Don't die,' he whispered to himself over and over. He knew she was old but he wasn't ready to lose her. She was his family. Once she'd gone there would be no one who would always be there for him.

Agonising minutes ticked by as he hung onto Marthe's hand as if hanging onto her life, anxiously watching the laboured breaths and constantly checking her pulse. It terrified him that if he stopped diligently monitoring her vital signs, either one would cease.

People had faded away, their voices subdued as if not wanting to intrude. Solange had come to sit beside him, while Hattie remained at his shoulder. Fliss and Alphonse had gone to open the gates to the orchard for the ambulance. He strained to hear the siren. Hurry up. Hurry up.

'It's okay, Marthe. Help is on its way. Hang on.' He kept talking to her. Could she hear him? He prayed they wouldn't be the last words she heard from him. There was still so much more he had to say. Had he ever said thank you to her? Told her he loved her? He could imagine her reaction. A brusque *tsk*. A dismissal of his sentimentality. But she'd be pleased. He knew it.

The wail of the ambulance made him grip her hand tighter, fearing it might be too late.

'Do you need me to come to the hospital?' asked Hattie, when the paramedics loaded Marthe into the bright white space of the ambulance. With an oxygen mask over her face and wrapped in a blanket on a stretcher, the indomitable Marthe had shrunk and looked every one of her ninety-five years. Fear skated over his skin and it took a moment for him to answer, as he stared into space.

Hattie saw his jaw clench and something inside her lurched when he finally shook his head.

'I'll be fine.'

He climbed into the ambulance and sat down in the functional square box, his eyes on Marthe as he reached for her limp hand. It was the loneliest sight she'd ever seen.

She watched as the paramedic shut the doors with a final clunk. The engine fired up and the ambulance, its blue light flashing, slowly drove away, lumbering down the track. As the others turned away, returning subdued to the orchard, Hattie stood watching everything as if from a distance.

'Hattie?' Chris called to her, coming towards her. 'What are you doing?'

'Thinking,' she said, starting to walk back to the orchard.

'She's very old,' he said, putting an arm around her. 'Someone told me she was ninety-five. She's had a good innings.'

347

Anger bubbled at his callous words and his arm felt like a boa constrictor draping itself across her shoulders. With an impatient shake she dislodged it.

'What?' asked Chris.

'I can't do it,' she said.

'Can't do what?'

'I can't come back with you. I'm sorry your mum is dead. Really sorry but...'

Chris suddenly looked wary, almost trapped, like someone caught out. 'She's not dead, exactly.'

Hattie stopped in her tracks. 'What do you mean?'

He lifted his shoulders in a boyish *oops* way. 'I never said she was *dead*. You ... well, you just sort of jumped to that conclusion and ... I mean, she is very poorly. In the hospital.'

Hattie stared at him. 'You let me think she was dead?' Her voice was full of disbelief. How could he?

Because he knew how to manipulate her. Fury built a small storm in her as her eyes bored into him. Sorrow filled her. How had she got things with him so wrong?

'I know. I shouldn't have done but I was desperate. But I have got a job now, for you. Everything is going to be different. I promise, Hattie.'

'No.' The word rang with emphatic denial.

'No?' he squeaked as if wasn't hearing correctly.

'No,' she repeated and for some reason poked him in the chest to reinforce her meaning. 'No. No. No.'

He took a step back and looked over his shoulder. Hattie realised that they had an audience, including Alphonse, Yvette, Solange and Bertrand. She caught sight of Fliss, who gave her a quick thumbs-up.

'Fliss was right,' she growled.

'Fliss? Who's Fliss?'

'I am an enabler. It's me that keeps enabling you to rely on me. But you're not my responsibility. You have to do things for yourself. I can't make you better.'

'I can do things for myself.' He was suddenly belligerent. 'I'm here, aren't I?'

'Yes, you are.' Hattie nodded sadly. Here because he wanted something. 'It's over, Chris. I'm not coming back.'

She heard a cheer and spotted Solange and Fliss doing an incongruous fist bump.

'But … but …' Chris's face crumpled in familiar distress but this time she steeled herself against it, determined to be honest with him – and herself.

'I'm in love with someone else.' As soon as she said the words, lightness settled on her.

Solange beamed at her like a proud mother hen.

'I need to go to the hospital,' she said, more to herself than to him, and ran towards the table where she and Fliss had set up their base. Grabbing the basket, she rummaged frantically for her car keys. Where were they? She tipped the basket upside down and pawed her way through the contents. They weren't there.

She turned to find Chris on her heels.

'My car keys. I can't find them,' she said in a panic.

Solange barrelled over, almost knocking Chris out of the way in her haste. 'No need. We'll take the minibus. Dorothea hasn't been drinking.'

When had Solange become so bossy? Hattie found herself hustled along to the ancient red minibus, which was supposed to be taking the wedding party to the restaurant and sandwiched in the first row of seats between Solange and Leonora. Dorothea climbed into the driver's seat and tossed her high heels into the passenger footwell.

'Don't worry about Marthe,' said Leonora, patting Hattie's hand. 'She's very strong. Like an old vine.'

'You fool, Leonora. She's worried about Luc. She's in love with him.'

'Ah,' said Leonora, sighing and straightening up, as if realising she had a part to play in a drama. 'Put your foot down, Dorothea. This is like one of those romantic films where you have to stop the hero flying away.'

'Luc isn't going anywhere. He'll be sitting in the emergency waiting room,' snapped Solange.

Hattie closed her eyes, praying that he was okay, vaguely aware of the three women bickering. A memory of Luc's stricken expression as the ambulance doors closed played over and over in her head. Dorothea, obviously deciding that she wanted to play her part too, had put on her racing stripes and applied her foot to the accelerator. She swung the minibus round corners at speed as they hurtled down the country roads towards Reims. They narrowly missed a white van coming the other way and passed within a paper's width of a cyclist but all Hattie could feel was gratitude and urgency. She had to tell Luc she loved him, that she wanted to stay. That he wouldn't be on his own. That she needed him as much as he needed her, even though he'd never said it. That was why she loved him. He didn't ask anything of her she didn't want to give.

Dorothea's handbrake turn in the car park of the hospital pulled Hattie out of her thoughts.

'Go, go, go,' said Leonora, pushing her out of the minibus. Hattie didn't need to be told twice. She ran into the hospital and in stumbling French asked about Marthe Brémont.

'Are you a relative?' said the middle-aged receptionist in perfect English.

Hattie shook her head. 'No but…'

'I'm very sorry but we can't give out information to anyone who isn't a close relative.' The woman smiled, her eyes softening with kindness even though Hattie knew she probably had to say the same thing every day of her working life.

'I know. Her nephew is with her. It's him I want.' She couldn't help but let her desperation show.

'All I can suggest is that you check the waiting room. If he's not there he'll be with her or with the doctors. But I think he'll be back soon. Why don't you take a seat?'

'Thank you.' Hattie nodded. Before she turned away the woman was already busy answering the next enquiry.

The emergency waiting room, like any other she'd ever visited, was almost full and she scanned the faces, mostly grey thanks to the harsh, unforgiving overhead lights. She spotted him almost immediately, hunched up in the corner, the bottle of champagne at his feet and his head in his hands, the protective curl of his body reminded her of an armadillo trying to keep scary things at bay. She'd never seen Luc look so vulnerable. He was always so sure of himself. Confident in his own skin.

She walked over to the row of shiny grey moulded plastic chairs and sat down, the silk of her dress whispering as she settled next to him. Without hesitation, she put a hand on his arm.

'Luc.'

He raised his head and blinked as if he wasn't sure what he was seeing.

'Hattie? What are you doing here?'

'I came to tell you I love you and I'm staying. Whether you like it or not.'

He stared at her. 'Can you say that again?'

'You heard me.'

'I know but I just wanted to be sure.'

'I'm sure. It took me a while to get here. Remember what you said to me the first time I saw you?'

Luc frowned, looking adorably confused.

'You said, "Are you going to knock or just stand there all day, hoping the door will open by itself?" Today I realised that I need to get on and walk through the door instead of being a coward and walking away.'

'What made you change your mind?' asked Luc, as if he were worried that she might change it again.

'Watching you get into the ambulance alone. I asked if you needed me and you said you'd be fine.'

'I lied. I wanted you to come but I knew you'd be torn. I saw you taking care of him. Was that Chris? He looked in a bad way.' Luc lifted his shoulders in a what-could-I-do shrug. 'It wouldn't have been right to make you chose. I love you. I want you to be happy. I want to look after you.'

She lifted a hand to cup his face and he turned his head to kiss her palm. 'Thank you.'

'You're welcome. What made you decide?'

'Because you didn't make me choose. You never tried to force the issue.'

'Marthe said in the ambulance I didn't fight hard enough for you.' He swallowed. 'I've grown up with the expectation that most people leave. Like the au pairs. My parents always did. I wasn't important enough for them to ever change their plans.'

'Not this time.' She took his hand and laced her fingers through his. 'I've got so much to stay for. You, Fliss, Solange, Alphonse, the château and the champagne.'

'Well, the champagne is on hold for the time being but, like I said, I'm not giving up.'

She'd been thinking about this all the way here. 'And you won't have to. With a wedding and events business at the château, we'll do our best to make enough money to buy the grapes from your father and outbid Roban. Maybe not this year, but next. Dorothea's already going to tell all her Parisian friends about the château and put a piece in her magazine. Apparently she's very well connected.'

Luc laughed. 'Just a bit. You must have made a good impression. She's an editor at *Paris Match*. She knows—'

'Monsieur Brémont,' a voice called from the door. Luc's grip tightened. 'It's the doctor.'

Chapter Thirty-Nine

I t took a second or two for Luc to round up his limbs. Swallowing the sharp acidic bite of fear, he rose, Hattie's hand still in his. 'Will you come with me?' he whispered.

In answer she wrapped her arm around his and squeezed. 'I'm right here.'

He bent to pick up the champagne.

Together, they crossed the floor towards the young doctor standing in the doorway through which Marthe had been rushed as soon as they'd arrived.

'You're here with Marthe Brémont?' he asked, looking up from the clipboard he held in the crook of one arm. 'I'm afraid it's family only,' he said, eyeing Hattie.

'It's all right. This is my wife,' said Luc. Hattie didn't so much as flinch, just gave his arm another quick squeeze and smiled beatifically at the doctor.

The doctor lifted one sceptical eyebrow and when Luc thought he might refuse to let them through, he said in a dry voice. 'Congratulations. Come with me. Although I don't think she'll be needing the champagne this evening.'

They followed the doctor and Luc steeled himself for the worst as he asked, 'I-Is she going to be all right?'

'Don't worry, my friend. She is made of strong stuff. This generation won't go down without a fight.' He led Luc along the corridor, their shoes squeaking on the shiny surface of the floor. Around them staff in blue scrubs, their name badges swinging on lanyards, worked with efficient calm, wheeling machines, conversing in even tones and bringing a sense of the everyday. For them this was all part of the job. It soothed his antsy nerves, as did Hattie's steady presence beside him. Marthe was in good hands and so was he.

They stopped outside a small bay with curtains drawn and the doctor pulled back the patterned fabric. Marthe lay on a bed in a hospital gown, stickers on her chest and a clip on her finger linked to a monitor.

'Here she is. You can stay for a minute but then she needs rest. We'll probably keep her in for a day or so to run a few tests to double-check everything is as it should be.'

Relief coursed like a hot flood through him. 'So she's okay?'

'Don't talk about me as if I'm not here,' Marthe's querulous voice reprimanded him. It immediately reminded him of being a young boy again.

'Nothing serious. A panic attack, which always looks alarming and for the patient it often feels like a heart attack or they're dying. But –' he gave Marthe a reproving look '– you're going to be fine. Outlive all of us.'

'Don't talk nonsense,' said Marthe, sharp as ever. Her beady eyes alighted on Hattie, and she gave a nod of approval.

'You'll be transferred up to a ward for the night. A porter will be along soon.'

The doctor sensibly beat a dignified retreat.

'Nice to see you, Hattie. You did a beautiful job in the

orchard. Everyone was very impressed. And that English girl, she can cook.'

'Thank you,' said Hattie. 'How—'

'How are you feeling?' asked Luc, steering Hattie to the plastic chair beside the bed and putting the champagne on the bedside table, while he perched on the edge.

Worry made him gentle, treating her with unusual care, even though he knew she wouldn't appreciate it.

'Foolish,' snapped Marthe. 'Fainting in front of all those people, spoiling Yvette and Bertrand's big day. And it's all your fault.'

Hattie shot him an amused look.

Luc rolled his eyes. 'You are feeling better.'

'There's nothing wrong with me. You heard the doctor. A silly panic attack. Even though he looks about twelve he does appear to talk some sense.

Luc didn't say anything. He couldn't. The overwhelming relief didn't leave room for much else and he knew Marthe wouldn't thank him for weeping all over her.

Hattie's reassuring smile made him feel better, especially when she leaned forward and took his hand again. Two together was so much better than one.

'Why couldn't you leave well alone?' She glared at him. 'Now you've gone and raked up history that was best buried. Although I suppose at my age they won't put me in prison. It's not going to do much for the family name.' She narrowed her eyes for a second, a glint of satisfaction shining. 'It's really going to piss your father off.'

Luc stared at her trying to make sense of what she was saying.

'So you knew about the fourth cellar?'

She nodded, her face pale. 'Of course I knew.' She turned to

Hattie. 'I suppose you'd better hear this too. Find out what you're taking on.' She turned back to Luc. 'Who do you think supervised building the doorway to the damn thing and had the shelves erected?' She scrutinised his face, a question in her eyes. He had a feeling she was screwing up her courage.

After a lengthy pause, she finally asked, 'Did you find anything else?' Her quiet, penitent voice was at odds with her previous sharpness.

'No, just champagne.'

Her face collapsed, wrinkle upon wrinkle, like an accordion. 'Nothing? No one?'

'No one?'

She pressed her lips together and winced, her shrewd eyes suddenly determined. 'A body?'

Hattie let out a little gasp, her eyes widening as she and Luc shared surprised expressions.

Shock flooded his body like a hot wave. Was she serious? The ramifications shook him, overtaking his mind. 'A body? Why would there be a body in there?'

'There's definitely no body?'

'Not that I saw and we walked to the far end and back again. The lights were on.'

'You're sure?'

'Yes.' He wanted to joke that he'd have noticed a body but from Marthe's sudden tension, he knew it would not be appreciated.

'Hattie?' Luc prompted.

'There was no body. I promise you. We'd definitely have seen it. Alphonse put the lights on. There was nothing but bottles down there.'

She drooped suddenly and exhaled. 'You're absolutely sure.'

'Yes,' said Luc again, taking her hand, now worried about her state of mind. 'Tell me what's wrong.'

'I thought he was dead,' she whispered.

'Who?'

'Paul. Paul Rey.' She closed her eyes. 'All these years, worrying and wondering.'

'That's why you didn't tell anyone about the cellar? Why the door was bricked up?' Luc said, the pieces all clicking into place.

'I couldn't. I know it was wicked but Henri told me he'd killed him.'

'Great-Uncle Henri?'

'Of course,' she said impatiently. 'Who else?'

'What happened?'

'Rey was *un connard*,' she spat, wrenching her hand away, both fists clenched, the tendons stark white against her veined skin.

He and Hattie both jerked in surprise at the vituperative tone.

Her mouth tightened, lines fanning out in displeasure.

'We were in the Resistance, Henri and me.'

Hattie leaned forward, as mesmerised by the story as he was.

'We used the cellars to hide English airmen who'd been shot down and helped them to escape to Marseille on the Pat line. One night we were expecting two airmen who were due to stay for a few nights while we arranged papers and clothes for them. Transport had been arranged for them but it was delayed. Paul –' her face contorted. '– that *salope* would have sold his own mother – heard of the arrangements and followed them to St Martin. Henri caught him snooping and he threatened to go to the high command at Reims if we didn't pay him.' She paused and stared off into the distance, lost in memories.

'What happened?' urged Luc, conscious that he was digging up an unwelcome past, but Hattie was nodding at him. Urging him to carry on.

Marthe stiffened and lifted her chin, looking him directly in the eye. 'Henri told me he had killed him and left him in the cellar. But before we could do anything about it, Henri was arrested and the Germans were searching for Paul. Henri told them that Paul had run off. We, me and Georges, bricked up the cellar so that the body couldn't be found and then Henri was sent to a labour camp and I never saw him again. I know it was wrong but Rey was dead and he had no family, so no one would miss him. That cellar door had been hidden, so we were already hiding the best vintages in there.'

Luc stared at her.

'It was an accident. Henri swore it was an accident. He hit him over the head with a champagne bottle.' She put her hands up to her face. 'Poor Henri, he was in such a state over taking a man's life, but Paul would have destroyed everything. Everyone would have been rounded up and shot. The week before, a whole family in Reims was executed for helping with the Resistance.' She stopped, her voice trembling. 'I know Henri didn't mean to kill him but he had to stop him.' She paused and he could see her thin chest rising and falling in rapid shallow breaths. He glanced at the monitors but they remained quiet.

'It's okay, Marthe,' said Hattie. 'Do you want some water?'

Marthe took the plastic beaker that Hattie held out. 'Thank you, *cherie.*'

She sipped and closed her eyes, clearly lost in unpleasant

memories. Hattie looked on with concerned sympathy. Guilt nudged Luc at having dredged it all up again.

He leaned forward and took her hand between both of his. She looked at him and her voice came out in a flat whisper. 'We would have lost everything. Piper-Heidsieck was sequestered after parachutes were found in the cellars. Paul Chandon-Moët was deported to Auschwitz and Moët & Chandon was sequestered. It was a terrible time. I was responsible for the vineyard. For the livelihoods of so many. I was just twenty.' She lifted her head. 'I bricked up the entrance to the cellar and I don't regret it for a minute but I don't understand. Henri said Paul's body was there at the back by riddling rack thirty-nine, but I couldn't bear to look.'

Luc sighed and squeezed her hand.

'Are you sure there is no body there?'

'I promise you.'

'So what happened to him?'

'Maybe he was just stunned and disappeared before you realised,' suggested Luc.

'Is there another exit from the cellar?' asked Hattie.

'Not to my knowledge. Besides Henri was so sure he'd killed him. But there would have been plenty of time. I didn't go back until the following morning.'

'You just said Henri was very shaken up by it,' said Hattie.

Killing a man would do that to someone, thought Luc.

'Maybe he didn't check properly,' she said.

'Yes,' agreed Luc. 'That must be what happened. And knowing Henri had tried to kill him, he didn't want to hang about to let him finish the job.'

'Maybe.' Marthe deflated. 'I just don't know. It's a mystery.' She gave a hollow laugh. 'And I've been so worried you would find that damn cellar before I died.'

Luc laid a hand on her soft, papery skin. 'I'm sorry for that. Although on the plus side, you don't need to worry anymore.'

'There is that.' She frowned. 'But now we have a mystery. Whatever happened to Paul Rey?'

'We could do some research and see if he ever turned up elsewhere?' suggested Luc.

Marthe's face relaxed. 'That's a very good idea.' She straightened up and once again she was the indomitable woman he'd always known, about to ride into battle. 'Now I'm tired. You can go but only after you tell me what's going on.' Her lips pursed. 'What I saw at the *vin d'honneur* was most unsatisfactory. You, Luc, were watching Hattie all the time and then pretending you weren't, and you, Hattie, were doing exactly the same to Luc until that Englishman turned up. Solange said you were going home. With him? That would be a great shame. You know you have to stop her.'

Luc started to laugh.

'And what is so funny?' Suddenly Marthe was back to being her starchy self.

'You were complaining about people talking about you in front of you,' Luc pointed out.

'That's different. I'm old. I can get away with bad behaviour.'

Hattie's mouth turned up at the corners. He could see her trying to hide a smile.

'Sorry, Hattie. He's not very good at fighting for people.' Marthe shook her head sadly. 'I remember the first time his parents left him with me.' She turned to Luc. 'You were resigned to it. Already at seven.' She leaned forward and this time she was the one that patted his hand. 'You always expect people to leave, so you don't put up a fight.'

'Not this time,' said Luc, winking at Hattie. He put his

hand in his pocket and pulled out her car keys, dangling them between his fingers.

'That's where they were!'

Luc grinned at her. 'I said it wouldn't be right to make you choose … but I never said I wouldn't.'

Hattie grinned back. 'You wouldn't have needed to. I'd already decided to stay.'

'Thank heavens for that,' said Marthe. 'I can't stand all this mushy stuff. Being young and in love and stupid must be exhausting. Now leave me alone. Like the doctor said, I need to rest. And if you're coming to see me tomorrow, make sure you bring some brandy.'

Luc pulled Hattie to her feet and kissed her. 'Let's go home to the château.'

She kissed him back. 'Home. I like the sound of that.'

'What about Yvette's wedding?' piped up Marthe. 'I don't see why we all have to miss it. You two should go. Perhaps you could take that to her. I happen to know there's plenty more where it came from.' She nodded to the dusty bottle beside her.

Chapter Forty

'Hattie, Luc!' Solange jumped to her feet, spotting them as they entered the restaurant. She swayed tipsily on the spot, waving a half-full champagne flute.

'Yay, you're here,' called Fliss, taking a swig straight from a champagne bottle as she sat on Alphonse's lap.

Around twenty people were seated at a long table which took up the entire restaurant. The place was closed to other patrons. Empty fat-bottomed bottles, running in a line along the centre of the table, and discarded napkins were testament to the celebration. Fairy lights twinkled from where they were draped across the rustic beams of the ceiling, peeking out from trailing vines wrapped around the wooden trellises. For some reason there were two large cardboard cut-outs of Yvette and Bertrand to which had been pinned varying sizes of envelopes with their names on. Hattie assumed they contained wedding gifts of money. She thought it a lovely idea.

Everyone began to cheer as they walked in, hand in hand, including Yvette and Bertrand, who were sitting at the head of the table like the king and queen of the day. It felt as if she and

Luc were triumphant heroes returning from a mission. Everyone was clearly pleased to hear that Marthe was going to be all right. They'd phoned the restaurant owner as soon as they'd left the hospital, to ask him to let the wedding party know that Marthe was fine. All the same, as they walked to the two empty seats next to Fliss and Alphonse, several people called out, asking after her.

'She's okay,' said Luc, reassuring them several times over.

Blundering into a chair, Solange wiggled her way through the seated guests who'd pushed their chairs back from the table and threw her arms around them both in a group hug. 'I'm so 'appy to see you.'

Hattie hugged her back.

'You are staying, *non*?'

'I'm staying,' she replied, her heart bursting with sudden happiness.

'She's staying,' yelled Solange in an uncharacteristic outburst that had both Hattie and Luc laughing.

Yvette rose to her feet, her face flushed with joy and champagne. She lifted her glass. 'A toast to Hattie. Everyone fill your glasses. I want to say thank you for making my day so special.' She paused and then added with a self-deprecating grin, 'Especially when I was such a bitch to you.'

Hattie laughed. 'It's okay. By the way, did you know mouse poo is quite different from rabbit poo?'

Yvette burst out laughing. 'It was not nice collecting it all.' She wrinkled her nose. 'It was a good punishment, no? Come, sit down. Drink some champagne.'

'We have a gift for you, from Marthe,' said Luc and raised the bottle of champagne from the cellar. 'She would like you to open it today.'

There was a sudden hush in the room. Everyone turned to

stare at the bottle with silent reverence as Luc handed it to Yvette. Alphonse had clearly already relayed the tale of how they'd found the cellar and the treasure hidden there.

'Everyone must have a taste,' she said and turned to her brother. 'Everyone will share a glass with their neighbour, I think. And you, Alphonse, must open it.'

Alphonse, wide-eyed with delight, took the bottle as Fliss shifted from his lap.

'Fresh glasses,' he called and someone scurried to the bar, collecting flutes on a tray.

Alphonse placed the bottle on the table and took one of the napkins. He carefully untwisted the wire securing the cork. Luc wrapped an arm around Hattie, pulling her closer. Everyone watched, breath well and truly bated, as Alphonse positioned the napkin over the naked cork and held it in one hand, using the other to twist the bottle.

As the cork was eased out with a satisfying pop, everyone cheered and began to clap.

Alphonse put the bottle back at the table and silence fell as the entire room stared at it, the anticipation almost palpable.

'Luc,' he said, with great ceremony. 'You must have the honour. To pour and the first taste.'

'Yes,' said Solange. 'It is your birth right and Marthe would want it, I know she would.'

Luc smiled and Hattie felt a delicious stab of love and pride as he squeezed her hand, gave her a kiss and then stepped forward. She watched as he carefully lifted the bottle and lined up ten glasses, and saw his Adam's apple dip as he poured the first glass. The room was so quiet, she thought that everyone could probably hear the gentle fizz of the liquid as it cascaded into the glass. Luc held it up to the light and tipped the flute this way and that.

'Good colour,' observed Alphonse as Luc dipped his nose into the glass.

'Aromas of caramel,' he pronounced before taking a sip. He closed his eyes and everyone watched as he swilled the liquid in his mouth.

When he opened his eyes, everyone in the room craned forward waiting for his verdict. A slow smile spread across his face before he nodded. 'Biscuit and honey.' He beamed. 'It's good.'

There was another burst of spontaneous applause and everyone began talking excitedly as Luc poured the champagne into the other glasses. Solange stepped forward to hand them out.

Once they were served to each pair, they jockeyed politely as to who would taste first.

'Santé,' said Luc, lifting his glass, and the lucky first tasters all took a sip and then handed the glass to their partners. He beckoned Hattie to his side.

'Taste.' He held the glass to her lips and she took a sip. She could taste the caramel nuttiness, a distinct contrast to the more acidic sharpness that she was used to, but even she could appreciate the subtle difference and its deep richness.

The room was filled with an underswell of awed murmurs as people swapped their glasses with each other.

Alphonse, who was sharing with Fliss, raised his flute. 'To St Martin champagne and the future.'

'St Martin,' everyone chorused.

Luc pulled Hattie to him, his blue eyes sparkling, 'To us.'

She smiled up at him, her heart bursting with love and happiness. 'To us.'

'To many dreams coming true,' he added.

'To new adventures,' she said, taking another sip and

closing her eyes, savouring the special vintage. She'd never forget this moment, sharing in the unique celebration of this wine. She knew that sharing this moment with Luc and this new-found community would always be one of her most treasured memories.

When she opened her eyes Luc was smiling down at her, love shining in his eyes. Then he leaned forward and whispered very quietly in her ear, 'There's nothing quite like seeing the woman you love enjoying herself.'

She reached up and kissed him, her lips soft on his mouth. There was nothing like knowing that love could set you free. It didn't have to be a trap and it could open your eyes to a whole new adventure. She had an enticing new future to look forward to and a dream to believe in. How could she have ever thought she could leave the château?

Acknowledgments

Without the added sparkle sprinkled by my fabulous editor, Charlotte Ledger, I'm not sure this book would ever have seen the light of day. Without the reassurance from my agent, the gorgeous Broo Doherty, I might not have soldiered on. Without the constant support of my dearest writing buddy, Donna Ashcroft, writing this book would have been even more difficult.

The French Chateau Dream was written during a stressful family time and while it was lovely to escape to France in my head, it was also difficult and there were times when I doubted I'd get the story right. What kept me going were the wonderful messages from readers which thanked me for my books, let me know that my novels had made a difference to them, and how much they'd enjoyed my stories. I might not always reply to messages, but I am so grateful to everyone who takes the time and trouble to contact me, to review a book or even just enjoy them. Thank you to each and every one of you.

I'd also like to thank the people that work behind the scenes and make the final book come together, gorgeous Emma Petfield, Marketing Manager at One More Chapter, new team member, Ajebowale Roberts, who's already made a big impression, the amazing rights team, the sales team and all of my wonderful overseas publishers. Particularly Ditta in Germany and Petra and Tereza in the Czech Republic who have made my books such a huge success in those respective countries.

YOUR NUMBER ONE STOP

ONE MORE CHAPTER

FOR PAGETURNING BOOKS

The author and One More Chapter would like to thank everyone
who contributed to the publication of this story...

Analytics
Emma Harvey
Maria Osa

Audio
Fionnuala Barrett
Ciara Briggs

Contracts
Georgina Hoffman
Florence Shepherd

Design
Lucy Bennett
Fiona Greenway
Holly Macdonald
Liane Payne
Dean Russell
Enya Todd

Digital Sales
Laura Daley
Michael Davies
Georgina Ugen

Editorial
Arsalan Isa
Charlotte Ledger
Ajebowale Roberts
Jennie Rothwell
Tony Russell
Caroline Scott-
Bowden
Kimberley Young

International Sales
Bethan Moore

Marketing & Publicity
Chloe Cummings
Emma Petfield

Operations
Melissa Okusanya
Hannah Stamp

Production
Emily Chan
Denis Manson
Francesca Tuzzeo

Rights
Lana Beckwith
Rachel McCarron
Agnes Rigou
Hany Sheikh
Mohamed
Zoe Shine
Aisling Smyth

**The HarperCollins
Distribution Team**

**The HarperCollins
Finance & Royalties
Team**

**The HarperCollins
Legal Team**

**The HarperCollins
Technology Team**

Trade Marketing
Ben Hurd

UK Sales
Yazmeen Akhtar
Laura Carpenter
Isabel Coburn
Jay Cochrane
Alice Gomer
Gemma Rayner
Erin White
Harriet Williams
Leah Woods

**And every other
essential link in the
chain from delivery
drivers to booksellers
to librarians and
beyond!**

Unwrap this gorgeous gift of a book for an escape to the snow-peaked caps of the Scottish Highlands and a romance that will melt your heart...

Izzy McBride had never in a million years expected to inherit an actual castle from her great uncle Bill but here she was, in the run up to Christmas, Monarch of her own Glen – a very rundown glen in need of a lot of TLC if her dream of turning it into a boutique bed and breakfast was to come true.

But when Izzy's eccentric mother rents a room to enigmatic thriller author Ross Adair and the Scottish snow starts to settle like the frosting on a Christmas cake, it's a race to get the castle ready before they're all snowed in for the holidays.

Available now in paperback, ebook, and audio!

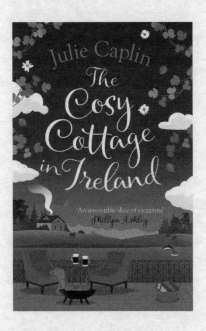

Snuggle up in your favourite armchair and take a trip across the Irish sea for comfort food, cosy cottage nights and a heartwarming romance…

Talented lawyer Hannah Campbell wants a change in her workaholic Manchester life – so she books herself a place at the world-renowned Killorgally Cookery School in County Kerry. But on her first night In Ireland, sampling the delights of Dublin, Hannah can't resist falling for the charms of handsome stranger Conor. It's only when Hannah arrives at her postcard-pretty home at Killorgally for the next six weeks that she discovers what happens in Dublin doesn't quite stay in Dublin…

Available now in paperback, ebook, and audio!

ONE MORE CHAPTER

One More Chapter is an
award-winning global
division of HarperCollins.

Sign up to our newsletter to get our
latest eBook deals and stay up to date
with our weekly Book Club!
<u>Subscribe here.</u>

Meet the team at
<u>www.onemorechapter.com</u>

Follow us!
 @OneMoreChapter_
 @OneMoreChapter
 @onemorechapterhc

Do you write unputdownable fiction?
We love to hear from new voices.
Find out how to submit your novel at
<u>www.onemorechapter.com/submissions</u>